murder california style

....murder
CALIFORNIA
STYLE ....

A COLLECTION OF
....
SHORT STORIES BY
....
THE SOUTHERN
....
CALIFORNIA
....
CHAPTER OF
....
MYSTERY
....
WRITERS OF
....
AMERICA

EDITED BY ....
JON L. BREEN AND JOHN BALL

A THOMAS DUNNE BOOK

ST. MARTIN'S PRESS
NEW YORK

Grateful acknowledgment is made for permission to reprint the following:

"Child's Play" © 1958 by HSD Publications; reprint by permission of the authors.
"Henry's Eighth" © 1977 by Elizabeth McCoy.
"House Call" © 1956 by Greenleaf Publishing Co.
"All-Star Team" © 1987 by Jon L. Breen.
"By Means Unlovely" © 1985 by Dan J. Marlowe; reprint by permission of the author.
"The Sweet Old Lady Who Sits in the Park" © 1987 by Maxine O'Callaghan.
"King's X" © 1987 by Brian Garfield.

(*Permissions continued on page 292.*)

MURDER CALIFORNIA STYLE. Copyright © 1987 by The Southern California Chapter of Mystery Writers of America. Introduction © 1987 by John Stevenson. All rights reserved. Printed in the United States of America. No part of this book may be used or reproduced in any manner whatsoever without written permission except in the case of brief quotations embodied in critical articles or reviews. For information, address St. Martin's Press, 175 Fifth Avenue, New York, N.Y. 10010.

Design by John Fontana

Library of Congress Cataloging-in-Publication Data

Murder California style.

"A Thomas Dunne book."
1. Detective and mystery stories, American—California, Southern. I. Breen, Jon L., 1943–
II. Ball, John Dudley, 1911–   . III. Mystery Writers of America. Southern California Chapter.
PS648.D4M854   1987   813'.0872'0897949   87-4448
ISBN 0-312-00620-9

First Edition
10 9 8 7 6 5 4 3 2 1

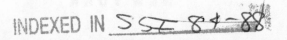

*In memory of Martha Axelrod, Dan J. Marlowe, and
Richard Levinson*

contents

introduction

Like most authors I graduated to writing from a long apprenticeship of reading—in my case, crime fiction. Also, like most authors, my first few attempts at fiction followed the pattern of those many years of reading. It was not until I had sold a few books, and could call myself an author without expecting to be struck by lightning, that I realized there were other people who lived a similar lonely existence. Other people who pushed pencils or hammered typewriter keys across a virgin sheet—the word processor was still on the way—to satisfy an innate urge to pour out all those pent-up emotions in the hopes of manipulating other people's vicarious feelings.

In my quest for soul mates I formed a great many friendships and became an avid fan of more crime and suspense novelists than I would have ever thought possible. It was not until a far-sighted editor persuaded me to try my hand at short stories that I became enamored of what is certainly the most difficult form of narrative communication. I had always thought of myself as a novelist, and the short story format to me was as foreign as watching seagulls and then expecting the wings of an airliner to flap. I tried it and after a record of considerably more failures than successes, I found that in my attempts I had more company than I could have reasonably expected.

With this allied expansion of my reading matter, one thing became crystal clear: I was expected to believe that all the good writers were on the East Coast; I was being brainwashed and it was anticipated that I would pay homage to this cliché. On the contrary, the more I saw of my neighboring writers the more respect I had for their work. I didn't need to fly to New York to rub shoulders with the best in the business; they were right on my doorstep.

At one of the monthly meetings of the Southern California Chapter of Mystery Writers of America, I suggested that we put together a collection of short stories, restricting them to those written by our multitalented local writers. Everybody who was a resident southern Californian and a crime and suspense writer was invited to submit a story. We already had two of the finest editors in the country present at our meeting, my colleagues John Ball and Jon L. Breen. Not everybody submitted a story, and not all the stories submitted were accepted, but what has been compiled here we sincerely believe are the best crime stories from southern California.

I feel honored that the story I submitted should be displayed together with the work of such geniuses as Richard Levinson and William Link and Robert Bloch and that of many other great names from the world of crime and suspense. I could list each of these famous people and tell you something of each story, but that would only set you looking for a central theme, and there is no central theme. The only thing that these stories have in common is the fact that their authors are residents of what we consider to be God's own country. Here, then, is the cream of the crop of mystery writers saying, This is what crime writing is all about in southern California.

John Stevenson

murder california style

Richard Levinson and William Link

The first story by William Link and Richard Levinson, "Whistle While You Work," appeared in *Ellery Queen's Mystery Magazine*, November 1954. In his introduction to the story, editor Queen (Frederic Dannay) wrote, "The authors, at the time of this writing, are twenty years old, and both attend the University of Pennsylvania. They first met in Junior High School, in Philadelphia, and discovered they had three hobbies in common: reading detective fiction, performing magic, and experimenting with wire recorders. These mutual interests led to an enduring friendship, and soon they began collaborating in their work, especially in the writing and directing of school shows."

More than thirty years later, the collaboration continues, in print, for the stage, and most notably in television. Levinson and Link created Columbo, perhaps the greatest TV detective of them all. They developed and produced the Ellery Queen TV series starring the late Jim Hutton. Most recently, they created with Peter S. Fischer the very successful "Murder She Wrote," starring Angela Lansbury. Winners of multiple Emmy and Edgar awards, they wrote such landmark teleplays as "My Sweet Charlie" (1970), "That Certain Summer" (1972), "The Execution of Private Slovik" (1974), "The Gun" (1974), and "Crisis at Central High" (1981), usually serving as executive producers as well.

And along the way, Levinson and Link contributed over thirty short stories to magazines. "Child's Play," one of their best, first appeared in *Alfred Hitchcock's Mystery Magazine*.

Richard Levinson and William Link

· ·

child's play

Camp Summit drowsed in the two o'clock heat. In the cedar cabins little boys lay in their bunks, staring out through screened doors at the lawns and sleeping tennis courts. Breezes stirred in the pines, but moved off toward the tent row and the lake. The boys, dreaming of afternoon triumphs, turned over and over in their bunks, waiting for rest period to end.

Arnold came slowly up the path from the lakefront. He wore khaki shorts and a T-shirt; his socks and sneakers were dripping wet. His round, solemn face, in the open sun, was curiously white.

He entered Cabin 12 and sat down on the bunk next to the door. A boy in the back glanced up from his comic book, but said nothing. Another boy, stretched out on his bed, picked up a tennis ball and stared at the newcomer. He watched Arnold kick off his sneakers and socks and change into a new pair of loafers. "You're lucky Uncle Jack isn't here," said the boy with the tennis ball. "You'd catch it for sure if he found out you just came in. You're supposed to stay in the bunk during rest period."

Arnold switched on the Hallicrafter radio set next to his bed and moved the selector band. He slid a pair of earphones over his large ears.

"Where have you been, Arnold?" asked the boy.

Arnold moved the selector band again.

"You can hear me. Those earphones aren't that thick, Arnold!" He threw the tennis ball at the little boy, but it hit the bunk ledge and rolled to a stop.

"Shut up," said Arnold.

"Where have you been? On another of your expeditions?"

Arnold adjusted the earphones.

The boy who had thrown the ball rolled over on his back and stared up at the raftered ceiling. "You don't know everything," he said abruptly. "There's a lot you don't know. There's a kid in Bunk 7 that knows three times as much as you do. And his father works up at Princeton. Arnold?" He looked over at the bed. "What are you listening to?"

Arnold cupped his small hands over the earphones.

"Arnold? What are you listening to?" The boy stared at Arnold for a few more minutes and then lost interest and took a comic book from his trunk. He turned away against the wall.

Arnold switched off the set and put the earphones down. He removed a key from his pocket and opened the trunk at the foot of his bed. It was a green trunk, new and unmarred by labels. Inside was a jumble of crumpled T-shirts and dirty pants; at the bottom, under some luminous white stones and the mechanism of a clock, was a sheaf of stationery. Arnold took out a piece and closed the trunk, locking it carefully. He removed a handful of pencils from his pocket and selected one with a point. Then, using the steel surface of the trunk top, he began to write in a clear, firm hand.

Dear Mother,

This is the third time I have written to you this week (and today is only Tuesday). I want to come home. You know that. In your last letter (which I received last Friday) you did not even refer to this subject, even though I told you about it in my last four letters and two postcards. You know why I want to leave here. Father can send Walter up with the car, it is only a five hour drive (I checked). I am quite sure that Mr. Whiteman will refund most of what you paid. Don't bother sending him a letter to find out, as that will waste too much time and complicate things. I want to come home.

Arnold

He was folding the letter when a bugle call sounded. There was an immediate yelling and shouting, the sound of feet pounding on the lawns. Youngsters raced by outside the cabin, their white shirts flashing against the summer dazzle of the lake. The bugle stopped abruptly, and there remained only the sound of boys' voices raised in the warm wonder of afternoon.

Arnold was left alone in the cabin. He addressed an envelope, slipped the letter inside, and placed it in his back pocket. Then he turned on the Hallicrafter and adjusted the earphones. He watched a group of boys in bathing suits walking down toward the beach.

"Arnold." A man stood in the doorway. He was short and balding, with a pleasant, tanned face. A whistle dangled at the end of a blue lanyard around his neck. "Arnold. Come on."

Arnold turned the selector band.

"It's activities period," the man said. He came in and stood looking down at the little boy. "Come on, Arnold."

"I don't feel like going."

"You have to. Look, you know what will happen if I tell Mr. Whiteman. He'll dock your free period. You don't want that to happen, do you?"

"You don't have to tell him."

"Yes, I do. I let you get away with this before, but I can't this time. Now come on. You've got riflery, and Uncle Paul will be checking on you if you don't show. Arnold?"

The boy hunched his thin shoulders.

"Take those earphones off. You can't hear me."

"Yes, I can."

The man wiped his sweaty neck with the front of his shirt. His nose was peeling. He sat down next to the boy on the bunk and tried a different approach.

"What are you listening to on that thing?"

"Radio Moscow."

"Is that so? What are they saying?"

"Lots of things."

"Like what, for example?"

"They claim we're going to have a depression."

"Do you think they're right?"

Arnold frowned and touched his smooth white cheek. "No. There are a lot of reasons why we won't. One is that—"

The man put his hand on his shoulder. "Arnold, will you come with me? If you don't I'll have to tell Mr. Whiteman. Now I mean that. I'm not kidding."

Arnold thought for a moment and then removed the earphones. The cabin was quiet except for the sounds of shouting and splashing from the lake.

"Okay, Uncle Jack," Arnold said to the man. He fingered the letter in his back pocket. "I'll go if you won't tell Mr. Whiteman . . ."

It was cool in the pine forest and the air smelled of summer leaves. A group of campers with .22 rifles lay stomach-down on a strip of canvas matting. Their firing sounded flat and ineffectual in the dim grove. After each round a young counselor would walk back to remove the little black and white paper targets from the rack.

Arnold sat in the shadow of a dwarf evergreen, waiting his turn with the second group of boys. He was drawing numbers with a stick in the soft earth.

"Okay. The rest of you guys." The counselor turned a red,

critical face to the new group and watched them tumble down on the matting. "And cut out the talk. You can't get a decent score unless you concentrate."

Arnold pressed the heavy rifle to his shoulder. The counselor stood beside him, his black moccasins almost touching the little boy's legs.

"Now concentrate."

The others began firing. Arnold yawned, closed his left eye, and pulled the trigger. He loaded and fired six times, and each bullet sang off into the dark underbrush.

"What are you doing?" cried the counselor. His foot pinned Arnold's rifle to the matting. "What's wrong with you? You didn't even have your barrel pointing at the target."

Arnold said nothing. He leaned his head on his elbow. The other boys stared at him.

"Didn't I teach you how to fire?" asked the counselor. "You squeeze the trigger. Sque-e-eze it. And you hold your breath. Didn't I teach you that?"

Arnold watched an ant cross a long gully in the matting.

"What's your name?" He waited for an answer.

"His name's Arnold," said one of the boys.

"Can't he talk for himself?"

"Can he talk?" said another boy. "You should hear him sometimes." The little boys snickered. A few threw stones into the bright sky.

The counselor bent down and tried to get Arnold's attention. "So you're Arnold. Well, I've been told about you."

Arnold lowered his eyes and puckered his lips as if to whistle.

"You've got the idea that you can do whatever you want around here. Well, not with me. Pick up that rifle."

Arnold watched the ant. The other boys were silent.

"I told you to pick it up," said the counselor.

Arnold looked at him. "I'm through using the rifle," he said.

"You're what?"

"Through using the rifle."

The other boys giggled.

"You're getting out of this period," said the counselor. "Right now. You go find Mr. Whiteman and tell him that I don't want you here with the rest of us. Tell him he'll have to reassign you to volleyball or arts and crafts. I'm certainly not going to bother with you."

Arnold got up.

"Do you hear me? Go tell Mr. Whiteman that. I'll check with him tonight to make sure you did."

Arnold turned his back and walked out of the clearing. He was on the path before the others began to talk. Then the rifles sounded again and frightened birds fluttered in the underbrush. He walked very slowly with his chin pressed down on his chest, his body swaying.

Soon he was out of the forest and standing on a grassy hill that overlooked the shining ring of beach and lake. There was a group of campers already there, including two of Arnold's bunkmates.

"Arnold!" called one of the campers.

The small boy came over.

"You're supposed to know everything," said the camper. "What's going on down there?"

Arnold looked. There were three automobiles and an ambulance parked in the shimmering sand. A few state policemen were walking out near the dock, and Mr. Whiteman was talking to another on the deserted beach.

"They won't let anybody down there," said the camper.

"They say we all have to go back to our bunks," cried a boy with glasses. "I think somebody was hurt."

"Did you hear anything?" asked the camper.

"No," said Arnold. He stood silently watching the activity on the beach and then turned abruptly in the direction of his bunk.

When he entered, the boys were waiting in line to take showers in the cramped bathroom. Uncle Jack wasn't around. Arnold opened his trunk, took out a book, and began reading. The campers were talking excitedly in the showers, and steam

7

poured through the canvas doorway. When they were finished they came out, wrapped in towels, and padded over to the front porch. They stood there in dripping groups, staring off through the clearing at the lake. Arnold continued to read.

Before dinner the campers usually gathered by the administration building for the lowering of the flag. Mr. Whiteman would tell them the evening's activities and read any necessary announcements. Tonight the ceremony had been called off, and the boys went directly to the dining hall from their bunks. Arnold had changed his clothes, and he strolled along the gravel path behind the others. On the steps of the old building he noticed a stone that gleamed in the fading sunlight. He picked it up and placed it in his pocket.

When he got inside he went slowly over to the mail table, where all late afternoon mail was stacked according to bunks. He shuffled through the Bunk 12 pile, but there were no letters for him. Angrily, he swept the other envelopes to the floor and went over to his table. Uncle Jack was sitting at its head, his peeling face disturbed. He still wore the same sportshirt, and there were dark perspiration stains at the armpits.

"Sit down, Arnold, you're late," he said.

Arnold took his seat. He glanced at Mr. Whiteman's table across the crowded, noisy room. The camp owner sat with three other men, and they were talking quietly. Arnold looked down at his grapefruit and attacked it with his spoon.

One of the little boys, who had been lost in thought at the other end of the table, suddenly said in a loud, clear voice, "Uncle Jack. What happened to Bobby Thompson? He drowned, didn't he?"

The large room was suddenly still. Mr. Whiteman and the three men glanced up. Uncle Jack frowned and waited for the rumble of conversation to begin again before he answered. "Keep your voice down, Teddy. I can hear you."

"But what happened, Uncle Jack? He's not here for dinner tonight, and one of the guys in his bunk told me—"

The counselor interrupted him. "Bobby Thompson had an accident, that's all. Mr. Whiteman will tell you all about it in the morning."

"I'll bet he's dead," said another boy, heaping sugar on his grapefruit. "I heard they found him after rest period underneath the old docks up at the lake."

"Now where did you hear a thing like that?" Uncle Jack tried a tentative smile. "The way foolish rumors spread around here. You boys dream up the wildest stories."

"It is not a wild story," said the boy stoutly. "Why would the cops be up here if something wasn't wrong? He's dead, all right."

"Maybe he was killed or something," another camper volunteered timidly.

"It was an accident," said Uncle Jack. "A simple accident. The police always come when there's an accident. Now I don't want to hear any more about it."

"Bobby was in Bunk 9, wasn't he?" somebody whispered to Arnold. "Uncle Paul's the head of that bunk, maybe he did it. Nobody likes Uncle Paul anyway. I wish they'd put him in jail."

Arnold shrugged and buttered a piece of bread.

Dinner progressed and the big room throbbed with high, young voices and the crash of silverware. A waiter dropped his tray and it rattled like a coin on the floor. His tables laughed and applauded. Someone near the windows began to sing, "Oh, the Deacon went down . . ." The song caught on, moving from table to table across the warm room. But the old verses failed to bring the usual enthusiasm, and the song died before it reached the head counselor's table. Mr. Whiteman got up, his eyes lowered, and left the room.

Arnold ate slowly, finishing a second plate of ice cream after most of his bunkmates had been excused. Uncle Paul came over and stopped beside the table.

"Hello, Paul," said Uncle Jack, mopping his mouth with a napkin. "What's up?"

The counselor frowned. "I had a little difficulty with this boy here on the rifle range today," he said, indicating Arnold. "He was causing trouble."

"Is that true, Arnold?" asked Uncle Jack.

Arnold licked his spoon carefully.

Uncle Paul shook his head. "His attitude is uncooperative. I sent him down to talk to Whiteman. Did he go?"

"Did you, Arnold?"

"No," said the little boy.

"Why not?" snapped Uncle Paul. "I told you to see him."

"I don't want to talk to him," said Arnold slowly.

"You're going to have to learn, fella, that you don't always do what you want."

Uncle Jack's face grew stern. "Arnold, go over to the office and see Mr. Whiteman right now. You'll probably catch him in. Then report to me after you see him."

"I don't want to talk to him. I already told you that."

"Maybe he'd better not, at least not tonight," said Uncle Paul. "Whiteman's got enough on his mind since this afternoon. Arnold can see him tomorrow."

"No, I want him to go tonight. Whiteman wants to see him sometime this week anyway. Now you go ahead, Arnold, and no back talk."

Arnold started to say something, but the two men did not seem in the mood for arguments. He slid back his chair. "Okay," he said. "But if any Special Delivery mail comes for me tonight, let me know about it." He got up and walked over to the door.

A light burned in the office of the administration building as Arnold came up the path. The place was constructed of white wood with mildewed window flaps that could be lowered in case of rain. It sat back near the clearing at the edge of the rippled lake, and Arnold could hear the cold waters sucking against the sides of discarded rowboats. He shivered a little as the night wind whipped along the path and pressed at his thin jacket. Off in the distance, orange lights went on in the recreation hall.

Arnold pushed quietly through the screen door and stood still in the room's mild darkness. Mr. Whiteman sat behind a desk, talking on the telephone. Arnold went over to a high bookcase near a row of filing cabinets and scanned the titles. He slid out one of the books and began paging through it.

Mr. Whiteman hung up the phone and swung around in his chair. "Oh, hello, Arnold," he said. "I didn't hear you come in." He was a tall, heavy man, with a brown face and short white hair.

Arnold put the book back and approached the circle of light on the desk.

"What were you reading, son?"

"*The Psychology of Children* by Klarmann," said the boy.

"Oh, yes. That thing's been kicking around this office for years."

"It's a new book," said Arnold. "You probably just got it this season."

Mr. Whiteman tilted back in his chair and looked at the boy. He took a pipe from a desk rack and tapped it on his palm.

"Well, sit down, son. You want a Coke or something? Some soda?"

Arnold shook his head. "I just ate a little while ago."

Mr. Whiteman packed the pipe from a small pouch and lit it. He puffed vigorously for a moment, then settled back even further in his chair. "What's the problem, Arnold? What can I do for you?"

"Uncle Paul and Uncle Jack told me to see you. Uncle Paul is mad at me because I didn't listen to him on the rifle range this afternoon."

"Well, why didn't you, son? After all, he's your instructor."

"He doesn't like me."

Mr. Whiteman laughed comfortably. "Of course he likes you. Why, that's downright silly, Arnold. Uncle Paul likes all of the campers."

The little boy was silent.

"Now come on, Arnold. You don't actually believe that any of the counselors has anything against you. Do you?"

Arnold looked up, his small eyes momentarily alive in the glow of the desk lamp. "My mother's been writing you, hasn't she?"

"What's that?"

"She won't answer my letters because she wants to keep me here. But she's been writing to you."

Mr. Whiteman expelled a long sigh. He pressed his fingertips against the edge of the desk. "Maybe we'd better have a real talk, eh, son? Now I'm going to level with you, and I expect you to be honest with me. Your mother *has* written to me. She said that you're not happy here. Is that true?"

"Yes."

"Well, why, Arnold? You're here for a vacation, to have a good time. Why don't you like it?"

Arnold compressed his lips and remained silent.

"Is it because the other boys don't understand you? Is that it? Frankly, son, we would have put you into an advanced bunk, but we didn't think you'd enjoy yourself there."

Arnold toyed with the zipper on his jacket, sliding it up and down.

"I'm not going to lie to you, Arnold. I've been checking with your counselor and some of the campers. I understand that you're being given a rough time. I heard that somebody cut all the strings off your tennis racket."

Arnold nodded.

"And I also know that somebody stole a tube from your radio set."

"I got it back." The boy's thin fingers snapped the zipper along its grooved track.

"That's not the point. If you're being bothered, I want to know about it. You should have come and told me these things." Mr. Whiteman's pipe had gone out and he relit it impatiently. "Now who's behind this, Arnold? Are they boys in your bunk?"

"No."

"How many are there? I can dock them their free period if they give you any more trouble."

"Only one boy's been bothering me, and you don't have to do anything."

"Look, Arnold," said Mr. Whiteman earnestly, "I'm not asking you to tell tales or anything. I just want to make things better for you. Your mother's been very concerned about your welfare, and I want to be able to tell her that you're getting along."

"Can I have a Coke now?" asked Arnold.

Mr. Whiteman frowned and went over to a small refrigerator. He removed a bottle, opened it, and handed it to Arnold. Then he sat down, rather wearily. "Now I'd like to know the name of the boy who's been picking on you. Arnold?"

Arnold wiped off the top of the bottle and drank the Coke slowly.

"Tell me, Arnold."

Arnold rolled the bottle between his hands. "It's not important now."

"Tell me."

"Okay. It was Bobby Thompson."

Mr. Whiteman paled. "Did you . . . say Bobby Thompson was the boy who was giving you trouble?"

"Yes."

Mr. Whiteman stood up very carefully and moved around the desk. He pulled on his jacket. "I want you to stay here for a few minutes, Arnold." His voice was uneven. "I want you to stay right here. Promise me that. I just have to see somebody for a minute. Promise you'll wait right here for me."

Arnold put the bottle on the floor. "Okay," he said.

"Read that book you were looking at. I'll be right back. All right?" He went over to the door and looked back at the boy. Then he left. Arnold heard him begin to run as soon as he reached the gravel path.

The little boy stood up. He wandered around the room, his hands in his pockets, then went over to the desk. He sat down

Richard Levinson and William Link

in Mr. Whiteman's chair, opened a drawer, and took out some stationery. He uncapped a fountain pen and began to write on the creamy paper.

> Dear Mother,
>   This is the last time I'm going to write unless I hear from you. I want to come home . . .

Elizabeth McCoy

·····················

"Henry's Eighth" was number 476 in the long parade of "first stories" published in *Ellery Queen's Mystery Magazine*. Its author, Elizabeth McCoy, holds an M.A. in English literature from the University of California and worked for several years as a civilian speech writer for top-ranked officers of the Air Force Air Material Command and Space and Missile Systems Division. Besides her fine short stories, she has published poetry, contributed television scripts to national network programs, including the well-remembered "United States Steel Hour," and is currently working on a novel.

Elizabeth McCoy

·····················

henry's eighth

Almost immediately after his third failure to kill his eighth wife, Henry concluded that Ellen was indestructible, and—to his immense astonishment—that he was glad of it.

He sat at the chrome and glass bar in the Marina apartment and swore softly to himself, then downed a neat slug of excellent brandy. Sea water from his smart sailing whites soaked into the

15

rich upholstery of the bar stool and squelched in his Adidas deck shoes while he contemplated this incredible new development.

The house doctor came out of the bedroom and said that he had given Ellen a mild sedative; she should sleep the clock around. She was a very lucky woman. So fortunate that those two young men should have arrived when they did to help with the rescue.

"Oh, God, yes," said Henry, meaning it from the bottom of his heart. "I'm not a strong swimmer at best, and I was so busy trying to get the boat under control after that lurch, that it was seconds before I realized she'd gone over the side. And I just wasn't doing too well at finding her in the water until they got there. I—" He stopped, aware that he was talking too much.

"Boating can be very tricky in weather like today's." The doctor's wistful eye was on the brandy. He accepted the proffered glass with satisfaction. "Have you done much sailing?"

"Not nearly enough." Henry was fervent. "And never again."

"Oh, now, you mustn't say that. These accidents will happen. You'd better get a long, hot shower and some dry clothes yourself, or you'll be the patient. Don't hesitate to call me if Mrs. Murchison isn't feeling right up to par within a day or two. Good constitution that girl."

Henry saw him out, then went and looked reflectively for a few moments at Ellen asleep, her damp hair straying over the pillow. Seen like that, reduced to fundamentals, she looked much younger than her thirty-odd years, and at the same time disturbingly like the Ellen he had first seen on that train to Baltimore three years ago. Ah, that other Ellen, the prematurely faded relict of a domineering mother, wearing a brooch too ugly to be anything but real diamonds, and no makeup, and scared to death of her first train ride alone.

He wandered into the bathroom, shed his clothes on the floor, and stepped into a shower with a control panel like a 747's. The hot water pulsed out over him. He did some of his best thinking in showers. Probably something about getting the blood moving in the brain that stimulated his normally very logical thought processes. Maybe he could sort out just what the hell was the matter with him now.

First of all, there was his absolutely inexplicable attitude toward those two young idiots who came churning out of nowhere to the rescue. He had actually pointed out to the blond one, frantically gulping half of the Pacific himself, exactly where Ellen had gone into the water. And the boy had dived there and dragged her up. Now what had made him point out the right place? Another minute or two of diving in the wrong places and it would all have been over, even if they found her.

None of his projects had ever been more painstakingly set up, or promised handsomer returns, than Ellen. Of all the women he had ever married she was the only one who could leave him an estate to keep him in comfort for the rest of his life, even if some of the present plush was from trusts. And everything that she could she had neatly and gratefully willed to him.

All of the others had been small-time. He had gotten a little inexpensive jewelry, some furniture and worthless clothes—and the insurance. God, that first policy had been for only $5,000. It was all he could afford. He and Ellen had spent more than that in their first week here at the Marina.

And the chances he had taken on some of them—for such small returns. It chilled him even yet to think of the danger. He adjusted the shower mixture to a hotter spray. That mean little redhead, Jeannie, who'd got wise to the setup and played him along, and then demanded all he had in his bank account—the one she knew about—and his watch, to stop her going to the police. And the fiasco with Angela and that insurance investigator with the soft voice and the facial tic like a jovial wink. That whole thing had been a loss, even his clothes left behind with the threat of that winking watchdog on his heels. And plump, slow-witted Myrna, who'd neglected to tell him she had an ugly, suspicious brother who would show up at the cheap funeral. For all he knew, that man mountain with the dull, stainless steel eyes was still looking for him. Fortunately,

Elizabeth McCoy

Homer—wasn't that it, Homer?—was as dim a bulb as his sister. No fear he'd ever catch up with him now.

He turned the dials to a soft, warm spray like summer rain, letting it patter down on the bald spot on top of his head that he always combed the hair over carefully.

For a while there, with one and another of them, he had just about gotten discouraged and given it up for good. Oh, those dreary little jobs when the pickings were scarce. Fitting tight shoes on fat females. The short order cook. The roofing con. Selling restaurants that silver polish he drank the sample of to prove how harmless it would be to their flatware. Peddling the encyclopedias. Then, Ellen on that train.

Really, he thought, rubbing the lather deliciously around on his chest, that was like a master violinist, down on his luck, finding a Stradivarius in the street.

Three years now to get it all in line, foolproof. No chances with insurance this time. No need. There was nothing but money, hoarded by three generations of eccentrics, the unspent income from the trusts piling up into its own comfortable fortune. She was the last of that infertile line. No one to pry on her behalf into his fabricated background or question his eager devotion that won her gratitude day by day.

He had had it made! Even when the auto accident and the fall downstairs misfired, there was no suspicion on anyone's part, least of all Ellen's. Her mother had long ago, in her everlasting put-down of the girl, conditioned her to acceptance of the fact that she was awkward and inept and that whatever mishaps overtook her were her own fault. This time, with the boat, it could have been a safe certainty. He had queered it himself. And, to top it all, he had this feeling of relief.

Dammit, why?

He twisted the dial savagely so that the water pounded down on him, pushing him gasping against the back of the shower.

Suddenly, under that stinging torrent, the truth hit him—like a religious revelation. He did not want to destroy Ellen, because she was his creation, the only thing he had ever created in his life. And she was beautifully wrought. Out of that wilting, rabbity, dowdy, emotionally arrested little creature on the train he had, by his own charisma and taste and skill, like a master craftsman, made a subtly lovely woman, good to look at, poised, happy, self-confident, loving, and grateful—always glowingly grateful.

He turned off the shower and leaned against the wall, stunned. Had he never really intended to kill her, then, after the first few weeks—even though he went through the motions out of habit? It was like finding a stranger within himself. Now that the light had burst on him, he could see how it had happened, of course. For safety's sake he had had to let some time elapse after the marriage before concluding the matter. He had been shocked when he realized how little actual good the wealth stacked up by her mother and grandfather had ever done Ellen. Given her utterly pliant nature, the time, and all that money, it had become a challenge to remold her to the real potential of her fortune—and herself.

And he had worked at it—the clothes, the face, the figure, the charm of a naturally affectionate woman flowering in the warmth of attention and what she assumed to be love. The setting afforded every opportunity and every facility to polish the gem. And she had responded to it all with totally unspoiled gratitude and eagerness to please, to repay him for having given her a new being and a new life.

In a way he had been like that professor in the musical comedy Ellen had enjoyed so much, who made a lady out of the flower girl.

Except, of course, he hadn't fallen in love with his creation. No. His strange behavior, now that he was beginning to understand it, was dictated by the soundest possible logic. Each of the others had been a dangerous step on the way to some longed-for goal, some vague, easy way of life for which he hungered. Now he had reached that goal. It was as simple as that. If he killed her, would he have more money? No. Less, because the trusts would be terminated. And she left handling the money, all the money, entirely to him, never questioned his use of it. Would he have a more desirable life-style or companion in life? How could that be when he had fashioned her so completely to his own desires and standards? She was attractive. She lived to please him. She was a breathing, blooming proof of his good taste, his success. With growing confidence she had even developed a fresh sexuality in the bedroom that stirred him as no woman ever had before. And she was at least four inches shorter than he.

Clearly, he had found the end of the rainbow and from sheer force of habit had almost thrown away the pot of gold.

He dried himself hastily, pulled on a terry robe, and went back into the bedroom. For just a moment there a strange, cold fear had tugged at him that she might be gone somehow, have slipped quietly away in her sleep.

But she was there, curled on her side, her breath faintly moving a fine tendril of hair that had fallen across her cheek. He pulled the blanket up carefully over her bare shoulder and stood looking down at her. What is it the kids say? he thought. "This is the first day of the rest of my life"? It is. Oh, God, it is. Such a flood of relief and well-being swept through him that he bent and kissed her gently, unmindful that there was no one there at all to see him.

"Henry?"

"Yes, sweet."

"Keep reading your paper and promise not to look around for two minutes."

"Darling, not *another* present?"

"Not really. Just—don't look yet! Now."

"It's the hybrid that Morris wouldn't part with. How in the world did you get it?"

"You wanted it. I talked him out of it."

"And paid plenty?"

"Not enough to matter if you want it. I don't know about money. That's your job. You're getting a very distinguished collection. Maybe we should get an assistant gardener to help out old Ames."

"Mouse, come here. You shouldn't spoil me like this."

"Ummmmm. I love to spoil you. You made me begin to live. I love you."

"Darling, darling. Please, again."

"So soon? It'd take Superman."

"Yes, oh, yes."

"Wanton!"

"Yes."

"Concentrate now, please, Henry. Do you want to go to Miami, Tahiti, Acapulco, that new place in Morocco where everyone wears bedsheets, or the lake?"

"Can't we just stay here and see the fall coloring before we close the house?"

"I wanted you to say that. You always say the right thing. No wonder that Stella Montrose is absolutely mad for you."

"She knows a good thing when she sees it."

"What an egotist you are. But so do I, darling. So do I."

"Open the door and then your eyes, and you will have a great surprise."

"Ellen, baby, it's beautiful. But the Mercedes isn't even a year old yet."

"But I could tell you liked Tony Harlowe's. And this is a prettier color than his, isn't it?"

"My God, yes."

"And it's a great occasion."

"What occasion? I forget."

"No, you don't. You never forget. Six years. I can feel a box in your pocket now. If I get a little closer—and just a little closer still and—"

"It's only a sprain, Henry. I hardly feel it with the foot up like this. Don't bark at the poor old doctor. He just isn't used to treating anything more complicated here than hangovers. He's done very well by me."

"I want you to have X-rays. It was a bad fall. You could have gone all the way down and off the ledge."

"Love, don't fret. I'm just awkward, that's all. Even you couldn't make that over. I fall—have ever since I was little—down stairs and over curbings and off boats and over rocks. I'm always all right, darling. Henry? Darling, don't look like that. I'm all right, I tell you."

"What would I do if something happened to you—if anything happened to you—now?"

"I see that Ames has moved those rose tubs onto the terrace at last."

"Not Ames, darling. His latest assistant. He's not very bright or pretty, but he is big—simply enormous. I told you I'd find some muscle power to help Ames if we could keep him a few more years before retirement."

"What would I do without you, Mouse?"

"What *would* you do if anything happened to me, Henry?"

"Oh, probably get a good toupee and marry Stella Montrose or Pamela Grant or some one of those dozens of women you're always telling me are frantic for me."

"Monster. I mean really. I would so much hate to go without having somehow expressed all I feel for you—the love and—and the gratitude."

"So very sober all of a sudden. You're talking as if Dr. Mason found something wrong today."

"Of course not, darling. Don't get so upset. He says the ankle is as good as new. He suggests that I learn to pick up my feet when I walk."

"A very sound idea indeed. And also to pay attention at cards. Gin."

"You have just got to be cheating. This is the third game in a row and—"

* * *

"Darling, I have a surprise for you."

"Before I even get my coat off? Do I shut my eyes?"

"No, silly. It's on the terrace. That is—well, let me take your coat."

"Is it something my tie needs fixing for?"

"No. I'm only stalling for time, really. I—well—you know I'm such a dolt about falling everywhere and having accidents, and—if anything should—well, the trusts would stop."

"Mouse, there's enough without the trusts for two lifetimes. Now let's not talk about—"

"Yes. We have to. I want you to have everything I can give you. It would never be enough for what I feel. There, your tie's fine. Let's go. What it is—well, I mean, I took out this absolutely huge life insurance policy—and the company says it's usual to meet the beneficiary on such a large one and— Mr. Lorimer, this is my darling husband, Henry."

The slow turning of the man near the rose tree, and the hand extended.

"Mr.—ah, Murchison?" Softly, softly, and the tic like a roguish wink at a good joke shared.

Howard Browne

Born in Omaha in 1908, Howard Browne worked for several years as credit manager of a Chicago department store before entering the magazine field, first as a contributor of short fiction and then as an editor for Ziff-Davis Publications. His first mystery novel, *Halo in Blood* (1946), written as John Evans, introduced private eye Paul Pine. Following the Pine novel *The Taste of Ashes* (1957), a classic of tough detective fiction written under his own name, Browne deserted the book field for a quarter-century, devoting himself instead to screenplays (among them, *Portrait of a Mobster* and *The St. Valentine's Day Massacre*) and television plays (127 episodes of such series as "Cheyenne," "77 Sunset Strip," "Playhouse 90," "Mission Impossible," and "Columbo"). A resident of Carlsbad, he has also been an instructor of writing at the University of California, San Diego, since 1973.

Now mostly retired from screenwriting, Browne has returned to the mystery field with *The Paper Gun*, (1985), a new Paul Pine novel published in a signed limited edition. "House Call" first appeared in *Rogue*.

Howard Browne

....

house call

At 8:15 on a heavily overcast morning in late October, Mr. Coombs awoke to the soft strains of a Bach fugue from the clock radio beside his bed. Because of his deep and abiding respect for the composer he waited until the selection ended before he threw back the blanket, slid blue-veined feet into a pair of slippers, and pattered into the bathroom.

After making sure there was no furry coating on his tongue and that his temperature was normal, he used some of the gargle strongly recommended by Mr. Latzos, the corner druggist who had suffered from a spastic colon for years. Next he brushed his teeth vigorously, then carefully shaved the graying stubble from his unlined cheeks, unaggressive chin, and narrow upper lip. Humming a slightly off-key accompaniment to a Mozart sonata from the bedroom radio, he adjusted the shower to lukewarm, shucked off his pajamas, and stepped under the needle spray.

This, Mr. Coombs told himself contentedly, showed definite promise of turning out to be a perfect day.

By the time he was dressed and had the bedroom and bath restored to their normal pristine neatness, it was a few minutes past nine. He polished the lenses of his horn-rimmed glasses,

25

switched off the bedside radio, and entered the apartment's small kitchen, where he immediately turned on the radio over the sink. This time there was something from Grieg's *Lyric Suite*. Mr. Coombs always spoke very highly of Grieg.

Alert to the dangers of overeating, Mr. Coombs put together his customary breakfast of prune juice, a slice of whole-wheat toast, and one cup of decaffeinated coffee. Through the open window he could hear the young couple next door arguing about something or other.

Presently a door banged and quiet was restored. The coffee came to a boil and Mr. Coombs, an ear cocked to the soothing sound of strings in a Schubert serenade, got down a cup and saucer. He was reaching for the pot when two sharp sounds like pistol shots rang out from across the areaway, instantly followed by a high, hard voice lifted in song:

> *Go on baby, make it again;*
> *Right on baby, ain't no sin.*
> *Come on baby, lay it out,*
> *That's what lovin's all about . . .*

Dropping the cup, Mr. Coombs sprang to the window and slammed it shut with such force that the glass nearly shattered. He was trembling violently, his no longer gentle features twisted with fury, his breathing quick and hard. Faint but still insistent, the barbaric chant went on:

> *Rich folks, poor folks,*
> *They all shout . . .*

Mr. Coombs ground his teeth together and twisted the volume dial on his radio, bringing in Schubert loud enough to drown out that nerve-crippling wail. How any human could deliberately pour such acid into his ears defied comprehension. He placed the fingertips of his right hand on the pulse in his left wrist. A definite quickening.

Frowning, Mr. Coombs sat down to breakfast.

At 9:40 the doorbell rang. A deliveryman in an unmarked jumpsuit shoved a parcel into Mr. Coombs's hands, used a grimy forefinger to indicate the line on a clipboard pad reserved for his signature, and went off down the hallway. Mr. Coombs closed the door, put back the safety chain, and carried the package into the kitchen.

It was the size of a shoebox and the brown paper wrapping bore the self-adhesive label of an exclusive Northside bootery. Near an upper corner the word RUSH had been rubber-stamped in red.

Instead of immediately removing the wrapping, Mr. Coombs used a fingernail to loosen one corner of the label itself, then delicately stripped it free. On the reverse side, neatly printed in ink, were a name and address. These he committed to memory, then dug a book of matches from a drawer, touched a flame to the label, and flushed the ashes down the drain.

Humming a reprise of the Schubert piece, Mr. Coombs returned to the bedroom, pushed back the closet door, knelt, and turned back a corner of the carpeting. After lifting up a small section of floorboard, he reached into the cavity and brought out a small silk underarm holster and a short-barreled .32 Colt Police Special.

With the holstered gun in place and the jacket of his dark gray suit buttoned, Mr. Coombs eyed himself critically in the dresser mirror. Even a practiced eye, he assured himself, would fail to detect the slightest hint of a betraying bulge.

Patronizing the right tailor was essential to a man in Mr. Coombs's line of work.

At 2:55 that same afternoon a very pretty blond woman named Myra Selvin was setting out lunch for her husband in the kitchen of their tract home.

Howard Browne

Selvin's Shack, as Bill Selvin called the house, was located in a still raw subdivision and a full block, thus far, from the nearest neighbor. This isolation was a constant source of worry to him since it meant sticking Myra and young Danny out there alone till one in the morning five nights a week. It had to be that way, for he normally worked the four-to-midnight shift on the copy desk at Universal News Service.

During the twelve years since Bill first found out there was a lot more to Myra than a pair of great legs and a superior superstructure, they had acquired an eleven-year-old son, an '84 Granada hardtop, and, four months ago, a staggering mortgage on an overpriced hunk of real estate.

It seemed they had something else, too—at least Myra did: a brand-new uncreased traffic ticket picked up three days ago for overtime parking. By this time she'd worked up enough courage to hand it to Bill, along with his second cup of coffee.

"Be a darling," she said, seeking the light touch, "and mail them a check when you get to the office. I'd do it myself but the household account is a little low. Like in zilch."

A single glance was all Bill needed. "Fifteen bucks! For Chrisake, Myra!"

"Could've been a lot worse," Myra said virtuously. "A smashed fender at least. If I hadn't been on my toes, that man in the blue sedan might've—"

"*What* man in *what* blue sedan?"

"The one parked in front of me. Scary-looking—the man, I mean. He comes tearing out of this apartment house next to the market and jumps into this blue sedan just as I was pulling out. Came right at me. If I hadn't cut the wheel—"

"Well, bully for you! Of course, if you'd parked in the lot instead of the street, there wouldn't've *been* a ticket and you wouldn't've *been* anywhere near this blue sedan and none—"

Myra put up her hands in surrender. "I might've known you'd get technical. Hurry it up or you'll miss your bus. And I have to be here when Danny gets home."

Bill was still sulking a little when Myra pulled up at the bus stop. "Fifteen bucks," he growled. "I could'a got me a new fly rod for—"

She kissed him fondly. "Not that I'm throwing you out, but here comes your bus."

She watched the bus pull away, then drove quickly back to the Shack. The school bus was due in twenty minutes; time enough for a cup of coffee and half a doughnut before Danny showed up.

It didn't work out that way. She'd barely filled her cup before the doorbell rang. Just her luck; some salesman, out canvassing the boondocks.

The caller turned out to be a neatly dressed middle-aged man of medium height and rather slight build. He had an unaggressive chin, a narrow upper lip, and a mildly apologetic manner. Not at all an impressive figure but his air of quiet authority was unmistakable.

He lifted his dark gray hat with a courtly gesture and bowed slightly. "Mrs. Myra Selvin?"

Myra nodded and fought back a smile. She couldn't recall the last time anyone had actually bowed to her. If ever.

"My name," the man said, "is Hayden. With the city Bureau of Urban Development."

He certainly looked harmless enough, Myra decided; but then you never know. "Could I see some identification, Mr. Hayden? If you don't mind."

Mr. Hayden didn't appear at all offended. "Very wise of you to ask, Mrs. Selvin." He got out his wallet and extracted a business card, handing it to her with something of a flourish.

Myra glanced at it, saw the wording bore out his statement. "I imagine it's my husband you'll want to see. He's at—"

Mr. Hayden's gentle smile and headshake stopped her there. "This is merely an inspection visit, Mrs. Selvin. No need to bother him. A few minor points about building-code requirements I have to check out. Should have been done long before this, of course, but city departments are notoriously slow."

Before Myra was quite sure how he managed it, the man was

past her and moving along the short entrance hall leading to the living room. She closed the front door and followed him.

His eyes seemed to dart around the room. "Such lovely furnishings. You certainly have an eye for color coordination, Mrs. Selvin."

Myra warmed to the praise. This time she led the way, into the dining room and along the inner hall. He no longer seemed so much an intruder, she decided, as a guest being shown through the house.

In the kitchen, Mr. Hayden said, "I see you have only the two outer doors, side and front. Personally I approve of these modern layouts; somehow a back porch always seems to end up as a storeroom." There was a kind of shy warmth in his voice, and Myra was almost tempted to say, *You and Mrs. Hayden must drop in some evening*.

The inspection of the second floor was conducted in tactful silence. Mr. Hayden contented himself with merely glancing into the bedrooms and through the open door of the bath before returning to the living room. "Thank you, Mrs. Selvin," he said politely and slid a hand under the left lapel of his suit jacket.

The hand froze briefly, then came out again, empty. He said pleasantly, "Someone's at the front door, Mrs. Selvin."

Myra looked at him blankly. "Are you sure? I didn't hear—"

The doorbell rang.

"Excuse me," Myra said and went off down the hall. Such a strange little man, she was thinking. For all his gentlemanly manner, there was something . . . well, *chilling* about him.

But then Mr. Hayden was suddenly forgotten as she saw Miss Anderson, the school nurse, in the doorway holding Danny by the hand.

Myra reached quickly for the boy with quick concern. "What happened, Danny? Are you—"

Miss Anderson said, "No need to be upset, Mrs. Selvin." She edged Myra gently aside and led the boy into the hall. "Danny's fine. He seemed sort of listless in class and we found he was running a slight fever; probably a cold coming on. Not the least

30

bit serious, but I thought I'd better bring him home instead of putting him on the school bus. You know how drafty they can be."

Myra turned away. "Come in, Miss Anderson. I'll call Dr. Evans."

The nurse shook her head, smiled reassuringly. "No need for that, really. Just put him to bed; if he's still running a temperature in the morning, then you might call the doctor."

"You're sure?"

"Of course. Youngsters Danny's age bounce back like a bad check."

They exchanged understanding smiles and Miss Anderson left. Myra hustled the protesting boy upstairs, gave him a hot bath, and put him to bed. Not until she was cleaning up the bathroom did she remember the man from the city housing bureau. Good Lord, what must he think of her.

But Mr. Hayden was not in the living room. Frowning, Myra went through the entire house. Without result. It seemed Mr. Hayden had left without bothering to say goodbye.

Vaguely repentant, she looked out the front window. As usual the street was deserted, with nothing beyond that but open prairie. Apparently Mr. Hayden, not wanting to disturb her further, had simply left by the side door and driven away.

Myra returned to the kitchen, reheated the coffee, and was sipping at it over the morning paper when the doorbell rang. This time the caller was a tall, square-shouldered man in his early forties wearing a blue serge suit badly in need of pressing.

"Lieutenant Greer, ma'am. Police department." He flashed something shiny and official looking pinned to the inner flap of his wallet. "You Mrs. Myra Selvin?"

Myra stared at him incredulously. "I simply don't believe it."

The lieutenant lifted a shaggy eyebrow. "Ma'am?"

"Sending a policeman out here. Just to collect a measly fifteen dollars. I only got that parking ticket three days ago."

Lieutenant Greer gave her a one-sided smile. "That's not why

Howard Browne

I'm here. At least not directly." He looked past her shoulder. "May I come in?"

Seated in the living-room lounge chair, Lieutenant Greer declined a cup of coffee and explained the chain of events that had brought him here. A notorious underworld figure, he said, had been shot dead three days ago in an apartment building near the Union Supermart.

"We understand the killer got away in a blue sedan," the lieutenant went on. "Nobody admitted getting a good look at him, leaving us at a dead end. Till this morning, that is, when Traffic came up with the information on your parking ticket. The officer who tagged you remembered seeing a blue sedan parked in front of your vehicle at the time." He spread his hands and looked at her hopefully. "We figured it was possible you got a look at the driver."

Myra leaned forward, her eyes sparkling with excitement. "I sure did. He was in such a big hurry he almost took my fender off."

The lieutenant's expression showed grim satisfaction. "Now we're getting somewhere. What'd he look like?"

Myra's forehead creased. "Well, he seemed kind of . . . big. His face was sort of . . . sort of ugly. And angry, you know? He had on a hat and a dark coat . . ."

Her voice ran down. Greer took a deep breath and managed to keep his disappointment from showing. "You think maybe you could recognize him from a mug shot? You know: a picture?"

"I'm positive I could," Myra said promptly.

"Fine." The lieutenant reached for his hat. "I'd like you to come down to Headquarters with me and go through some of them. I'm sure we can narrow down the number beforehand, so it won't take much of your time."

Regretfully, Myra shook her head. "I can't, Lieutenant. Not right now. My little boy's upstairs, sick, and my husband's at work. How about tomorrow morning? I could drive over then."

After a brief discussion, Lieutenant Greer arranged to meet

her at the precinct station the following morning, bade her good-bye and drove off down the empty street.

That was at 4:25. At 4:40 a small gray Chevrolet coupe drew up at the curb a short distance from the Selvin residence and on the opposite side of the street.

Myra Selvin first noticed the gray car shortly after five o'clock. She was in the master bedroom straightening her bureau drawers when she caught a glimpse of it through the gathering darkness beyond the window.

Absently she wondered what a car was doing there at all. The only house on the block was her own. Probably some salesman, she decided, filling out a report, or whatever salesmen did at the end of a day.

But when, twenty minutes later, she realized the Chevrolet was still there, a dim sense of alarm began to rise within her. Suddenly Lieutenant Greer's story of the killer in the blue sedan flooded back—and the sense of alarm was no longer dim.

She peered cautiously from behind the bedroom drapes, trying to learn if anyone was actually in the car. But at 5:30 in late October dusk had already filled the street, making it impossible to see into the car's interior.

It was then she remembered the field glasses hanging from a strap in Bill's closet. She got them out with unsteady hands, knelt at the open window, and focused the powerful lenses on the front seat of the small gray coupe.

Someone was sitting there.

Because of the downward angle she could not make out the upper half of the man's body, but she could see his upper thighs . . . and his hands. Something was in those hands; some small object she could not identify. If only there was more light . . .

As though in response to her silent plea, the street lamp almost directly above the car came on. In the yellow rays the magnified image of the object stood out sharply before Myra's straining eyes.

A gun.

The binoculars dropped from Myra's nerveless fingers. A wave of weakness washed over her and for a long moment she could not rise from her knees. Finally, trembling with mounting fear, she got to her feet, ran from the bedroom, and down the stairs.

The phone receiver came into her hand with the heartening feel of a life preserver to a drowning man. Thrusting a palsied finger into the last hole, she spun the dial and put the receiver to her ear.

No answering buzz, no faint crackling sound of an open wire. Just an empty silence that seemed slowly to spread and engulf her. Frantically she moved the bar up and down. *Please!* a voice screamed inside her. *Please answer!*

Nothing. Nothing at all. Slowly her eyes moved along the cord toward the wall. A dry sob tore at her throat and the receiver fell from her hand.

The cord had been ripped from the wall box.

Bill Selvin filled his cup from one of the office coffee carafes, took off his green eyeshade, and got up to stretch his legs. The wall clock put the time at 4:50. Why not, he thought, call Myra, tell her he really wasn't sore about that parking ticket. Hell, he'd paid off a few tickets himself that Myra didn't even know about. Not that she was sitting around crying her eyes out, but a guy ought to be understanding about such things.

After the tenth ring he slowly put back the receiver. Funny; she *had* to be home. If she'd gone out for any reason, she would have called him first. Unless she'd taken Danny to McDonald's for a burger . . . No; even then she'd have called to let him know.

He tried the number again. Still no answer. Scowling, he depressed the cutoff bar, released it, and dialed the operator.

Myra sat huddled on the floor at the downstairs front window, peering past a corner of the drawn drapes. The burst of panic that had sent her flying to the telephone had dissipated, leaving her limp with terror. *You're trapped*, her mind shrilled; *there's nothing you can do!*

She closed her eyes, shivering, her fingers digging into the carpet. She had seen the face of a murderer; for that she must die. She knew now that when Mr. Hayden had slipped a hand inside his jacket he was reaching for a gun. Naturally he had been the first to hear Miss Anderson and Danny at the front steps. He was a killer—a hired killer, and would possess the sharpened senses of a stalking tiger. The moment she had left him to answer the bell, he had slipped out the side door. There had been no one to see him arrive, no one to see him go.

And now he was back again. Sitting out there where he could keep an eye on both outer doors, waiting till the last trace of daylight was gone before forcing his way in and doing what he had been hired to do.

Suddenly Myra was on her feet. There *was* a way! Yank open the door and *run!* Run screaming into the night, away from where he waited. If he dared shoot at all, there was so little light that he *had* to miss a moving target. It was worth trying. Anything was better than waiting to die cowering in a corner like a helpless child . . .

Danny. My God—*Danny!*

Her knees seemed to melt and she leaned, shaking, against the wall. Some strange alchemy of the mind had managed to block Danny out, leaving only the thought of her own danger. Briefly, she weighed the possibility of getting him hurriedly dressed and, together, making a run for it. But the thought of Danny out in the open as the killer took slow and deliberate aim . . .

What if she simply left Danny upstairs in his room? If he didn't *see* Mr. Hayden there would be no reason to harm him. The man wasn't a maniac; he was a cold, controlled executioner, killing only the person he was paid to kill.

A crazed kind of gratitude welled up within her toward the man outside. Her tormented mind became a twisted prism

35

through which he was revealed as a good man, a kindly man, a man who would never senselessly harm a child . . .

She straightened as a sudden thought sent her spirits soaring. Hurrying to the living-room desk, she found a thin plastic letter opener in one of the drawers, then sat down on the floor in front of the telephone box fastened low on the wall. Her fingers were steady as she removed the screws on either side and took off the black metal cover. Then her spirits plummeted as she stared helplessly at the maze of wires, their number and confusion magnified by fear as she poked at them with the double-pronged end of the loose cord.

He knew you couldn't fix it! her mind shrieked. *He doesn't make mistakes.*

She put her face in her hands. *This is the way he wants me to be,* she thought. Helpless, defeated, knowing that nothing could save her, that no door, no lock, would bar his way.

Her churning thoughts went back to Danny. At least he could be spared. She hurried up the stairs and found him propped up on the pillows leafing through one of his books in drowsy contentment. She forced a smile. "How do you feel, darling?"

Danny eyed her with open calculation. "Can I stay home tomorrow?"

"Of course you can. Tomorrow's Saturday."

His expression changed. "I'm not sick, Mom. It's just that ole Miss Anderson said so."

"But I want you to stay in bed. That's very important. Do you understand, Danny? No matter what, you must stay in bed!" She bit her lip, afraid she'd made too great a point of it, stirred his curiosity. He might . . .

"Can I play my radio, then?"

"After a while, darling." She bent and kissed him, careful to keep the caress from being the fiercely possessive act she yearned to make it. She straightened and looked down at her son for a long moment, then turned and went stiffly down the steps.

Mr. Hayden was waiting in the living room.

All during the timeless period of terror since she had first seen the gun, a corner of Myra Selvin's mind had dwelt on how the killer would act at the last moment. Would that narrow upper lip twist into a sneer? Would he strike her first? Or would he merely point the gun at her and pull the trigger?

There was no violence. He did not sneer. He stood there facing her, his expression serious, his hand holding the gun along his leg.

"I saw him," she said dully, the words forming without conscious volition. "I wish I hadn't, but he looked back, you see."

A flicker of interest stirred in the gray face. "Who was it you saw, Mrs. Selvin?"

"Why, the man. The man in the blue car. The man who killed somebody. Isn't that why you . . ."

The man who called himself Hayden, Coombs, or any of a dozen other names stared at her and said nothing.

"You mustn't k-kill me," Myra said in a small voice. Her nails were biting into her palms.

"I'm sorry, Mrs. Selvin. I'd much rather I didn't have to."

"Then go away," she whispered. "Just go away. Tell the man I won't say anything to the police."

"I'm afraid I wouldn't know how to do that," he said regretfully. "I never know the names of my . . . clients. It isn't at all necessary, you see."

He began slowly to bring up the muzzle of the gun. *Why don't I scream?* Myra wondered dazedly. *Why can't I turn and run? Or get down on my knees and beg?*

She forced out a last whisper, a shattered prayer. "You won't hurt my boy—upstairs?"

The gun was level now, pointed at her heart. It seemed to swell, to grow in his hand. "Of course I won't, Mrs. Selvin."

"Thank you. Oh, thank . . ."

There were two very loud shots. But they came from upstairs, not from the gray man's gun. A blast of raucous sound followed; Danny had turned on his radio.

Go on baby, make it again;
Right on baby, ain't no sin . . .

Howard Browne

Both Mr. Hayden and Myra reacted sharply; the former with a snarl, a visible shudder, a turning of his body toward the stairs. Myra, seeing only the snarl, knew that Danny was in danger. She threw herself at the man with instinctive and unreasoning ferocity, driving a shoulder into him at about the level of his belt buckle. Since Mr. Hayden was not a robust man it was not at all surprising that he toppled backward.

The gun fell from his hand as his head snapped back sharply on his thin neck, striking a leg of the couch with surprising force. His body seemed to contract convulsively, then go completely limp.

Myra crawled on hands and knees along the carpeting, her staring eyes glued to the gun. The blast of music from upstairs decreased sharply as the volume was adjusted. Myra's hand closed around the weapon's chill length and everything within her seemed to stop functioning. She sat there, one leg stretched out, and stared at the blued metal . . .

A bell was ringing. The doorbell. She wondered in a kind of detached way who it might be. She went on wondering, not moving, not calling out, and presently a cautious face appeared around the edge of the living-room archway. A young man's face under a shock of black unruly hair. Wondering eyes took in the scene. He stared at Myra. Myra stared at him.

"Telephone Company, lady. We got a rush out-of-order report on this number."

"The cord," Myra said. "It's been pulled out."

"I'll get it fixed right up, lady."

"Thank you."

It was completely mad. The way they spoke, the politely commonplace things they were saying. Like two friends witnessing something indecent while out for a stroll and hiding their embarrassment with casual conversation.

Ridiculous.

Then Myra fainted and the telephone man took over.

Jon L. Breen

....

Jon L. Breen has been contributing fiction and criticism to the mystery field since 1967. Born in Montgomery, Alabama, in 1943, he now lives in Fountain Valley. Two of his books, *What About Murder?: A Guide to Books About Mystery and Detective Fiction* (1981) and *Novel Verdicts: A Guide to Courtroom Fiction* (1984), won Edgar awards in the biographical-critical category. Between 1977 and 1983 he was mystery reviewer for *Ellery Queen's Mystery Magazine*. With his wife, Rita, he edited the anthology *American Murders* (1985). His parodies of other writers were collected in *Hair of the Sleuthhound* (1982).

A radio play-by-play broadcaster in his college days, Breen has used sports backgrounds for many of his mysteries, notably horse racing in the novels about track announcer Jerry Brogan, *Listen for the Click* (1983) and *Triple Crown* (1986), and baseball in the series of short stories about major league umpire Ed Gorgon. "All-Star Team" is a new Gorgon story, written especially for this volume.

Jon L. Breen
....
all-star team

I have resented telephones the whole of my natural life. After umpiring an eighteen-inning game at New Hopton Stadium, getting back to the hotel at 1:30 A.M. with a day game scheduled for the next afternoon, finally dropping off to sleep a little after 2:00, and then hearing that obscene ringing in my ears, I especially resent telephones.

With commendable restraint, I grab the phone off its cradle and say "Hello." Just "Hello."

"Ed Gorgon?" says the voice on the other end.

Do I admit it? Probably some disgruntled fan wants to chastise me for that call at third base he thinks I blew in the bottom of the sixteenth. I didn't blow it, by the way. Oh, I've blown a few, but not that one.

"Yeah, this is Ed Gorgon."

"This is Rojas."

"Good to hear from you, Sarge, but you've picked better times to call. What's up?"

"Sorry to wake you, Ed, but you and I have to talk a little baseball."

"I'd talk about murder at this time of night, that being my hobby, but baseball is my profession and I'm off duty."

"Professionals are never off duty. Don't you think I'd like to be home in bed? We'll talk murder, too, but first baseball. What do you think of this all-star team?"

I fall back groaning on the bed, letting the receiver fall gently against my ear. If this is going to be a discussion of the comparative skills of Eddie Murray and Wally Joyner, I'm going to sleep through it.

"Abbott at first base, Best at second, Dilnot at third, Kott at short, DePuy in right, Adey in center, Fox in left, Adimov pitching, Elms catching. Horst is the designated hitter. Coors and Fry are warming up in the bullpen. Jopp, DeGhoort, and Hill are available for pinch-hitting duty."

I feel like I've just walked into *Alice in Wonderland*. Has Sergeant Rojas, a normally level-headed and competent member of New Hopton's police force, been drinking? Is he playing some kind of game with me? Drawing a deep breath, I decide to play it straight.

"Not much of an all-star team. Most of those guys I never heard of. Nelly Fox was a second baseman, not a left fielder, or was it Jimmy Foxx with two *x*'s? Jim Kaat was a pitcher, not a shortstop, though he about fielded well enough . . ."

"It's K-o-t-t. Spelled differently. So these aren't real players?"

"They don't ring many bells with me. Who did you say the first baseman was?"

"Abbott."

"No, Who's on first, What's on second . . ."

"Ed, this is serious."

"Well, if it's so damned serious, quit playing games and tell me what it's all about. You said something about murder."

"I was hoping you could tell me what all those players had in common."

"Oblivion. Come on, Sarge, I don't work without the facts."

41

Jon L. Breen

I've played into his hands. Now instead of being angry at getting woken in the middle of the night, I'm begging him for details.

"A man named Clarence Fortune, partner in a large corporate law firm, was found murdered in his office at about nine o'clock last night. Actually, we can pinpoint it at exactly 8:53, because a cleaning woman heard the murder take place. She was sweeping out an adjacent office and heard Fortune talking to a visitor. She says he said something like, 'You could make my all-star team. Here, look.' She didn't hear the other person speak, but she did hear a shot and somebody running out of the office.

"She was scared out of her wits and sort of stood there frozen for a couple of minutes, though she had presence of mind enough to note the time. Finally, she got up the courage to go around to Fortune's office and found him dead. She called us at once.

"We were able to determine from the watchman on duty that no one had left the building since the murder, so we could narrow our range of suspects to three other people who were working late on Fortune's floor. One was Mabel Hollister, a secretary in Fortune's firm who was working in an office down the hall."

"Did she hear the shot?"

"She says not. The offices are fairly soundproof and she says she was typing all the time. Actually, the only reason the cleaning woman could hear the shot was that the wall between her and Fortune's office was a temporary partition.

"Now the other two were Wilbur Chow, an importer of Asian art who was also working late—he thinks he heard the shot but says he's used to unexpected noises in the city and thought nothing of it—and Gilbert Formby, a tax accountant, very nervous and edgy guy. He says he didn't hear the shot either."

"Funny time for him to be working overtime. It's long past April 15. What about the weapon? Did you find it?"

"Yeah, dropped in the wastebasket of the office. Very clever. No prints, of course, and the killer must have been pretty confident the gun couldn't be traced to him. Or her."

"Any connection between Fortune and the three others?"

"Well, they all knew him. Mabel Hollister used to go out with him, but they'd broken it off some months ago. She said she couldn't stand his game-playing."

"Did she mean that figuratively or literally?"

"Maybe both, but for sure literally. He loved puzzles and word games and all that stuff. She had it up to here. Formby had done some work for Fortune's firm in the past, and Chow had sold him some Chinese art. No apparent motives, but we'll keep digging. We can handle the ballistics and the doorbell ringing, though, Ed. I called you because of the baseball angle."

"This all-star team . . ."

"Yeah. At the time of his death, he was making out lineups for this all-star team of his. Mabel Hollister said he was always making up imaginary teams of guys who were all under six feet or whose names all started with Y or who came from Connecticut or whose names were kinds of food. Things like that. Only he always used real players' names. But this team he was working on when he was killed didn't seem to use real players. And we couldn't figure out what all the names had in common. And what the killer's name might have had in common with them."

I have a sudden glimmering in the back of my mind. A theory is taking shape.

"So you were lucky I was in town—your baseball consultant, huh? I don't think you have to know a baseball from a volleyball to figure this one out, though. What did you say the cleaning woman's name was?"

"I don't think I did. But it's Clarice Singleton."

"Uh-huh. And give me those names again from the top. Abbott was on first . . ."

"Yeah, no Costello."

"Costello couldn't make this team. And Best was on second. Yeah, that checks. Give me a spelling on all of these."

He runs them down. The one that has me worried is Adimov. "That's not Adamov?"

"No, it's A-d-i . . ."

Jon L. Breen

"Good, good." I finish the list and look it over carefully, looking for a loophole, inviting Rojas to do the same. After a couple of minutes, I say, "Now do you see what they have in common?"

"No."

"I suggest you take a long look at Mr. Wilbur Chow. He killed Fortune. How did I know that?"

"I don't know."

"Third base!"

"Ed, quit kidding around."

"You wake me up in the middle of the night to figure out a puzzle any school kid should be able to do. I have the right to a little fun. Look at the names again, Sarge. What do they all have in common? Nationality? No. Number of letters? No. Association with some special field of endeavor? No. But look closely at the names, at the letters in the names. It's as simple as A, B, C."

After a slight pause, Rojas says, "Oh, geez . . ."

"You mean you finally got it?"

"Yeah."

"And did you have to know anything about baseball?"

"Not a damn thing."

"And are you going to arrest Wilbur Chow?"

Rojas laughs. "Not just yet. I don't think we can convict a guy of murder just because the letters in his name are in alphabetical order."

Dan J. Marlowe

....

Born in Lowell, Massachusetts, in 1914, Dan J. Marlowe worked in accounting, insurance, and public relations and served on the city council and as mayor pro tem of Harbor Beach, Michigan. Between 1959 and 1976, he wrote numerous well-received paperback-original crime novels, the best known of which, *The Name of the Game is Death* (1962), introduced professional thief Earl Drake, later to turn secret agent in the course of a dozen-book series. One Drake adventure, *Flashpoint* (1970), earned Marlowe an Edgar for best paperback of its year.

Marlowe, a resident of Tarzana at the time of his death in 1986, called the story that follows "a perfect example of my devious mind at work . . ."

Dan J. Marlowe

....

by means unlovely

E ddie Anderson looked up from his morning task of removing the lightweight linen dustcloths from the glass showcases. A customer had entered through the wide doors of Stone's Jewelry. The man walked directly to the trays containing the most expensive watches the store had for sale.

45

Dan J. Marlowe

Eddie moved in behind the counter. The subdued, indirect lighting, the thick carpeting, and the elaborately simple individual displays all contributed to the cathedral-like atmosphere that was the hallmark of Stone's. An ornate marble staircase wound upward to the second-floor offices.

"Yes, sir?" Eddie inquired.

"Are you Anderson?" the customer asked. "Tom Jenkins told me to look you up. He said you carried the Medallion watch in the Donada line."

Warmth came into Eddie's voice. He couldn't recall a Tom Jenkins, but he had no difficulty at all in recalling that Donada's Medallion was the top of the line.

"I'm Anderson," he agreed. "And we do have the Medallion, sir." He opened a drawer beneath the counter and removed a glistening, minuscule watch. He displayed it on the black velvet pad atop the showcase. "It's an exceptional value, sir," Eddie continued in his most sincere salesman's tone.

The man picked up the elegant-looking ladies' watch and examined it appraisingly.

"It has the very finest movement," Eddie assured him. "And just look at the styling. It's the very—"

"I'll take it," the customer announced.

Eddie nodded. He turned at once to pick up a gift box from the back counter. It was a bit disconcerting to have the animals walk in from the street and just about jerk the merchandise out of your hand, but a sale is a sale is a sale. Never offer to show them anything after they've spoken the fatal words "I'll take it." Procrastination is the thief of commissions.

"Charge, sir?" Eddie asked.

"Cash."

The customer fingered out a dozen new-looking crisp bills from his wallet. He picked up the tiny package that Eddie had deftly gift-wrapped for him, a very small amount of change, and departed as rapidly as he had entered the store.

Eddie shrugged as he closed the drawer of the cash register.

Not a bad start on the day.

He moved back in the direction of the still-covered show-cases, then detoured toward the front of the shop. He paused behind the shop's front window. He was concealed from the eyes of passersby by the heavy, dove-gray drapery that served as a front-window backdrop. Eddie moved an end-fold slightly to one side and looked across the street.

Harry was there.

Harry Williams was standing behind the front window of Williams' Jewelry Store across the street. Watching. Just standing and watching. As he had yesterday, last week, and last month.

You didn't even really need to see him, Eddie thought. You could feel him, standing and staring across the street. It was a feeling that made Eddie nervous, increasingly nervous as time passed.

He forced himself away from the front window. Stop thinking about it, he told himself. You're getting as bad as Harry. Forget about Harry. An ulcer you need? Harry would like that. Harry would like that fine, but an ulcer was far too good for what Harry would wish for Richard Harrington Stone, Jr., Eddie's boss.

Eddie returned to the showcases in the rear of the shop, but even as his quick hands nimbly folded and creased and laid away dustcloths, his treacherous mind reverted to the front window of the jewelry shop across the street. Cut it out, he told himself for the thousandth time. You weren't Harry's partner. Richard Harrison Stone, Jr., had been Harry's partner, and you didn't see Richard Harrington Stone, Jr., worrying about Harry.

Richard Harrington Stone, Jr., had insisted that his former partner, Harry Williams, buy him out. Stone had had a number of reasons, all of which Harry had sought to brush aside. Harry hadn't wanted to buy out his young partner.

Harry had the money, but he was satisfied with things the way they were. Harry was interested in amateur theatricals, and the partnership gave him time to enjoy his hobby, which included the writing of one-act plays. Harry had had four plays produced by regional theatrical companies.

Still, if your partner wants out, what can you do? Harry had called Derwood Cheney, his lawyer for twenty years, and Derwood had drawn up the reduction-of-partnership papers. Once begun, the dissolution had moved forward swiftly.

And then three months later Richard Harrison Stone, Jr., had opened up this brand-new store right across the street from Harry's store. Harry had just about torn the door off his safe getting out his reduction-of-partnership papers and had then found out there was no restrictive clause preventing Richard Harrison Stone, Jr., from opening up another jewelry store in the same area for a specified period of time.

Harry had found out, too, in his first semihysterical telephone call to Derwood Cheney that Cheney had both lost and gained a client. The new client was Richard Harrison Stone, Jr. The legal papers that had been mailed to Harry informing him of the abridgement of Harry's and Cheney's former legal relationship must have gone astray, Cheney informed Harry suavely.

The originals were in Cheney's office, signed by Harry. For twenty years Harry had signed the hundreds of papers Cheney had presented for Harry's signature. Harry had never read the papers. Cheney was his lawyer, wasn't he?

Harry had found all this out just a little bit too late, Eddie Anderson told himself defensively. In business a man protected himself, or else he stood in windows staring across the street.

The street doors opened again, and Eddie was glad for the interruption of his thoughts. A fat man hurried to the counter and thrust a magazine clipping into Eddie's hand. "I need six of these," he declared breezily. The man's manner was bluff and hearty. His grin was toothy. "Promotion job. Got to be identical. Can you fix me up?"

"Six," Eddie repeated. He looked down at the clipping that showed a Medallion wristwatch. He thought quickly. He could call a couple of stores and pick up the watches he needed to complete the order. "Certainly, sir. By two o'clock this afternoon I can—"

"Not a chance, son." The fat man's tone was positive. "I'm

due at a sales meeting in half an hour. How many Medallions do you have?"

"I have four. In an hour, even, I can get—"

"Any in the window?" the customer interrupted.

"No, sir."

"Any in the vault?"

"No, sir. There's not another one in the shop."

"Gimme the four." The fat man tossed coarse wads of money down upon the countertop. "My girl'll have to shoot out and pick up a couple more while I stall them in the meeting."

The man wouldn't even wait for gift-wrapping. He hustled out the door, almost trotting. Eddie looked after his rotund figure thoughtfully. It surely had to be a monstrous promotion if the sales prizes were Medallions. Something on the order of steam shovels, perhaps. Or locomotives.

Eddie wished he'd had the other two Medallions. How could you figure this business? You might sell one or two a month, ordinarily, if you were lucky. Now they had snatched five away from him in a morning. In a morning? He glanced at his watch. In less than an hour.

He made a note on the Out pad beside the cash register, then looked up as the street doors parted again.

Richard Harrison Stone, Jr., entered the shop with his usual arrogant stride. He gave Eddie a curt nod. Eddie's eyes followed the ascent of the lean, aristocratic-looking figure up the marble stairs. Eddie shook his head. Working for Richard Harrington Stone, Jr., was a far different proposition than working for Harry had been. Stone was a hard-nosed boss.

The street doors flew open and the morning's first customer reentered almost at a run. His face was flushed as he plowed toward Eddie at the counter. He was obviously trying to repress strong emotion. He slapped down upon the countertop the still-gift-wrapped package Eddie had handed him earlier.

"Like to return this," the customer said hoarsely. He was trying to smile. "The lady wouldn't even look at it. Or at me."

49

Dan J. Marlowe

"Sorry," Eddie murmured. "It happens." He toed the buzzer under his foot that would bring Emile the watch repairer from his cubicle behind a curtain. Eddie unwrapped the package, then handed the watch to Emile when the little man appeared.

Emile examined the Medallion, checked the itemization on the refund slip Eddie was making out, then silently returned the watch to the drawer under the counter. You never knew, Eddie reflected as he made the refund and watched the customer depart again. Even in a shop like this you could find someone trying to work a switch. It was never a problem, though. On any refund, he had only to call Emile from behind the curtain to identify the merchandise.

The girl must really have given that poor guy a hard time, Eddie thought. He'd be a woman-hater now, until the next time. Eddie looked at his watch. Eleven o'clock. And as though linked by an invisible wire he drifted along the counter and out to the front window, where he again raised a fold of the drapery and looked across the street.

Bright sunlight reflected from Harry's window, dazzling Eddie. He dropped the fold of drapery. So you can't see, Anderson. You need to see? Harry is standing there. Watching. Watching and waiting.

Eddie's mouth twitched. Harry was mad at Stone, all right. Harry was purely-out-his-mind mad at Stone, but Harry was mad at Eddie, too. Eddie had worked for Harry, before and after the breakup of the partnership.

Then Stone had come after Eddie and made him a very, very good offer. Eddie had given Harry a chance to match it, but Harry, out of control by that time about anything connected with Stone, refused to even talk about it. So Eddie had gone with Stone.

At the time it had seemed the thing to do. Eddie had liked Harry, but it really hadn't been a difficult decision to make. There was the money, but even more there was the difference in the two stores.

Harry's was old, comfortably dusty-looking, and seemingly

50

down-at-the-heels although Harry carried only the best merchandise. Stone's was new, sparklingly bright and clean, and prosperous-looking. No, it hadn't been a difficult decision to make.

Except that on mornings like this Eddie wondered increasingly about his decision. Not that Harry would really do anything. Not that Harry really could do anything. It was just . . .

Eddie turned at the sound of the outer doors opening. He found himself gazing at an overdressed big blond pushing her way inside. She was followed by a hawk-faced man in a dark suit and a huge man in a rich-looking sport coat and light-colored slacks.

Eddie examined the blond more closely as she marched toward the counter. A little warning bell jangled in his mind. A beef. Even in a place like this you had to get a beef once in a while. The blond confronted Eddie with a triumphant air, and he waited for the lightning to strike.

But it was the huge man who spoke. "That's the clerk?" he demanded. His voice was fantastically deep. The woman nodded, and the voice boomed at Eddie. "You, there!" He dangled a wristwatch in front of Eddie. "You sold my wife a phony watch. Don't try to deny it."

"If I could just see the watch," Eddie said in his most patiently courteous salesman's voice, regarding the spinning object held up at eye level, "I might not have to deny it."

"Here." The large man thrust it at him. "It's lost thirty minutes every day she's had it, and I've—"

"Sometimes even a new watch needs a slight adjustment," Eddie managed to wedge into the roar of the waterfall of words. He looked at the watch in his hand. A Medallion. Another Medallion. On Medallions this morning they were in a rut so deep it was a trench.

Eddie looked at the blond again and then he remembered. She had bought the watch the previous week. He turned back to

51

the basso profundo. "I'll have our watch man take a quick look at it and see what he recommends. It will only take—"

"Will you listen to me?" the basso profundo interrupted. He had never heard such a voice, Eddie decided. It was a wonder the crystal on display wasn't shattering. "I know they need adjusting sometimes! When Nora told me she was having trouble with it, I took it to my own jeweler, thinking I'd save her a trip across town. And get this, buddy—when my jeweler looked at it, he said the watch has a cheap movement worth about ten dollars."

"That's impossible," Eddie returned at once. He made sure that his tone was polite but firm. He toed the buzzer again for Emile and handed over the Medallion when the little watchmaker once again appeared in the front of the shop.

Emile listened to Eddie's hurried explanation. Then he inserted his jeweler's loupe in his eye and delicately unscrewed the back of the watch. His head came up after his first look. "The watch came from here?" he asked carefully.

The blond fumbled in her handbag and produced a sales slip that she waved triumphantly at Emile.

"I remember the sale," Eddie said. He thought his voice sounded a little faint. He tried to strengthen it. "I recall it clearly."

Emile cleared his throat. "It is not a Medallion movement," he said in his precise-sounding voice.

Eddie stared at him. The man in the dark suit who had been standing off to one side spoke up for the first time. Eddie observed that he had a hard, authoritative-looking face. "You got any more of these watches here?" the man demanded.

"No," Eddie began, and then remembered the lovelorn suitor. "Wait. We do have." He opened the drawer under the counter and removed the returned watch. "Here."

"Open it up," the man said, handing the watch to Emile. His tone was brusque. Eddie found himself leaning toward Emile to see better. When the back was removed from the watchcase and he saw the expression on Emile's usually stolid features, Eddie felt as if his own stomach had been punched.

The man in the dark suit had seen Emile's expression, too. He took both watches from Emile, then removed a leather billfold from his jacket pocket. He opened it, and Eddie caught a flash of a badge. "District Attorney's Rackets Squad," the man said to Eddie. "You the owner here?"

"No." Automatically, Eddie's glance went toward the marble staircase. "Mr. Stone is the owner. Perhaps—"

The man didn't give Eddie time to finish. "Let's all go upstairs and talk to Mr. Stone."

Eddie watched in disbelief while the red-faced, violently protesting Richard Harrison Stone, Jr., was loaded into the summoned squad car. "Lock up here until I can get this . . . this idiocy straightened out!" Stone called in a strangled voice to Eddie, who was standing in the shop's doorway.

The squad car started up, turned the corner, and disappeared. Eddie locked the doors of Stone's Jewelry and walked deliberately across the street to Harry's store. He could see Harry in the window again, watching Eddie as he approached. Eddie could see that Harry was grinning widely.

"*You* did it!" Eddie cried out as he burst through the door. "I don't know how, but *you* did it!"

"Sure I did it," Harry agreed. He sounded complacent. Gleefully complacent. He was unwrapping the cellophane from a cigar that he placed in a corner of his mouth. "How'd you like the play I wrote?"

"Play? Play? Stone's going to *jail*, Harry! He'll be ruined! He'll be—"

"It's only a fine. I checked." Harry lit up his cigar.

"But his business will be trashed! This kind of thing gets around! Stone will be—"

"So?" Harry cut off Eddie's excited comment. "You expected maybe I'd send him tickets to a musical?"

Eddie was silent for a moment. Then he shook his head. "I'm surprised you didn't think of something for me, too," he said finally. "Like life on Devil's Island."

"Hey, Eddie, if it was still the first week you went across the street with Stone, I'd have figured something for you, too. Believe it. But I got over being mad at you. Stone, now, him I stayed mad at."

Harry exhaled what was plainly a self-satisfying lungful of smoke. "I made up my mind I'd use that character up until there was nothing left but gold fillings in a crematorium ash pit. So I cold-cocked him. Figured out yet how I did it?"

"Go ahead and gloat," Eddie said gloomily. "Right now I'm trying to think where I can get another job."

"It took me six months to fit the pieces together," Harry went on, unheeding. "Then I wrote the script, and like I said, I put all the words right into the mouths of the four actors I hired."

"Actors?" Eddie said blankly.

"Just listen, okay?" Harry was looking more pleased with himself by the moment. "First I sent the woman to you to buy a Medallion, right? She brought it to me and I removed the Medallion movement and substituted a cheap one. I gave her back the watch and told her to wait till she heard from me again."

"But why—" Eddie stopped when Harry held up a hand.

"Then this morning I sent the guy who wanted a Medallion for his girlfriend," Harry resumed. "And right behind him came the loudmouth who wanted six Medallions, but you could sell him only four. His job was to get every Medallion you had in the shop. From the trays, from the counter, from the front window, from the vault. Did I say I wrote all the dialogue?"

Eddie nodded.

"So then the lovelorn suitor came back and gave you *his* Medallion for a refund, okay? Only he brought it to you *after* he'd brought it to my back door and I'd switched the movement in it, too. I know Emile is a very careful man, but not even Emile takes the back off a watch he's just seen you take out of the original gift wrapping. So now you had a Medallion with a cheap movement in the drawer under the counter."

Eddie was silent, mentally reconstructing the sequence of events Harry was relating.

"Then I called the woman and sent her and the guy with the bass voice to walk in on you with *her* Medallion with an inferior movement. And they brought a Rackets Squad detective with them. And when the only other Medallion you have in the shop, courtesy of the lovelorn suitor, also turns out to have an inferior movement, what's a Rackets Squad detective supposed to think? Exactly what he did think, and bingo, Richard Harrison Stone, Jr., takes a ride downtown."

Eddie took a deep breath as the 24-karat perfection of the frame became clear to him. "You must have spent—"

"So I spent a few dollars." Harry waved his cigar airily. "It was a pleasure."

"But you're not really going to let it go all the way, are you?" Eddie protested.

"Let's see how mad I still am after the arraignment," Harry said. "My actors all had phony I.D., so if I say disappear, there'll be no witnesses." He took another pull at his cigar, squinting at Eddie through the emitted smoke. "As for you, birdbrain, you come back to work for me here. At your old salary." He grinned. "Talk to me in six months and I might write another script about what you'll be making then."

"Yes, sir," Eddie said meekly.

Maxine O'Callaghan

According to Robert A. Baker and Michael T. Nietzel's valuable reference source, *Private Eyes: One Hundred and One Knights*, Tennessee native Maxine O'Callaghan "was raised on a cotton farm that her family sharecropped and was the first member of her family to graduate from high school." Early jobs included waitress, secretary, and long-distance operator. Now a resident of Mission Viejo, O'Callaghan is best known as the creator of Delilah West, the capable and believable female private eye of *Death Is Forever* (1981) and *Run from Nightmare* (1982). She has contributed short stories to *Ellery Queen's Mystery Magazine* and *Alfred Hitchcock's Mystery Magazine*. Her latest book, *Dangerous Charade* (1985), was written under the pseudonym Marissa Owens.

"The Sweet Old Lady Who Sits in the Park" appears in these pages for the first time anywhere.

Maxine O'Callaghan

························

the sweet old lady
who sits in the park

Mrs. Hartley settled into a shady corner of the park bench
to wait for Mr. Smith. Not his real name, of course. It was a
code name she had made up—strictly unnecessary—but besides indulging an old lady's love of intrigue, it served a useful
purpose by keeping things at an impersonal level.

The park was a favorite place for the community's older generation to congregate on a sunny afternoon, to play cards and
checkers, or simply sit, dozing in the sun. There was plenty of
activity to watch if you were interested. The park formed a
buffer zone between the northern boundary of the intercity's
business district and an old residential neighborhood with a
pleasantly homogeneous population.

Mornings, young mothers pushed strollers beneath the elm
trees. At lunchtime businessmen crossed the park to eat at
Fritz's, a restaurant serving both areas of the community. All
day long people hurried to appointments and home again.

After four weeks the others had automatically left this par-

Maxine O'Callaghan

ticular spot, a bench facing the main walk that bisected the park, for Mrs. Hartley. She sat and knitted and smiled at everybody who passed. Most of the people smiled back, sometimes adding a cheerful "Hello." A great many of them thought wistfully that all grandmothers ought to be comfortably round with soft white curls, lively eyes, and skin like faded pink silk.

Mrs. Hartley knew the picture she made. To tell the truth she enjoyed it. It was difficult to remind herself that in a few hours her job would be finished and she would never come here again.

I'm getting too old for this, she thought. The argument had been going on for several days inside her head. She had been very careful with her money. After today there would be enough so that she could quit working and find an apartment. Not in this neighborhood, unfortunately, but someplace equally nice. *If inflation doesn't flare up again and eat up my savings,* she amended. *If I don't get sick.*

She hid trembling hands in the blue wool on her lap. No use trying to reason with fear. She had learned when Edward died what it meant to be alone and destitute. It was a lesson she wasn't likely to forget.

"Emma?"

Startled, she looked up to find Jacob Morrison bending over her. "I'm sorry, Jacob. I was far away."

"Not a happy journey, I think." He leaned heavily on his cane as he folded his long body into a sitting position beside her.

For the past week Jacob had stopped to chat briefly before his daily chess game. Today she would have preferred to be alone but she couldn't be unkind to him.

"I was thinking about my husband," she said.

"Ah. You have spoken very little about him. He died of a heart attack, I think you said. It must have been a shock."

"Yes. A great shock."

"What was Mr. Hartley's profession?"

"Edward had his own business. He fixed things." *And so do I. If you knew, Jacob . . .*

58

"Nice for you. I was never mechanically inclined. My wife, God rest her soul, used to say I was all thumbs. Was he good at his work?"

"Quite good." Dear Edward. There must have been plenty of money. Not his fault that he was such a poor manager, or that he wanted to give her every luxury.

"I was a musician before my arthritis," Jacob was saying. "Always on the road. At least you had a settled life."

"Not really. Edward's work was specialized and he traveled quite a bit. Since we never had children, I always went along."

"Well, you were lucky to be together."

"Yes, we were."

Especially that last night when Edward had had his attack. At the time it had been a shattering experience but later she was thankful that he had died in her arms rather than in a strange room in an indifferent town.

"You'll excuse me, Emma." Jacob pushed himself erect with his cane. "I see my opponent has arrived. Till tomorrow?"

"Till . . ." She stared at him with an overwhelming sense of loss. "Till later."

Now don't you get maudlin, Emma Hartley, she told herself severely as she watched Jacob hobble away.

She pictured cold dark rooms, hunger, the smell of poverty and despair. The vision dispelled any guilt feelings and pulled her up straight on the bench. She had done what she had to do that time eight years ago when Edward died. People were not lining up to offer jobs to fifty-nine-year-old widows with no marketable skills, so she simply took over Edward's business. Thank God he had made notes in his spidery handwriting, enabling her when she finally became desperate to take up where he left off. It still amazed her that she could do the work so efficiently and that it bothered her not at all. After all, men like Mr. Smith . . .

He was coming down the path, briskly as always, looking very *dapper*, to use an old-fashioned and extremely descriptive word. A slim man with ears laid closely against his head, pale blue eyes, and a thin moustache. His charcoal silk suit looked as though it just came out of a cleaner's bag and he always carried, even though it was summer, a pair of thin gray gloves. Another man followed closely behind. Mr. Smith never walked alone. Mrs. Hartley felt a tremor of fear when she saw it was the big man today, the one with enormously muscled shoulders and long, hairy arms. He looked very much like the gorilla in Lincoln Park Zoo, all that brute strength and feral cunning that made you shiver and stand a respectful distance from the cage.

Trying to ignore the quivering in her stomach, Mrs. Hartley stood up and her knitting bag went tumbling, practically beneath the feet of the two men. She herself staggered and would have fallen except that Mr. Smith grabbed her arm to steady her.

"Oh my, how clumsy," Mrs. Hartley cried. "Please excuse me. Sometimes when I stand up suddenly, I get a bit dizzy and . . . Thank you so much," she said as Mr. Smith motioned to the Gorilla Man to pick up her things.

"You all right?" he asked. "Do you need a doctor?"

"Heavens, no. Just a bit wobbly but otherwise I'm perfectly fine." She accepted the tangle of wool offered awkwardly by the Gorilla Man and called, "Goodbye," with a wave as Mr. Smith walked on, a self-satisfied smile hovering on his thin lips.

His good deed for the day, Mrs. Hartley thought dryly, and very few of those to warm his soul. She waited exactly fifteen minutes, packed her knitting bag efficiently, and without the slightest unsteadiness headed toward Fritz's, where Mr. Smith always had his lunch.

The two men were seated at a corner table, a protective wall behind Mr. Smith; the Gorilla Man was positioned so he had a view of the room. He grunted something as Mrs. Hartley swept past the maitre d' straight for their table with excitement coloring her cheeks and shortening her breath.

"I thought you might be here. I'm so glad I caught you." She grabbed the edge of the table for support and put her hand against her throat. "Oh, dear, I—I hurried too fast. Do you suppose I could . . ."

Mr. Smith looked wary and very slightly put upon but he nodded curtly toward a chair and Mrs. Hartley collapsed with a huge sigh. A waiter hurried over. Mr. Smith shook his head but Mrs. Hartley didn't see that. "Some tea would be very nice. You wouldn't mind?" she asked guilelessly.

"No, of course not. Tea," he said sharply to the waiter and fastened his ice-chip eyes on Mrs. Hartley. "Now, was there something you wanted?"

"Of course. You really must think me a silly old woman. First falling all over you and now interrupting your lunch." She opened her handbag. The Gorilla Man stiffened as though ready to lunge across the table, then relaxed when she took out an elegant gray glove. "You dropped this on the sidewalk. Oh, marvelous," she said to the waiter as he put down a steaming pot and cup. He had coffee on the tray and attended to refills.

Mr. Smith pocketed the glove and reached for the sugar bowl. "Thanks for bringing the glove. They're favorites of mine." The graciousness was stilted.

Doesn't have much practice, Mrs. Hartley thought.

She beamed as she poured the tea. "I thought they must be, such lovely leather. I do appreciate beautiful things. Once, well . . ." She didn't notice the look of bored resignation that passed between the two men as she chattered away with the bright intensity of a lonely old lady while she stirred, sipped, wrinkled her nose. "Dear me, I am getting absentminded. I forgot the sugar."

She put down the cup to reach for the sugar bowl, but failed to put it straight in the saucer. It teetered there and a brush of her sleeve turned it straight toward Mr. Smith's lap. Mrs. Hartley leaped up with a wail, grabbing napkins to mop at the spill but only succeeded in upsetting the Gorilla Man's coffee, too. Both men jumped up to avoid the hot liquid and Mr. Smith swore savagely.

61

"Get a waiter," he snarled to the Gorilla Man. "Don't stand there like a fool."

Poor Mrs. Hartley had managed some semblance of order by the time the waiter arrived and insisted on helping the man put the table in order. Mr. Smith, disgusted, was ready to leave but by then the food was ready and Mrs. Hartley, flushed with embarrassment and with tears trembling on her lashes, pleaded, "Oh, do sit down and eat. I'd be so upset to know I'd spoilt your lunch. I'm so sorry."

She gathered her things and hurried from the room, pausing only once to make sure he had indeed sat down and, with a final muttered curse, picked up his coffee cup and ordered the waiter to bring the knockwurst.

It was several days before Mrs. Hartley allowed herself to relax. She had gone directly to the airport from the restaurant. A cab was waiting, dispatched according to her earlier instructions, first to the apartment building to pick up her luggage and then to the corner a block from Fritz's. She made the two o'clock flight with minutes to spare. Her only link with Mr. Smith had gone into a trash can as she walked briskly to her taxi. Mr. Smith had, after all, cooperatively dropped a glove in the park. The pair she bought had not been needed. She doubted that anybody noticed her disposing of them; all their attention had been focused on the sirens screaming through the streets.

And who would attach any importance to the clumsy old woman and the incident preceding Mr. Smith's sudden heart attack? A fast-acting, undetectable drug in his coffee? Nonsense! All that greasy food—cholesterol, the doctors would declare; cholesterol and stress, a deadly combination.

Now, days later and a thousand miles away, Mrs. Hartley sat on a park bench in a shady corner. A palm tree waved overhead and a hummingbird darted in a mass of scarlet hybiscus. She took out her knitting and smiled at everybody who passed. Any minute now she'd have her first glimpse of Mr. Jones. Not his real name, of course, but . . .

Brian Garfield

Demonstrating the high respect in which he is held by his fellow professionals, Brian Garfield is the only writer to have served a term as president of both Mystery Writers of America and Western Writers of America. Born in New York in 1939 but educated in Arizona, Garfield first attacked the Western pulp magazine market as a teenager under the tutelage of famed Western author Luke Short (Frederick Glidden). His first novel, written when he was eighteen, was published in 1960, and he has been a prolific writer ever since. *Hopscotch* (1975) won an Edgar for best novel of its year. Though he may be most widely known as the author of *Death Wish* (1972), made into a highly successful and controversial film with Charles Bronson, Garfield is on record as deploring the distortion of his work that film has created. Since 1974 he has been president of his own motion picture production company.

"King's X" appears in these pages for the first time anywhere.

Brian Garfield

....

king's x

S he found Breck on the garage floor, lying on his back with his knees up and his face hidden under the car. His striped coveralls were filthy. There was a dreadful din: he was banging on something with a tool. When there was a pause in the racket she said, "You look like a convict."

"Not this year." He slid out from under the car and blinked up at her. He looked as if he'd camouflaged his face for night maneuvers in a hostile jungle. He didn't seem surprised to see her. All he said was, "You look better than I do."

"Is that supposed to be some sort of compliment?"

"My dear, you look adorable. Beautiful. Magnificent. Ravishing." He smiled; evidently he had no idea what effect the action had on his appearance. "That better?"

"I wasn't fishing for reassurance. I need to talk to you."

He sat up. The smile crumbled; he said, "If it's anything like the last little talk we had, I'd just as soon—"

"I haven't forgotten the things we said to each other. But today's a truce. Time out, okay? King's X?"

"I'm a little busy right now, Vicky. I've got to get this car ready."

"It's important. It's serious."

"In the cosmic scheme of things how do you know it's any more important or serious than the exhaust system I'm fixing?"

She said, "It's Daddy. They've ruined him." She put her back to him and walked toward the sun. "Wash and come outside and talk. I can't stand the smell of grease."

The dusty yard was littered with odd-looking cars in varied conditions of dissassembly. Some had numbers painted on their doors, and decal ads for automotive products. The garage was a cruddy cube of white stucco, uncompromisingly ugly.

Feeling the heat but not really minding it, she propped the rump of her jeans against the streetlight post and squinted into the California sunlight, watching pickups rattle past until Breck came out with half the oil smeared off his face. He was six four and hadn't gained an ounce since she'd last seen him three years ago: an endless long rail of a man with an angular El Greco face and bright brittle wedges of sky-blue glass for eyes.

"Shouldn't spend so much time in the sun," he said. "You'll get wrinkles."

"It's very kind of you to be concerned about my health."

"Anybody tell you lately how smashing you look?"

"Is that your devious way of asking if I'm going with someone?"

"Forget it," he said. "What do you want, then?"

"Daddy's lost everything he had. He was going to retire on his savings and the pension—now he's probably going to have to file bankruptcy. You know what that'll do to him. His pride—his blood pressure. I'm afraid he might have another stroke."

He didn't speak; he only looked at her. The sun was in her eyes and she couldn't make out his expression. Stirred by unease she blurted: "Hey—Breck, I'm not asking for myself."

"How much does he need?"

"I don't know. To pay the lawyers and get back on his feet? I don't know. Maybe seventy-five thousand dollars."

He said, "That's a little bit of money."

"Is it," she said drily.

"I might have been more sympathetic once. But that would've been before your alimony lawyer got after me."

"You always loved Daddy. I'm asking you to help him. Not me. Him."

"What happened?"

"He was carrying diamonds and they arrested him. It was all set up. He was framed by his own boss. He's sure it was an insurance scam. We can't prove anything but we know. We just know."

"Where is he?"

"Now? Here in town, at his place. The same old apartment."

"Why don't you give him the money yourself?"

"I could, of course. But then I'd just have to get it back from you, wouldn't I."

"You mean you haven't got that much left? What did you spend it on—aircraft carriers?"

"You have an inflated opinion of your own generosity, Breck."

She smiled prettily.

He said, "I can't promise anything. But I'll talk to him. I'll finish up here about five. Tell him I'll drop by."

The old man blew his top. "I'm not some kind of charity case. I've been looking after myself for seventy-two years. Women. Can't even trust my own daughter to keep her nose out of my business. Breck, listen to me because I mean it now. I appreciate your intentions. I'm glad you came—always glad to see you. But I won't take a cent from you. Now that's all I've got to say on the subject. Finish your drink and let's talk about something less unpleasant."

The old man didn't look good. Sallow and dewlappy. His big hard voice was still vigorous but the shoulders drooped and there were sagging folds of flesh around his jaw. It had been what, two years since Breck had seen him? The old man looked a decade older. He'd always been blustery and stubborn but you could see now by the evasiveness in his eyes that his heart wasn't in it.

Breck said, "I'm not offering you money out of my pocket. Maybe I can come up with an idea. Tell me about the man you think set you up. What's his name? Cushing?"

"Cushman. Henry Cushman."

"If he framed you for stealing the money, that suggests he's the one who actually got the money."

"Aagh," the old man said in disgust, dismissing it.

"Come on," Breck said. "Tell me about it."

"Nothing to tell. Listen—it was going to be my last run. I was going to retire. Got myself a condo picked out right on the beach down at Huntington. Buy my own little twenty-two-foot inboard, play bridge, catch fish, behave like a normal human being my age instead of flying all over the airline route maps. I wanted a home to settle down in. What've I got? You see this place? Mortgage up to here and they're going to take it away from me in six weeks if I can't make the payments."

"Come on," Breck said. "Tell me about it."

"I worked courier for that whole group of diamond merchants. I had a gun and a permit, all that stuff. No more. They took it all away. They never proved a damn thing against me but they took it all away. I carried stones forty years and never lost a one. Not even a chip. Forty years!"

Breck coaxed him: "What happened?"

"Hell. I picked up the stones in Amsterdam. I counted them in the broker's presence. They weren't anything special. Half-karat, one-karat, some chips. Three or four bigger stones but nothing spectacular. You know. Neighborhood jewelry store stuff. The amount of hijacking and armed robbery lately, they don't like to load up a courier with too much value on a single trip."

"How much were the stones worth altogether?"

"Not much. Four hundred thousand, give or take."

"To some people that's a lot."

The old man said, "It's an unattainable dream to me right

now but hell, there was a time I used to carry five million at a crack. You know how much five million in really good diamonds weighs? You could get it in your hip pocket."

"Go on."

"Amsterdam, okay, the last trip. We wrapped them and packed them in the case—it's that same armored steel attaché case, the one I've carried for fifteen years. I've still got it for all the good it does. The inside's divided into small compartments lined with felt, so things don't rattle around in there. I had it made to my own design fifteen years ago. Cost me twelve hundred dollars."

"Amsterdam," Breck said gently.

"Okay, okay. We locked the case—three witnesses in the room—and we handcuffed it to my wrist and I took the noon flight over the Pole to Los Angeles. Slept part of the way. Went through Customs, showed them the stones, did all the formalities. Everything routine, everything up-and-up. Met Vicky at LAX for dinner, took the night flight to Honolulu. In the morning I delivered the shipment to Cushman. Unlocked the handcuffs, unlocked the attaché case, took the packets out and put them on his desk. He unwrapped one or two of them, looked at the stones, counted the rest of the packets, said everything was fine, said thank you very much, never looked me in the eye, signed the receipt."

"And then?"

"Nothing. I went. Next thing I know the cops are banging on my door at the hotel. Seems Cushman swore out a warrant. He said he'd taken a closer look at the stones that morning and they were no good. He claimed I'd substituted paste stones. He said the whole shipment was fakes. Said I'd stolen four hundred thousand dollars' worth of diamonds. The cops put an inquiry through Interpol and they got depositions and affidavits and God knows what-all from the brokers in Amsterdam, attesting the stones they'd given me were genuine."

Breck said, "Let me ask you a straight question then."

"No, God help me, I did not steal the damn stones."

"That's not the question."

"Then what is?"

"How come you're not in jail?"

"They couldn't prove it. It was my word against Cushman's. I said I'd delivered the proper goods. He said I delivered fakes. He had the fakes to show for it, but he couldn't prove they hadn't been substituted by himself or somebody working for him."

"Did they investigate Cushman and his employees?"

"Sure. I don't think they did an enthusiastic job of it. They figured they already knew who the culprit was, so why waste energy? They went through the motions. They didn't find anything. Cushman stuck to his story. Far as I can tell, none of his employees had access to the stones during the period of time between when I delivered them and when Cushman showed the paste fakes to the cops. So I figure it must have been Cushman."

"Did the insurance pay off?"

"They had to. They couldn't prove he'd defrauded them. Their investigator offered me a hundred thousand dollars and no questions asked if I'd turn in the stones I stole. I told him he had five seconds to get out the door before I punched him in the nose. I was an amateur light heavyweight just out of high school, you know. Nineteen thirty-one. I can handle myself."

Right now, Breck thought, he didn't look as if he could hold his own against a five-year-old in a playpen. But what he said was, "What else do you know about Cushman?"

"Snob. I don't know where he hails from but he affects that clenched-teeth North Shore of Long Island society drawl. Mingles with the million-dollar Waikiki condominium set. I guess they're his best customers for baubles."

"What'd they do to you?"

"Revoked my bond. I can't work without it. I tried to sue for defamation, this and that, but you know how these lawyers are. The case is still pending. Could be years before it's settled. The other side knows how old I am—they know all they have to do is wait a few years."

Breck said, "Maybe I'll have a talk with this Cushman."

"What's the point?"

"Maybe I can persuade him to give you back what he owes you. Don't get your hopes up. He's never going to admit he framed you—he'd go to jail himself if he did that. The best you can hope for is to get enough money out of him to pay off your debts and set you up in that retirement you talked about. The condo, the boat, the bridge games. That much I may be able to persuade him he owes you."

"Aagh."

The shop was a pricey-looking storefront at 11858 Kalakaua Avenue; the sign beside the door was discreetly engraved on a small brass plaque: CUSHMAN INTERNATIONAL DIAMOND CO.

Inside, every inch a gent in nautical whites, Breck stood looking down at several enormous diamond rings spread across a velvet background.

"My fifth wedding anniversary. I want to give my wife the most beautiful present I can find. You were recommended— they told me they were sure you'd have what I'm looking for."

The man across the counter was bald and amiable. He looked fit, as if he worked out regularly. He wore a dark suit and he'd had a manicure. "Thank you, sir. You're very kind."

"Are you Henry Cushman?"

"That's correct. May I ask who recommended me?"

"A couple of people at a party for the governor. Let me have a look at that one, will you? The emerald cut."

Cushman picked up the third ring. Breck gave him the benediction of his best smile. "Mind if I borrow your loupe?"

Clearly a trifle surprised, Cushman offered him the small magnifying glass. Screwing it into his eye Breck examined the stone. "Very nice," he opined.

Cushman said softly, "It's flawless, sir. Excellent color. And there's not another one like it."

"How much?"

"Four hundred and fifty thousand dollars."

Breck examined the ring even more closely. Finally he said, "Make it four twenty."

"Oh, I wouldn't be at liberty to go that low, sir." The bald fellow was very smooth. "You see, diamonds at the moment—"

"Four thirty-five and that's it."

There was a considered pause before Cushman murmured, "I think I could accept that."

"I thought you could." Breck smiled again. And then, a bit amused by his own air of tremendous confidence, he went around to the proprietor's desk and took a checkbook and a gold pen from his pockets and began to write out a check. "I want it gift-wrapped—and I'll need it delivered to my suite at the Kahala Towers no later than seven o'clock tonight."

He beamed when he stood up and handed over the check, accompanied by a driver's license and a gold credit card; Cushman scribbled lengthy numbers across the top of the check and Breck didn't give the jeweler a chance to get a word in edgewise. "Of course my wife'll have to approve it, you understand. I don't want to spend this sort of money on a gift she doesn't really like. You know how women can be. But I don't really think it'll be a problem. She's a connoisseur of good stones." Then he was gone—right out the door.

He went two blocks to the beach and shoved his hands in his pockets and grinned at the ocean.

Henry Cushman stood momentarily immobilized before he came to his senses and reached for the telephone. The bank's telephone number was on the check in his hand but he didn't trust anything about that check and he looked up the bank in the directory. The telephone number was the same. He dialed it.

It was a frustrating conversation. A bank holiday, this particular Friday. "I know you're closed to the public but I've got to talk with an officer. It's important."

"I'm sorry, sir. This is the answering service. There's no one in the bank except security personnel."

Cushman hung up the phone and made a face and wasn't

quite sure what to do. He paced the office for a moment, alternately pleased to have made the sale but disturbed by suspicion. Finally he picked up the telephone again.

The lobby bustled: people checking in, checking out—business people and tourists in flamboyant island colors. In this class of hotel in this high season you could estimate the fifty people in the lobby were worth approximately $20 million on the hoof. Mr. Fowler watched with satisfaction until the intercom interrupted. "Yes?"

"It's Mr. Henry Cushman, sir."

"Put him on."

"Jim?"

"How're you, Henry?"

"Puzzled. I've got a little problem."

Jim Fowler laughed. "I told you not to bet on the Lakers. Can't say I didn't warn you."

"It's serious, Jim. Listen, I've just sold a very expensive diamond ring to . . . a Mr. F. Breckenridge Baldwin. I understand he's staying at your hotel."

"Baldwin? Yes, sure he's staying here." And by the sheerest of meaningless coincidences Fowler at that moment saw the extraordinarily tall F. Breckenridge Baldwin enter through the main entrance and stride across the vast marble foyer. In turn Baldwin recognized Fowler and waved to him and Fowler waved back as Baldwin entered an elevator.

"What's that, Henry? Hell, sure, he's reputable. He and his wife have been here three weeks now. Royal Suite. They've entertained two bishops and a Rockefeller."

"How long are they staying?"

"They'll be with us at least another week. She likes the beach. I gather he has business deals in progress."

"What do you know about him? Any trouble?"

"Trouble? Absolutely not. In fact he's compulsive about keeping his account paid up."

"He gave me a damn big check on the Sugar Merchants Bank."

"If you're worried about it why don't you call Bill Yeager? He's on the board of the bank."

"Good idea. I'll do that. Thanks, Jim."

"That's all right. You're certainly welcome."

It took Henry Cushman twenty minutes and as many phone calls to find Bill Yeager. In the end he tracked him down at the Nineteenth Hole Clubhouse. There was quite a bit of background racket: a ball game of some kind on the projection TV, men's voices shouting encouragement from the bar. Yeager's voice blatted out of the phone: "You'll have to talk louder, Henry."

"Baldwin," he shouted. "F. Breckenridge Baldwin."

"Is that the big tall character, looks like Gary Cooper?"

"That's him."

"Met him the other night at a luau they threw for the senator. Nice fellow, I thought. What about him?"

"What does he do?"

"Investments, I think. Real estate mostly."

"Does he have an account with Sugar Merchants?"

"How the hell would I know?"

"You're on the board of directors, aren't you?"

"Henry, for Pete's sake, I'm not some kind of bank teller."

"It's important, Bill. I'm sorry to bother you but I really need to find out. Can you give me a home number—somebody from the bank? Somebody who might know?"

"Let me think a minute . . ."

"That's right, Mr. Cushman, he's got an account with us. Opened it several weeks ago."

"What's the balance?"

"I can't give out that kind of information on the telephone, sir."

"Let me put it this way, then. He's given me a check for four hundred and thirty-five thousand dollars. I need to know if it's good."

"I see. Then you certainly have a legitimate interest . . . If Mr. Yeager gave you my name . . . Well, all right. Based on my knowledge of that account from a few days ago, I'd say the check should be perfectly good, sir. It's an interest-bearing account, money-market rate. He's been carrying a rather large balance—it would be more than adequate to cover a four hundred and thirty-five thousand dollar check."

"Thank you very much indeed." Hanging up the phone, Henry Cushman was perspiring a bit but exhaustedly relieved. It looked as if he'd made a good sale after all.

Breck's hand placed the immaculate ring onto the woman's slender finger. Vicky admired it, turning it this way and that to catch the light, enraptured.

"It's the loveliest present of all. My darling Breck—I worship you."

He gave her a sharp look—she was laying it on a bit thick— but she moved quickly into his embrace and kissed him, at length. There was nothing he could do but go along with it. Over her shoulder he glimpsed Henry Cushman, beaming rather like a clergyman at a wedding.

Politely, Cushman averted his glance and pretended interest in the decor of the Royal Suite. If you looked down from the twelfth-story window you could see guests splashing around the enormous pool, seals performing in the man-made pond beside it, lovers walking slowly along the beach, gentle whitecaps catching the Hawaiian moonlight.

Finally she drew away and Breck turned to the room-service table; he reached for the iced champagne bottle and gestured toward Henry Cushman. "Like a drink before you go?"

"Oh no. I'll leave you alone to enjoy your evening together. It's been a pleasure, sir. I hope we meet again."

As if at court the jeweler backed toward the door, then turned and left. Breck and Vicky stood smiling until he closed it. Then the smile disappeared from Breck's face and he walked away from her. He jerked his tie loose and flung off the evening jacket.

She said, "You might at least make an effort to be nice to me."

"Fire that alimony lawyer and let me have my money back and I'll be as nice as—"

"*Your* money? Breck, you're the most unrealistic stubborn stupid . . ."

He lifted the bottle out of the ice bucket and poured. "We're almost home with this thing. I'll keep the truce if you will. Time out? King's X?"

She lifted her champagne in toast. "King's X. To Daddy."

He drank to that. "Your turn tomorrow, ducks."

"And then what?"

"Just think about doing your job right now."

AVAKIAN JEWELRY—BY APPOINTMENT ONLY.

It was upstairs in an old building in Waikiki village. Patina of luxury; the carpet was thick and discreet. Past the desk and through the window you could see straight down the narrow street to a segment of beach and the Pacific beyond.

There were no display cases; it wasn't that sort of place. Just an office. Somewhere in another room there would be a massive safe.

The man's name was Clayton; he'd introduced himself on the telephone when she'd made the appointment. His voice on the phone was thin and asthmatically reedy; it had led her to expect a hollow-chested cadaverous man but Clayton in person was ruddy-cheeked and thirty pounds overweight and perspiring in a three-piece seersucker suit under the slowly turning overhead fan. He was the manager. She gathered from something he said that the owner had several shops in major cities around the world and rarely set foot in any of them.

Clayton was examining the ring. "Normally I don't come in on Saturdays." He'd already told her that on the phone; she'd dropped her voice half an octave and given him the pitch about how there was quite a bit of money involved.

He turned the ring in his hand, inspecting it under the high-intensity lamp. "I suppose it's a bit cool for the beach today anyhow." His talk was the sort that suggested he was afraid of silences: he had to keep filling them with unnecessary sounds. "Raining like the devil over on the windward side of the island today, did you know that?" It made her recall how one of the things she'd always admired about Breck was his comfort with silences. Sometimes his presence was a warmth in itself; sometimes when she caught his eye the glance was as good as a kiss.

But that was long ago, as he kept reminding her.

Presently Clayton took down the loupe and glanced furtively in her direction. "It's a beautiful stone . . . shame you have to part with it . . . How much did you have in mind?"

"I want a quick sale. And I need cash. A hundred and fifty thousand dollars."

He gave her a sharp look. He knew damn well it was worth more than that. He picked up the hinged satin-lined little box. "Why don't you take it back to Henry Cushman? They'd probably give you more."

"That's my business, isn't it?"

"I may not have that much cash on the premises."

She reached for the box. "If you don't want the ring, never mind—"

He said, "No, no," accepting the rebuff. "Of course it's your business. I'm sorry." He got to his feet. "I'll see what I've got in the safe. If you'll excuse me a moment?"

She gave him her sweetest smile and settled into a leather armchair while the man slipped out of the office. He left the ring and the box on the desk as if to show how trustworthy he was.

She knew where he was going: a telephone somewhere. She could imagine the conversation. She wished she could see Henry Cushman's face. "That's my ring all right. What's the woman look like?"

And the manager Clayton describing her: this tall elegant

auburn-haired woman who looked like Morristown gentry from the horsey fox-hunting set. In her fantasy she could hear Cushman's pretentious lockjaw drawl: "That's the woman. I saw him put the ring on her finger. That's her. Wait—let me think this out . . ."

She waited on. *Patient, ever patient, and Joy shall be thy share.*

Henry Cushman would be working it out in his mind—suspicion first, then certainty: by now he'd be realizing he'd been had. "They set it up. They've stuck me with a bum check."

She pictured his alarm—a deep red flush suffusing his bald head. "They must have emptied out his bank account Thursday evening just before the bank closed. They knew I'd inquire about the account. But the check's no good, don't you see? I've given them one of the best stones in the islands and they've got to get rid of it before the bank opens. If you let her get away . . . by Monday morning they'll be in Hong Kong or Caracas, setting up the same scam all over again. For God's sake stall her. Just hold her right there."

She smiled when Clayton returned.

He said in an avuncular wheeze, "I'm afraid this is going to take a few minutes, madame."

"Take your time. I don't mind."

Breck sat in the back seat of a parked taxi, watching the building. He saw the police car draw up.

Two uniformed officers got out of the car. They went to the glass door of the building and pressed a button. After a moment the door was unlocked to permit them to enter.

After that it took not more than five or six minutes before Breck saw Vicky emerge from the shop, escorted by a cop on either side of her. She was shouting at them, struggling, forcing them to manhandle her. With effort the cops hustled her into the police car. It drove off.

In the taxi, Breck settled back. "We can go now."

* * *

Henry Cushman looked up at him. Cushman's eyes were a little wild. The smooth surface of his head glistened with sweat.

"A terrible blunder, Mr. Baldwin, and I can only offer my most humble apologies. I'm so *awfully* embarrassed . . ."

On the desk were the diamond ring and Breck's check.

Breck impaled him on his icy stare. With virulent sarcasm he mimicked Cushman's phony accent:

"Your *awful* embarrassment, Mr. Cushman, hardly compensates for the insult and injury you've done to my wife and myself."

The quiet calm of his voice seemed nearly to shatter Cushman; the man seemed hardly able to reply. Finally he managed a whisper:

"Quite right, sir."

Breck stood in front of the desk, leaning forward, the heels of both hands against its edge; from his great height he loomed over the jeweler.

"Now let's get this straight. You called the bank this morning . . ."

"Yes sir."

"And you found out my check's good." He pointed to it. "*Isn't* it. The money's in the bank to cover it."

Henry Cushman all but cringed. "Yes sir."

"But because of your impulsive stupidity, my wife was *arrested* . . . Do you have any idea what it's like for a woman of Mrs. Baldwin's breeding to spend a whole night locked up in whatever you call your local louse-infested women's house of detention?"

Cushman, squirming, was speechless.

Breck was very calm and serious. "I guess we haven't got anything more to say to each other, Mr. Cushman." He wheeled slowly and with dignity toward the door. "You'll be hearing from my lawyers."

"Please—please, Mr. Baldwin."

He stopped with his back to the jeweler, waiting.

"Mr. Baldwin, let's not be hasty. I feel sure we can find a solution to this without the expense of public litigation . . ."

With visible reluctance Breck turned to face him. Very cold now: "What do you suggest?"

"No, sir. What do *you* suggest."

Breck gave it a great deal of visible thought. He regarded the check, then the ring. Finally he picked up the ring and squinted at it.

"For openers—this belongs to me."

He saw the Adam's apple go up and down inside Cushman's shirt collar. Cushman said, "Yes sir."

"And I can see you haven't deposited my check yet. So here's my suggestion. You listening?"

"Yes sir."

"I keep the ring—and you tear up that check."

Cushman stared at him. Breck loomed. "It's little enough for the insults we've had to suffer."

In acute and obvious discomfort, Cushman struggled but finally accepted defeat. Slowly, with a sickly smile, he tore up the check.

It earned the approval of Breck's cool smile. "You've made a sensible decision. Saved yourself a lot of trouble. Consider yourself lucky."

And he went.

She said, "Don't you think we make a good team?" She said it wistfully, with moonlight in her eyes and Remy Martin on her breath. "Don't you remember the time we sold the same Rembrandt three times for a million and a half each? I remember the Texan and the Iranian in Switzerland, but who was the third one?"

"Watanabe in Kyoto."

"Oh yes. How could I have forgotten. The one with all the airplanes around the pagoda in his yard."

A breeze rattled the palm fronds overhead. He looked down into her upturned face. "I've got a race next week in Palm

Springs, which means I've only got a few days to get the car in shape. Besides, you still need to learn a man doesn't like paying alimony. It feels like buying gas for a junked car."

"Don't talk to me about that. Talk to my lawyer," she said. "Are you going to kiss me or something?"

"I don't know. I seem to remember I tried that once. As I recall it didn't work out too well. Turned out kind of costly." He began to walk away.

"Hey. Breck."

Her voice pulled him around.

She said, "King's X?"

He threw up both arms: his eyes rolled upward as if seeking inspiration from the sky. And shaking his head like a man who ought to know better, he began to laugh.

John Stevenson

....

Though his books and stories have a thoroughly American flavor, John Stevenson was born and educated in England. Following World War II service with the British Army commandos in India and Burma, he lived in Singapore, Australia, and Canada. He moved to Los Angeles ("Canada was too cold for anything but a martini shaker.") in 1961. Retiring from a successful business career in 1970, he took up writing, producing romantic suspense and men's action novels under various pseudonyms and house names. He is best known as Mark Denning, author of several paperback spy novels featuring the CIA's John Marshall as well as the hardcover *Din of Inequity* (1984), one of the great punning titles, about a new character, Mike Wade. Stevenson put his acquired know-how to work for other writers in *Writing Commercial Fiction* (1983). Since recovering from a near-fatal stroke, he has served two extremely productive terms as Southern California regional vice president of Mystery Writers of America.

Previously published in an adapted version for young readers, "The Blind Alley" appears here in its original adult version for the first time.

John Stevenson

·······················

the blind alley

I sat in my swivel chair and ruefully contemplated the gold lettering on the window that proclaimed JIM KATT, INVESTIGATIONS. My office is the room over Pop Arniento's grocery and liquor store. When I moved in there I had furnished it with an old desk that was missing half a leg, a swivel chair that had a tendency to collapse if I didn't sit down very carefully, and a two-drawer filing cabinet that now contained a jar of instant coffee, a supply of paper cups, and my current bottle of bourbon. The most expensive thing in the entire establishment was that gold lettering, and the reason I was looking at it so mournfully was that there were three deep parallel scratches running from top to bottom. I didn't need to hire another investigator to tell me how they got there. My associate Gregory, the black cat, had been chasing a moth or a fly and got him backed up to my sign for the coup de grâce. Unfortunately, moths and flies have a disconcerting habit of moving even faster than the fastest cat at dinner time.

Sometimes I think the only reason Gregory adopted me is that he's superstitious and he needed somebody whose path he could cross at regular intervals. I hadn't worked for a week, so maybe there was more to my theory than I had first thought. I looked at Gregory, exuding an air of absolute innocence from his perch on top of the filing cabinet, the most profitable station for spotting his favorite aperitif, cockroaches.

I heard somebody walking up the stairs. They were walking slowly and carefully. I heard the creak of the stair second one down, and then the doorknob rattled.

I called, "Come in." My office door is never locked because the last thing I want to do is to discourage clients. The door opened slowly and Gregory took a leap from the top of the filing cabinet to the windowsill.

When the door was fully opened a man stepped in and said, "You must be Jim Katt." He was unusual in only one respect: he wore dark glasses and he was led by a large black Labrador.

I jumped up from my chair. "Let me help you to a chair," I said, sweeping a pile of magazines and today's half-finished crossword puzzle to the floor from the visitor's chair. I took his elbow and steered him to it, my only stable chair. The dog sniffed at my ankles and I bent down to pat him to the accompaniment of a hissing noise from Gregory.

My blind visitor put his hand out and said, "I'm Willard Barclay."

I shook his hand, came back behind my desk, sat down gingerly, and said, "What can I do for you, Mr. Barclay?"

He said, "Do you have a cat in here?"

"I prefer to call Gregory my associate. Does he bother you?"

"No. I thought I heard him hiss at Blackie. Don't worry. Blackie would never chase a cat."

I said, "Gregory has won many a battle with a dog. I'll put him out."

"Please don't bother. I've never known Blackie to be bothered by a dog or cat. They seem to know that he's working."

As though to prove his point Gregory jumped down and inspected Blackie from a respectful distance. Deciding that it was only a dog and that he should be on hand to protect me, or

83

maybe share the odd cockroach with him, he leaped back to the top of the filing cabinet and resumed his vigil.

"Now," I said, "you were about to tell me what I can do for you."

"I want to hire you."

"That's what I'm in business for," I told him. "My rates are two hundred dollars a day plus expenses, payable in advance with a minimum of one day's work. And I will not do anything illegal. What is it that you want me to do?"

"I want you to make a payoff for me."

"Payoff—as in blackmail?"

"Right. My sins are catching up with me."

I said, "My experience has been that a blackmailer always has a nasty habit of coming back for more until he has bled you dry. Are you sure you don't want me to scare him off or bring the police in on it?"

"And have everybody in town, including my wife, know of my indiscretions? It is difficult enough for a blind man to operate in this world of sighted people without adding to the disadvantages by hearing that a story has appeared on the back pages of the paper, or have my friends cross the street when they see me coming. And if you don't think it's difficult for a blind man to operate, just close your eyes and keep them shut while you pour yourself a drink of bourbon. It is bourbon you've been drinking, isn't it? Go on, I challenge you."

I thought about that. The bourbon was in the bottom drawer of the filing cabinet, or was that the paper cups and the instant coffee? And did I throw those magazines between my desk and the filing cabinet or did I dump them on the floor in front of the desk? His sense of smell must be as acute as his hearing. Of course I could do it with my eyes open, but his hearing seemed to be sharp enough that he would hear my eyelids pop open.

Gregory stood up and stretched. He seemed to have accepted the presence of the dog, and as he sometimes does he walked around in a tight little circle, his claws tapping the top of the filing cabinet before he lay down to maintain his watch on the

most likely spot for a cockroach to appear. Word must have
gone out about him: several days had gone by since he last
caught a cockroach. As soon as my client left I would have to
open a can of cat food.

"Can I ask you something, Mr. Barclay?" I said, in a desperate attempt to change the subject. Without waiting for a reply
that might change the subject back again, "How did you come to
pick me? Was I recommended, and how did you find my office?"

It was highly unlikely that I had been recommended. Even
my best friend, Dave Willows of the LAPD, calls me a lush to
my face although he has managed to steer a couple of clients my
way.

Willard Barclay said, "Obviously I didn't stick a pin in that
page of the telephone directory and see where it landed, but I
did the next best thing. I took a cab, had the driver get a directory, and read me all the names listed under private in-
vestigators. When he got to your name I just decided on you.
When I had my sight I was an animal lover, and I figured that
with a name like yours you too must be an animal lover, so I had
the cabbie drive me over here and guide me to the foot of the
stairs."

I couldn't follow his reasoning, but I wasn't about to turn
away my first client in over a week. "So what is it that you want
me to do?" I asked.

"I want you to pick me up this evening, drive me to the meeting place, impersonate me, and hand over the briefcase with the
money, then bring me back again."

"I'm not sure if I can impersonate you," I said.

"It shouldn't be any problem. It will be a dark night, and the
meeting is to take place in a dark alley. You will wear dark
glasses, and Blackie will lead you, while I sit in the car and
wait for you."

"Will Blackie lead me?"

"It won't be that dark. You will be able to see the entrance to
the alley. When you return you will recognize your car. If you
get lost you can always take your dark glasses off."

John Stevenson

"It sounds very simple. What time do I pick you up and where?"

"I don't want you to come to my house. My wife has a friend who comes over to play gin rummy with her, something that I can't do. She will be there at eight, so I will leave at seven forty-five for a walk with Blackie, and I will meet you at the newsstand two blocks south of my house."

He pulled a wallet from his pocket and passed me a card. "That has my address on it, and now I'll give you your fee."

He took a stack of twenties from the wallet and started to count them out. When he got to ten he said, "That's two hundred, and here's another twenty for your expenses."

I said, "That's not right. The third bill you counted was a fifty, not a twenty." I took the fifty and pressed it into his hand.

"You're quite right. It is a fifty; I just wanted to make sure you were honest." He tucked the fifty back in his wallet and put another twenty down. "You will be carrying five thousand dollars of my money, so you must excuse me for checking up on you; and please no drinking before we start out."

I said, "You're the client, so you call the shots. Can I get you a cab?"

"The cabbie who brought me is waiting for me, but thanks anyway. I shall meet you at exactly seven forty-five tonight."

I marveled at the way Blackie steered him to the open door of my office and then to the top of the stairs. They went awkwardly down the stairs and disappeared from my sight. Gregory leaped to my shoulder from the filing cabinet and rubbed his head on my ear, although I couldn't be sure whether that was to tell me just how hungry he was or relief at the disappearance of the dog.

However, I was never one to take chances so I opened a can of cat food and put some cottage cheese in his bowl of milk. At six o'clock I took a good stiff belt of bourbon, then went home to my one-room apartment for a shower and a change of clothes. I had promised Willard Barclay that I wouldn't take a drink before going out on the evening's errand, but I didn't stipulate how long before. I munched a handful of breath mints while I hung up my only suit and changed into an old sports jacket and slacks that were more suited for wandering down dark alleys. At seven forty-four I was discussing the latest results of the Democratic primary election with the news vendor when I heard Willard Barclay approach. To be more accurate I didn't hear Barclay because he was wearing crepe-soled shoes, but I heard Blackie's claws tapping their way toward me.

"Is that you, Katt?"

"Right here, sir. My car is just around the corner." Blackie was on his left, so I took his right arm and with the briefcase bumping between our legs I guided him to my '63 Oldsmobile. I settled him in the passenger seat, with the briefcase on his lap and Blackie at his feet.

The address he gave me was in Venice, and since I had picked him up in Santa Monica it was only minutes before we arrived at the corner. He said, "You're parked at the corner, and the ocean is off to your right?"

"Just like you said."

"Now get out of the car and come round to my side and I'll give you the briefcase and let Blackie out. Carry the briefcase in your right hand and Blackie's harness in your left. When you get past the second house there will be an alley. Go down the alley and a man will be waiting to take the briefcase from you. Then you come back here and drive me home again."

I slipped my dark glasses on and fumbled around until I felt Blackie's harness. I started off, responding to Blackie's pull on the harness, only stopping once when he steered me around a tree that was growing too close to the sidewalk. There was no moon and a layer of smog hid the stars, and for the first time in my life I appreciated what it must be like to be blind. Even with the dark glasses I could sense the gap between the houses. As I made toward the alley, Blackie took the lead and steered me down the alley. I was just getting used to being led when the dog came to an abrupt halt and would go no further forward, to the left or right.

John Stevenson

All I needed was a stubborn Seeing Eye dog. I said, "Is there anybody there?"

"Right behind you," a gravelly voice declared. I dropped Blackie's harness and swung around to see a shape a little darker than its surroundings. I stepped back and felt my heel catch on something just as there was a blinding flash and a loud report and I fell flat on my back. I felt the briefcase being snatched out of my grasp, and I fought to maintain my consciousness.

I couldn't say how long I lay there, but when I was able to get to my feet again I felt a lump on the back of my head like a hairy billiard ball. I took a few deep breaths, but there was no sharp pain or wet, sticky blood to tell me that I had been shot in the chest, and I've recovered from bruises before. I snatched my dark glasses off and scraped a few matches into light while I looked around me. The briefcase was gone. I would have been surprised had I found it there. Neither was there any sign of Blackie standing by patiently.

I stood up and fumbled my way out of the alley to my car, which was as empty as a whore's protestations of love. The entire stock of first-aid equipment that I carry in the glove compartment of my car is a one-pint flask of bourbon, and it was about half empty when I put it back again. I turned the ignition key and drove over to the address that appeared on Willard Barclay's card. The driveway was a jumble of police cars and an ambulance, so I parked on the street and walked into the house, where Sgt. Dave Willows was talking to the medical examiner. The uniformed cop on the door was so used to seeing me hanging around Dave that he let me pass with no more than a nod of vague recognition.

"What the hell's going on around here?" I asked.

Dave said, "Your breath smells like an abandoned moonshiner's still. Are you down to chasing ambulances now?"

I held the lump on the back of my head so that my head wouldn't fall off when I drew myself up to my full height and said, "My client lives here."

"Well, you're in bad shape then. Your client was found shot to death, by a friend who stopped by for a friendly game of cards, and the place has been ransacked."

If Dave thought that I had been working for Mrs. Barclay I wasn't about to disillusion him. I have always found it expedient to have a good hole card when I start playing the game.

A uniformed officer came through the door and said, "Sergeant, there's a blind man out here who says he lives here. Says his name is Barclay. Shall I let him in?"

"Yeah," Dave growled. "The more the merrier." He stepped toward the door, but I stopped him with a hand on his arm. When he looked at me I placed my finger on my lips and shook my head.

Dave may have had a sarcastic attitude toward me, but he's no dummy and if I didn't want my presence revealed he knew that I must have a good reason for it. I went to the far side of the room and sat down as Willard Barclay, carrying the briefcase, came through the door led by Blackie.

He said, "What's going on here? Who's in charge? I find cars all over my driveway and policemen everywhere I go, and all they will tell me is that there's been an accident. What is it? Has something happened to my wife? Did she have a heart attack, or a stroke?"

Dave said, "You'd better sit down, Mr. Barclay." He led him to a chair, where he sat down, with Blackie at his feet and the briefcase beside the chair. Dave went on, "An intruder broke in while you were out, shot your wife, and ransacked your home."

"Shot Nancy? My God, I can't believe it. How badly is she hurt?"

As if on cue, two ambulance attendants came through the room bearing a stretcher with a sheet-draped corpse on it, followed by the medical examiner. Barclay said, "Who's there? I can hear people all around me. Who is it?"

Dave said, "Don't get upset, Mr. Barclay. They're taking your wife to the morgue."

"I walk in here and you tell me that they're taking my wife to the morgue, and I'm not to get upset."

Dave said, "I'm sorry you had to learn of this disaster in such a coldhearted way, but believe me, we're only doing our job."

I took a notebook out of my pocket, found an empty page, wrote on it "Ask him where he's been," and handed it to Dave. He looked at me as though I really should stop drinking, then turned to the blind man. "Just for the record, Mr. Barclay. Would you mind telling us where you were when the intruder broke into your home?"

He looked up with the light reflecting off his dark glasses. "I went for a walk." He reached down and fondled Blackie's ears. "I always do, at this time, and if I need an alibi, I'm sure a lot of people saw me, but I can't tell you who they were, because I couldn't see them."

I said, "How about the guy who drove you to Venice?"

He put his head to one side and said, "Is that you, Katt?"

"Yes," I said, "it's me. The guy you left for dead in that alley."

"I heard what sounded like a shot, but I couldn't find the alley. Eventually Blackie came back to me and I had him bring me home."

Dave said, "What the hell's been going on between you two?"

I said, "Willard Barclay came to me this afternoon and hired me to make a blackmail payoff for him tonight. I was to wear dark glasses and be led by his dog into a dark alley in Venice. What actually happened was that Barclay, who has exceptionally keen hearing, shot his wife from the sound of her voice and made the place look as though it had been ransacked by pulling a few drawers out and emptying them on the floors. Then he met me at the newsstand down the road, knowing that his wife would be found by the friend who was due to arrive at eight o'clock to play cards with her. I drove him to Venice, where he guided me to the alley and gave me the briefcase, then followed me and the dog into the alley in his noiseless shoes. He shot me from the sound of my voice, and hid the gun in the briefcase because he couldn't see to hide it anywhere. Then he had the dog bring him back home."

"Then if I shot you, why aren't you dead?" he demanded truculently.

I said, "Ain't no way I'm going to be suckered into wearing dark glasses and walking down a dark alley without taking some precaution. I went home and put a bulletproof vest on under my shirt."

"That's just talk. You don't have a shred of proof."

"When the police find that the bullet in your wife's body and the one lodged in my bulletproof vest were fired from the gun in your briefcase, they'll have all the evidence they need."

He grabbed for the briefcase, but Dave beat him to it, and opening it laid a Colt .38 automatic on the table.

Barclay said, "That still doesn't prove anything."

"You followed me into that alley, fired at the sound of my voice, took the briefcase to hide the gun, and then had Blackie lead you home. It was supposed to look as though when the intruder found nothing in your house he followed us to Venice and shot me for the contents of the briefcase. What you didn't know was that I was not completely unconscious and I heard Blackie lead you out of the alley. Next time you try anything like that, get the dog's claws clipped. I heard them tapping all the way up the alley."

Dave said, "I think you'd better leave the dog here and come down to the station and make a statement. It's first-degree murder, but I don't think they would do much to a blind man."

One of the uniformed officers read him his rights, and they took him out to a squad car for the ride downtown. When he'd gone, Dave turned to me and said, "I don't think we'll have any trouble getting a confession from him, but just to sew it up tight, you'd better let me have that bulletproof vest so that I can dig the slug out of it for the DA's office."

"What bulletproof vest?" I said. "I tripped and fell flat on my back and he missed me."

Not too long ago Nan Hamilton entertained a very distinguished dinner guest—Ellery Queen. Queen (Frederic Dannay) sat down with her and encouraged her to write. "I know you have the talent," he said. "Now use it." She did. She wrote nine short stories that were all accepted immediately. Most of them dealt with some phase of Japanese culture, a subject on which she is very well informed. Her first book, *Killer's Rights* (1984), about Japanese-American police detective Isamu "Irish" Ohara, scored a considerable success. Her second, *The Shape of Fear* (1986), was accepted within three days. Hamilton, who is married to author John Ball, is now busy on her third book.

"Made for Each Other" is a new story published here for the first time.

Nan Hamilton
• • • • • • • • • • • • • • • • • • •

made for each other

Hubert Peabody felt extraordinarily pleased with his decision to marry Rose Makem and put an end to such wasteful widowhood. The fine spring afternoon prompted his inner man to an unseemly twirl of his gold-headed cane, as he whistled a bar of Irving Berlin's latest hit. The sight of the Rev. and Mrs. Stonewater across the street, however, sobered him at once; with a genteel tip of his gray homburg he resumed the dignified tread befitting Elmhurst's leading banker. He was well aware that he had to work overtime on dignity, since his cherubic Santa Claus appearance detracted considerably from his impressive self-image.

He knew himself to be at the pinnacle of success, having taken only ten years from teller to owner of Grange Security Bank. It had not come cheaply; he'd toadied to old Ledbetter, Security Grange's owner, and walked a painfully undeviating line of rectitude. In ultimate sacrifice, he'd married Ledbetter's daughter, Emma, the apple of her father's eye and repository of all his worst features. Earlier sacrifices had been his ambitions as a pro baseball player and popular ladies' man. But even in the sports-minded twenties, banking paid better.

He sublimated by becoming a walking encyclopedia of players, scores, and teams, never missing a "business trip" to Chicago whenever the White Sox played at Comiskey Park. His aftergame activities made up for the long evening with Emma.

Emma, who'd been stunned into rapture by Hubert's proposal, had actually been the least of his troubles, but the worst of his installments on the road to the top. He quite enjoyed living in the Ledbetter curlicued frame mansion on Elm Street, even more so when the old gentleman died and he became at last lord and master of the home, bank, and Emma's fortune. Being careful in everything, Hubert had bided his time while indulging his penchant for hand-tailored British worsteds, Italian silk cravats, and other niceties. His Model T was the latest, and his business trips to Chicago frequent.

Emma, bereft of her father's vigilant support, protested in whining truth that Papa's fortune was being thrown away and none of it on her. The only thing left to her to enjoy was ill health, which she made the most of, taking pleasure in timing her attacks to coincide with Hubert's trips. She knew he would never risk public criticism by leaving an ailing wife. Unfortunately, she died to regret it. Hubert, with a firmly applied feather pillow, assisted her out of her misery; no one questioned that the poor sick soul had died in her sleep, which, of course, she had.

Hubert had just emerged from a suitable period of mourning when Mrs. Rose Makem had come to town. She'd opened a sizable account at the bank and eagerly sought Hubert's advice on a provident investment. When her wide blue eyes, intriguingly shadowed beneath the lacy veiling of her hat, beseeched his help and wisdom, it quite unmanned him. Only prudent self-control, and his massive desk, prevented him from reaching out to touch the provocative red-gold curl lying against her cheek. As he talked facts and figures, he estimated the span of her waist and pictured appreciatively the curving swell of bosom beneath her starched white blouse. Face, figure, and money—the lady had all the attributes of a perfect wife.

He dragged his mind from future possibilities to present necessity. "A first-class boardinghouse should do quite well here, my dear." He accompanied his advice by patting her soft white hand lying invitingly on his desk.

The following weeks passed for Hubert in a happy daze, as he helped the Widow Makem find a suitable house, painters, carpenters, and hired help. The genteel home for cultivated ladies and gentlemen, as its advertisement read, became a reality. The first clients were a junior accountant at the bank, a spinster librarian, a drummer named Jones, and the star boarder, Hubert. His excuse was an impulsive decision to have the Ledbetter mansion renovated. These pleasurable activities and other more practical considerations decided him. Hubert was ready to propose.

As he turned up the walk to his temporary home away from home, he savored the coming moment. In the entrance hall, he hung up his hat and cane, shot his cuffs, and smoothed his mauve silk cravat, then headed for the parlor. The tantalizing smell of roast beef teased his nostrils and Rose's pretty laugh delighted his ears. Then another laugh, loud and masculine, joined it.

Abruptly Hubert entered the room and waited for his usual perfume-scented greeting from Rose. It was not forthcoming. She was too absorbed in smiling up at a tall man with big shoulders and thick curly hair. He was relating some nonsensical story in a mellow voice just touched with brogue.

Hubert's hackles rose. An Irishman! Those people were getting in everywhere these days. It took two sharp coughs before he got Rose's attention; then she came toward him with the young giant in tow.

"Oh, Hubert, this is our new lodger, Mr. Michael Donovan. He'll be with us a while as he's thinking of opening a business in town." She smiled again at the new boarder. "Michael, this is Mr. Peabody, president of Grange Security Bank. I'm sure he can be helpful to you."

Michael pumped Hubert's hand enthusiastically. "I'm glad to know you, Mr. Peabody. You look just the boyo to give a man a leg up."

Not if I can help it, Hubert thought glumly, and sat down to wait for dinner, uncheered by his afternoon sherry, increasingly annoyed by Donovan's witty stories and dazzling white-toothed smile. He consoled himself by thinking that at dinner he would be restored to his proper place beside Rose, recipient of her full attention.

It was not to be. The rare roast beef and featherlight biscuits might have been sawdust. Michael Donovan sat at Rose's left, paying her extravagant compliments on the food, the house, her intelligence, so that her head was completely turned, certainly away from Hubert.

After dinner, she went with Donovan for an evening stroll around town. Hubert was left to sit disconsolately on the front porch. Jones, the drummer, puffing away on one of his odious cigars, joined him. "That fella, Donovan," he said, "I keep thinking I know him from somewhere. Can't place yet, but it'll come to me. I never forget a face; my former training as a cop, you know."

Nan Hamilton

Hubert coughed pointedly and waved away a stream of smoke. "In what connection would you know him?"

"Could be a salesman. But I don't think so."

The days that followed were a misery for Hubert. From breakfast eggs to afterdinner coffee, Michael Donovan held sway. In the evenings he either squired Rose around or bellowed Irish ballads in a syrupy baritone, while she accompanied him on the piano. Only the necessity to maintain his territorial rights kept Hubert sitting in the parlor during the nightly concerts. The repeated renditions of "My Wild Irish Rose" had quite ruined his digestion. His proposal was still unspoken. Then at last he obtained Rose's promise to attend the band concert with him on the coming Saturday.

Fortunately for Hubert, he could not see into Rose's mind as, in the privacy of her bedroom, she assessed her prospects. She knew Hubert would not hold still much longer. Six months' careful cultivation had brought him to the brink of proposal. She hated to throw all that tiresome work down the drain—but, oh, that Michael was a lovely man!

She felt a little pleasure was overdue after all she'd accomplished in the last ten years. Born Maggie Duffy, oldest girl in an impoverished family of twelve, she had learned early to take what she wanted fast and first, or go without. She looked sixteen, and decided to cash in her assets—a ripe young body, a pretty face, and iron determination.

A baby nurse job had been the first step. Before long, the master of the house saw her bending curvily over the crib and he, too, required her services, when the mistress wasn't looking. Maggie saw no future in that but was accommodating enough to strengthen her hand. When she judged the time was right, she threatened the gentleman with a nonexistent pregnancy and was packed off with a tidy sum.

When she went home again to consider her next move, a picture postcard arrived from her mother's brother, Tim, in Chicago. Judging from the picture of the Palmer House, where he said he was staying, Uncle Tim was doing very well. Maggie decided it was time for him to share.

She located him without trouble. Any reluctance he may have felt at the arrival of a penniless relative dissipated when he got a look at Maggie. He greeted her with as many avuncular hugs and pats as he could get away with. Upon hearing that she wanted a job, not money, he smiled even more and offered her a place in one of his class "houses" that catered to only the best clientele. It quite astonished him when Maggie jutted out a chin as pugnacious as his own and said she had better things in mind. She asked for a two-year loan that she promised to repay with interest.

"You're just like meself, Maggie. I don't want to work for nobody. They works for me. That's how I'm going to own Chicago one of these days. I'll give you the money, but I'll collect from you, darlin', one way or another and don't you forget it."

The loan she at once invested in a course in practical nursing. The road to riches, not Florence Nightingale, had been her inspiration.

After graduation her first patient, a wheezing octogenarian, took one look at his relatives and decided he preferred her. He held her hand when the end inevitably came and remembered her liberally in his will. She paid off her Uncle Tim and went back to work.

Her next few cases netted her little more than salary, except that she providently began to build up a cache of unused medicines—a little chloral hydrate here, some digitalis there, a bonus of nitroglycerin, an ampule of morphine, and a few other oddments that she thought might come in handy.

At last one William Martin, recovering under her solicitous care, asked her to marry him. As Mrs. Martin she enjoyed a trip to Niagara Falls, a new wardrobe, and a large sapphire engagement ring. Unfortunately, William proved to be a tightfisted bore, so she had to resort to her little leather case of medicines for a solution to the problem. In no time, William died in his

Nan Hamilton

sleep. The doctor conceded his old ailment had carried him off, and Widow Martin inherited a modest estate that she promptly turned into cash. She then left the state, presumably to forget her grief.

Practicing her profession under different names, in different states, she nursed, wed, and dispatched two other gentlemen. An engraved diamond and emerald wedding band joined the sapphire ring, as well as a fine string of pearls. Her last husband's daughter rather spoiled things by contesting his will. She lost, and the forlorn and lovely widow's picture appeared in the newspaper. On a whim, Rose kept it when she set out for greener and safer pastures in the Midwest. A small town would do nicely, she thought, and selected Elmhurst, a wealthy suburb of Chicago. There she'd found an excellent prospect in Hubert.

But Michael! Rose snuggled cozily into her satin pillows as a smile curved her lips. He didn't fool her; he was as money-hungry as she was and just like her father, all brawn and blarney. "A girl's entitled to a little sparkle now and then," she said aloud, thinking of the years of bedpans and gruel, bald heads, gold-chained paunches, and teeth that stayed on the dresser at night. She stood up and surveyed her lush curves and flawless peach-glow complexion in the mirror. They were much too good for Hubert. She imagined herself running her fingers through Michael's thick, dark hair and could almost feel his arms folding her against his broad chest.

After pouring herself a brandy from a crystal decanter on the table, she curled up on the bed again like a contented cat. Too bad for Hubert; he wouldn't know what he'd missed.

The night of the band concert, Hubert ate his dinner in glum silence. Donovan was holding court as usual, dropping names of the great and near-great like crumbs to sparrows. Hubert fumed in silence until he heard a sacred name.

"Ty Cobb's not in the same class with Ruth," Michael was saying. "The Babe's the greatest hitter in baseball."

Jones came alive from the end of the table, as Hubert almost stuttered in indignation. "If Ruth wants to beat Ty's record, he'll

98

have to win ten championships in thirteen years. I know base-ball better than banking. I'd like to see anybody steal ninety-six bases in one year like Ty did."

"Well, gents," Jones joined in, "wouldn't like to decide be-tween 'em, even though I know my ball, too. I was on duty in Comiskey Park when the White Sox threw the series. Papers started calling 'em the Black Sox, remember?" His snorting laugh set the fat afire.

Hubert and Michael were for once united in defense of the team. When they paused for breath Jones said, "Was either of you gents there?"

"I was there," Hubert snapped. "I saw every single game. They had bad luck, that's all."

Jones grunted disbelief. "They threw it."

Michael took aim and fired. "You're wrong, Jones. I saw every play from a field box next to the commissioner's. The lads played it straight. I had inside dope." He stopped abruptly. "I mean, I was friends with some of the players."

Rose ended the argument. "Gentlemen, I think we're all fin-ished." She looked around, smiling. "I'll just go and change for the concert, Mr. Peabody. I won't be long."

In his excitement Hubert had forgotten his long-awaited date with Rose. With a triumphant look at Donovan, he hurriedly left the table for his room and a few last touches of bay rum. At the foot of the stairs, however, Jones caught up with him and plucked at his sleeve. "I've got it. I know who the Irishman is. He just gave himself away."

Hubert grabbed Jones by the arm and led him out to the porch. "Where? How?"

"I told you I used to be on duty at Comiskey Park when the White Sox . . ."

"Never mind the White Sox, what about him?"

"The box he said he was sittin' in was Boss Gerrity's."

Hubert looked blank.

"You've never heard of Gerrity? His mob runs Chicago. Don-ovan was his strong-arm boy then. Called himself Mike Haggerty. Put more than one guy in the hospital, maybe even in the Chicago River, but nobody could prove nothin'."

"Ah . . ." Hubert exhaled in sheer bliss. "I'll tell Mrs. Makem." He handed Jones two prime Corona Coronas. "Corroborate what I say, Jones, and there'll be something in it for you."

Jones pocketed the cigars. "Got it, partner."

Michael had not missed the excited conference at the foot of the stairs. He drifted close enough to the front door to hear Jones's damning revelations and sighed with regret. "Me old Dad always said I'd hang myself with me tongue."

Hubert would see to it that Rose's money and curves were lost to him, and if Jones should put out the word of his whereabouts to Chicago, he'd be a goner. The bundle of protection money he'd lifted from Gerrity would buy him a cement overcoat.

But it would be too bad to leave empty-handed. As soon as Rose and Hubert had gone to the concert, he'd nip up and have a quick look in Rose's bedroom. He might pick up the odd bit to repay his investment in time and charm.

Since ladies' boudoirs were more or less his natural habitat, Michael had no trouble in uncovering even the most secret of hiding places. This time his compensation was a sapphire ring, a string of pearls, and a diamond- and emerald-studded wedding band engraved "James and Norah." The case of medicines puzzled him until he found the newspaper picture at the bottom. After a moment of teasing thought he had it . . . the Fairweather case. It had been in the paper the day he'd arrived in Richmond. The tubes of lethal medicines gave him the rest. He rolled on the bed in silent laughter.

"Me love, you're a girl after me own heart. Too bad we couldn't have run in double harness."

He pocketed the jewelry, then, taking a piece of letter paper from Rose's desk, wrote a note that he laid on her pillow along with the empty medicine case.

Sorry to be leaving you so abruptly, darlin'. We might have made a team, but I've no fancy to end up

like old James in Richmond. Marry Hubert, luv', and
get a little richer. I'll only be asking a small share
from time to time. The jewelry will do for a down
payment. You're a beauty.

Michael.

It was during intermission, after he'd bought Rose an Italian
ice, that Hubert revealed the truth about Donovan. It seemed to
him that she took it all a little too calmly. She went on eating
her ice and said only that she would do something about Michael tomorrow. He had to be content with that, since the band
blared into "Semper Fideles" and put an end to further conversation.

Hubert's news had not surprised Rose; she'd suspected that
Michael was a rogue. But she had plans for him and if he got out
of line, or she grew tired of him, there was always a solution to
be found in her little leather case.

On the walk home, she held Hubert's proposal at bay with the
promise to join him for a lemonade in the parlor at home. When
they arrived she excused herself for a moment to go upstairs and
"powder her nose." Passing Michael's door she saw a light and
smiled. In a few minutes she would go downstairs and get rid of
Hubert.

The coming interview and his imminent proposal so excited
Hubert that he too sought the upstairs accommodation to relieve
his very natural pressures, both mental and physical. When he
noticed the light under Michael's door, he decided to take matters into his own hands.

His preemptory knock was answered almost at once, and
Donovan, leaning carelessly against the doorjamb, said, "Well,
Hubert?"

With as much pleasure as he got in refusing a shaky loan,
Hubert told him the game was up, and why. "I've told Miss
Rose," he concluded, "so you'd better get out now. She's much
too distressed to even speak to you."

With a short laugh, Michael walked lazily over to the bed and picked up his already packed bag. "Worry no more about the competition, Peabody," he said, "I was just leaving. Miss Rose is all yours, and I wish you luck of her. I've left her a note and my rent's paid up."

Feeling somewhat deflated, Hubert heard Rose's door open and turned to claim his reward. "I've just been getting rid of him . . ." he began.

Rose looked more alarmed than pleased. "Be quiet, Hubert. Don't interfere." Her voice was cold but her face was flushed and her breathing strained.

"You got my note, Rose?" Michael's bold eyes held her, his smile was amused.

Being ignored this way stung Hubert to action. He grabbed at Donovan's bag. "I think we should have a look in this, Miss Rose. He's just the sort to lift the silver."

Rose's face turned from red to white. "No!" She clutched at his arm. "Leave his case alone."

Michael's smile broadened, then he jerked Hubert's grip loose from the bag and brushed past him. Taking Rose's hand, he kissed it with gallant charm. "I'll never forget you, Rose. Sorry to be brief, but I've a train to catch."

He turned to Hubert and gave him a wink, then ran lightly down the stairs. Strains of "My Wild Irish Rose" marked his progress until they were cut off by the slam of the front door. Rose looked wilted but Hubert, with a comforting arm around her shoulders, led her downstairs and settled her on the love seat in the parlor. "Forget the blackguard," he soothed. "I've something to say to you that will make up for everything." He took breath, got down on his pudgy knees, and began.

He took Rose's subdued "yes" in his stride, realizing she must be quite overwhelmed, then seated himself beside her on the love seat. He beamed above her golden head nestling on his chest and talked of future domestic bliss. Rose thought grimly about the long years ahead. The loss of her medicines was a real handicap. She'd have to find another way. Something would have to be done about Michael, too. He was a threat that couldn't be ignored.

When at last she could disentangle herself from Hubert, she went to her bedroom and carefully closed the door. Picking up the gold French telephone on her desk, she gave a long-distance number and waited for her connection. "Uncle Tim?" she said softly. When she heard his reassuring rumble, she came straight to the point. "I need a favor, and whatever it costs, I'll pay." She explained what she wanted done.

Big Tim Gerrity's laughter finally abated enough for him to say, "Sure it'll cost you nothing, Mavourneen. It's family business. I've been waiting to get my hands on that boyo for some time now. He owes me a bit and I mean to collect."

Rose's stomach turned over at the thought that Michael might pay off with what he had on her. She had no illusions as to what Uncle Tim would do with it, family or not. She tried a bluff. "It's just a suitcase with a few bits and sentimental value, mostly." She wondered if he believed her.

"Don't you worry. I'll have a couple of the boys meet his train, get your suitcase, and put the fear of God in him."

As she put down the phone, Rose hoped they'd do more than that. If Michael talked . . . but she had to take the risk. She put her hope in the thoroughness of Gerrity's boys. If they ran true to form, Michael wouldn't be doing any talking. She was taking a chance, but maybe her luck would hold.

She poured herself a drink of brandy and sat down. Now she needed to think about her long-range plans for Hubert.

Joseph Hansen

Joseph Hansen's major contribution to mystery fiction has been the creation of insurance investigator Dave Brandstetter, the first sympathetic and realistically presented homosexual sleuth in the genre. After a three-year struggle with reluctant publishers, Hansen sold the first Brandstetter book, *Fadeout*, in 1970. Another seven novels in the series have followed, interspersed with non-series books both in and out of the mystery field. Born in Aberdeen, South Dakota, in 1923, Hansen has been a self-employed writer for most of his life and has achieved considerable success as a teacher of writing at UCLA. His short story "The Anderson Boy" won an Edgar award in 1984.

"Snipe Hunt," a novella which first appeared in *Ellery Queen's Mystery Magazine*, features Hack Bohannon, Hansen's second series detective, whose cases prove Hansen can write excellent mystery tales outside of the gay milieu.

Joseph Hansen

snipe hunt

O utside, on the long covered boardwalk that fronted the ranch house, a cat clawed the aluminum frame of the screen door. It was morning. The wooden door stood open. Good smells filled the kitchen—of coffee, of sputtering sausage and slabs of cornmeal mush turning golden in cast-iron skillets. But it wasn't the hope of food that brought the cat. Something glittery dangled from his jaws. He was a big black and white tomcat with massive jowls and clear, indifferent yellow eyes.

"Should have named that cat Magpie."

Stubbs, a stocky ex-rodeo rider gone white in the whiskers, said this. He came hobbling to the big deal table with plates of food that he set in front of Hack Bohannon, owner of this place, a boarding stable up a rugged canyon on California's central coast, and Rivera, a slender, dark youngster, studying for the priesthood at a seminary on a nearby ridge, who helped Bohannon out part-time.

"Or Pack Rat," Stubbs added and went back to the stately white enamel and nickelplate cookstove for his own breakfast and a platter of sourdough biscuits. "No—Magpie. Them's his colors, same as the birds." He plunked down the plates, scraped chair legs on smooth planks, and sat down. His blue eyes took in Bohannon's plate. "Right. Sunny-side up on the eggs again. I told you, it's the only way I know how." He took a biscuit in arthritic fingers, broke it open, buttered it. "Never claimed to be a chef. Just a chuckwagon cook, is all. You want it fancy, cook it yourself, Hack."

"I will," Bohannon said. He often did. He filled his mouth with sausage, egg, fried mush, washed these down with coffee, and rose to go open the screen door. The cat came inside and dropped the glittery thing with a small rattle at Bohannon's feet. It was a wristwatch. Free of it, the cat was able to make a few remarks, and it made them. Bohannon smiled, said, "Thank you. Very nice, right." He bent, gave the sleek black and white back a couple of strokes, and picked up the watch. On the face of the watch was printed CARTIER. Expensive. The cat crossed the room and jumped up easily onto the counter beside the stove, to stick its head out and sniff at the hot pans there. Bohannon went back to the table, sat down, laid the watch next to his plate. It was undamaged. The time was right—6:10. Bristles of dry grass were caught in the reticulated metal band.

"A nice watch," Rivera said.

"How far does he go, collecting things?" Bohannon said.

Rivera's slight shoulders moved. "Not far, I don't think."

"He likes his comforts too much," Stubbs said. "He sticks around the stables mostly. Mostly sleeps."

"He thinks he is a horse," Rivera said with a smile.

Bohannon doubted it. Eating now, drinking coffee, he watched the cat jump down from the counter and come to the table. He stood looking up first at Stubbs, who ignored him, then at Rivera, who shook his head, then at Bohannon, who nodded. The cat sprang lightly into his lap. Bohannon broke off a bit of sausage and set it between the cat's teeth. The cat growled as if someone was threatening to take the food away from him and jumped down on the floor to eat it, still growling, shaking his head as if he had a mouse in his jaws. "He knows he's a cat," Bohannon said, "and he wouldn't have it any other way. I've got a theory. It explains the mystery of Man. Cats invented Man to look after them."

"I will tell the Monsignor," Rivera said. "He has been giving us the wrong information."

". . . Feed them, shelter them, keep them out of trouble," Bohannon said. He frowned and turned the watch over. Initials were engraved on its back. "T. K.," he said and looked at Stubbs's ruddy face and Rivera's smooth brown one. "Mean anything to you?"

"Had a Mrs. T. K. here the other day," Stubbs said. "Rented Seashell and Mousie for a morning's ride. Young fellow with her she says was her nephew, but she didn't look at him like a nephew. Mrs. Thomas Kruger. She didn't give me the boy's name."

"The first time?" Bohannon asked.

"First time with him," Stubbs said. "But she's been up before. Mostly with women her own age, women friends. Middle forties. New little red roadster. Rich women. Time on their hands. Lunch afterwards, I expect. Lots of margaritas."

"With the girls," Bohannon said. "Not with the nephew."

"No, she'd find something else to do with him," Stubbs said, "if memory serves me."

"I think"—Rivera pushed back his chair—"the conversation is slipping from its usual high spiritual plane, here. There is work to do." He rose, smiling a little. "Among our speechless friends, the horses, who are God's innocents, and will not trouble my mortal thoughts."

"Sorry about that," Bohannon said.

"Stay and offer a prayer for that nephew," Stubbs said. "Woman looked like a man-eater to me."

"I will see you later." Rivera went down the room to the screen door. When he pushed it open, the cat slipped out between his boots. He followed it, and the door rattled shut. Stubbs sighed, belched softly, used his napkin. "Fine day. Wasn't for the annual giant community rummage sale and flea market in Madrone, we'd be busy. Maybe I'll run down there myself, later. I could use a couple new shirts." He rose, started off, paused, glanced back at Bohannon, and changed course. From a cupboard, he took down a gray mottled cardboard file shaped like a shoebox and limped to the table with it. "Her number will be in here."

Bohannon was pouring coffee. He nodded his thanks. But no one answered the telephone at the number Mrs. Thomas Kruger had given Stubbs. Bohannon finished off his new mug of coffee and two more cigarettes, went to the wall phone, and tried the number again. It rang in an empty house. Not even an answering machine. Bohannon went along a knotty-pine hallway to a plank bedroom where Rivera had earlier made up the poster bed under its patchwork quilt, as he made the beds up every day. Bohannon pulled on socks and boots, checked the kitchen stove to see that Stubbs had turned off oven and burners—he sometimes forgot— then went out into the bright morning and his pickup.

The cat in fact went far afield. Bohannon clattered the old GM along a lot of dusty back trails and side canyons before he caught a glint of metal down among brush in a barranca sheltered by big old oaks. He braked, climbed out, slammed the door with a clang that echoed in the stillness, and slipping, sliding, scraping hands and the seat of his britches, followed the slurred swath a car had made chuting down here. It was a red European sports car of some kind that looked new. It rested on its top, wheels up. Bohannon crouched to see inside. Nobody. He straightened up and looked around. All he saw was dry brush and drier rock bleaching in a streambed that wouldn't run with water until winter, when it would run hard and deep. Boots crunching rock, he circled the car, squinting against stabs of sunlight down through the dusty trees. A lizard scuttled away, claws whispering agitation in the stillness. It scampered over a shoe. Bohannon went for this, picked it up, saw a second shoe—and this one had a foot in it. A stout, gray-haired man in a pricey tweed jacket and wool trousers sprawled face down among boulders like something broken and thrown away. He had leaked blood, and flies buzzed around this. Bohannon crouched and touched a hand. It was cold. He climbed back to his pickup and used the two-way radio there.

Brown sheriff's department cars stood in a loose row along the back road half an hour later. Also a brown ambulance, a converted van with a row of lights along its top and an electroplated howler that glittered in the sun. Men in chalky lightweight jumpsuits toiled up the slope with the body of Thomas Kruger in a zippered bag on a gurney with its shiny tubular metal legs folded. Deputies in crisp suntans nosed around the red car, took photographs, used a steel tape for measurements. It took Bohannon back to where he had no wish to be anymore. He'd been a deputy for fourteen years and loved it, and then had come to hate it, and had quit. Because people kept coming to him for help, he held a private investigator's license now, but he wished they would stop coming, would forget about him, leave him alone. He was content with the horses, for the same reason as Rivera, he supposed. They were innocent. Human beings were rarely that—himself least of all.

"Lieutenant?" A young deputy with freckles called this from beside the car. The call went echoing down the canyon. Someplace far off, as if answering, a crow cawed, and another. The man beside Bohannon grunted and went skidding, teetering down to the freckled kid. The man was Gerard. Bohannon had worked with him for a long time, and they had been friends— until Gerard was part of a whitewash that let an officer get away with shooting dead an unarmed latino boy in Cayucas. Now they were civil when they met, but that was the extent of it. Bohannon followed Gerard. The young deputy said, "I don't think it was an accident, sir. It looks to me like the brakes were tampered with. A slow leak in the line. Back at the garage, we'll be able to tell for sure."

"Somebody wanted him to drive off the road?"

"I'd say so." Up on the road, the doors of the ambulance slammed. The kid lifted his head, squinting in the sun glare. "Yes, sir."

"It's a stupid plan for murder," Bohannon said. "Too much could go wrong. Why would someone try it?"

Gerard shrugged. "Money? He was well off. Senior vice president of Mountain Savings and Loan."

"What was he doing driving up here?" Bohannon asked.

"Looking at land?" Gerard wondered.

"It happened in the dark," the young deputy said. "His headlights were on. The doc said the body temp makes it someplace around midnight when he died."

"Not looking at land," Gerard said, and turned to Bohannon. "You know all these canyons. What's here, who's here?"

"Nothing and nobody," Bohannon said. "And he wasn't heading over the ridge for Atascadero or Paso Robles. Not on this road. Anyway, he was pointed back. Only it would take him a hell of a lot of chopping and changing to get there."

"Maybe he was lost." The young deputy wiped sweat off his forehead with a hand. "But why come so far to get lost?"

Bohannon said, "Maybe somebody lied to him."

"A snipe hunt?" Gerard said. "I'll ask at the savings and loan. I'll ask his wife."

"She's not home," Bohannon said. "I tried the number twice this morning."

Gerard frowned. "You knew who he was before you even found him? You want to explain?"

"My cat brought this in at breakfast time." Bohannon dug the watch out of a frayed Levi's pocket and laid it in Gerard's hand. "His initials are on the back. Stubbs took a stab at guessing what they stood for. His wife rides my horses sometimes."

"Why would she lose his watch for him?" Gerard said.

"Exactly what I asked myself," Bohannon said.

"You found the answer," Gerard said. He ventured a smile and in a country-western twang repeated something they used to say to one another when they'd worked together young. "You done good, son."

Bohannon kept his face stiff, and felt sad and angry. There was no use in Gerard's trying, even less use in Bohannon's encouraging

110

him. It could only be fake now. Up on the road a truck engine rumbled, gears clashed. Bohannon winced and peered upward. The wrecker had arrived to winch the pretty little red car out of the barranca. He said, "I don't think that's his car. I think it's hers." He started up the steep slope, rubble rattling down behind him with each step. "Let me know what happens."

But it wasn't Gerard who let him know what happened. It was a very young woman in baggy white sheeting pants and jacket yards too big for her, a Union 76 blue and orange globe printed on her T-shirt, and panic in her eyes. He was waiting under the overhang of the white and green stable building while a young father leaned against the wall, writing him a check for riding lessons given. It was late afternoon. The kids seemed relieved the lesson was over. They were about nine or ten. The blond one had grabbed the dark one's hat and was running and dodging with it, and jeering. Out in the yard, with its white rail fences, flower beds, shaggy old eucalyptus trees throwing long shadows, the girl had hopped out of a new compact and was talking shrilly to Rivera, pushing at her crazily cropped pale hair, and waving her arms. The young father tore the check out of its folder, handed it to Bohannon with a wan smile, pushed the folder away, and went to collect his boys. Bohannon tucked the check into a shirt pocket. Rivera pointed, and the girl came running to Bohannon, jogging shoes, no socks.

"You have to help me," she panted. "You have to."

Bohannon took down a bucket from a nail beside a box stall door. "Why me?" He walked away with the bucket.

She ran alongside him. "Mr. Fitzmaurice said you would."

"Archie?" Bohannon bent to a tap and turned the valve. Water splashed into the bucket. "Are you his client?"

She shook her head. "Melanie Kruger—that bitch."

Bohannon glanced at her. He turned off the tap and set the bucket down. "Mrs. Thomas Kruger?"

The young woman nodded. She licked her lips and eyed the

water in the bucket. "They arrested her. At the rummage sale. For killing him—her husband. Last night."

Bohannon frowned. That was fast, wasn't it? He said, "But you call her a bitch, so it isn't her you want help for—her and Archie."

"No, it's Dennis," she wailed. "Dennis Toomy."

Bohannon couldn't stop a small smile. "Would that be her nephew? The one she came here with the other morning?"

"Her nephew!" She scoffed. "Is that what she said? Oh, wow. What a hypocrite."

"There was a husband." Bohannon took a dipper off a hook, plunged it into the bucket, brought it up filled, offered it to her. "Thirsty?" She took the long handle and drank, water dribbling off her chin, darkening the 76 globe between her pert little breasts. She handed back the dipper and wiped her chin with a hand. Bohannon hung the dipper up again above the tap. "If he isn't her nephew, what is he?"

"A graduate student at Davis—an arboriculturist. Trees, all right? And when she drove in for gas the other week, Mrs. Kruger told me about her oaks dying, and I said maybe Dennis could help her, okay? So she called the university, and he went, didn't he? And what does she do—invite him in. For lunch. Oh sure, for lunch." Hurt and disgust were in her voice.

Bohannon's mouth twitched. "Those things happen. It's his age. And hers. Don't take it too hard."

"I'm liberated," she said. "But it wasn't just once. He kept going back. She gave him presents. He's a poor boy. A Rolex watch, gold chains, a camera? Why wouldn't he?"

"Not for love?" Bohannon said.

She stared, outraged. "Have you seen her? She's old."

"He left you for her," Bohannon said.

"I'm not jealous," she said stoutly. "Is that what you think? Well, you're wrong." An old bay gelding called Bearcat put his head out over the closed lower half of his stall door and nibbled at her puffy windbreaker. She jumped. "Hey!" Bearcat, who had a sense of humor, lifted his head, curled his upper lip over long yellow teeth, and nickered. Bohannon laughed and led her two steps out of the horse's reach. Then he held the water bucket up and, shaggy black mane falling into his eyes, Bearcat drank—noisily, splashily. The young woman said, "I just hated seeing her using him. I knew it would lead to trouble. I went and begged her to leave him alone. She sneered at me. Now look what's happened."

Bohannon set the bucket down. Bearcat grabbed his hat by its brim. Bohannon grabbed it back, grinning, and gave the big soft muzzle a push. "Get in there and behave yourself," he said. And to the young woman, "What has happened?"

"They've arrested him, too. They say she paid him to murder her husband." She waved her small hands. "But he didn't do it, Mr. Bohannon. He couldn't."

Bohannon's brows rose mildly. "Paraplegic?"

"Stop that. Of course not. But he's not that kind of boy. I've known him all my life. He's gentle. He can't hurt anything living. He wouldn't. Kill another human being? Never." She shook her head fiercely. "Never."

"The sheriff doesn't make arrests for murder without a reason. What's the reason?"

She stopped looking at him. She turned away to watch or pretend to watch Rivera helping an old couple down off horses. Both were rail-thin. They wore black Mexican outfits with silver braid, silver belts, silver bands around black gaucho hats. The saddles on their palominos were heavy with silver. Once the couple must have cut a dash, but they were frail and stiff in the joints now, and Rivera had a time of it to keep them from breaking bones dismounting. The young woman said glumly, "The sheriff has letters they wrote. And her check made out to Dennis. That he cashed."

"What kind of letters?" Bohannon said.

"What kind do you think?" she asked bitterly.

"I see." Bohannon sighed. "I don't see what I can do. It sounds open and shut to me. I'm sorry."

She turned to him sharply. "Don't say that. He didn't do it." Tears filled her eyes. "You have to help him."

"What's Mrs. Kruger doing?" Bohannon said. "Keeping Arch Fitzmaurice all to herself?"

"You better believe it," the young woman said.

"He'll have a public defender, then," Bohannon said. He touched the girl's shoulder. "Don't worry about it. If he didn't do it, it will come out at the trial."

She shrugged his hand away. "No, it won't. She'll blame it all on him. She'll say it was his idea." Her laugh was sour. "Haven't you ever heard about one law for the rich, one law for the poor? She'll get away, he'll go to death row."

"When you're older," Bohannon said, "you'll learn that things almost never turn out as badly as we fear."

"Don't patronize me," she said. "I tell you—Dennis didn't do it. I know he didn't. There—is that good enough for you?"

Bohannon looked away, over her tufty blond head, past the yard where the shadows had stretched, purple on the yellow hardpan. A breeze had risen, as it did about this time every day, bringing coolness and a smell of the sea. It rustled the high trees. Over the canyon rim, colors other than blue began to change the sky. Soon it would look like the inside of an abalone shell. Then it would streak with reds and, almost before you could blink, it would be black and strewn with stars.

He asked, "Are you being very careful with your words?" He looked into her eyes. "What makes you so sure?"

She dropped her gaze and her voice. "I can't tell you." Then quickly she looked up again and gripped his arms. "But I am sure. I swear it. Now, will you help him—please?" She poked into a pocket of the blowsy white jacket and brought out a wallet. "I'll pay you. I have a job." She held out two twenties. "And I can always sell my car, if I have to."

"Let's see if I'm any use first," Bohannon said. "What's your name? Where can I find you?"

"Billie Shears," she said, and gave a Madrone address.

Rivera looked wounded in his feelings and shook his head. "Next time, you must take one of us with you," he said. He dipped a fragment of fried tortilla into a big bowl of guacamole and stuffed his mouth with the green stuff. "You are an artist." Chewing, he nodded at Stubbs's drawings on the kitchen walls—horses mostly. When the weather was warm and dry and his joints weren't too stiff from arthritis and old breaks, Stubbs liked to draw and he did it well. "But you have no taste in clothes." Rivera washed down the food with orange soda. "That is a terrible shirt."

Stubbs worked at breaking long elastic strings of white Mexican cheese. Bohannon had fixed beef enchiladas with his own secret sauce and the cheese melted on top. Holding a forkful of enchilada high, Stubbs sawed at the strings of cheese with a knife. He glanced at Rivera. "For any man that can drink that stuff with perfectly good food to talk about taste," he said, "don't add up to much." He gave up, laid the knife down, stuffed his mouth, and wrangled the cheese strands in as best he could with the fork. He looked down at the shirt. "It's got all its buttons. It covers me up decent. What's wrong with it?"

"It makes you look like a sofa," Bohannon said.

Outside in the red sunset light a car door slammed, steps sounded on the porch planks, a figure appeared at the screen door. Knuckles rattled the frame. "Hack?"

"Come in." Bohannon stood up and started for the stove. "You want supper? Enchiladas."

"They give me heartburn," Gerard said. "Thanks. My wife will be expecting me." While the screen door rattled shut behind him, he read his watch. "Jesus, it's late. But I wanted to fill you in." He moved a chair out at the table and sat down. "If you've got a beer around . . ."

Bohannon took down a glass and brought a brown bottle from the refrigerator. He set these in front of Gerard and resumed his place and his eating.

"I seen you arrest that Kruger woman," Stubbs said. "Right in the middle of the rummage sale she was running. Surprised hell out of folks. Even me."

"Oh, then it's not news," Gerard said. He tilted the glass and let beer run out of the bottle slowly into it. He regarded Bohannon. "What more do you want to know?"

"How come it happened so fast?" Bohannon said. "Did you settle on her first, or did you find those letters first?"

Gerard tasted his beer, smacked his lips, wagged his head in appreciation, and read the label on the beer. "Anchor. It's still the best, isn't it?" He reached across, picked up the orange soda bottle, shuddered, set it down again, and asked Rivera, "How can you drink that stuff?"

"It is an old Aztec tradition," Rivera said.

Gerard said to Bohannon, "The mail gets to my house about eight-thirty. A brown envelope was in the box, and my wife noticed that it didn't have any stamps on it. Also it seemed a little damp, and the rest of the delivery didn't. As if it had been in the box all night. She phoned me about it, and I sent a car around for it. And it had these letters in it—from this Davis student, Dennis Toomy. And I phoned the Davis police, and they went around to ask questions of Toomy, and they found Melanie Kruger's letters to him. And they fit together. They made a picture."

"Love letters?" Stubbs said. "That the nephew?"

"If you'd stayed here instead of going shopping for awful shirts, you'd know all about it," Bohannon said.

"Love letters of a sort," Gerard said. "Sex letters is more like it. But with a nasty turn to them. All about how wonderful the world would be for this twenty-three-year-old kid and this forty-five-year-old woman if only her husband was dead. She couldn't leave him, because he'd cut her off without a dime. And she didn't have any money of her own. He wouldn't politely divorce her. It would disgrace him. So wouldn't it be nice if he met with some kind of fatal accident."

"No specifics?" Bohannon said.

"Better than that. A check for five hundred bucks. The D.A. is delighted. To any jury the meaning has to be plain, in the light of what happened to Kruger. He doesn't figure to have any trouble with it."

"Billie Shears is having trouble with it," Bohannon said.

"That pest," Gerard said. "Was she here, too?"

"She's very much in love with young Toomy."

"Yeah, well"—Gerard grunted—"love is blind." He gulped his beer and filled the glass again. "How did she happen to hunt you up? What does she expect you to do?"

"Get the boy off," Bohannon said. "She must have pestered Archie Fitzmaurice, and he sent her to me to get rid of her." Bohannon finished his enchiladas and laid down his fork. "Who left those letters in your box in the middle of the night?"

"Kruger himself," Gerard said. "We asked neighborhood dog-walkers. Heavy-set, middle-aged, white-haired. Who else could it be? Before he drove off to die. Ironic, isn't it?"

"You said he didn't want a scandal," Stubbs said.

"If the county prosecuted her for conspiracy to commit murder," Gerard said, "what could he do about it? It wouldn't reflect on him—and it would punish hell out of her."

"If you want proof there is a God"—Rivera rose and went into gathering shadows to fetch the coffeepot from the stove—"just look at how miserably people act without Him."

"I want to talk to Toomy," Bohannon said. "Who's his public defender?"

"May," Gerard said. "Fat Freddie."

Madrone was a cluster of spindly, jigsaw-work houses in foothills above the coast highway. The houses had been fixed up inside, and outside painted candy colors. A good many of them now housed antique stores, gift shops, small restaurants. The names were quaint and quaintly painted on swinging signboards. The sea wind creaked them a little tonight. He saw the gilt lettering spark through the drooping branches of fine old roadside pepper trees. Main Street had showed a lot of dull brick storefronts not long ago. Now these had been covered by cedar and redwood planking, so the street looked like a set for a Western.

Bohannon made a face and rattled the old pickup onto the lighted tarmac beside the pale brick sheriff's station. He parked in a slot reserved for official vehicles, and grimly pushed the heavy

117

glass doors into the place. He hated coming here, hated the smell of the place, the familiar sounds echoing down familiar hallways from familiar offices. The officer at the desk, with a padded phone at one ear and a slim tubular microphone at mouth level, was a dark young woman, slightly buck-toothed. She raised thick, dark brows above lustrous eyes and sketched a smile for him.

"Hack Bohannon," he told her. "May's expecting me."

She widened the smile and pointed down a hall. "Interrogation room. She glanced at a wall clock. "He has Dennis Toomy with him." She tilted her head. "He must have known you'd be on time. Are you always?"

"You can test me," Bohannon said. "Tomorrow night. At six-thirty. The Briary Bush. Dinner? They serve great salmon steaks there—fresh-caught from the creek."

She laughed, a sound pleasant as bells. "And they charge twenty dollars for it. Are you rich, Mr. Bohannon? Can you afford to throw your money away on nameless deputy sheriffs?"

"Your name is T. Hodges," he said. "It's on your badge."

She touched the badge with slim fingers. "I'd forgotten that. Who are you? What do you do?"

"Keep stables up Rodd Canyon. For town people who haven't anyplace to keep a horse. I also rent horses to people who can't afford them but like to ride."

She watched his left hand scratch his ear. "That's a wedding band." Her glossy brown eyes mocked him.

He said stiffly, "My wife's in a mental hospital." Linda had been held hostage on a filthy drug smuggler's boat, half-drowned, beaten, and repeatedly raped. Afterward she had crept inside herself—it looked like forever. "I'm not asking you to sleep with me, Deputy. Only to have dinner with me."

A telephone with a broad, flat display of Lucite buttons on her desk began to buzz and wink. She said, "Perhaps some other time," gave him a gentle, regretful smile, pushed one of the buttons, picked up the receiver, and spoke into it.

Bleakly, Bohannon walked to the interrogation room. Fred May was twenty pounds heavier than he used to be, which brought him to about three hundred pounds. He also had less hair. But the tic that tended to make jurors wonder if he was serious when he pleaded with them and kept winking—that seemed gone. He wasn't dressed for a courtroom tonight. He wore a blue T-shirt stenciled SAVE THE SEA OTTER, and his belly bulged over cutoffs bought when he was thinner. His arms and legs were furry. He sat at a scratched yellow oak table on a bentwood chair his bulk made appear fragile.

Across from him sat a big-boned blond boy, long hair pulled back in a 1960s ponytail. He wore yellow jail coveralls, unzipped to the navel, showing a deep chest, gold hair glinting on it in the sour overhead light. The sleeves of the coveralls were short, and the boy's arms were thickly muscled, gold hair glinting on them, too. With his big, strong hands, high cheekbones, blue eyes under a heavy brow ridge, he looked as Paul Bunyan must have, just out of the egg. What he failed to look was bright.

"What's this all about?" he said to Bohannon.

"Billie Shears wants me to help you." Bohannon pulled out another bentwood chair and sat on it. He looked at Fred May. "How can I do that?"

"If I was going to kill him by fixing the brakes on a car," Toomy said, "I'd fix them on his, not hers."

"Not if you knew she'd be using his car last night," Bohannon said, "to haul things over to the park for the big yard sale. Lieutenant Gerard says she was doing that all day, and the better part of the night. His is a big car. Hers is too small for the purpose."

"I didn't know about the sale," Toomy said.

Bohannon looked at May. May shook his head. The white, bare top of his scalp shone greasily in the light. "He says he was in Davis, but I can't scare up a witness."

"I was in my room," Toomy said. "Studying. I'm going for my masters, now. I'm going for a doctorate." He looked ready to cry. "I should have gone to the library. Then everybody would have seen me. I go almost every night."

"Is there a phone in your room?" Bohannon said.

"Nobody phoned me," Toomy said. "I wish they had. It's a

119

wall phone, down the hall. The landlady answers it and calls anybody that's wanted."

"You didn't call out?" Bohannon said.

"I told you—I was studying," Toomy said.

"But you keep a stock of quarters," Bohannon said, "so you can call when you need to. Madrone, for example. The Kruger house?"

Toomy's mouth twisted. "I keep a stock of stamps," he said with grim humor. "We wrote letters."

"So I hear," Bohannon said. "But somebody telephoned Mr. Kruger last night. That's how it looks. And lured him up into those canyons above Mandrone, where he drove off the road and died because the brakes on his wife's car had been monkeyed with. All the fluid dripped out."

"I don't know anything about cars," Toomy said.

May unwrapped a stick of chewing gum and folded it into his mouth. "That checks out. We had the Davis police ask his friends on campus. Dennis is famous for his ignorance of mechanical matters." He gave the boy a brief, unhappy smile.

"All the letters say," Toomy told Bohannon, "is how great it would be for Melanie and me if Tom had an accident and died. They don't say anything about rigging an accident."

"You use the library all the time," Bohannon said. "What would stop you from looking up in an auto repair manual where the brake lines are? They're easily accessible. Anyone could poke a hole in one with an ice pick."

"I don't have an ice pick," Toomy said. "What kind of helper are you supposed to be, anyway?"

"You wanted him dead so you could live off his widow—the money, insurance, property she'd inherit. That's a motive, Dennis. It would help if someone else had one. Didn't Melanie ever mention anybody else who'd want Tom Kruger dead?"

Toomy gave his head a shake. "All she said was Mountain Savings and Loan was his whole life. He'd forgotten about her, years ago—never took her anyplace, hardly spoke to her. His focus was down to making money." Toomy sulked. "Greed. It's ruining the planet."

"And that's why you killed him?" Bohannon said.

"I didn't kill him," Toomy shouted.

"What was the check for, then?"

Toomy flushed. "It was a gift. She said I needed clothes. That's how she is. Beautiful and fine and giving."

"Uh-huh. You should have stuck to Billie Shears." Bohannon looked at May. "Has bail been set?"

The fat man nodded. "Fifty thousand each."

Bohannon asked Toomy, "Have you got five thousand bucks for a bail bondsman?" Toomy only stared. "Because if you haven't, you'll stay locked up till your trial."

"That's not true. Melanie's not like that. You don't know her." But Toomy's bravery was all noise. He turned to May and his voice was small. "She wouldn't leave me here."

May chewed his gum. "She walked out an hour ago."

"You're no use to her anymore, Dennis." Bohannon rose. "But don't take it too hard." He went to the door. "Billie still loves you." He pulled open the door. A uniformed officer waited outside. Bohannon turned back. "Billie says she knows you didn't do it. How does she know that?"

Toomy said dully to the tabletop, "Figure of speech."

"I hope not," Bohannon said.

Bohannon remembered this place as a meadow. He recalled a particular afternoon, though it may have been several afternoons overlaid in his memory and probably was, when twenty or more deer had come out of that stand of oaks over there, hesitant, watchful, big ears moving, and stood statue-still in knee-deep spring grass and wildflowers, watching his car pass. Sunset time it had been, really. Now it was bright morning, and in the meadow stood three large houses. The building-over was happening fast. Before he died, Rodd Canyon, too, would have filled up with people, houses, kids, dogs, cars. He'd move on when that happened—though God knew where he'd move to. He swung in at a curving driveway between patchy new lawns and flower beds, and halted behind a white BMW parked at the front door of the house.

121

Joseph Hansen

The woman surprised him by being small and slim. *She's old,*
Billie Shears said in Bohannon's memory. But she did not look
old. She was as fair as Billie, or fairer, her hair in a fashionable
short bob. She wore jeans and a plaid shirt and soft leather
boots, and carried a glass of orange juice. To his question, "Do
deer come down out of those woods anymore?" she answered
without surprise, "Yes, sometimes, still. It's the raccoons that
give trouble, though." Her smile made age lines around a gener-
ous mouth. "What bandits they are." She looked him up and
down. He wore jeans, too, and a plaid shirt and boots, but all of
a tougher sort and not new, like hers—far from new, in fact.
His hat was mapped by stains of sweat and weather. She
frowned a little, which didn't make her look younger, either.
"You own the riding stables, don't you? What brings you here?"

"I'm also a private investigator." He took out a folder and
showed her his license. "I'm inquiring into your husband's
death." He looked into her eyes. They were greenish gray. "I'm
sorry for your loss."

"Thank you." She said it mechanically, dismissively, and
turned from the doorway. "Come in. I'm glad you came. Something's wrong here. I was about to phone the sheriff."

The house was New England saltbox, gray and white outside.
Inside it was comfortably formal, the furniture traditional. There
was a lot of wallpaper and white paint. The staircase had var-
nished treads. He closed the door behind him. "Wrong how?"
he asked, and she led him up the stairs. She opened a white
door to a rear room the designer probably meant to be slept in,
but that was outfitted instead with a desk and file cabinets, a
computer in glossy beige plastic, a multiline telephone, shelves
with books about banking and finance. He saw what she meant
by wrong. Drawers hung open, papers strewed the hardwood
floor, the oval braided rugs. She had showed him inside past
her. She hung back, standing outside in the hall.

"He didn't like me to come in here," she said.

Bohannon looked around at the mess. He turned back to her.

122

Those letters Dennis Toomy wrote you. Did you see them when they questioned you at the sheriff's station?"

"Oh, yes," she said glumly, "yes, indeed."

"And they had all of them? There were no others?"

She shook her head. "I still don't know how Tom found them. He wasn't the suspicious type. He trusted me. They were hidden in a small department store gift box in my closet." Her smile was amazed. "You didn't think I'd hide them here."

"I didn't," Bohannon said, "but someone else might." He pushed at computer printouts with his boot, frowning, listening to them rustle. "Have you had break-ins before?"

"Never," she said. "Of course, we only moved out here a few weeks ago. But it's not common in this area, is it?"

"You think it happened last night?" Bohannon crouched, picked up an armload of the folded sheets, and squinted at them. "What made you look in here this morning?"

"I came home tottering with exhaustion after Archie arranged my bail," she said. "I showered to get the smell of the jail off me, took a sleeping pill, and slept very hard. It was early, but I didn't care. I wanted oblivion. But sometime in the night I woke. Had I heard someone in the house? I didn't know, and I fell asleep again right away. But when I got up this morning, I remembered the noise. And I looked through the house. Not thoroughly, really. I half thought I'd dreamed it. But that's how I happened to look in here."

"So it could have happened the night he died, when you were both away," Bohannon said. "Or during the day."

She shook her head. "No. I have a daily woman. Inez."

"Right." Bohannon let the printouts whisper onto the desk, and studied the room. "He brought work home. So where is his attaché case?"

Startled, she came into the room, orange juice glass still in her hand. "That's a very good question." She walked around, peering into corners, into a closet stacked with storage files and office supplies. She shut the closet door and regarded Bohannon. "Private investigator? Working for whom?"

"Dennis Toomy," he said, "at the request of Billie Shears."

"That brat," she said coldly.

"What was in the attaché case?" Bohannon asked.

"Good God, how would I know? Me—a mere woman?"

"What did it look like?" Bohannon said. "Color, make?"

"Mark Cross. Tan cowhide. With his initials in gold. I gave it to him for his fiftieth birthday. It was something he took with him everywhere. I thought"—she sounded for a startling moment as if she might cry, and tears brightened her eyes—"he might be reminded of me now and then."

"Do you think Dennis Toomy arranged for that accident?"

She shrugged fragile shoulders inside the plaid shirt and turned away. "What a fool I was. A college boy. Dear God." She walked out the office door, halted, turned back. "The things loneliness can make a person do. How I wish I could change it, go back to that morning, not feel what I felt, just let him look at the oaks and tell me, and then send him on his way. I'd give everything to change that."

"I know what you mean," Bohannon said, and he did. "But do you think he went ahead and fixed those brakes? Do you think he telephoned your husband here that night, while you were out hauling tarnished toasters and lopsided lamps down to Seaside Park for the sale, and told him something that would get him up into those mountains, those canyons, those crooked dark little trails at midnight?"

She opened her eyes wide. "Wait. Maybe the attaché case was in the car. He could have taken it with him. Maybe that was what whoever called asked him to bring."

"Did Dennis know anything about your husband's work?"

"All Dennis knows is trees," she said.

"The attaché case wasn't in the car," Bohannon said.

"Perhaps after the crash, the killer took it."

"Afraid not," Bohannon said. "I was the first person to come upon the car. There were no human tracks down there. I don't think he took the attaché case." Bohannon came out of the office room and closed the door behind him. He told her, "You think Dennis did it. That's why you left him in jail."

"He's emotional," she said. "A child. I shouldn't have wept on his shoulder. He hated Tom for what he'd done to me. But I never meant for him to—" She closed her mouth.

Bohannon grunted and started down the stairs. "It's a beautiful house," he said. "A beautiful setting. A way of life most people only dream about. You forgot all that?"

"Exactly," she said. "I was a fool."

"And Dennis Toomy has to pay?" Bohannon stood on the polished oak floor of the entry hall and glanced into the handsome lifeless rooms on either side, morning sunlight slanting into them. "It wasn't Dennis who rifled those files upstairs."

"I suppose not." She shrugged, passed Bohannon, pulled open the front door. She gave Bohannon a wan smile as he put on his hat and stepped outside. "I don't want to think about it. I'm a selfish, spoiled woman, used to having everything—almost everything— as I want it. I want to forget Dennis Toomy. All about him. As quickly as I can. If I can." She used the woebegone smile to mock what she knew herself to be—though she didn't really care. She laid a hand for a moment on Bohannon's arm. "He'll be all right. You don't think he did it. You'll find out who did."

"You broke it," Bohannon said, "and I pick up the pieces?"

"Something like that," she agreed.

He thought of Rivera. "You don't believe in hell?"

"Oh, yes," she said. "It's right here on earth."

Meritt Fletcher rocked in a high-backed padded rawhide chair behind a glossy desk. Executive director of Mountain Savings and Loan, he was a hefty man in his mid-fifties, white-haired, rosy-cheeked. His blue eyes had a way of twinkling, and laughter seemed always ready to shape his mouth. He didn't have Thomas Kruger's taste in clothes, however. His linen jacket was a loud plaid in rust red and three shades of green. Fletcher said:

"She could have rifled those files herself. Why not? I've known

Melanie Kruger for years. Close friends with a man, close friends with his wife, right? But I never liked her. Had no reason for that, so I tried to overcome the feeling." He sighed and waggled white eyebrows. "But now it looks as if my instincts were right. She blamed Tom, said his career left no time for her. It wasn't that way. She was cold, cold as she looks. I'd have divorced her. I've done that twice. Not Tom." Sorrowfully, Fletcher shook his head. "For him, she was the only woman in the world. Poor bastard. What else was there for him but his work?"

Bohannon said, "She could have done it herself, yes. To furnish Archie Fitzmaurice with an argument in her defense—that somebody else wanted Tom Kruger dead."

"It wouldn't have worked for long," Fletcher said.

"That's why I don't think she did it," Bohannon said.

"Rifled Tom's files, you mean," Fletcher said. "She killed him all right. Nobody else had a reason."

"He had a lot of work at home, there," Bohannon said. "Stuff he'd brought from here."

Fletcher sighed, lifted big, expensively kept hands, and dropped them to the desktop again. "I tried to interest him in golf, tennis, sailing—I have a boat: he was always welcome. 'All work and no play,' I told him, 'will kill you, Tom. You have to learn to relax.' But he didn't listen. You're right. He took mountains of work home. Had a computer set up there, interfaced with our system here."

"Right," Bohannon said. "And what would somebody break in and steal? Why would they?"

Fletcher lifted beefy shoulders. "Can't imagine. I mean, if this was a high-tech manufacturing business, a research laboratory, yes. But we're a simple savings institution. Nothing of value but our integrity."

Bohannon rose from the leather chair that faced the desk and went to gaze out a window. Across the highway below, the tall, lean pines of the hills that hid the ocean swayed in a forenoon wind. The sun was bright, the sky blue. "You know," he said carelessly, "drugs come in on this stretch of coast. On supposed fishing boats? Illegal aliens with cash to pay the fare? Money changes hands. That money has to go someplace, if only to wait to be sent south for laundering."

"Now, listen here." An angry flush replaced Fletcher's rosiness. "If you're implying—"

"Relax," Bohannon said. "I didn't mean you knew where the money came from. But suppose some of it is here? Suppose Tom Kruger discovered some customer, maybe more than one, has been making bigger deposits and withdrawals than he could explain?"

"Ah, yes, I see. Sorry." Fletcher's anger seemed to subside, though wariness lurked in his eyes. "Putting it like that, maybe you're right. But there's this college boy. Those letters between him and Melanie."

"I don't think the break-in took place at the Kruger house till after Tom Kruger was found dead, and they were arrested. It worries me, Mr. Fletcher. It worries me that Tom Kruger's attaché case is missing."

"It worries me," Fletcher said with sudden heaviness, "that Tom is gone. I'm going to miss him terribly. Not just here, where I relied on him, his sharpness, his integrity. We were close as brothers. Family. We had keys to each other's houses, could talk anytime, about anything, and did."

"Who broke into his house? What for?" Bohannon said.

Fletcher's phone pulsed softly on the desk. He lifted it, listened, said, "Right away," hung up the receiver, and rose. "I don't have any idea," he answered Bohannon, "but you can be sure I'll look into it." He touched Bohannon's card that lay on the desk, a horse head printed on it. "And if I find anything the least suspicious, I'll get in touch with you." He let his smile loose now, a little ruefully. "Meantime, I'll ask you to excuse me. The state auditors are here on their semiannual visit." He shook Bohannon's hand, pulled open his office door, and with a hand between Bohannon's shoulder blades, showed him out, and turned his attention to bespectacled men in poplin suits, who came in carrying attaché cases.

127

Joseph Hansen

*   *   *

The sea had done nothing for it, nor had the nets, nor the long fall with thousands of glistening fish into a wallowing boat. It was wet, scuffed, scarred, but the initials T.K. still gleamed gold in the hard light of Gerard's office. The case gaped empty on his desk. Empty except for one thing. A Smith and Wesson .45 revolver. Bohannon stared.

"Who belongs to that?" he said.

"Kruger's wife—widow—the ice princess says he never owned a gun," Gerard said. "Not of any kind. He gave money to the anti-handgun movement."

"Circumstances alter cases," Bohannon said. "It looks new. If he bought it recently, maybe it means he felt threatened. Maybe by the people who broke into his house and stole the briefcase—and whatever was in it."

"It is new," Gerard said. The corners of his mouth twitched in suppressed amusement. "I just put it back in the case to show you how the fishermen found it. It's been through the lab. The cylinder was full. There are no fingerprints on it. If they were drug dealers or coyotes, do you think those types would throw away a brand-new name-brand gun? That had nothing incriminating about it, not a bullet fired?"

"I don't think so." Bohannon picked the gun up. It was cold and damp because the suede lining of the attaché case still held water. He turned the heavy thing over in his hands, puzzled, and laid it back in the case. "Why would anyone?"

"A call will come in on the registration soon," Gerard said. "But what was in this case before the gun got there?"

Bohannon wasn't listening. He frowned out the window, where patrol cars sat in the parking lot and big eucalyptus trees rose out of the ground lighting into darkness. "Emotion," he said, "revulsion. When I was about ten, I stole a handful of cigarettes and sneaked out to a storage building full of rusty old tools and cobwebs to smoke them. I got through maybe three and, God damn, was I sick!" He laughed at the memory. "I looked at the

128

ones I had left, and took and threw those suckers as far as I could into a corn patch. I never wanted to see another cigarette."

Gerard grinned. "Happened to you, too, did it?" His face sobered. "Yeah, I see what you mean. Somebody bought it to kill him with, and lost his nerve."

"Somebody with a boat," Bohannon said.

"Not a smuggler. They don't give a damn what they do."

Bohannon said grimly, "Tell me about it."

"Sorry," Gerard said. "So—who does that leave?"

"One man," Bohannon said. "Meritt Fletcher."

Gerard's brows went up and he blinked. "Director of Mountain Savings and Loan? Are you serious?"

Bohannon said, "You could ask him. He owns a boat. He wears jackets that belong only one place—where horses run and horses' asses bet. Auditors were due at his bank today. Last night somebody stole papers from the office in Kruger's house. In that attaché case. Why hadn't Kruger found out Fletcher was embezzling to cover his losses at the track?"

"Jesus." Gerard said it softly and looked pale. "You think it was Kruger who did the phoning—said I've got this proof you're creaming accounts, and we better talk about it, and meet me someplace in the mountains at midnight?" Gerard reached for a telephone, said into it, "Terry, get me the harbormaster's office," and set the receiver down again. "If he went out last night to jettison that attaché case, maybe he was seen." Gerard closed the attaché case, snapped the catches, sat staring at it. "But he wouldn't dump the papers at sea."

"His house is that big white Gothic fright down on the point, alone there in the pines. It has a lot of chimneys. He probably used a fireplace."

"Probably." The phone rang. Gerard picked it up and spoke to the harbormaster's office. And smiled. Yes, Fletcher took his boat out—around one A.M., and came back in an hour. Gerard hung up, pushed back his swivel chair on squeaky wheels, stood, and picked up the attaché case. "You are one smart son-

129

of-a-gun." He went to lift down his jacket from a hook by the office door. "Fletcher is going to love seeing this again."

"Did they see him carry it on board?"

"No. But I just remembered something." Gerard set the case down and shrugged into his jacket. "He's a thick-set, fiftyish man with white hair, right?" He carried the case into the hall and Bohannon followed. Down the hall the clack of typewriters echoed, the moan of a siren from outside. Gerard stopped at the reception desk and told T. Hodges where he was going. She gave him a nod and Bohannon a long look he couldn't translate. Gerard led Bohannon outdoors, where a wind had risen, the smell of rain on it. He said, "Same type as Kruger."

"Meaning," Bohannon said, "it could have been Fletcher who left those letters in your mailbox."

"Stubbs was right," Gerard said. "It didn't make sense for Kruger to do it. He wouldn't have wanted a scandal."

"And Fletcher, on his way to kill Kruger, left the letters to cover his ass, to throw suspicion on the wife and her lover."

Bohannon followed Gerard to the parking lot, bending into the wind. "Just one thing—how did he get hold of those letters?"

"I'll ask him." Gerard stopped beside a patrol car. "She went riding at your place with Toomy. I don't call that keeping the affair a secret, do you?" Gerard tossed the attaché case into the patrol car, got in, slammed the door. "She runs with a gaggle of idle rich women, close friends. Maybe she bragged about Toomy. Maybe she even showed off those letters." The worn engine clattered into life. "Women get carried away."

"They aren't the only ones," Bohannon said.

"What?" Gerard began to back the car.

"You're forgetting." Bohannon walked beside the car, wincing, holding the brim of his hat to keep the wind from snatching it. "Kruger wasn't killed with a gun."

"You're forgetting." Gerard halted the car. "Fletcher's gun wasn't fired. He lost his nerve and fixed the brakes, instead. That way, he wouldn't have to watch his friend die."

"You don't even know the gun is his," Bohannon said.

"You're going too fast. Back off. He's a power in these parts. I
don't want you tangling with him on a half-assed theory of mine.
You could lose your job."

"Thanks." Gerard blinked at him soberly. "I appreciate that,
Hack. But . . ." He backed the car fast, turned it sharply, tires
squealing on the blacktop. The car rocked to a stop, the gears
clanked. Gerard said, "I don't think it's half-assed. And I have
to see what's in that fireplace." The car shot forward, jounced
out of the parking lot, and roared away up the night street,
where the tops of trees were tossing in the wind.

Rain had come on that wind, all right, but the storm had blown
on past by midnight, and this morning the sky was a new-
washed blue. Patrol cars crowded the sheriff's station parking
lot, still patched with damp clumps of litter. But there was an
empty slot, and Bohannon left his old pickup truck in it. The
station house smelled of coffee in paper cups. Officers stood in
groups, drinking coffee, munching doughnuts, talking. Some of
the older ones knew Bohannon and gave him nods as he went
past. Gerard, red-eyed, looked at him, told him to come in and
shut the door, told him to sit down. He half-heartedly lifted his
Styrofoam cup and raised his eyebrows over it in a question.

"No, thanks," Bohannon said. "What was in the fireplace?"

"Very fine ash. I don't think the lab can make anything of it,
but Fletcher thinks they can." Gerard smiled. "I don't know
where he got that idea, but it was enough to make him talk."

"So he is a compulsive gambler," Bohannon said.

"You know that. His jacket told you. And you know how that
goes, don't you, for a man who handles other people's money
every day. You know he heard about those letters from a woman
friend, you know he had a key to the Kruger house so he could
hunt till he found them, and then he could search Kruger's
workroom and remove the proof that he, Fletcher, was ripping
off Mountain Savings and Loan. And you know he removed the
proof in that attaché case and burned the papers and diskettes

131

in his fireplace, and dumped the case at sea." Gerard snorted. "Half-assed theory? You were right on target."

Bohannon shrugged and lit a cigarette. "But?" he said.

Gerard held up a hand. "Wait. Let me finish reciting everything you know. You know he bought the gun. That didn't seem to me to equate too well—how could he have done that so fast? The answer has two parts. A week or more ago, Kruger had told him he'd run across irregularities that made him think someone inside the institution was draining off interest on accounts. At that point, of course, Kruger didn't dream it was Fletcher, but Fletcher knew, and it panicked him. That's when he bought the gun, on the pretext that it was to arm a security guard. But when he got it in his hands, he knew he couldn't use it. But you know that. The second part is that it was Fletcher who phoned Kruger that night. Just as you thought in the first place. He told Kruger he'd confirmed his suspicions and asked Kruger to meet him you know where. But only to get Kruger out of the house, so he could sneak in and get Kruger's proof to destroy it."

"A snipe hunt." Bohannon smiled. "As you said."

"That's exactly what it was."

"Not exactly," Bohannon said. "Not if Fletcher tampered with the brakes on that little red car."

"Yeah, well," Gerard said gloomily, "that's where you missed the target and hit the cow."

"He couldn't have fixed the brakes," Bohannon guessed, "because he was out of town at the time? Left early, didn't get back until very late? How am I doing?"

"You're being too modest." Gerard drank from the white cup, made a disgusted face, said, "Cold." He looked at Bohannon. "Tell me where he was. You know where he was."

Bohannon had to laugh. "Not Santa Anita."

"Give the gentleman a cigar," Gerard said. "And not alone. He picked up friends—one in Ventura, two in Santa Barbara. We've had them checked out. It's true." Gerard looked sourly into his cup and made to rise. "So, we're back at square one."

"I told you it was a half-assed theory." Bohannon stood.

"He's still an embezzler," Gerard said. "Around three hundred thousand, he estimates. You did a good thing, Hack. It helped a lot of people."

"It didn't help Dennis Toomy," Bohannon said.

The rain had washed the shaggy, drooping heads of the old pepper trees that sheltered the brick and glass filling station by the highway out of town. Above the trees on a tall steel pole the revolving orange ball with its blue and white 76 gleamed glossy as new. A bony man in crisp blue work clothes unlocked the office door of the filling station as Bohannon swung the pickup in off the highway, where there was little traffic yet, it was so early. The man had faded red hair and a worried look. He puttered at a steel desk for a minute, then came out and undid the padlock on a wide garage door that he swung upward. It looked almost too heavy for him. He went inside, puttered at a workbench there for a moment. Bohannon stopped the pickup and climbed down out of it. The man turned, called, "Help you?" and came at a quick walk.

Bohannon said, "Mrs. Thomas Kruger a customer of yours?"

The man tilted his head on a scrawny neck and looked doubtful about answering. Maybe he thought confidentiality existed between garage mechanics and their clients. Bohannon showed him his license. The man thought about it for a minute and said, "Both of them." He nodded. "Too bad, what happened." His naturally worried look deepened. "You think you know folks. You never know. I sure wouldn't have pegged those two for that kind of trouble. Plenty of money. Not a worry in the world." The mention of money reminded him, and he headed back to the office. Bohannon followed. "And damn if he doesn't drive off a road and get killed, and they're saying she did it—her and some college boy."

"That's what they're saying," Bohannon agreed.

The man crouched, slid back a panel under a counter, opened a safe there, and took from it packets of paper money and bags of coins. He closed the safe, rolled the panel shut, and carried the money past Bohannon and out to the slant-top steel boxes on posts beside the gas pumps.

"But maybe it wasn't that way," Bohannon said. The man unlocked the first of the steel boxes and began laying bills into it, then rattling coins into it. "Did Mrs. Kruger leave her car here, day before yesterday—for a lube job, oil change, wheel alignment, something like that?"

"She didn't." The man closed down the lid of the first box, locked it, angled off to the second. He had a rickety walk. "He did. Says he was using her car because she needed his big one to haul stuff down to the park for the rummage sale." He clattered open the padlock on the second change box and glanced at Bohannon as he opened it. "Yeah, an oil change. That's what it was." He began laying in the rest of his bills and coins. "Said he'd pick it up at four-thirty—which is what he done." The man paused and looked again at Bohannon, startled this time. "Was that the car he crashed in?"

Bohannon nodded. "Little red sports car. Do you have a college girl working here, name of Billie Shears?"

"That's right." The man finished with the money, shut down the lid, locked it. "Part-time, is all. But she's a good little worker. Don't mind getting her hands dirty."

"Did she get them dirty on Mrs. Kruger's car that day?"

"Here she comes now." The man pointed. A new little hatchback curved down the off-ramp from the highway, windshield flashing in the sun. "You can ask her yourself."

"I'd rather you told me," Bohannon said.

The man tilted his head again, guarded. "What for? She do something wrong?" Bohannon said nothing. The man looked worriedly at the car Billie wheeled to a stop under a pepper tree, dry berries crackling beneath the tires. "Well, yes, she was the one. She wasn't here when Mr. Kruger left the car, and she was gone by the time he picked it up, but she was the one that worked on it. It'll be written on the repair bill."

"Good," Bohannon said. "Thanks for your help."

Billie Shears, in a clean blue jumpsuit with the 76 logo

stitched to the pocket, flung herself out of the compact and came running. Her hair was still spiky. "Mr. Bohannon," she panted, "have you found out anything to help Dennis?"

"Morning, Billie," the filling station owner said.

"Oh." She gave him a quick, distracted smile. "Morning, Mr. Zimmerman." She peered up at Bohannon, anxious, begging. "It's me you're here to see, isn't it?"

"That's right," Bohannon said. "And the answer is yes. Just as you said—Dennis wasn't the one who fixed those brakes."

"Oh, that's wonderful," she cried, and hugged him.

"It was you," he said, and hugged her back.

Allowing for the heat, Stubbs had very early this morning made potato-leek soup, and now it was chilled through. They ate it with thick chunks of new-baked bread and a crisp white wine from a vineyard the other side of the mountains. They were alone at the noon kitchen table. Rivera was up at the seminary.

"The green-eyed monster," Stubbs said, "never dies."

Bohannon said, "And she isn't sorry. She'd do it again. She's a good hater for one so young." He gnawed a crusty chunk from his slab of bread, swallowed some wine, followed it with a spoonful of the icy soup. "Cool customer, that Billie—until Dennis was arrested. Then she lost her head."

"So, now he's free—does that make her happy?"

"Not with me, it doesn't." Bohannon glanced ruefully at his left hand. His old doctor friend, Belle Hesseltine, had cauterized, stitched, and bandaged it. But Billie had bitten to the bone. The hand ached and throbbed. "She hates my guts."

Footsteps sounded on the long porch, a slender shadow fell on the screen door, there was a light rapping. He told the shadow to come in, and a slight woman entered, the cat with her. In the backlight, it took him a moment to make the woman out. T. Hodges, in a crimp-brimmed straw hat, gingham shirt, trim jeans. Crouching to pet the cat, she smiled faintly.

"I thought it might be nice to ride a horse today."

Bohannon stood. "Have some lunch first." He pulled out a chair. "Then maybe we can go riding together."

Raymond Obstfeld

· ·

Along with a full-time teaching schedule as an English professor at Orange Coast College in Costa Mesa, Raymond Obstfeld has become one of the most prolific writers of paperback fiction extant, producing action-adventure, Western, and mystery novels under a variety of pseudonyms and house names. Best-known works under his own name are a series of humorous mysteries about Orange County detective Harry Gould. One of them, *Dead Heat* (1981), was nominated for an Edgar.

Obstfeld is also adept at writing poetry, plays, film scripts, literary criticism, and, as "Someone's in the Kitchen with Dinah" shows, short stories. This story originally appeared in *Mystery*.

Raymond Obstfeld

· ·

someone's in the kitchen with dinah

D inah had always liked her name because it reminded people of Dinah Shore. And since most people liked Dinah Shore, Dinah figured they'd like her, too. She was right. Most people did like her.

someone's in the kitchen with dinah

Most people.

But someone didn't. Someone who called on the phone at 3:00 in the morning to threaten her. To tell her of what was going to happen to her one night when she was all alone. One night when she was in the bath. Or in the living room watching television. Or in the kitchen. Someone was going to kill her. Slowly.

At first, Dinah had been frightened. She felt her space had been violated, as if someone had broken into her house and read all her old love letters. But she felt better when her husband returned the next day from his sales trip. He wanted to call the police right away, but she told him it was probably just some kids fooling around. He said nothing to that, but he did take her out for the best dinner they'd ever had, followed by dancing at a disco for the over-thirty crowd, and home to bed.

And then the second call.

Two weeks after their big night out, when Doug was away again, the phone rang. Dinah ran to answer because it was 8:00, the time Doug always called.

"Hello, sweetheart," she panted, trying to catch her breath.

"Hello, darling," the voice snickered.

Dinah felt her mouth dry up instantly, her tongue became swollen and lazy. It wouldn't move. She knew the voice, knew it wasn't Doug's, knew she'd heard it before. Her teeth began to ache. She swallowed the vomit that had boiled up into her mouth.

"Hi, there, sugarplum." He laughed. The voice was a half whisper, the way they always portray these guys on TV. She felt better somehow at that thought. How could someone who watched the same programs as she did really hurt her?

"I see you're all alone tonight. Again."

How does he know? Dinah wondered. She looked quickly around her house, eyes swinging from doors to windows, but the drapes were all drawn, the doors and windows all locked.

"But you won't be alone for long. It won't be long now."

She wanted to hang up, slam the phone down, or blow a police whistle in his ear. But she was afraid. Afraid to make him mad, hoping that as long as she kept him on the phone he wouldn't come to her house. She wanted to cry now to show him what he was doing to her. She wanted to cry and be told everything was okay, it was just a joke. But her eyes were too dry. So dry that it hurt to blink, as if the eyelids were scraping across her eyes, gouging them, leaving deep scars.

"Someone's in the kitchen with Dinah," he sang hoarsely. "Someone's in the kitchen I know . . ."

She hung up.

The phone rang.

She snapped it up automatically, wanting to put it back down even as she saw it come to her ear. She listened but said nothing.

"Sweetheart? Are you there? Hello?"

"Doug!" she screamed. "Doug."

"What's the matter, honey? Come on now, calm down."

She tried to tame her breathing. She remembered a celebrity talking about yoga on TV. How whenever she was upset while driving in heavy freeway traffic, she would always hold her breath for a few seconds, sigh deeply, and hold her breath again, repeating this process until she was calm. She swore that this had changed her whole life. Dinah had wondered why someone as rich and famous as this star didn't have a chauffeur drive her and avoid the whole thing.

Wooossshhh. Dinah released the air from her lungs. By God, it really did work.

"I'm okay, Doug. I'm okay now." She was calm and in control, the way Doug liked her to be. In control. "I guess being alone and hearing him sing like that was just too spooky, like something out of 'Twilight Zone.'"

"That does it," Doug barked, "we're calling the police. I'm leaving here right now and catching the first plane back. You call the police."

"No, no, Doug. Don't rush back. I'm okay now," she said, in control.

"I'll be there in a few hours. Stay in the house, I'll take a cab from the airport."

"Well, if you insist." She sighed, relieved to have lost that argument.

"I do. I love you, sweetheart, and I'll be there soon. In the meantime, call the police and keep everything locked. Trust no one."

Dinah dialed information for the number of the police department. The recording told her to look it up in the phone book and quit wasting precious phone company time. Dinah hung on. She was in control. It disturbed her not to have the number of the police where she could dial it in an emergency. After this she would tape it to the phone.

"Cabrillo Bay Police Department," the voice announced. Suddenly Dinah realized that she'd never before called the police and now she wasn't sure what to say. She wondered if you had to talk to them in a special way. Maybe in code. Ten-four.

"Complaint Department, please," she whispered, her voice sounding as hoarse as her caller's.

"Sure, lady," the officer replied. "You want to return a pair of shoes or something? Wrong style, huh?"

"I'm sorry. I mean I want to talk to someone about a man who's been calling me up and threatening to kill me. I wanted to make a criminal complaint."

"Could I have your name, please?"

Dinah hesitated. She had an uneasy feeling that giving your name to the police was somehow asking for trouble. Then they would know who you were. They'd always keep an eye out for your name. If they had your name, never mind for what, somehow you would always be known as a troublemaker.

"Mrs. Dinah Bradford."

"Just a moment, Mrs. Bradford, I'm switching you to Sergeant Denny. He can help you."

She started to say thank you, but they were already disconnected.

"Sergeant Denny here. What can I do for you?"

Raymond Obstfeld

*   *   *

"What do you mean there is nothing you can do?" Dinah shouted. She was no longer frightened; she was angry.

"Now, I didn't say that, Mrs. Bradford," Sergeant Denny said, getting up from the sofa and pacing toward the window. "I said there is very little that we can do right now. We can authorize a tap on your phone and try to trace the caller, but even a twelve-year-old kid knows enough to get off the phone before a trace can reach them. Television, you know.

"Or we can post a guard for surveillance, but we can't do that indefinitely. If he doesn't make his move within three days we have to pull out. Time is on his side."

"So what am I supposed to do, wait here until he kills me and hope that he leaves a fingerprint somewhere so you will finally have a clue?"

Sergeant Denny swallowed. He was always embarrassed in the face of other people's fear. "For now I suggest that you change your phone number. Then if the calls continue, we'll set up a tap and hope that he hasn't watched too much 'Baretta.'"

"Oh, well, that's different," she said sarcastically. "Now at least I have something to hope for."

"I'm sorry, Mrs. Bradford, that's all we can do. But most of these guys never really do anything. They just get their kicks scaring women. It makes them feel powerful."

"They are powerful, Sergeant. Good night."

Sergeant Denny hesitated, as if to offer encouragement or advice, but he said nothing. "Good night."

Dinah turned the lock into place and started to cry. She was no longer scared or angry, just tired. Just tired. She wanted to go to bed, but she should wait up for Doug. She should look frightened for Doug, not tired. After all, he'd rushed back a day early from his sales trip to comfort her. She should look like she needed comfort.

The phone rang.

Maybe it's the police.

Or Doug.

140

She let it ring.

Maybe Doug couldn't get a plane. Maybe he was stuck at the airport.

The phone was ringing.

"Hello?"

"You talked to the police, Dinah. They can't help you. You should . . ."

She slammed the phone down into the cradle. Then she slammed it down again, and kept slamming it down until she was too short of breath to continue. She held her breath, sighed, held her breath, until she was in control again. Then she put the phone to her ear.

He was laughing.

"You did the right thing," Doug assured her, pulling the covers up over their shoulders as he huddled against her back, his body and legs following the contour of her body and legs exactly like two pieces of a jigsaw puzzle.

"But unplugging the phone, see, is like giving up. It allows him to tell us how to live. Some stranger has forced us to change our life to suit him. It seems wrong."

"It is wrong, but it isn't permanent. I'll have our number changed tomorrow. From now on we'll be the Unlisted Bradfords. Quite exclusive, those Bradfords, don't you know," he joked and Dinah laughed to please him.

"What about Becky and my mother?"

"I'll call them tomorrow."

"I feel like such a rotten mother to send Becky away like that."

"Come on, honey. Let's not talk about that now, okay? Let's try and get some sleep."

Dinah nodded.

"I just wish he'd call once while I was home," Doug muttered, punching his pillow up. He kissed her and went to sleep.

"I'm not going to work," Doug announced over the breakfast he had cooked to surprise Dinah. "I'm taking the week off and we're going away together. Away from this house and away from this chilly weather."

"And away from the phone?"

"Away from all phones. I want you all to myself." He smiled, raising his arms like Bela Lugosi and biting her on the neck.

"I don't know, Doug. It isn't right."

"Come off it, Dinah. I don't care what's right. I care about us. Six weeks ago we were talking about divorce . . ."

"*You* were talking about divorce."

Doug stopped. Now *he* was controlling his breathing. Soon everyone Dinah knew would be holding their breath, sighing, and holding their breath.

"Dinah," he said quietly.

"Oh, God, I'm sorry, Doug. It's my fault and I know it. You had every right to want a divorce." Dinah would never forget the look on Doug's face when he returned home a day early only to find Dinah in bed with a man she had just met that day. It was like a cartoon out of *Playboy* or something. Outraged husband, flustered lover. Everyone seemed to speak slowly and in comic strip balloons. There had been no fighting or clumsy violence, everyone had controlled their breathing. Hold, sigh, hold.

At least Becky had the chance to be spoiled by her grandparents for a few weeks while Doug and Dinah straightened out their lives again. Returned to order.

"I love you, Doug," Dinah said, and meant it.

"I love you, too, sweetheart. God, how I love you. We're just getting everything back to normal again and we don't need this crap from some nut. Maybe it is running away; I don't care. We need to be alone together, otherwise we may just end up alone."

Dinah nodded. "You're right. Let's go."

"Okay, lady, prepare yourself for some kind of vacation," he said, rubbing his hands together as if he could physically pump some gaiety into Dinah. "We'll get a cabin up in Tahoe and see if we can break our honeymoon record."

"I think we already have." Dinah smiled.

"Well, then we can do it again. I'll make the arrangements.

First I go **to** the phone company, then to the travel bureau to make reservations."

"Okay, I'll stay here and pack."

"Maybe you should come with me for the ride. Keep me company."

"No, I'll pack. I want us to get out of here as soon as possible. Maybe we can even stay in the hotel at the airport tonight."

"Great idea. I'll take care of everything." He kissed her solidly on the lips. "Will you be alright?" She nodded. "You sure?" She nodded.

"I'll just give them a call at the office and tell them to send someone else on my route this week. Then I'll go into town and take care of the details of our little getaway. Everything is going to be just fine, I know it. Trust me."

Doug had been gone an hour when the phone rang. At first it merely startled Dinah because she had forgotten that Doug had plugged the phone back in to call the office. He must have forgotten to disconnect it again. Dinah was prepared to be frightened, but strangely she felt a certain sense of relief, like someone who expects the worst for so long they are glad when it finally comes.

"Yes?" she said.

"Your husband wasn't dressed for work this morning. I guess he doesn't trust you alone. Are you planning a trip, maybe? I hear Tahoe is nice this time of year."

"Officer, it's him!" Dinah shouted, hoping to scare him.

He laughed. "There's no one there, Dinah. You're all alone. But you won't be for long. Soon," he sang, "someone will be in the kitchen with Dinah. Someone in the kitchen I know."

Dinah jerked the plug of the phone out of the wall. That gravelly voice still sang distantly in her ear. Someone in the kitchen I know. Why couldn't Doug be there now? Why couldn't he ever be there when the man called? Maybe a man's voice would scare him away. Dinah began to shiver slightly. Control, she thought. Stay in control. Hold breath, sigh, hold breath. Much better.

143

Raymond Obstfeld

Obviously he knew when Doug was gone and waited until then to call. Soon the phone number would be changed, maybe that would stop him. He could start calling someone else.

Dinah returned to the bedroom to pack away the last few toilet articles and wait for Doug to return home. They could leave immediately. It would be good for Doug and her to be alone together. To curl up and watch TV, to take walks around the lake, to go to the casinos for a little gambling. Dinah loved the slot machines. Doug told her that the slots were for suckers, but she liked them anyway. She always lost money, but it was worth it to her. Besides, Doug always won money so everything evened out.

She closed the suitcases and carried them into the living room. Nothing to do now but wait for Doug. She leafed through the *TV Guide*. Nothing on. She was grateful never to have become interested in soap operas. That kind of addiction killed too much time. She paged through *Time* but wasn't inclined to read anything important. She was already three weeks behind in her *Time*s.

Might as well finish off the last of the coffee, she decided, drifting into the kitchen. And a piece of cake. She slid the thin blade out of its wooden sheath on the wall and sliced the cake in half.

Thank God, Doug was so understanding. She wouldn't have known what to do without him. Six weeks ago when Doug had threatened to sue for divorce and to take Becky away from her, Dinah had seriously, for the first time in her life, considered committing suicide. Without Doug and Becky she had nothing, no life. But Doug had calmed down. They had talked. Yes, there were others, but they didn't mean anything. I was just lonely.

Thank God, Doug was understanding.

She sipped at the hot coffee and suddenly the chills returned. Her teeth were aching again. Doug was very understanding. Wasn't he?

She sipped her coffee. She was shivering.

Would she have been so understanding had she walked in on Doug? Probably not. But then she wasn't Doug. He was kind and gentle. He was in control. He liked others to be in control, too. Now everything would be good.

Someone in the kitchen I know.

Why had Doug left the phone plugged in? He was the one who had insisted it be disconnected. Probably forgot. He's not used to having to unplug the phone after making a call.

How does the caller always know when Doug is gone? Must watch the house. But she hadn't seen anyone outside. It couldn't be one of the neighbors, could it? Of course, Doug always knew when he was out.

Someone in the kitchen I know.

Dinah felt a sharp pain in her left eye. It was throbbing. She had to keep it closed. She needed to scream.

"My God, not Doug!" she cried.

But she knew. Doug was in control. There would be no divorce, but there would be punishment. He would break her down until she begged to be put away somewhere safe. Away from Doug; away from Becky. Doug had known when to call, Doug had left the phone connected.

But maybe Doug didn't want to just drive her crazy. Maybe he wanted to kill her. He could tell everyone he had gone out to make reservations for their second honeymoon. They would sympathize. The maniac who had been calling had broken in while he was gone and had killed his wife. The police knew about the calls. Doug had insisted she tell them.

Someone in the kitchen I know.

Dinah raced into the living room, plugged in the phone, and started to dial the police. She had forgotten the number. And she hadn't written it down. She called information and the recording told her to look it up in the phone book. She waited for the operator, then dialed.

"Cabrillo Bay Police Department," the voice announced.

"Let me speak to Sergeant Denny. It's an emergency."

145

Raymond Obstfeld

"I'm sorry, but Sergeant Denny just stepped out for a cup of coffee. He'll be back in a few minutes. Who's calling, please?"

"This is Mrs. Bradford. Dinah Bradford. Please have the sergeant call me as soon as he gets back."

She hung up, but paced around the phone, waiting for it to ring. How long could it take to get a cup of coffee?

Dinah returned to the kitchen for more coffee to warm herself up. She had never been so cold before, so ice cold. Her fingers were stiff and numb.

She had to do something. But what? The car was gone, the windows and doors were all locked. But Doug had keys. She ran to the front door, frantically pushing and tugging furniture to barricade the door. Now the kitchen door, she said, running in that direction.

In the kitchen's back doorway stood Doug. He smiled and came toward her.

It was all so clear to Dinah. Hold breath, sigh, hold breath. She moved slowly but powerfully through the kitchen like a swimmer. Doug's arms opened to her as she got closer. There was no stopping. Her hand swept up the knife from the cake, and as she stepped into his arms she drove the knife firmly into his stomach. His dreadful scream frightened her and she twisted away sharply, the thin blade of the knife breaking off at the handle.

"Oh my God, not me," he whispered hoarsely. "Not me." He tried to pull the blade out, but it was too slippery from the blood. And he was too weak now.

He weaved drunkenly and collapsed.

Control, Dinah thought. Hold breath, sigh, hold breath.

Dinah ran into the living room and snapped up the ringing phone, shouting, "Sergeant Denny! Hurry, he . . ."

First came the hoarse laughter, then: "Someone's in the kitchen with Dinah. Someone in the kitchen I know . . ."

146

John Ball
· · · · · · · · · · · · · ·

Few writers have had as multifaceted a life as John Ball. He served on the staff of *Fortune* magazine and as a New York *World-Telegram* columnist. An accomplished musician, he once worked for Columbia Records and was music critic of the Brooklyn *Eagle*. A commercial pilot since 1947, Ball served in the Army Air Corps in World War II and still holds the rank of lieutenant colonel. He has been a radio commentator and an assistant curator of New York's Hayden Planetarium. In recent years, he has enhanced the credibility of his procedural novels by serving as a reserve police officer with the Los Angeles County Sheriff's Department.

Ball's *In the Heat of the Night* (1965) immediately established him in the front ranks of mystery writers. The first case of black Pasadena homicide specialist Virgil Tibbs won an Edgar for best first mystery novel of its year as well as a Gold Dagger Award from Britain's Crime Writers' Association. The film version, starring Sidney Poitier as Tibbs, won five Oscars, including best motion picture of its year. Tibbs has been featured in several subsequent cases, most recently *Singapore* (1986). Ball has also introduced a second series sleuth in Jack Tallon, chief of police of a small Washington city, who stars in *Chief Tallon and the S.O.R.* (1984).

The Virgil Tibbs story that follows appears in these pages for the first time anywhere.

John Ball

················

good evening,
mr. tibbs

I t was only a few minutes past ten when Officer Rick Sorenson thought he saw something lying in the middle of the street a
half block ahead. It was a poorly lighted street, so he had to
wait a few seconds until the headlights of his patrol unit had it
in their range, then there was no doubt. He pulled his car up
fifty feet short of the spot and made a quick check. Then he
used his radio.

"I have a victim lying in the middle of the street," he reported. "Female Caucasian, approximately thirty-five to forty
years of age. No signs life, no visible injuries. Request backup,
supervisor, and paramedics. Possible one eighty seven."

That broadcast got action and a lot of it—fast. Within a minute another of the all-white Pasadena patrol units came up the
block, its roof lights on. Seconds later another car rolled from
the other direction. The field sergeant called in with an ETA of
three minutes. By the time the two backup units had the ends of

the street blocked off, the siren of the paramedic ambulance could be heard coming up Colorado Boulevard.

The full homicide team would not roll until the field sergeant had confirmed the situation, but the "possible one eighty seven" was heavy. That grim number meant murder, which would make it a new ball game. As Sergeant Hetherington sped toward the scene it was already in his mind that a victim in the middle of the street was much more likely to be a hit-and-run victim, but that was still manslaughter at the least and called for a full response. He had handled many similar instances in the past and he knew exactly what to do.

Sergeant Hetherington pulled his car up well short of the place where the victim lay. He was careful to leave plenty of room for the paramedic team that automatically had first priority. He adjusted the side spot to illuminate the silent form that he was already quite sure was a corpse: if there had been any evidence of life, four officers would not be maintaining a perimeter as they were—they would be rendering first aid pending the arrival of the paramedics.

The red ambulance unit came code three—with lights and siren—and stopped within twenty feet of the woman lying in the street. The men inside jumped out, grabbed their equipment, and knelt beside the still, silent form. A minute or two later one of them got up and shook his head. Hetherington saw it and reached for his microphone. He quickly gave the location and then added, "The victim is S-5. Notify Virgil." That last was not strict police code, but he knew he would be understood. It was a lot better than asking for the homicide team in the clear when so many civilians had scanners in their homes and cars. The less crowd, the better.

There were some people already, of course, being kept back by Sorenson and one man from each of the two initial backup units. Five patrol cars were on the scene by that time and there was plenty of manpower, all of which might be needed.

It took Virgil Tibbs six minutes to get to the scene after

Hetherington's report had come in. He hopped a ride in a car going to the scene and was the first out when the vehicle stopped. The inevitable spectators, who were quiet and orderly, saw a trim-looking Negro who was very neatly dressed and who obviously knew what he was about. There was no racial discrimination whatever in the Pasadena Police Department and there had not been for a generation. Tibbs nodded to the paramedics and was given the word immediately.

"The victim is dead, gone not much more than half an hour. The body is still very warm, and someone would have seen it if it had been there much longer."

Tibbs had already come to that conclusion himself, but he continued to listen. "It's your department, but I don't think it was a hit-and-run," the paramedic added. "It looks as if she dropped right where she is. Good luck."

The paramedic unit drove off, ready to return to its regular and vital job of life saving. It was now up to the coroner's office and the Pasadena Police Department.

Hetherington came over to confer. He had done much homicide investigation himself and he knew the ropes. He stood by as Tibbs dropped to one knee and began to make a careful check of the body.

As Virgil worked, he passed his findings on to his colleague. "There's no evidence of abrasion on either the palms or the knees, so the victim probably fell right where she is. No visible skid marks or tire tracks to suggest a hit and run. No readily available marks on the external clothing. Purse, if any, missing." He did not need to add that there most certainly would have been a purse, because no woman would be out alone at night unless she had stepped from one of the houses in the immediate vicinity. That was highly unlikely, but officers were already ringing doorbells, looking for possible witnesses or an identification of the dead woman.

After five more minutes Tibbs got to his feet. By that time the full homicide team was on hand and the photographer was waiting to take his shots. Virgil moved away to give him room and spoke with Hetherington. "Time of death within the hour," he said. "Sorenson was accurate: it's a Caucasian female close to forty. I'd say five feet four, a hundred and thirty pounds. She's used to working, because her fingernails are worn way down, not bitten. Her dress is from that big Pennsylvania mail-order house. Sensible shoes, good quality, but not above that. Limited use of cosmetics and no expensive scents. Obviously a respectable lady and married; the ring on her finger is well seated in the flesh and probably couldn't be slipped off in the normal way. Limited circumstances, lived carefully within them."

"Hardly a sex crime or one of passion," Hetherington noted. "Anything in the way of indicators?"

"Two," Virgil answered. "Her hair: she was a natural ash blond, which suggests Scandinavian origin. She could have been a lot more attractive, to men at least, if she had tried, but she obviously didn't think in those terms."

"The other point?"

"Oh, the position of the body. Notice, Ben, that she is lying at about a ten degree angle to the curb. Does that suggest anything to you?"

"Frankly, not at the moment. Let's have it."

Tibbs, who seemed about to respond to that, clammed up instead. "I'd like to see the coroner's report first," he said. "And I want to check with the telephone company."

On his way back to Headquarters, Virgil Tibbs could not erase the image of the victim he had just examined. Everything about her spoke of respectability on a limited income. She had done the best that she could with what she had, and that very thought bit into Tibbs. He had never gotten used to seeing people who had been cut down in the midst of their normal and decent lives.

As soon as he was in his office, he began to set in motion the machinery to identify the victim. Both the watch sergeant and the incoming watch commander had been briefed and would handle any incoming inquiry calls with the usual tact; notifications of death were almost never given over the telephone. Before the night would be over, there was a 90 percent chance that a call would come in and that an identification would be made.

Because there was nothing more that he could do for the moment, Virgil Tibbs went home to get some sleep.

He was back a little after eight the following morning despite the fact that he was technically working the second shift, beginning at four in the afternoon. He had a case on his hands and he was not one to leave it to someone else to clean up.

There had been several calls during the night that were of interest. Tibbs read them all carefully, considering each possibility even though it appeared unlikely.

Reported missing: Madeline King, motion picture and TV actress. Left a party early claiming that she was not feeling well. Failed to arrive at her home. Location, Hollywood. Age twenty-nine, divorced. Report made by her boyfriend with whom she was sharing an apartment. Preliminary investigation revealed that despite the relatively early hour, she was already quite drunk and had been advised to take a cab home. After she had left the party, no one knew what had happened to her. Her car had not been taken. Height five feet six, brunette.

Tibbs put that one aside for the moment.

Reported missing: Mrs. Esther Sommers, age forty-nine, female Negro believed to have been visiting in Claremont. Wife of the Reverend Henry Sommers of South Pasadena, black pastor of a small white church that had called him to its pulpit. Highly respected in the community. Five feet three, 135 pounds. Her husband had not seen her go out and could not be certain what she had been wearing. If she had decided to stay overnight with friends, she would have called. She always did.

He also put that report temporarily aside.

Reported missing: "Ms." Yvonne Didelot (informant refused to state whether Miss or Mrs. Claimed the report-taking officer was chauvinist pig). Age twenty-five, five feet five, slim, owner of a beauty parlor. Yvonne Didelot admitted to be a professional name, but informant refused to supply real name. On being pressed, admitted that "Ms." Didelot was twice divorced and was at present residing with the informant.

Unlikely as it was, Tibbs called the number given and found himself talking with a lofty-voiced female who mixed concern with a carefully cultivated snobbery. The conversation did not take long. He identified himself as a police officer and asked about the missing woman's fingernails. He was assured that they were exquisitely long and shapely. He presumed that Didelot, whatever her real name was, was having an affair and dismissed it from his mind.

Reported missing: Marion Horowitz, aka Marcy Dawn. Age thirty-two, divorced, five feet four, known to the Burbank police as a prostitute. That called for another phone call, this time to a lieutenant he knew on the Burbank department.

"Marcy," he learned, was a well-behaved prostitute who gave satisfaction and who never went in for robbing her clients or using shakedown devices. Apart from her occupation, a good citizen. She was the ex-wife of an aerospace engineer who had had a drinking problem.

Pressed for a fuller description, the lieutenant mentioned that "Marcy" was given to expensive cosmetics and perfumes. She probably deducted them as a business expense. One of her professional friends thought she might have gone to Las Vegas with a client who looked her up regularly.

Tibbs discarded that possibility and called the coroner's office. When he had one of the medical examiners on the line, he put his question. "You have a Jane Doe that came in from here last night. Thirty-five to forty, plainly dressed, no visible external injuries."

"I know the one," the doctor said. "We're going to do her shortly."

"Let me know what you find. Meanwhile, would you take a careful look and see if there are any indications that the victim may be black?"

"Virgil, she's a Caucasian."

"Yes, but you can get fooled. Do you remember Walter White?"

"Vaguely."

"He was a pioneer Negro leader who was very light skinned; people constantly took him for white. There's a famous story about him: he was on a train coming up from the South and he had eaten his dinner in the diner. Shortly after that some tough rednecks came through the train when it was stopped. When White asked them what was wrong, they told him that they were after a light-skinned nigger who had dared to enter the diner."

"Good God," the doctor said.

"That's how it was," Tibbs said, without emotion. "Now, will you have a careful look at my Jane Doe and see if you can find any evidence at all that she may be either wholly or partly Negro?"

"Call you back."

Twenty minutes later he kept his promise. "I've checked her very carefully, Virgil, and I'll bet my reputation that if she has any Negro blood at all it would be generations back—and that doesn't figure. She's a definite Nordic type and here's something else: she has some dentistry, probably done a while back, that's definitely European."

Tibbs spoke his thanks and hung up. He had four other cases on hand that required attention, so for the moment he put aside his Jane Doe problem. The odds were better every minute that someone would call in and resolve the matter.

At two in the afternoon he got another call from the coroner's office. "On your Jane Doe, Virgil, you can relax. Death was due to natural causes. She had a very bad heart condition, possibly due to rheumatic fever earlier in her life, and it took her. There's no evidence whatever of physical attack or injury. I just signed the certificate."

"I thought that might be the case," Tibbs said, "but I wanted it confirmed before I went any further."

"How come?"

"The position of the body when it was found, for one thing. Now I've got to check with the telephone company."

He drove back to the scene of the incident and parked his car. In the center of the street a wooden barricade protected the chalked outline that had been drawn the previous night. He went first to the southeast corner at the north end of the block. There he found a public telephone. He dropped a coin and called the telephone repair service. He got his coin back and a representative on the line who confirmed that that number had been out of order. Tibbs thanked her and hung up. Then he looked carefully down the block and saw that there was a filling station on the opposite side of the street. It was clearly visible from where he was, and he knew for a fact that it was open until midnight.

If the unfortunate woman had been stricken while standing on the corner, waiting for a bus, she would try to use the telephone to get help. Assuming she was in pain, she might well try to walk to the filling station where there would be someone to help her. In that condition she followed instinct and took the shortest possible route—diagonally down the block. If a car came by, so much the better, she could signal for help.

Her body had been pointed in just that direction when she fell. Someone had found her before Sorenson came by in his patrol unit and had taken her purse. The thief probably hadn't given a damn if she were alive or dead; he had her simple possessions and that was what he wanted.

She had been like a doll that someone had tipped over. Somehow Tibbs was relieved that, while premature, it had been a natural death.

He got back into his car and drove to the modest church where Reverend Sommers was the pastor. The man he wanted to see was not in, but the church secretary was. She was a middle-aged woman, awkward in appearance; when she got up to assist him, she walked with a definite limp. However, she was most pleasant and willing to help.

155

Tibbs identified himself. "I understand that Mrs. Sommers is missing," he said. "I'm the officer investigating the circumstances."

"Oh, I'm so glad you've come, sir. Pastor is out. He's terribly upset, of course, but he's making his hospital calls—there are a number of them this week. He puts his duty before everything else, you know. He does call in frequently to ask if there is any news."

"I'm sorry," Tibbs said. "I didn't get your name."

"Oh, excuse me. I'm Miss Morgan, Dorothy Morgan." She looked at him, anxious to be of help.

"Miss Morgan, you know Mrs. Sommers, I assume."

"Of course. A wonderful lady, and so very well liked. We are friends."

Tibbs hesitated a bare moment. "Miss Morgan, I understand that Pastor Sommers is black."

"Yes, but that doesn't make any difference to us here. He couldn't be a better pastor to our church. And he's a Ph.D., did you know that?"

"No, I didn't; thank you. Pardon my asking this, but I haven't had the pleasure of meeting either Pastor or Mrs. Sommers. Is she black also?"

For a moment the church secretary looked at him as though the question was offensive. Then she understood and relaxed. "No, Mr. Tibbs, that's right, isn't it? Mrs. Sommers is Swedish. But they are a wonderful couple and . . ."

There was only one thing more to do. Virgil drove to the South Pasadena station and asked to speak to the officer who had taken the report on Mrs. Sommers. He wasn't in, since he worked the late shift, but they got him at his home.

"The pastor came in personally," the desk man reported. "When he told me that his wife was missing, I made out the report. He gave me her age, height, and weight, but I didn't ask about her race. I put her down as Negro, obviously. It never occurred to me . . ."

"I quite understand," Tibbs interrupted. "He should have

told you, but he probably assumed that everyone knew in a fairly small community where he was in a conspicuous position. But next time ask, will you?"

"Definitely."

Virgil was at his desk when he was called and told that the Reverend Dr. Sommers was in the lobby asking if there was any news of his wife. Virgil asked to have him wait.

He got up, put on his coat, and braced himself for the unpleasant duty he would have to perform. Frequently the police chaplain assisted in death notifications, but in this instance it was probably unnecessary.

He went down the stairs to the main floor, walked down the corridor, and opened the door into the lobby.

A tall, very carefully dressed man was waiting for him. He was not wearing clericals, but his profession was written on his features. And since Virgil had come down to see him, there was a good chance that he had already guessed.

He made it easy, because that was his path in life. Dr. Sommers held out his hand, offering moral support, and said, "Good evening, Mr. Tibbs."

Helene Juarez Phipps

Since her first sale to *Playgirl*, Helene Juarez Phipps has contributed short fiction to publications as varied as *Texas Quarterly*, the Mystery Writers of America anthology *Cop Cade*, and the distinguished anthology series *Grito del Sol*. Her story "The Running Lovers" won first prize in a 1984 short story contest sponsored by the Southern California chapter of MWA and subsequently appeared in *Ellery Queen's Mystery Magazine*. Her book *Authentic Mexican Cooking* (1984) led to a television appearance with Phil Donohue. A graduate of Stanford, Phipps served as art and food editor of the magazine *Impresion* and is currently state-wide coordinator of the California Democratic Council. "The Answer" is a new story and one of her best.

Helene Juarez Phipps

the answer

H e hadn't expected to find snowflakes in the desert. Coming from New York, he had always pictured the desert with dunes and mesas and unending wastes of sunlit sand. Not dung-colored and covered with scrub and thorny brush and an occasional saguaro reaching skyward. Not like the dreary flatlands that he was viewing from the windows of the airport bus.

He held the image with him and when he reached his destination at Lamy, it began to snow. He lifted his backpack and his two boxes of canvases from the luggage compartment and set them on the station platform to wait for whatever transportation the town had to offer. The large flakes came down like dampened feathers and their cold touch sent his thoughts back to the farm in Connecticut where he had spent a winter day hunkered down on his closet floor while he pieced together old snapshots of his grandmother and smoothed out crumpled sheets of newsprint that he had salvaged from the trash bin.

As the desert began to whiten with the sudden snowfall, he wasn't worried about himself or the cold. But he worried about his canvases. They were his cards of introduction to the grandmother he had never seen, portraits of women he had never known. He hadn't packed them so watertight that they wouldn't be harmed by the moisture in the air, and it was important that he get them somewhere inside, where it was dry. The nearest shelter was the Red Garter Saloon across the semblance of a road from the bus station.

He made two trips across the pathless snow, one with his boxes and then his pack, before he settled in for the remainder of the afternoon at the long rough-hewn bar.

By nightfall, he had to make a choice. Either the advertised room to let, upstairs, or the house, according to the bartender, owned by the lady painter up the street who occasionally welcomed an overnight visitor.

So she was prepared to take in guests and was acknowledged as an artist by the townsmen. She had covered her identity well. It had taken him years to track her down.

From the front porch of the saloon, he could see the lights of the adobe building up the street, its irregular contours being obliterated gradually by the slanting curtain of snow.

Back at the bar, he ordered a drink that he thought went with the territory.

Helene Juarez Phipps

As the bartender set two glasses before him, a jigger of tequila and a large mug glass for beer, he pondered whether he should arrive announced or should he give her warning.

He placed the filled jigger inside the mug. When the bartender handed him a bottle of Mexican beer he poured it carefully, inundating the smaller glass. The foam rose swiftly to the rim.

With his first swallow, the heat of the strong liquor and the coolness of the foam-capped beer settled his mixed inner feelings. He decided to make the call.

On the phone, from the house only three blocks away, she sounded as though she were in the room beside him. Her voice was strong, not feeble and raspy with age as he had anticipated.

"What took you so long?" she said. "It's been years . . ."

"What made you think I could find you?"

"Because you're just like your father. He had a crazy curiosity. It never subsided until he died."

As he listened, he was sorry that he had called her. He didn't even know whether he could bear to see her.

"Now that you're found me, pack your gear and come on."

He could hardly settle the receiver on its cradle. His hand was still shaking when he paid the bar tab.

"The old lady made you that nervous?" the bartender asked.

"No. Just the circumstances all around," he said.

It was late for the old girl to still be up. But he was committed and he'd have to spend the night. He'd be more comfortable in one of the rooms above the bar, but this way, he could conclude his business sooner. His hands were shaking as he gathered up his gear. He wondered if her house would be any warmer.

There was no street, really. Just a wide cowpath and a tin-roofed shanty along the way. And then there was the long, deep-set adobe house that took up an entire corner, if there had been a corner. But no surveyor had set this town out.

Close up, the house was the color of putty mixed with coffee, lightly creamed. Snow mounds were beginning to build up in the corners of the low, flat roof. He peered in through the front window and saw the jawbone of a bull ox hanging on the fire-wall. The light from the raised and rounded hearth cast shadows formed like moving spears.

Then he saw her, seated before the fireplace, dressed in a long black robe like a monk's. She was smoking a thin cigar and the smoke from it flowed in stripes and layers up to the ceiling beams. In the newspaper reproduction that he had snatched from the incinerator when he was a boy, she had looked like Garbo, with a slouch-brimmed hat pulled down over one eye, broad-shouldered and in man-tailored suits. Then, she had a certain gaunt elegance that even now, sitting in her bentwood rocker, she still retained. There was no semblance of her past beauty, but he had no doubts from her posture that she was the model for the pictures he had kept hidden from his mother all these years.

The string of drying peppers that hung from the outside eaves rattled against his head as he walked along the veranda toward the front entrance. When the door opened before he knocked, he saw the lean, black-garbed figure standing there with hair cut short like a man's, vigorous and bristling. He thought there must be two women in the house. He couldn't believe that anyone that old could move so quickly from the fireside.

"I haven't got all night," she said. "What took you so long?"

"I left the Red Garter as soon as I hung up."

"I don't mean now . . . I've been expecting you for years."

"There must be some mistake," he stammered, twice-surprised. "You couldn't have been expecting me. I wasn't sure I was coming myself." He was embarrassed. He didn't like to keep anyone waiting, and she, for some reason, appeared unreasonably annoyed.

The crease in her forehead made a deep *V* between her heavy brows. The sunken hollows in her cheeks that must have been fleshed out and rounded when she was younger appeared to be covered with dull-grained leather. Her forehead shone as though it had been polished with a chamois and, oddly, there were no lines above the wrinkles of her frown.

On the whitewashed wall behind her were paintings of flowers, iris and orchids and lilies, larger than life, opening up like blackened vulvas. They made him feel uncomfortable, revealing depths of mysteries he had not yet plumbed.

"How old are you?" she asked.

"Twenty-four." He wondered when she was going to ask his name. There was no way that she could have known it.

"You don't know much, then, do you?" she said.

"I only know myself. I can't talk about me, though. My paintings speak for me." He pointed to the two narrow boxes that he had set inside the door. The wood was dampened by the snow and drops of moisture were forming on the outer surfaces.

"They look like they are sweating," he said. "Maybe I should take them from the packings and let them air?"

"They're not ready," she said. "They should stay boxed until they ripen."

"They're paintings, not cheeses," he said, offended.

She seemed to forget him as she turned back to a pine table and lit a candle behind a cut-out shield of stenciled tin. Then she pushed the box toward him. It held the long cigars she was smoking. "Your paintings aren't important, they mean nothing. How could they? You're too young."

He declined the cigar. She offered to show him to the quarters she kept ready for him. They walked together through an alcove to a room behind the kitchen. He could see a narrow monk's bed with a carved wooden headboard. He had to bend down to enter and his foot caught in the fringe of the indigo-striped rug. He knew it was of value and tried to walk around it, but the floor tiles were slick from the snow that was drifting in from the open window.

"Is there a way to close this?" he asked. Then he realized it had no pane of glass and the carpet of snow was deepening.

"Stuff it with one of your canvases, if you feel cold," she said. "That's as good a way as any." She left him to settle in.

The room was like an iced-over cave. He dropped his back-pack on the bed. He could hardly wait to get back to the fire that had turned almost totally to ash.

"Can't I spark this up for you?" He looked around for extra wood. There was a pile of logs at the far end of the kitchen and he found her standing by the stove heating up some wine. When she followed him back through the kitchen door, she was carrying a tray with a ceramic pitcher and two heavy glasses.

"You won't need more fire. This will warm you up."

He took the drink from her. It smelled of cinnamon and cloves. He was shivering from the cold, but he had to grasp the glass at the top to avoid burning his fingers. He gulped the drink and felt it scald his throat. "Are you having one, too?" He could feel his tongue beginning to swell. He could hardly swallow.

"Yes, but mine is cold. I'm used to the weather. I always feel too warm. Why didn't you come sooner? Why did you wait so long? I've watched for you every day."

"I had to wait until my mother died. She was buried this last week." He thought he saw a faint smile relax her tightened lips.

"A big boy like you. You had to wait for her permission?"

She rested her head against the back of her chair and began to laugh. "You didn't dare risk her fury. She would never have allowed you to come. You should have had the guts to seek me out on your own. You wanted these paintings, didn't you? They're worth a fortune." She gestured to the walls around her. "The world is waiting for them. Do you think they'll all go to you?"

He took another swallow of his drink. It was warming, but the dregs were bitter. He shrugged. "I don't need your paintings. I'm painting my own. I've inherited my father's talent."

She sat upright and glared at him. She thrust a long index finger toward his eyes. "Don't you forget. He got all that from me."

He looked around him at the erotic garden specimens hanging on the walls. "My father didn't paint like that. Nor do I. There's absolutely no connection."

"What do you paint?" she asked.

"Don't you want to see them?" He began to expand. He was proud of his prowess. "They're going to give me a show at the Whitney. It's quite an honor . . . at my age."

"The Whitney! What do they know? What school are you? This crazy minimal art? Conceptual stuff? Symbolism?"

"No," he said. "The school of naturalism. I paint murderesses. I do very realistic portraits of women who had to kill."

Her eyes began to glow as the fire died completely. "What do you know of such women?"

"Only what my mother told me."

"The family had plenty to say, too. I'm sure of that."

"Never. They never mentioned your name. I found all the newspapers before I even knew how to read. I hid them and held onto them until now. They thought they had kept the news from me. Later, I figured it all out. I put two and two together and then, when I was in college, I read it in a book."

She sat up suddenly, very straight. "I was in a book?"

"It was a factual book about violence and killings. There were stories of Winnie Ruth Judd and the 'Pig Woman' and a fellow they called 'The Fox.'"

"I shouldn't have been lumped in with them." She gave a derisive cough. "I killed because I had good reason. And I was subtle about it. I used a poison only an artist, or a photographer, would know about."

"But I have to know why you did it. That's why I finally came here. I had to find out. I called the prison, years after your sentence was commuted. I traced you through your attorney. Did you really have a reason?"

"Of course," she said. "A very valid one."

"Can you tell me . . . will you tell me . . . why?"

She sat back in the chair and began to rock. There was no sound in the room except the runners of the rocker scraping on the uncarpeted floor. He couldn't stand the sound. It was like a metronome tapping out the time. He had to bring her back into the conversation. "I heard you built this house, yourself, with your own hands. I don't know how you did it."

"My hands were always strong." She was pleased to be talking about herself. "I wanted to be a sculptress. They said I had talent. I planned to go off to Florence, but then I met your grandfather. He changed all that for me."

"Some women marry," he said, "and continue with whatever they started on before."

"They don't. They can't," she said. Her eyes grew bright and crafty. "It's the family, the family that ruins everything. One thing leads to another. It's the continuation of the line that is so destructive."

He had to reach for a smoke. He needed something to hold onto. The fumes in the room were going to his head. The rocker appeared to be moving about the room. She was quickening her pace. But he had to speak what was on his mind. He had to say it. "How could you have done it? Your own son? My father?"

The rocking stopped.

"It's all here. My answer is right on these walls." She stood up and pointed to her canvas garden of larger-than-life flowers. "Isn't that reason enough for you? They are all pictures of your mother. She thought she could take him from me."

"So you took him from her, instead." His vision was getting blurred. "But those are flowers. They're not women."

"You say that because you're blind."

His eyelids were growing heavy. He could hardly keep his eyes open.

"But you didn't solve anything," he said. "You forgot about me. My mother's dead. When you go, I'll be the head of my line. I can start a whole new generation."

She settled back in her rocking chair and watched as his eyes finally closed. She began to rock more peacefully as she kept her vigil. "That's what you think," she said softly, so as not to disturb him.

Harry Prince

....

A native of Boston, Harry Prince spent most of his adult life in business before retiring in 1976 for a more enjoyable career as a writer. Many of his most successful stories have a Damon Runyon flavor, the result of fifteen years spent as a buyer of ladies' furs in New York "in the days of the mobs." Other stories have foreign settings, inspired by travel to every continent except Australia. Prince has won four awards in contests sponsored by *Writer's Digest* and four more from the National League of American Penwomen, two for first prize in fiction. His first story, "Drop Dead, Chink Martin," appeared in *Cavalier* ("My wife and I were quite surprised when we opened it to pages and pages of open vaginas") and he subsequently appeared in *Short Story International*, and *The Saint Magazine*.

"Requiem for a Busted Flush" originally appeared in *Alfred Hitchcock's Mystery Magazine* under the title "Game Plan."

Harry Prince
· · · · · · · · · · · · · · · · · ·

requiem for a busted flush

I t was no news to anyone—except the cops—that on the night in question Frenchy smoked a young Jersey mobster who drew first when he got caught with six cards in his duke—which is considered most unorthodox among practitioners of five-card stud.

Frenchy didn't realize that the Jersey player only had a busted flush, even with the six cards, when he called him. He was sorry he had to ventilate the Jersey player, who was young, like himself—and, what was worse, still had eighteen hundred potatoes in his jeans to lose.

Frenchy didn't wait around to explain this unfortunate happenstance to the gendarmes, since he felt sure no cop would have the good sense to listen to his side. Besides, he expected reciprocal heat from the Jersey side. The baffled police later came up with a Death by Natural Causes ticket.

Frenchy was a native of Montreal and spoke French as well as he spoke English. He was of medium height and weight and had medium brown hair, but he had a face that attracted better-than-medium-type women. He was an orphan who'd once said that he'd trade a year's good poker luck to have had a family of his own.

In the early morning after the poker blast, Frenchy hopped on a boat as it pulled away from the Fulton Street pier.

The captain said, "Welcome aboard. We're just leaving for Newfoundland and we can use another hand. When the cod start running, it's all we can do to keep up with the cleaning."

"All right," Frenchy said. "I'll go to Newfoundland, but I don't want any cod for myself—except maybe on Friday. But I'd like to see how it's done. I may decide to take it up myself. I'll just go along for the ride and pay the same fare as everybody else."

As the boat was already out on the river and it was probably against the ecology laws to throw him overboard, the captain said, "If you want to eat, you must work like the rest. You'll like my fish soup."

They didn't catch many fish before they got to Newfoundland, but they caught enough so that Frenchy learned the fishing industry wasn't his bag. In fact, he swore that separating fish guts was strictly for the gulls, who seemed to do it with a great deal of relish. He also got tired of the fish soup, which was on the menu three times a day.

When they were east of Newfoundland, Frenchy asked the captain about a beautiful low-lying island.

"That's Bird Island," the captain said. "It's owned by Pierre Roget, who lives there. Many years ago Pierre struck oil back in Edmonton and became a millionaire."

"Why does he live on the island?"

"He married, and his new wife couldn't stand the smell of oil wells, so he brought her to Bird Island where the sea air is good and there are no oil wells, only fishing and farming."

"I think she made a sucker bet," Frenchy said. "I'd rather

smell an old oil well any day, because you know that's as bad as it's going to get. But old fish get riper all the time."

He peered at the landscape. "What's that big stone building?" he asked. "It looks like some kind of a fort from the old days."

"No, that's Pierre Roget's manor. He built it to cheer up his wife. She had a son many years ago—a wild one. When little Jean was only eight he rowed out in a dory and was never seen again. Pierre took it bad, but Madame Roget never recovered. They never had any more children. She still dresses in black and it's said she spends most of her time in the chapel praying that little Jean is still alive and will come back to her someday."

Frenchy considered. The island would be a very nice place for a vacation from fish guts and the fish soup. "I don't think I'll go into the cod business after all," he told the captain. "Let me off here. I'll stay a short while, and you can pick me up on your way back."

"We'll miss you," the captain said. "You did a first-class job chucking the fish guts overboard once you learned not to throw them into the wind. But I must warn you, they eat only fish on the island too—except for an occasional crab or lobster now and then."

When they put him ashore, Frenchy looked around the pier and asked an old geezer if the island had a lawyer. If there were any games or scams going on a lawyer would be sure to know about them.

The old geezer was scraping the bottom of a boat. He looked up, scratched himself, spat some tobacco juice at a bait can, and said, "Lawyer? Why do you want a lawyer? You only been here three minutes and already you want to sue us! I advise against it—and that's the only free advice you'll get on this island. If you sue, the only winner will be old Skrim. He's the local shyster. You'll find his office across from the pier. But if I

169

am you, sonny, I will keep my mitts in my pockets while talking to Skrim."

Frenchy thanked the old geezer and walked along the pier to the lawyer's office.

"Glad to see you," the shyster said. "I'm Cyrus Skrim. What can I do for you?"

"I'm Henri Dubois, but I answer faster to Frenchy. Tell me, Cyrus, where do you go when there's a tidal wave on such a little bitty island?"

"I see you're new on our beautiful strand," Skrim countered. "Will you be staying for the boating and fishing?"

"I'd like to look around a while and see what kind of game plan you have here. I'm a sporting man."

"I'm afraid there's no gambling on Bird Island."

"Not even a racetrack?"

"No, but I can represent you if you'd like to build one. Of course, we have a population of only one hundred and eighty-two, and nine plowhorses—which might present a problem. However, we do have a croquet tournament every summer where a few side bets are tolerated. Only last summer Jed Groper won a bushel of crab apples, which his wife spiced. May I suggest a fish cannery, Mr. Dubois? Or perhaps a nice bit of farmland?" The shyster rubbed his hands together. "Ben Pickelberry's mule started sitting down last spring and won't get up to pull the plow anymore. Ben sees no way out but to sell. You can make a good deal and I can get Ben to throw in the mule."

"I don't think I'd make a good farmer," Frenchy said.

Skrim studied him. "What kind of business are you interested in?"

Frenchy observed the sly look on Skrim's face. "I'm ready for any hand you deal," he said. "I'm twenty-two and I'm a gambler. I left the States ahead of the homicide squad and I've packed a rod since I was eighteen. I cooled a poker player who couldn't count to five. This information should save us a week of sparring. As client to lawyer, this knowledge is confidential."

"Why tell me at all?"

"Because you have something wrinkling the front of your brain. I've told you about me, so you tell me the table stake you have in mind, without any more fencing."

"I'd like to do a blessed deed for a bereaved family," Skrim said, then proceeded to tell Frenchy the same tale the captain had told him about the Rogets.

"Pierre promised me ten thousand dollars," the shyster concluded, "if I could get information that would return Jean to his mother. With a little patching, there's no reason you couldn't be Jean."

"That's very nice," Frenchy said, "but I don't think I could walk in and say, 'Here I am, *maman*. I am Jean. Give Skrim the ten grand.' No, life tells me it's got to be harder than that. So far all you've got is a four-card flush."

Skrim coughed. "First of all, I'm not after ten thousand. I'm after a hundred thousand, and it's easier than splitting a salmon. I've been inside the manor many times on business with Pierre. He has an office safe where I've seen what must be more than a hundred thousand dollars in cash. The safe is always open in the daytime. No one on the island ever locks his door. But even if the safe were closed, it's the kind of breadbox you could open with a butter knife."

"I accept your arithmetic," Frenchy said, "but what makes you think a total stranger can walk into the hive in broad daylight and walk out with the honeycomb? There must be a million guys in Canada who are twenty-two."

"When I was only a short order," Skrim said, "I lived in Halifax. My father was a tattoo artist and taught me his trade. I worked my way through law school on the waterfront putting dragons, twining hearts, and sexy ladies on deep-water salts. I even did a few girls who had different ideas about where tattoos would do the most good."

He turned his eyes to the window. "Jean had a strawberry birthmark behind his left earlobe. You look enough like him to pass after all these years. Growing up changes people."

Frenchy's eyes widened. "Can you tattoo me with something

that'll wash off? I don't know if I want to go around forever with a strawberry mark on my neck. I'm sure you do a fine job, but the cops will be looking for a joe with a strawberry. It would be like a card mechanic wearing spare aces in his hatband."

"As long as you stay south of the border no one will connect you with the theft. As for the inconvenience, your share of the profit should soften the pain and may even buy a laser-removal job." Skrim rubbed his jaw. "I can tell you all you need to know about the island and the family. I even drew up the Rogets' wills. You'll have enough information to keep you afloat."

"How long do you think I'll have before Madame Roget starts to nose a bad oyster in the stew?"

"It should only take a few days for you to look around, open the box, grab the money, and get out. I'll have my cruiser ready to take you to Halifax. From there you can catch a flight to the States." Skrim walked around his desk and sat down.

"I'll square my end," he said. "The strawberry mark will be so good I may even insist on the other ten thousand."

He looked hard at Frenchy. "As for the split, I'm the brain and the tattoo artist. I will also supply the boat you'll live on for the next ten days while the tattoo heals. So it will be more than fair if I take sixty percent—that's not including the ten thousand from Pierre. That was always mine."

"A fifty-fifty split would be nicer," Frenchy said, "but I see your point. Deal me in and I'll play the hand for you."

Skrim gave Frenchy the strawberry and sent him out on the cruiser. He headquartered at Badger Bay on the mainland, where they'd heard about steaks and chops.

He spent the time sunning and cruising, and he came back in nine days, healed and suntanned.

Skrim examined the strawberry. "It'll fool the Rogets, and even a bumblebee, if necessary. I think if you went to a strawberry festival you'd be picking forks out of your neck." He went to the phone and called the manor.

172

"I have a party here in my office who claims his name is Jean Roget," he said.

Twenty minutes later the Roget launch circle-swept into the pier in a high spray. The boathand helped Madame Roget and Pierre off the craft. They walked arm in arm to Skrim's office. Madame Roget's face was wet with tears under the black veil. She was a worn-looking forty-eight, her eyes sad and lined. Pierre Roget was fiftyish, on the heavy side, and had a pleasant enough face. He held onto her as if he was afraid she would vanish.

Frenchy was trim and handsome. Madame looked at him and tried to smile.

"Jean?" she asked.

"Oui, maman," Frenchy said.

"Are you well? Where have you been?"

"I rowed the dory onto a rock and it sank. I was picked up by a ship and taken to New York."

She walked around him, looked at his neck, and began to sob.

"Jean!"

They grabbed each other and Frenchy said softly, "I'm home, *maman.*"

Pierre was overwhelmed and offered many thanks to Skrim. The lawyer broke out a bottle of wine and there were toasts. *Maman* wept into her burgundy until it looked like she was drinking pink chablis.

A month went by.

One day Frenchy buffered the Roget launch into the pier. He walked into Skrim's office with a big smile on his face. "You've made me a very happy man," he said.

"Where have you been?" Skrim snarled. "Do you have the money?"

"No, but I have good news for you. Papa sends you this check

173

for ten thousand dollars and says to thank you no end. It's your fee for finding me."

"Fee, shmee. Where's the bundle?"

"It's in the safe," Frenchy said, "and it's nearer to a quarter of a million. And the safe is open all day, just like you said. But I can't steal from Papa. I am very grateful to you but I love my parents and I would never spoil it, not for a *million* dollars."

"So you think you can grab it all for yourself?" the lawyer screamed. "I'll show you! I'll not only show you, but I'll show you up for the creep you are!"

"Take it easy," Frenchy said with a smile. "Think about it for a minute. If I'd failed, you'd wind up with zero for your trouble. This way you get ten grand and my eternal gratitude. I only want to bring them some happiness—"

"Bring them some happiness!" Skrim shouted, "You can't do this to me! I'll expose you for the tinhorn murderer you are!"

Frenchy's smile faded. "You shouldn't have said that." He walked over to Skrim, grabbed him by his tie, and dragged him up out of his chair. Pulling a gun from his pocket he jammed the muzzle into Skrim's neck. "They must never know, you hear?" he said. "You'll either take the ten grand or I won't leave enough of you for a wake. Make up your mind. *Maman* is waiting for fresh fish for the soup."

Skrim's eyes were popping. "Let me go! I'll take the check! Get the gun out of my neck!"

"Say thank you," Frenchy said.

"Thank you! Now put that gun back in your pocket before someone sees it."

Frenchy returned Skrim to his chair and holstered the piece.

"My name is Jean Roget—*Jean Roget*—and you'd better not forget it for as long as you live, because you'll only live as long as you remember it."

"You're going too far," Skrim said. "You haven't a prayer of getting away with it. I should have done it my way. Jean was old enough to remember the plush cocoon he came from. Sooner or later he'll come back to get what's his—and then you'll get yours."

"I don't think so," Frenchy said. "Remember the Jersey player I cooled in that poker game I told you about? He had a strawberry birthmark behind his left ear."

Robert Bloch
....

How highly Robert Bloch is regarded in the three closely related genres of mystery, science fiction, and horror can be demonstrated by at least two things: his record as a guest of honor at various fan conventions—the World Science Fiction Conventions of 1948 and 1973, the first Anthony Boucher Memorial Mystery Convention (1971), and the World Fantasy Convention of 1975—and his pervasive presence on anthology contents pages. Long before his novel *Psycho* (1959), filmed memorably (and faithfully) by Alfred Hitchcock, extended his fame and helped open the doors to screenwriting success, he was regarded as one of the finest writers of horror and suspense, especially in the short story length. He has won numerous awards, including both a Hugo and an Edgar, and has served a term as president of Mystery Writers of America. Among his recent novels are *Psycho II* (1982) and *Night of the Ripper* (1984).

Bloch is especially noted for his macabre humor. He is famous for the line "I have the heart of a small boy; I keep it in a jar on my desk," and he once dedicated a book "To Clayton Rawson, A man after my own heart—with a knife." "Final Performance," one of his best stories, could have been written by no one else. It first appeared in *Shock*.

Robert Bloch

....

final performance

The neon intestines had been twisted to form the word EAT.

I squinted up at it, the sand stinging my eyes, and shifted my overnight bag to the left hand. As I opened the sagging screen door a trickle of perspiration ran down my arm.

Two flies accompanied me into the restaurant. One of them headed for a pile of crullers on the counter and the other alighted on the bald head of an elderly fat man who leaned behind it. The man looked up and the fly buzzed away.

"Evening," he said. "What'll it be?"

"Are you Rudolph?" I asked.

He nodded.

I slid onto a stool. "Fellow named Davis sent me."

"From the garage?"

"That's right—the place up the highway. My car conked out on me coming through the mountains. He had to phone Bakersfield for a new connecting rod. They're bringing it out first thing tomorrow morning, and he figures he can get it installed before evening. But tonight I'm looking for a place to stay. He told me to try here—said you used to run a motel."

"Not anymore. Isn't enough traffic along this route."

"I noticed a couple of cabins out in back."

"Closed up." The fat man reached under the counter and came up with a half-empty bottle of beer. He took a long gulp; when he set the bottle down again it was empty. "Look, you could hitch a ride into Bakersfield and come back tomorrow."

"I thought of that, but I hate to leave all my belongings. Everything I own is in that car—guess it broke down because it was overloaded. You see, I'm moving to Hollywood, and I packed all my books and—".

"Hollywood?" The fat man blinked. "You in show biz?"

"I'm a writer."

"Television?"

"Short stories and books."

He blinked again. "That's better. TV is lousy. I can't understand what they think they're doing out there. Now you take a guy like that Ed Sullivan—" He broke off abruptly and stared at me. "Book writer, you say. Ever run into Arnie Pringle?"

"No, I can't say that I have."

"Before your time, I guess. Probably dead by now. He used to write my act."

"You were in show business?"

"Are you kidding? Rudolph the Great. Twenty years top billing, Pantages, Albee, Keith-Orpheum time. Why, I've got three press books full of—"

I rose from the stool.

"Here, where are you going?"

I shrugged. "Sorry, but if I'm hitching a ride into Bakersfield I'd better get out there on the highway before dark."

"Never mind that. Guess we can fix up a cabin for you. Put some clean sheets on the bed." He swayed along behind the counter, and it suddenly occurred to me that he was just a little bit drunk.

"Look, I wouldn't want to put you to any trouble," I told him.

"No trouble. My pleasure." He jerked his head toward the swinging door behind him. "Rosie!" he yelled.

Rosie came into the room.

She was a tall girl, blond and amply proportioned, her hair done up in a ponytail. She wore a blue sleeveless smock and her legs were bare.

"Rosie, this is Mr.—"

"Chatham. Jim Chatham." I nodded at her and she wrinkled up her nose at me. It took a moment before I realized she was smiling.

"Had a little trouble with his car," Rudolph said. "Davis is fixing it up at the crossroads. He needs a place to stay overnight. You think you can find some clean bedclothes for Number One?"

She nodded at him, still looking at me.

"Better take him out with you. Let him have a look."

"All right." Her voice was soft, deeper than I'd expected.

"Keys in my desk, right-hand drawer."

"I know. I'll get them."

She turned and left the room. Rudolph reached under the counter into the cooler and brought out another bottle of beer, a full one this time. "Care for a brew?" he asked.

"Later, perhaps. Let me get settled and then I'll come back for dinner."

"Suit yourself." He bent to open the bottle, then raised it to his lips.

Rosie came back into the room; she carried a bundle of sheets wrapped around a pillow. "All set?" she asked.

I picked up my bag and followed her outside. The sun was setting and the desert wind was cool. Joshuas cast their shadows along the path leading to the cabins in the rear, striping the sand and the backs of her bare calves as she walked along before me.

"Here we are." She halted and opened the door of the tiny cabin. The interior of the little shack was dark and stifling hot. She switched on the light. "It'll cool off in a minute with the door open," she said. "I'll make up the bed for you."

I put down the suitcase and slumped into the single chair

next to the gray-filmed window. She went to work, bending over the bed. She had fine breasts. As she moved around to tuck in the sheet, her leg brushed mine.

All at once, for no reason at all, my mind was filled with corny dialogue. *What's a nice girl like you doing in such a god-forsaken hole? Let me take you away from all this . . .*

Suddenly I noticed she had stopped working. She stood there with the pillow in her arms, staring at me.

"I heard you talking to him," she said. "About being a writer. What are you going to do out in Hollywood, work for the movies?"

"I doubt it. Probably just keep turning out stories the same as usual. But the climate's better."

"Yes, the climate." She nodded and wrinkled her nose at me. "Take me with you."

"What?"

"I said, take me with you."

"But Mrs. Rudolph—"

"His *first* name is Rudolph. Rudolph Bitzner."

"Mrs. Bitzner, then—"

"I'm not Mrs. Bitzner either."

"Oh, I just thought—"

"I know what you thought. Never mind that. Just take me with you. All I'd do is ride along. There wouldn't be any trouble." She let the pillow fall on the bed and moved closer. "I wouldn't be any bother at all. I promise."

I stood up, but I didn't reach for her. I didn't reach for her, because she came right into my arms, and she said, "Please, please, say you'll take me. You've got to. You don't know what it's like all alone out here. You don't know what he's like. He's crazy—"

She had this trick of talking without opening her mouth, keeping her lips puckered up, waiting to be kissed, and she wrinkled her nose and I could see the tiny freckles on the bridge, and her skin was marble-cool in all this heat. And it's one thing to sit back and make sophisticated remarks about cheap waitresses named Rosie *(Rosie, for God's sake!)* and another thing entirely to feel a waiting, willing woman stirring hard against you and whispering, "Please . . . promise me you will . . . I'll do anything . . ."

So I opened my mouth to answer, then let it remain open in bewilderment as she stepped back quickly and picked up the pillow again. Then I heard him scuffling along the path and understood.

"Rosie!" he yelled. "You almost finished? Customers!"

"Be right in," she called.

I stepped over to the doorway and waved at Rudolph.

"Everything all right?" he asked.

"Everything's fine."

"Come and eat, then. You can wash up inside."

I glanced back at Rosie. She was bending over the bed and she didn't look at me. But she whispered, "I'll see you later. Wait for me."

That's what kept me going through the long evening.

I followed Rudolph, cleaned myself up a bit in the filthy washroom, and shared a steak and french fries with the two flies and their cousins. The customers were in and out for the next couple of hours, and there was no chance to talk to Rudolph or even catch a glimpse of Rosie out in back. Then, finally, it was nine o'clock and the place was empty again. Rudolph yawned and walked over to the door, switching off the EAT sign.

"This concludes the evening's performance," he said. "Thanks for the use of the hall." He went over to the swinging door. "You fixing yourself something?" he yelled.

"Yes, just a hamburger. How about you?" Rosie asked.

"Never mind. I'll have myself another beer." He looked at me. "You ready for one now?"

I shook my head and stood up. "No, thanks. It's about time I turned in."

"What's your hurry? Stick around. We'll go in back and chew the fat a while. To hell with the beer—I've got some hard stuff there."

Robert Bloch

"Well, I—"

"Come on. Got some things that might interest you. Man doesn't get much chance to talk to anybody halfway intelligent around here."

"All right."

He ran his wrist across the gray stubble around his mouth.

"Tell you what, I'll check the register first. You go right on back, through that door at the end. I'll be along."

So I went back, into the little room on the side of the restaurant that served as a parlor. I saw the overstuffed couch and the easy chair and the desk, the lamp, the TV set, but I didn't do any more than glance at them.

Because I was staring at the walls—the walls of another world.

It was the world of the twenties and the early thirties, a world that belonged to the half-forgotten faces that peered out at me from a thousand photographs reaching from floor to ceiling. Some of the pictures had peeled and faded, just as my memories had peeled and faded in the long years since early childhood. But I could still remember the familiar countenances, and I had at least heard of most of the names scrawled in autograph fashion beneath the unfamiliar ones. I moved around the room, moved around the mementos of what had once been a world called vaudeville.

Here was a skinny, gangling kid called Milton Berle and a buxom young woman named Sophie Tucker. Here was a youthful Bert Wheeler holding an apple and a smiling Joe Cook holding an Indian club and explaining why he would not imitate the Four Hawaiians. There was an entire section of faces in burnt cork—Cantor, Jolson, Lou Holtz in the pre–Sam Lapidus days, Frank Tinney (way before my time), and one mournfully humorous countenance that needed no spurious blackface; the signature read, "To Rudolph from Bert Williams."

And there were the teams and the acts—Moran and Mack, Gallagher and Shean, Cross and Dunn, Phil Baker and Ben Bernie, Smith and Dale (Dr. Kronkheit, I presume), and a surprisingly handsome young couple who signed themselves "George and Gracie." And there was an incredible Jimmy Durante—with hair—and Clayton and Jackson.

"See? It's like I told you, I knew 'em all." Rudolph had come up behind me, carrying a bottle and glasses. "Here, let me fix you a snort and I'll show you my press books."

He made me a drink, but he didn't get around to the press books. Instead he sprawled out on the sofa, uncorked the bottle again, and uncorked himself.

I don't know how long he rambled on about the old days and the old ways; about the Six Brown Brothers and Herman Timberg and Walter C. Kelly and Chic Sale. At another time, under other circumstances, I might have hung onto his every word. But right now I was hanging onto other words—"I'll see you later. Wait for me."

So I really didn't listen to him, to Rudolph the Great who used to do Orpheum Time until vaudeville died and then wandered out here into the desert to do a twenty-year layoff as Rudolph Bitzner. Twenty years—why, Rosie couldn't be much over twenty herself! And here was this fat old man wheezing away on the couch, drinking out of the bottle now and slobbering. He was getting ready to pass out. He had to pass out soon, he *had* to . . .

"Have 'nother drink?" He sat up, blinking at the bottle. "Oh, 's empty, well, whaddya know?"

"That's all right," I told him. "I've had enough."

"Well, I haven'. Got more 'round here someplace. Rosie!" He yelled her name, then lowered his voice as he turned to me. "She's out front. Told her to clean up the joint. Won't come near me when I'm drinking, anyhow, you know?" He chuckled. "Don't matter—I locked the door before I came back. Got the key ri' here, so she can't get away. Never get away, not from me."

He swayed to his feet. "Know what you're thinkin'—just an old lush, that's all, just an old lush. But wait till I show you the press books. Then you'll see who I was. Who I *am*." He stumbled back against the sofa. "Rudolph the Great. Tha's me. Keep in practice. Jus' as good as I ever was. Better. Why, I could go on Sullivan's show nex' week . . ."

Then the color drained from his face and he fell back on the couch. I never did get to see those press books. By the time I put his feet up on the sofa he'd started to snore.

I took the keys from his pocket and went back into the restaurant. She was waiting for me in the dark. And we went out through the dark to my cabin, and she clung to me in the dark, and that's the one thing I want to remember, *have* to remember now.

Afterward she told me about herself. She'd been ten when she'd come to Rudolph—her parents stopped by on their way to Texas and dropped her off while they filled a fair date. They were a couple of ex-vaudevillians themselves: the Flying Keenos. They knew Rudolph from the old days and they accepted his suggestion to leave her in his care while they traveled on, because they were down on their luck.

"Only they never came back," she said. "They never came back. And he tried to find them. He wrote to *Billboard* and everything, but they just disappeared. So I stayed on. Rudolph—he wasn't so bad then, you know. I mean, he didn't drink so much or anything. He sent me to school on the bus, bought me clothes and things. Treated me just like he was my father—until I was sixteen."

She started to cry, very softly. "He isn't even in love with me, not really. It's because of living out here all alone in this crazy desert and knowing he's getting old. Before it started he used to talk about making a comeback on TV. He said it was just like vaudeville, he'd always known there'd be a revival. Then, that summer when I was sixteen, he decided the time was right and he took me with him out to L.A. He went around and saw some agents, had a few auditions. I never did find out what really happened. But when we came back here in the fall he started to drink right away, and that's when—"

That's when she tried to sneak off, and he caught her, and he closed up the motel so she couldn't see anyone or attempt to hitch a ride. He kept her inside the restaurant, didn't even allow her to go up to the crossroads for supplies, wouldn't let anyone come near her.

There were times when she thought of running away in the night, but something always stopped her. She realized she owed him something for all the years he'd taken care of her, and he needed her now. He was just an old man, not quite right in the head, and he seldom bothered her anymore. Most nights he just drank and passed out. She'd resigned herself to putting up with it until this evening. Then, when she saw me—

"I know. You figured you *could* get a ride, and maybe I'd even take care of you out on the coast for a week or so, long enough for you to find a job. That's it, isn't it?"

"No!" She dug her nails into my arms. "Maybe I *did* think something like that at first. But not *now*. Believe me, not *now*."

I believed her. I believed her voice and I believed her body, even though it was incredible that I should be lying here in the desert night with this stranger whom I'd known forever.

"It's all right," I said. "We'll go away. But I'd feel better if we told him. Maybe if I talked things over with him, explained, I could make him understand."

"Oh no—you can't do that! He's crazy jealous. I didn't want to tell you, but one time he caught this truck driver talking to me outside—just talking is all—and he took after him with that big butcher knife. He would have killed him if he caught him, I know he would! And he beat me up so that I couldn't even get out of bed for three days. No, he mustn't even suspect. Tomorrow afternoon, when the car is fixed . . ."

We made our simple plans. The restaurant was closed on Sundays, and it would be better if I didn't attempt to take a meal there—just went straight to the garage and saw to it that Davis got the car fixed as soon as possible. Meanwhile Rosie would have her suitcase packed and ready. She'd encourage Rudolph to drink—not that he generally needed any encouragement from her. Maybe he'd even pass out. If not, she'd go so far as to cut the phone wire, if necessary; just so she could slip out to me with the assurance of getting a head start.

So we talked it all over, calmly and sensibly, and she slipped out of the cabin, and I lay there and tried to sleep. It was almost dawn when I closed my eyes, and the bats were out, flying against the gaudy desert sunrise.

I slept for a long time. When I left the cabin and cut across to the highway, it was almost two o'clock. I walked the mile to the crossroads garage and found Davis working with the car up on the rack. We talked for a while, but I didn't listen to what he said, or to what I said either. From time to time somebody drove up for gas and Davis would have to stop and give them service. The car wasn't ready until a little after five; it was already getting dark.

I paid him and drove off. The motor hummed smoothly, but I almost stripped gears as I shifted. I was nervous, that's all, just nervous. I didn't feel any guilt and I didn't feel any fear. Certainly I didn't feel any horror.

That came later.

That came when I parked in the deepening shadows on the side of the darkened restaurant and went up to the door.

This was it. If something had gone wrong—

But nothing could go wrong. I squared my shoulders and took a deep breath, then rattled the doorknob. That was the signal; she'd be waiting to hear me.

Nothing happened. A few flies buzzed against the glass awaiting entry. I rattled the door again softly. It was locked.

Then the figure emerged from the back room.

I recognized Rudolph.

He moved briskly; there was no shuffle in his gait and no stagger either. His face was gray and puffy, but his red-rimmed eyes weren't blinking. He stooped and unlocked the door, motioning for me to come inside.

"Good afternoon," I said. There was nothing else I *could* say, not yet, not until I knew what had happened.

He nodded, moving behind me to lock the door again. I could hear the click of the key and I didn't bother to look around.

That's when the horror came.

Horror is something cold and sharp, biting against the back of your neck.

"Let's go into the other room," Rudolph said. "Rosie has something to say to you."

"What have you done to her?"

"Nothing. She just wants to talk to you. You'll see."

We went down the aisle past the counter, the flies buzzing in our wake. Then we were in the back room and they were all waiting for me there—George and Gracie, Frank Tinney, Lou Holtz. They were all staring, as I stared, at the open torn heap. For a moment, in the dim light, I thought it was Rosie lying there.

But no, Rosie was sitting on the sofa and she was looking at the suitcase, too. She didn't say a word when I came in because there was nothing to say now.

I could feel Rudolph's breath on my neck, right behind me. And I could feel the coldness, too, the sharpness, the horror. All at once it went away. I heard the knife clatter to the floor.

"You can thank her for that," Rudolph murmured. "I could have killed you, you know. I wanted to kill you. But she talked me out of it. And now she has something to say to you. Go ahead, Rosie, tell him."

He left me standing there in the doorway and walked over to where Rosie was sitting. He slid down on the sofa beside her and put his arm around her, smiling. Rosie looked up then, but she didn't smile.

The shadows crept across the walls, across the faces of Williams and Bernie and Jolson, across his face and hers. But I wasn't watching the shadows. I was listening to the girl.

"You see how it happened," she murmured. "He walked in while I was packing. He found out."

"All right," I said. "So he found out. I wanted to tell him in the first place. And now that he knows, he can let us go."

Robert Bloch

I was already moving before I finished my last sentence, crossing the room in two strides and scooping up the big, broad-bladed butcher knife from the floor.

"Look," I said. "I've got the knife now. He can't hurt us and he'd better not try. We can walk out of here whenever we please."

She sat there, turning her head to stare at the knife. And he stared, too, tightened his arm around her and stared and smiled while she said, "No. I've changed my mind. I'm not going with you."

"But I don't understand—"

"We talked it all over before you came. I can't go. He needs me so. It's right that I should stay. I belong with him. Can't you see that?"

I shook my head. There was something wrong with her words, something wrong with the way she stared and he smiled. And all at once it came to me as I looked into his fat face off in the shadows. "Maybe I can see," I said. "Rudolph the Great. You were a hypnotist, weren't you? That's the answer, isn't it? You've hypnotized her, that's what you've done—"

He started to laugh.

"You're wrong, mister," he said. "Tell him how wrong he is, darling."

And then she was laughing, too, in a high, hysterical titter. But there was no laughter in her face, and her words, when they came, were soft and somber.

"He's no hypnotist. I know what I'm doing, believe me. I'm telling you to get out. Just get out, do you hear me? Go away and don't come back. I don't want to go to the coast with you. I don't want you pawing me in some dirty cabin. I know what you are. You're a—"

She began to curse me then; the filth and the foulness poured out of her mouth and she bobbed her head at me in rage, while he just sat there and smiled.

Finally she was finished. "All right," he said. "Have you heard enough?"

188

"I've heard enough," I said. "I'll go." And I dropped the knife again. It rolled across the floor, and a thin ray of light from the dying sunset streaked the dulled and darkened blade.

I turned to go, and neither of them rose. They just sat there, arms entwined, and stared at me. The shadows blotted out their faces, then pursued me all the way down the hall.

The car stood waiting for me in the twilight. I climbed in, switched on the ignition, pulled away. I must have driven two or three miles before I remembered to turn on my lights. I was in a daze. There was nothing but the shadows, the strange shadows. Shadows in the room, on their faces, on the dulled and darkened knife. *The dulled and darkened knife . . .*

Then it hit me, and I speeded up. I found a phone just ahead in a filling station outside Pono and put in my call.

The state troopers arrived in fifteen minutes, and I told my story as we roared back to the restaurant in their patrol car.

"He must have done *something* to her," I said. "That knife blade was dark with dried blood."

"We'll see," the sergeant told me.

But at first we didn't see, because Rudolph must have heard us coming, and that's when he used the knife on himself. We found it sticking out of his chest there on the floor in the back room, and he was quite dead.

Rosie still sat there on the sofa, staring at us. It was the sergeant who discovered she'd been strangled.

"Must have happened a couple of hours ago," he told me. "The body's getting stiff."

"Strangled? A couple of hours? But I was just here. We were talking—"

"See for yourself."

I walked over and touched her shoulder. She was stiff and cold and there were purple marks on her neck. Suddenly she toppled forward, and that's when I saw how the knife had been used—saw the huge, foot-long gash extending from the back of her neck down across the shoulders. The wound was incredibly deep; I couldn't understand why. Not even when the sergeant called my attention to the blood on Rudolph's right hand.

It wasn't until I saw the press books that I really knew. Yes, we found his press books, and I finally saw them there at the last, finally found out what must have happened in his dark room, in his dark mind, when he walked in and discovered her getting ready to leave.

That's when he'd strangled her, of course, strangled her to death in a crazy rage. But he was sane enough to realize I'd be coming by to get her and that he'd have to find a way to get rid of me.

So he used the knife then and cut the hole, cut it wide and deep. Wide and deep enough so that she could bow and nod and turn her head when he had his hand behind her. Of course I'd heard her talking to me, but the press books explained all that.

He wasn't lying about his notices; they were raves.

And he wasn't lying about hypnotism either. Rudolph the Great hadn't been a hypnotist. He was just one of the best damned ventriloquists in the business.

In a distinguished academic career, Lois Du Lac attained B.A. and M.A. degrees as well as membership in Phi Beta Kappa while attending UCLA and has subsequently received a J.D. degree with honors from Western State University. In addition to her short stories, she has published poetry, edited the third edition of Vincent Schmieder's *Constitutional Law,* and made sales in four non-fiction fields. The wife of fellow writer Leo Du Lac, she is the mother of five children.

"What's Cooking? Murder?" illustrates the originality and offbeat point of view that typifies Du Lac's fiction.

Lois Du Lac
· · · · · · · · · · · · · · · · ·

"what's cooking? murder?"

"**F**ood, Horace Cassata." Jennifer flung the words as she continued to pack. "You don't love me. You don't love anything. Just food. You . . . career *Italian* eater."

She was, indeed, walking out on him. Sixteen years of marriage in a suburban, split-level mansion down the garbage disposal. And that well-shaped index finger of hers would, any moment now, flick the switch.

"Honey," he coaxed, "why spoil such a nice April evening? Ah, come on," he added. "Kiss and make up."

"Your mouth's greasy." She slammed the suitcase shut. The sound conveyed a metallic finality.

"Your delightful dessert," he said, trying to sooth. "You know, that low-calorie Bavarian cream always makes me yodel." He sang romantically, "O, de, layee, oo."

She shrugged.

"Say, I've an idea, dear—a trip to Venice. We'll glide along in a gondola; I'll sing 'O Sole Mio' to you."

"No." Her blond curls bounced from side to side with refusal. Cosmetic bag in one hand, suitcase in the other, she marched to the door.

"Jenny," he begged, "what's wrong?" His hands pleaded.

"You!" she exploded. "All three hundred pounds of you. When we met on the *Roma Aeterna*, you called yourself 'sturdy.' That description—and your clothes—fitted then. Also, you had brains and ambition. You're fifty now, a strolling can of lard."

She reached for the knob. "I don't want to be around, waiting for you to keel over." Her voice quivered, then steadied. "I can't take it, Horace. You hear?"

He did. He nodded, then made his offer. "On our next cruise, we'll celebrate our anniversary with delectable meals and wine; and maybe you'll . . ."

His arms began to feel the effects of gravity.

Jennifer warmed to her subject. "We go out in summer, you in that vanilla ice cream suit of yours; and you fall asleep, slumped in a chair like a wedding cake crumbling apart at the layers. You embarrass me."

She looked away. He let his arms drop.

He took his defense directly to her. "We can stay home, swim in the pool, if you want."

"You swim?" She laughed. "Hah! All you ever do is float in a chair and drink from a mint julep in each fist."

"We could play billiards or read." He stretched a fleshy hand toward an adjacent room. In his early years of wedded life, he'd given thought to it as the future nursery, the throne room for his princeling of a son. Or little girl.

Jennifer, however, had finally remodeled the space into a game room and library with glass-fronted cases.

"Read what? *Cookbooks?*" She turned the knob.

"Why, a connoisseur would give a gold-plated filet mignon for our collection! Don't you agree?"

"All cookbooks!" she snapped. "Except for *Motherhood à la Mode*. And that *I* bought."

"But everything you make tastes marvelous. Can I help it if I'm tempted to have more? Or run out of the dieter's goodies you keep in the 'frig'? They never seem enough."

"Horace, why bother to visit the specialist at the weight-control clinic? What good does it do?"

"Not much," Horace admitted with a sigh. Yet he had met the most fascinating people there: a superb R.N., an elderly attorney, a jail matron, a young dietician, and a heavy-set police detective.

Italians all. Naturally.

"*Motherhood à la Mode*. Fat lot of good it did me." Jennifer slammed the door.

"Jenny," he cried. "Don't leave me!"

The entry showed a crack that enlarged. A sign of relenting?

"Tomorrow a cook will come out from an employment agency. Please let her help you eat with some sense. Maybe you'll listen to a stranger, even if you *never* pay any attention to me."

She threw a white, lace-edged handkerchief over her eyes.

"I'll come by, now and then, make sure you're all right." A sob caught in her throat. The door closed once more.

Women. Always emotional.

Some hours later, he managed a midnight snack on his own.

Lois Du Lac

He did not relish the thought of facing, alone, the endless weeks ahead. The possibility lay as heavily as swallowed, unbaked pizza.

In the morning, he constructed a sufficiently satisfying breakfast, then settled down to await the arrival of the new cook.

The door chimes called.

"I'm Lucinda." Her voice sounded like the touch of a sterling silver spoon against a champagne glass, and she was obviously floating on the cream of her twenties. He didn't quite catch her last name, but what did that matter? An Easter box of candy drifted unbidden through his mind.

He saw a heart-shaped face, aglow with a perfect olive complexion. Brown eyes lifted meltingly to his. She spoke again. "Most of the night, I was dreaming up recipes; so I overslept. Can you forgive me?"

Wordless with joy at the gourmet beauty of her figure, he nodded; and only then did she draw the warmth of her soft, little hand from his.

"I do hope you haven't had to make yourself breakfast?"

"Well, just a tiny bite or two." He escorted her to the kitchen.

"Oh, no, you mustn't watch." She placed her hand firmly over his pounding heart and shoved him delicately away. "It would make me nervous, what with the responsibility and all."

As he waited in the dining room, he fell into slumber. Her fingertips on his forehead summoned him to a heaping platter of golden fluff. "Baker's Dozen," she cooed. "My very own creation. You'd swear it was made with thirteen eggs."

One bite and he sensed that her cooking would leave Jennifer's forgotten in yesterday's darkest shadow.

After a marvel of a luncheon and an English high tea, he dozed again, then awakened to find Lucinda dusting. She mustn't work like this! He put his hand over hers.

"Why, Mr. Cassata, I do believe you bite your fingernails." She was scolding him and he loved it.

"A man gets hungry at times." He sighed. "Especially fighting midnight thoughts of the 'frig' and the leftovers."

"Tell you what. I could stay, if you wish. Tonight only, of course; get a fine, early breakfast ready that way."

Thus Lucinda took over. She knew what she wanted and how to go about it. Slow simmering on a back burner would tenderize the situation.

So it was that later, but not much later, Horace found himself in his attorney's office. Lucinda had decided Horace should no longer postpone changing his will.

The next day, he returned to sign. "I'm surprised she asked for only that one thing. It would seem so little."

"My thought exactly," the lawyer murmured, an echo from a mournful cavern. He could speak openly; Horace and he had that close a relationship. He, however, said no more.

Afterward Lucinda continued her career in the kitchen, and elsewhere, in what she and Horace both thought of as "their little place." At the stove she would sing snatches of English versions of Verdi and in the bathtub hum Puccini.

Jennifer, meantime, kept her word. She often stopped by, bringing Horace cheer, gifts of food, and protestations of undying love. Lucinda always managed to be out then on some discreet errand. Weeks had passed and the walls of the house had never witnessed any face-to-face meeting between the two women.

Until the last day.

Jenny had dropped in for part of the previous afternoon, urged on Horace her latest offering, a teasingly thin slice of what she termed Slim Trim Fruitcake. She generously left, unasked, the remainder of her cake, along with a new brand of wine.

Swept away with what appeared to be gentle emotion, he pressed into her hands one of his cherished miniature decanters.

Vying, Lucinda made enormous bowls of Ersatz Rum Sauce. Horace presented her with a little decanter, too.

Lois Du Lac

The final noon, Luigi, the heavy-set detective from the weight clinic, hurried up the steps and rang urgently.

Horace, in the dining room, held a spoonful of dessert. He tried to push himself up from the table, but made it only halfway.

Suddenly he doubled over, one hand clutching at his shirt front. Then he straightened up valiantly and pushed the chocolate mousse onto his tongue. He reached for the glistening, oversized maraschino cherry he'd saved 'til last.

His eyes opened wide, his body jerked, half-swiveled into a heap. As he fell, he grabbed for the tablecloth.

A disdained raw apple rolled off and landed in Horace's mouth.

Luigi called through the mail slot, "Horace, it's me." He sang the words "La donna mobile" in a strong lyric tenor, Sicilian born.

No answer. He tried the door, found it unlocked, and entered.

Roman nose lifted lovingly into the pervasive scent of lunch, he called, "What's cooking, ol' chum?" and headed by instinct and inclination toward the kitchen. Seeing the varied delicacies, he had to steel himself to pass through, check out the patio, and return via the master bedchamber.

Deep-set brown eyes alert, he went to the dining room where Horace lay in a heap by the table, his fingers dribbling blood from the jagged pieces of his wineglass.

Anything but murder, this, it would seem. A man grown as heavy as Horace had to expect a heart attack.

They'd even joked about it at the specialist's one day. Luigi had shoved Horace in the ribs. "What a way for a fathead to go." The last time he had ever heard Horace laugh.

Tears rose into Luigi's eyes. "I'm sorry," he all but blubbered, "for saying you'd die looking like a stuffed pig."

That very morning Luigi had visited their doctor.

"I've given Horace the best possible literature on his condition," the physician had said. "But as you've guessed, he hasn't

196

made an appointment for far too long a time. Why don't you look in on him? With his wife gone, the atmosphere should be cordial."

Luigi, he had a theory. Some people booze; others don't. Some people go wild for the opposite sex; a few can't stand them. Most persons live and do business in an honest fashion, or at least legally. A certain portion rate as crooks.

But everybody eats. He reasoned that 99.99 percent of murderers and their victims would have eaten sometime in the twenty-four hours preceding the crime. *Cherchez la cuisine* and locate not only the *femme* but the suspect, too.

Luigi's hands trembled as they gently, reverently closed the sight of Horace's body away behind the dining room doors.

He made a few quick phone calls from the kitchen.

Then the front entry opened. "Horace?" The tone wavered. While Luigi watched, a slender figure hurried in, put her purse down. Light footsteps moved toward him.

"Who are you?" the blond demanded, her voice a needle scratching damage across a record.

"Mrs. Cassata, I presume?"

"Yes, but—?"

"Where's your husband?"

"Here. I mean, he's got to be here. He is, isn't he?"

"When you left him, would you say he was in any condition to travel anywhere?" The steady gaze of his dark eyes bored in on their quarry.

"What are you talking about?" Jennifer's face paled, then flushed. "You'd better leave before I call the police."

"Mrs. Cassata," he said in a tone as soft as high-piled meringue, but frozen glacier cold. "You don't really want a detective nosing around, do you?" He noted her eyes widen.

"Why don't we sit down and wait for Lucinda, instead?" He chose the breakfast nook as she dropped heavily onto the telephone chair. "That's what you intended to do, I'm sure."

Soon Lucinda entered on a run with a bundle of groceries that towered above her and atop of which rode her purse.

Lois Du Lac

She turned back to the door, gasped, reached out to the woodwork to steady herself. "Jenny," she stammered, "who's that man? When did *he* get here?"

"Shut up," Jennifer snapped.

"Ladies, let's adjourn to the living room. We can talk in comfort there." He herded them, at once shaken and defiant, to chairs at a distance from the front door.

The three sat in wordlessness. Except for the troubled expressions passing over the women's faces, it would have seemed to an onlooker a moment of meditation in a Japanese tea ceremony.

Luigi sighed. He spoke softly. "You finally managed it, Jennifer, Lucinda. You murdered him."

"That's a lie," Jennifer cried out. "But I'm not surprised if he's dead. The way he ate and drank." She touched a lace-edged handkerchief to her eyes.

"I had nothing to do with it," Lucinda asserted hotly.

"You both did."

"Well, if he's dead, he dug his own grave with his fork, knife, and spoon," Lucinda declared. "Nobody, *nobody* could do a thing about it. Like a drunk you can't keep from the bottle."

"Precisely! The tines of that fork both of you sharpened. You honed the knife to a dagger point, the spoon into a stiletto. And plunged them all into him again and again."

"Nonsense," Jennifer objected. "You talk like a lunatic."

"Horace, being intelligent," Luigi said, "chose as his confidants persons who would be aware of anything amiss, those capable of coping with difficult situations. He told me how each of you always conversed with him solely about food and drink. How you egged him on. He found the diet literature where you'd thrown it, unopened, into the trash barrel. He discovered and photocopied your fiendishly concocted recipes, Jennifer. Yours, too, Lucinda. Horace concealed his findings in a hiding place that reflected his inner longings, his real love."

The women leaped up, ran, Luigi trailing, for the library.

In the paneled room, the curly blond head was rushing in one direction, the sleek brunette in the other. Small feminine hands, nails lacquered in apple blossom pink, carefully lifted out from behind a large volume a strong box, winnowed through its contents. The other fingertips, with pimiento red nails, kept adding to a cascading heap of books.

"Try these," Horace's boon companion suggested. *"Diet Regimen for Metabolic Disorders. Authentic Recipes of Ancient Sicilia.* You'd consider them likely, wouldn't you, Jennifer, Lucinda? Well, you're wrong. Both of you. Dead wrong."

He gestured toward the living room. They obeyed. Luigi's hands stabbed downward through the air. The women seated themselves. He remained standing.

"You had disappointed his hopes, Jennifer. So he turned to Lucinda. He believed he had every possibility there."

"Now what are you babbling about?" Jennifer inquired.

"He wanted children. He found out you never intended to have any. At least not his. Neither of you."

"Neither?" Jennifer whispered.

"I've my reasons, ladies, to state that a certain nurse is distantly related to the doctor, cousin Enrico—"

"He's no relative of mine," Lucinda retorted.

"He's first cousin to Horace; remotely related to you."

"What's all this?" Jennifer, gazing from one to the other, punctuated her words by half rising from her chair.

"Many generations back," Luigi resumed, "two immigrant cousins arrived in America. One kept close to the old ways. The other let that heritage become lost in the melting pot. Horace and his doctor, Enrico, belong to the branch of the elder immigrant. Lucinda derives from the younger."

"Now, ladies, let me read you your rights." The ritual sounded like a chipmunk practicing speed-reading.

Luigi's ten furious fingers commanded Jennifer and Lucinda to rise.

Lucinda asked, "Where did he keep the diet lists?"

"In *Motherhood à la Mode*, which neither of you ever bothered to read and thought Horace never would. He knew you both

199

had no intention of following the lists or having a child for him. He turned the book into a hiding place for the unopened envelopes."

"You've no right to rummage through the library!" Lucinda declared. "Horace's will gives that to me. Those rare manuscripts, banquets even of the Medicis. Literally priceless. The cookbooks. His current and past editions of *What's Cooking at Home and Abroad?* The restaurant columns."

Luigi laughed. "Who's sure of living long enough to enjoy it all?"

Silence washed over the three.

Then Lucinda ventured a question. "What's it like? The cells . . . and the food?"

His fading smile revived as he ignored her. "You're very quiet, Jennifer. Hoping for help from the desk sergeant or matron? No chance there. And the dietician, a *very* close friend. Like a blood brother."

Lucinda moaned.

"Ladies, you will wonder with every meal and lose your appetites. And afterward, get hungrier and hungrier. Now let's pretend I'm escorting you into the station. Such a pleasant beige interior." He led them back to their chairs. "And deserted, except for the desk sergeant."

Jennifer's voice narrowed to a squeak. "The law says you can't keep us more than forty-eight hours. I . . . think."

"Depends on the day of arrest. How can we arraign you when the weekend's coming up and the courts are closed?" Luigi, sliding behind a desk, had assumed the role of the officer. "A lawyer, the best, is beating through his books to make an airtight case against you. You'll get a sentence you deserve."

His eyes seethed, cauldrons of anger. His close-cropped head bobbed notice to both women. "Welcome to our jail, cousin Lucinda." He hovered on the brink of bel canto. "Cousin Jennifer."

Under its tan, Lucinda's tense young body shivered. The lips of Jennifer's blotching apricot and cream face parted. Her blue eyes stared.

"Enticing Horace to eat without cause. Willfully failing to prepare his food properly. Plying him with alcohol. *Very* dangerous for hyperlipoproteinemia. *His* disorder. And you knew it. Both of you."

He glared at the women. "The sleepiness that would come over him unexpectedly for brief periods clued you in that his body was not coping. How much saturated fat, excess sugar, did you use? Skill with such ingredients means everything."

His voice sharpened. "Key personnel, known to me and brother Horace, when he was alive, await your eventual arrival at the hospital prison ward. There, thirstier and thirstier, you'll gnaw on your lips for the blood. Because the water may seem to have too much . . . chlorine sometimes and sometimes not enough. Hungrier and hungrier you'll get; so that if you could find a dead rat, you might eat it raw.

"But . . . if you take a chance on what the dietician orders for your menus, don't expect it to return the roses to your cheeks. You see, my dears, you're not the only ones good at adding substitutions such as whipping cream for skim milk, extracts to food: a pinch of this and a dash of that. It began before the Borgias; remember, they were Italian, too."

He formed a steeple with the fingers of his thick hands. "Had you been interested in Horace and his beloved Sicily, Jenny, we all might have met under more enjoyable circumstances."

"Show me respect," she managed. "I'm Mrs. Cassata."

Leaving the desk, Luigi seated himself between the women. "I'm related to you, Lucinda, and you, Jennifer, by marriage. As you're related to one another. Distantly, all around, of course."

The sound in Jennifer's throat resembled a windpipe squeezed by thumbs.

"Horace respected his Old World heritage, dear ladies. It caused him twinges of conscience. He hoped to straighten out his life by legal steps, giving you, Jenny, an annulment of your shipboard marriage and a big money settlement; then see if he could marry you, Lucinda, according to the church."

A police siren, a shrill banshee, seemed to be headed in their direction.

"Hungry, ladies?" Luigi asked. "Right this way for recipes from Sicily, home of the vendetta, feud to the *death*!

"I've notified cousin Gilda, our matron. I won't wait for her to speak to the head of the food services; I'll do so myself, make doubly sure of the finest culinary accomplishments. I'll tell all about you, what you've done, your names.

"Before we go through the routine of booking you, ladies—for murder—let's have a little talk." He led them into the dining room. Jennifer and Lucinda gingerly skirted Horace's body.

"Please make yourselves comfortable. Take a chair. And remember you can speak openly to me. It's my *job* to protect you." Sympathy. Understanding.

"We have such a cozy little jail here, a real home away from home; and, oh, the food!" A shiver of ecstasy. "All the meals are done elsewhere."

The women's bodies relaxed. Their hands dropped onto the table.

"Now for a little something Horace chose to leave undisclosed until his last moment. How well hidden it was, beneath the ever-loaded tablecloth!

"This acronymic poem, ladies. Without a byline. Typical modesty. Don't miss reading downward the first letter of each line:

> *Arrange a little garnish on the top.*
> *Rodent doom? That's a too common way to stop.*
> *Strychnine, wouldn't you say, is much too swift?*
> *Enough is what seems ample for a lift.*
> *Now find something slightly fatal. The spoon to lick.*
> *Ingredient in amount meager, to make somebody sick.*
> *Cause of death must not be guessed as . . .*

"Arsenic!" the women cried out in duet.

"I surmise you got your signals mixed and each dosed him, oh, just the teensiest bit, each thinking the other hadn't." Oil of smile, salt of scorn.

"So may I propose a cooking contest, not necessarily for the best cook, but the fastest?" He put his hands over the twenty twitching fingers. "That way, one of you might survive. The quickest one to squeal on the other."

His grip tightened. "If you decline, we can't have a winner, can we? And by the way, I have noted two of Horace's precious miniature decanters missing. That collection has a most unusual added touch, guaranteed slowly but surely to . . . Dear ladies, has your digestion today seemed a bit . . . off?"

His voice deepened. "Silent still? From shock? Must I so inform the incoming maestro of the purveyor of meals to jails and prison hospital wards? If such be the case, I'll check personally with Cassata Food Services, for the appropriate cuisine with special ingredients . . . for the *two* of you."

The tape recorder and other equipment under his coat rose and fell with his heart. His face darkened into doom. "Cassata Food Services. Based at Luigi's Godfather Café. My own little ristorante Italiano."

Vengeance, all black and white, its long scream changed to a moan by the curb, was stopping just outside.

The moment had come.

The upper and lower lids of one glaring brown eye closed together as if a sarcophagus—its marble top clanging shut over a corpse. "And, please, dear ladies, always feel free—to ask me, 'What's cooking? Murder?'"

Michael Collins

....

Michael Collins is the best-known pseudonym of Dennis Lynds, a notably prolific and versatile writer who has also written as William Arden, John Crowe, Mark Sadler, and Carl Dekker and shared with other writers such house names as Nick Carter, Maxwell Grant, and Brett Halliday. Born in St. Louis in 1924 and educated in New York, Lynds served in the U.S. Army Infantry during World War II, was awarded the Purple Heart and three battle stars, and spent several years as an editor on various chemistry periodicals before becoming a full-time writer in 1960. In addition to his mystery fiction, he has contributed numerous short stories to little magazines, some of which were collected in *Why Girls Ride Sidesaddle* (1980).

Lynds/Collins now lives in Santa Barbara, home to a distinguished list of mystery writers (including Margaret Millar, William Campbell Gault, and the late Ross Macdonald), and many of his novels have vivid southern California settings. Most of his novels about one-armed private eye Dan Fortune, however, are notable for their sharply observed background of New York City. The first Fortune novel, *Act of Fear* (1967), won an Edgar for best first mystery novel of its year.

"Hot Night Homicide" is the only short story signed by Michael Collins that does *not* feature Dan Fortune. It has not been reprinted since its original magazine appearance in *Mike Shayne Mystery Magazine* in 1968.

Michael Collins
· ·

hot night homicide

It was the kind of homicide that called for one inch of copy at the bottom of an inside page. Or that was how it looked when Lieutenant Mastro of the precinct detective squad first arrived on the scene.

The facts were simple and obvious. John Thomas Renzo, male Caucasian, forty-two years old, taxi driver by occupation, was shot twice through the plate glass window of the Tugboat Bar & Grill by Rose McCoy, female Caucasian, aged forty, at 10:29 P.M. on a hot Friday night in August.

There were seventeen witnesses inside the tavern, and six more on the street outside. John Renzo was dead when the first patrolman arrived two-and-a-half minutes after the last shot. The deceased, according to all witnesses, did not say anything after he was hit and before he died.

The fifteen men and two women inside the Tugboat Bar & Grill were exact about the time of the shots, because the commercial had just started at the midpoint of the TV show most of them had been watching.

They had all been trying to order drinks at the same time

during the break when they were interrupted by the explosions of the three shots and shattering glass.

The bartender, Charles Crowe, hit the floor in the reflex of an ex-infantryman with his eyes focused on the clock: 10:29. The assistant medical examiner later confirmed the time of death as probably exact.

The identity of the killer was equally certain. On the street outside the six witnesses there had been no farther than ten feet from Rose McCoy when she stopped outside the window of the Tugboat, took a 9mm Luger from her handbag, and fired the three shots with the pistol held steady in both hands.

These witnesses all testified that Rose McCoy had been swearing when she fired, and all agreed that she had swayed as if drunk. Later tests proved that she had been very drunk.

John Renzo was struck by two of the three shots. One shot struck him in the back just under the left shoulder, tore a hole in his old World War II field jacket, and lodged against the bone at the shoulder joint. A second bullet hit him in the back of the head and was the fatal wound. The third shot embedded itself in the end of the bar that faced the window.

Rose McCoy made no attempt to escape. After she had fired she sat down on the sidewalk, let the pistol fall, and began to cry. Two of the men on the street, and three from inside the Tugboat Bar & Grill, restrained her while other men went for the police.

All this was quickly learned by the first patrolman and the men in the first squad car, and reported to Lieutenant Mastro when he arrived some ten minutes later.

The lieutenant came personally because it was an exceptionally hot night and all four men of his precinct detective squad were out on other calls. A hot night in the city meant a busy night for the police. The shooting of John Renzo was a typical hot night violent death. Mastro had seen hundreds of such homicides.

The lieutenant set the uniformed men to taking the names of the witnesses, including those of the ones who had decided not to be involved and had vanished—if those names could be gotten from others. He himself checked the identity of the victim, John Thomas Renzo, through his papers and by questioning the witnesses who had known him.

The medical examiner arrived and went to work, although there was little for him to do, and other patrolmen arrived to disperse the curious.

Mastro then turned his attention to Rose McCoy, who still sat on the sidewalk, crying and babbling. The lieutenant made his mandatory statement concerning Rose McCoy's rights to silence and counsel, and then showed the woman the Luger.

"This is your pistol, miss?"

It was at this point that the trouble began.

"Poor Roger," Rose McCoy said, sobbed.

Mastro held the Luger. "What?"

"I killed him," Rose McCoy said to some vast and empty space she seemed to see before her swollen and bleared eyes. "Poor Roger. I loved him, you know? He was a louse."

"Roger?" Lieutenant Mastro said.

"I told him, yessir," Rose McCoy said. "I told you, Roger!"

Mastro rubbed his beard-shadowed chin as he studied the drunken woman. The bartender, Charles Crowe, was standing close to him. Mastro continued to contemplate Rose McCoy as he spoke to the bartender.

"The victim's name was John Renzo? John Thomas Renzo?"

"That's right, Lieutenant," the bartender said. "Johnny Renzo. He was a regular in here."

"You're sure his middle name was Thomas?"

Another witness chimed in. "Tommy, yeah, Lieutenant. I remember this girl called him Tommy. Tommy the Terror."

"Roger," Mastro said. "Did he use an alias? Nickname?"

"Not that I ever heard, Lieutenant," the bartender said.

"What about the woman?" Mastro asked. "Know her?"

"Never saw her before," the bartender said.

Mastro nodded. Then the lieutenant shivered slightly. He

could see the headlines: INNOCENT MAN GUNNED DOWN. A hot night death.

"Miss—" Mastro began.

Rose McCoy waved her arms wildly in the hot night. "I wait! I wait, wait! His pay he drinks up. Two months rent we owe. Women? I know about the women! No more women, Roger. No more—nothin'! All alone, you know? I wait. In that sweatbox. He don't come. I wait. He don't come—he don't come—"

"You were waiting," Mastro prompted, "but Roger didn't come. So you took the gun and went out looking for him. You thought you saw him in the Tugboat, at the bar. So you—"

Rose McCoy waved her wild arms, her bleared eyes red with anger and whisky. She tried to stand. She failed and slumped back against the building wall. Her voice was vicious.

"He told me!" she cried. "He called and told me Roger's out drinking again! All night I wait and Roger's out boozing it up again. With a woman! With some tramp! He told me where Roger was so I took the gun, yeah. No more! No more!"

"Someone told you where Roger was?" Mastro asked quickly.

"Yeah, he told me," Rose McCoy cried. "I wait, wait! It rings, you know? The phone. Roger's in the Tugboat drinking and with a woman. Boozing! A woman! Alone in that sweatbox! I get the gun! I run out! I find him! I find—"

Rose McCoy swayed halfway up to her feet. Almost screaming now. Swayed, blinked, and fell over flat on her back.

Mastro bent over the fallen woman. She had passed out. The lieutenant stared down at her for a full minute while the witnesses licked their lips and waited. Then Mastro told his men to put her in the patrol car and take her to the precinct. He stood on the sidewalk in the hot night and stared off after the patrol car long after it had vanished.

The M.E. finished and had his men remove the body. The uniformed patrolmen cleared the sidewalk. The witnesses were released. The tavern was closed down for the night. Soon everyone was gone except the bartender, who did not seem to know what to do next. And still Mastro stood on the sidewalk staring at nothing.

Then he let out a deep sigh. There was no way out of it. He was going to have to work on the death of John Thomas Renzo.

Mastro started with the home address of Rose McCoy. It turned out to be a single shabby room in a West Side rooming house less than two blocks from the Tugboat Bar & Grill.

He questioned all the tenants in the rooming house. He waited in the room until Rose McCoy's husband came home— Roger McCoy. He took the husband down to the precinct to wait for Rose to sober up.

Next, Mastro went to work on the life and history of John Thomas Renzo. He plodded from witness to witness, talking to each one. He interrogated the bartender, Charles Crowe, for two hours.

He checked the telephone company.

It all took three days. Then he sat in the office of the captain and made his report.

"Her husband," Mastro said, "is Roger McCoy. Male Caucasian, aged forty-five, electrician, same general height, weight, and coloring as John Renzo. When he came home on the night of the killing he was wearing an old World War II field jacket and gray work pants. Renzo had gray pants on, too. From the back, to a drunk, they would have been twins in that bar light."

"Where was McCoy?" the captain asked.

"Working late," Mastro said. "For real. I checked it. He admits he often lied about working late. The wife knew that. McCoy admits he sometimes drinks in the Tugboat. The wife knew that, too. Only that night he was really working late."

"Mistaken identity," the captain said. "Damn."

"Maybe," Mastro said. "Or maybe murder."

The captain blinked. "Murder? The McCoy woman and Renzo playing under the table, Nick?"

"I don't think so, no," Mastro said. "When she sobered up she still thought she had shot McCoy. She cried like a baby. She wanted us to burn her fast. When I told her New York doesn't burn them anymore she said that was unfair, she deserved to die. When I brought McCoy in she fainted dead away. When we brought her around she was so happy she cried in his arms and hung on like a Band-Aid."

"So she can act," the captain said. "They're all Academy Award material."

"It took us a day to make her believe she'd shot anyone after she saw McCoy alive. She thinks she must have missed McCoy. She never heard of John Renzo. She thinks we're out to get her."

"Do you believe her?"

"Yes," Mastro said. "I checked from Renzo's end, and the McCoys' end, and the witnesses' end."

"Sum it up," the captain said wearily. It was still too hot. Sleepless weather. Temper and boredom weather.

"Renzo was a cabdriver," Mastro summed up. "He lived alone in an apartment a block from the Tugboat. He'd lived in the same apartment for twelve years. He'd lived in the neighborhood for twenty years. He was a regular in most of the taverns around. No one can connect him to either of the McCoys."

Mastro lighted a cigarette. "The McCoys came from Detroit three months ago. Nothing connects them to Renzo. The Detroit police report they had a record of brawling, but no record of her playing around, and no hint of any John Renzo but they're still working on it.

"Renzo was never west of Jersey City, according to fourteen people who've known him for twenty years. He had two girlfriends and neither of them ever heard of Rose McCoy. The two girls couldn't pick Rose out of the show-up. Six of Renzo's best friends couldn't make Rose McCoy in the show. The same with Roger McCoy."

The captain spread his hands. "So? Mistaken identity. Open and shut, Nick. An accident. You know we get them. A hot night, a skinful of whisky, a hate on, a gun in her hand."

"Yessir," Mastro agreed, "except for the phone call."

"Phone call?" the captain said warily.

The captain's eyes told Mastro that he was not in the mood to hear about a clever murder, or any murder. It was too hot, the complaint sheet was full, and the captain did not like a simple homicide to turn into clever murder at any time. But—"

"She and McCoy had been brawling ever since they moved into that rooming house," Mastro said. "All the other tenants on three floors had heard the fighting. The McCoys screamed so loud the tenants even knew what the fights were about—his drinking up his pay and chasing women in bars. The landlord was considering throwing them out because they broke things."

Mastro blew smoke. "That night it was like an oven in the room. Rose was alone, drinking. I found an empty fifth and a half-full pint. No ice. McCoy was still not home at ten-fifteen. She was boiling. The other tenants say they'd heard her yelling to herself, throwing things, for a couple of hours. They were considering calling us by ten o'clock, or so they say."

The captain swore. "But they never do call us. They think about it, but they don't call, and guys get killed."

Mastro chewed his lip. "About ten-fifteen she got a phone call. No name and she didn't know the caller, so she says. The caller told her that McCoy was in the Tugboat drinking and with a woman. I've got her exact statement."

Mastro opened his notebook and read. "Here it is. 'Someone, I don't know who, called me and told me that my husband was in the Tugboat Bar and Grill. The caller told me that my husband was drunk and with a woman. Then this person said that my husband and the woman were going to do something bad later.'"

Mastro closed his book. The captain swiveled in his chair until his back was to Mastro. The captain swore again.

"Damn!" the captain said.

"She thinks the voice was a man," Mastro went on, "but it could have been a woman. The voice was 'funny.' Kind of high and laughing."

"A hophead?" the captain suggested.

"Or a psycho, or a drunk with a big joke, or someone talking

falsetto to disguise the voice," Mastro said. "Anyway, Rose Mc-
Coy exploded, grabbed the gun, ran to the Tugboat, saw what
she thought was McCoy through the window, and shot him."

The captain shook his head. "Not a psycho. Please, not a
psycho."

"That call killed John Renzo, Captain," Mastro said.

The captain swiveled back to face Mastro. "A setup? You're
trying to tell me that someone set Renzo up to be shot?"

"The call was the trigger. Without the call we've got a simple
accident, and we close it. With the call—"

"All right," the captain said. "Tell me about Renzo. He had
an enemy? A mob of enemies?"

Mastro chewed a knuckle. "Renzo played with women. He
played the numbers, the ponies, and poker. He drank and had
people who didn't like him much. But the women and gambling
was pretty minor league, the drinking was small-time, and no
one seems to have really hated him."

"Swell," the captain said.

"None of it looks enough for killing, but I'm still digging,"
Mastro said. "You never know what a killer will think is enough
for a killing, and maybe the caller didn't have killing in mind.
Maybe the caller figured that Rose McCoy would just give Renzo
a scare. Maybe it was a big joke."

"Some joke. What about the call?"

"Local, no trace."

The captain considered the ceiling. "To make it play the
caller would have to have known that Renzo was in the bar, that
he was dressed like McCoy, that McCoy wasn't there, and that
Rose McCoy was drunk, mad, and had a gun. It's crazy."

"Crazy and a long chance," Mastro agreed. "We've both seen
crazier, and we've both seen longer chances. And it wouldn't
have been so hard to set up, not for someone in that damned
rooming house."

"In the rooming house?" the captain echoed.

Mastro leaned in his chair. "They all knew about the McCoys'
fights, and what they were about. Anyone in that rooming house

knew that Rose was alone, drunk, mad, and had a gun. Anyone in the rooming house could have known how McCoy was dressed."

"How about them knowing Renzo?"

"Anyone in the Tugboat would know how Renzo was dressed, and where he was standing, and that McCoy wasn't there. Any regular in the Tugboat probably knew McCoy drank there."

"Put it straight," the captain said. "Tell me your story."

Mastro sat back. "Someone heard Rose McCoy in her room. He knew what Roger McCoy looked like. He went into the Tugboat. He saw Renzo. He had a hate for Renzo. He saw how much Renzo looked like McCoy that night. He got the idea. He went to the telephone and called Rose and waited to see what would happen."

A silence settled over the heat in the captain's office. There was an aura of unreality. Both men seemed to move sluggishly, as if under thick water. The captain brushed at the air as if trying to clear away the murky liquid.

"Crazy," the captain said. "Just crazy."

"Someone telephoned Rose McCoy," Mastro said.

"Yeah, someone called," the captain said. "Okay, dig. I want whoever made that call."

Mastro went back to work. He questioned all the witnesses again, checked into their lives to look for some connection to Renzo or the McCoys or both. He went around the list of Renzo's friends, enemies, associates, and bookies again looking for anyone who had been in the bar or had had any connection to the rooming house of the McCoys.

He concentrated on the tenants of the rooming house, looking for any of them who might also have known Renzo. He then branched out to look for anyone who had known Renzo, even briefly, and who had also had some possible reason to have been around the rooming house, no matter how slim the reason. A milkman, maybe, or a gas man, or a repairman.

Three days later he had found nothing.

"Do you want Homicide, Nick?" the captain asked.

"No, dammit," Mastro said. "I'm going to find that caller myself."

"Two more days, then I give it to Homicide," the captain said. "Let Gazzo worry. I need you on some nice, clean muggings."

Mastro nodded gloomily. He hated to turn a case over to Homicide. He put in another day as fruitless as the three before it. It was a big city and a crowded neighborhood. He could not connect anyone to both Renzo and the rooming house of the McCoys.

At six o'clock that evening he again sat in the captain's office finishing his written report.

Two furious middle-aged women stormed into the office with the desk sergeant close behind them.

"Taxpayers you keep out?" one irate woman demanded. "Maybe you don't want we should see what you're doing. Nothing, that's what you're doing! Taxpayers you give trouble!"

The captain waved the sergeant out. He smiled at the ladies. Mastro went on with his work. He was not the captain.

"What's the trouble, ladies?" the captain asked politely.

The women were worked up to full steam. Their words tumbled out in a chorus of anger.

"We want these phone calls stopped!"

"Children! Where do they learn such filthy ideas? Baby voices they got, and such terrible, terrible words, such lies!"

"Our husbands are drunk, they say. Our husbands are with women. I'm afraid to answer the phone."

"Kids telling us our husbands are in that dirty Flamingo Club, with women in that awful Tugboat Bar and Grill! Laughing at us. Telling such lies! It must be stopped immediately."

All the captain said was, "Telephone calls? Lies? Kids?"

Lieutenant Mastro slowly put down his pen and stared at the two women.

R. R. Irvine

....

A native of Salt Lake City, Robert Ralstone Irvine had a successful career in radio and television news before turning to full-time fiction writing. He planned the transition of Los Angeles' KNX-radio to an all-news format and served for three years as news director of KABC-TV, winning two Emmy awards for Channel 7 documentaries. Disturbed by the drift of TV news from journalism to show business, Irvine left to write mystery novels, usually using his television experience for a fresh background. *Jump Cut* (1974) and *Freeze Frame* (1976) were both nominated for Edgars in the paperback-original category. In Irvine's latest novel, *Ratings are Murder* (1985), TV reporter Bob Christopher makes his first hardcover appearance.

Bob Irvine, who now lives in Carmel, believes that "In the Dead Hours" is the best of his several short stories from *Ellery Queen's Mystery Magazine*.

R. R. Irvine

· · · · · · · · · · · · · · · ·

in the dead hours

Trakker had become a vampire. He didn't suck blood exactly—he filmed it.

But he did keep Transylvanian hours, rising at sunset to spend the night hunting the streets of Los Angeles seeking his lifeblood, tragedy. His battered pickup truck sported a maze of aerials connected to police-band radios, fire frequencies, and sheriffs' shortwaves. They allowed him to monitor the pulse of the city, a beat he'd been auditing for more than twenty years.

Shootings, freeway fender-benders, calamities of all kinds transfused him, but only to the point of bare subsistence. Yet like all stringer cameramen, he never gave up hope that someday his big story would come along and make him rich and famous.

Such a story would have to break between midnight and 6:00 A.M., the hours when the big TV stations all but closed down their newsrooms. Otherwise, why pay him when they could film it themselves?

So on each nightly run Trakker kept fingers crossed, praying that the stations' overnight men—hapless creatures sentenced to oblivion because they had incurred the wrath of management—

216

were their usual vigilant selves. That is to say, by all odds they should be asleep. Hell, Trakker had been around the business long enough to know how things worked. Of course, it was no longer like the pioneering days of TV news, the 1950s, when anything went, when the tools of the trade were an old shoe, a white sheet, and a child's broken doll.

Trakker laughed at his memories. Scenes of tragedy danced in his head. Clearly, as if it had been only yesterday, he saw himself lying beneath his sheet, simulating a body, and yelling "Roll it!" to other members of the camera fraternity, who were invariably late at the scene of disaster. Re-creation had been easier and cheaper than installing reliable two-way radios.

He remembered the countless shoes dropped at the scenes of traffic accidents, as if to show that the victims had been hurled into eternity by the impact.

And the memory of his own special doll brought a grin to his face. It had been so poignant—its little dress torn, one arm completely ripped away. In closeup that doll had said everything there was to say about fatal childhood accidents. Besides, what was the harm in a little stage-managing?

But Trakker had no need for re-creation this day. He had a story that was all his own, his ticket to a bonus. He laughed out loud. There had been no skill involved. He'd been on his way home after a fruitless night when the DB (dead body) call came over the police band. DBs were seldom worth much, a few feet of film at most, but he'd been less than a mile from the location, so he said, "What the hell!"

He'd arrived just ahead of the first patrol car.

Now, whistling cheerfully, he drove toward Hollywood. Excitement surged in him the moment he pulled up before Channel 3's main gate.

Trakker leaned out of the pickup window to shout a greeting at the guard. But the sentry, decades beyond Trakker's fifty-five, eyed the stringer sourly, without a flicker of recognition, though they'd been through the procedure countless times before. "What's your business?" the guard demanded truculently.

"Film for the newsroom," Trakker replied, as always.

"Who ya wanna see? I got to put a name down on my log."

"Wayne Gossett, the assignment editor."

"He don't get in till six."

"It's that right now," Trakker said.

Without so much as an acknowledging grunt the guard thumbed Trakker on his way. The stringer maneuvered his pickup into a no-parking area directly in front of the news building and then, with a weary sigh, eased his potbelly out from under the steering wheel and lumbered inside to face Gossett.

The assignment editor, who looked like a mere kid to Trakker, twenty-five at the most, got busy on one of his phones when he saw the stringer coming. He usually did that; he liked to make stringers wait.

Trakker lit a cigarette and wheezed out a cloud of smoke. Assignment editors were all alike, he knew. They hadn't changed in all the years Trakker had been hawking film. They made each sale a tough fight.

"Hurry it up," Trakker grunted. "I've got a good one."

Gossett answered with a gesture and then made a show of turning his back on the stringer.

That would never have happened in the old days, the days before the big unions took over and made it almost impossible for a free-lancer like himself to make a decent living. In those days he hadn't been limited to overnight pickups. Hell, no! Then he'd been in demand. Often as not he'd fill in for a regular staff cameraman and have his own sound man, a bond-servant attached by audio umbilical to follow his every whim.

Back in the fifties there was hardly anyone who'd ever heard of TV news, let alone knew the workings of a 16mm camera. It had been a stringer's market. Reporters had called him by his first name, bought him lunches, laughed at his jokes; they never knew when their careers might depend on his film.

Trakker muttered a silent curse, condemning the unions and the slick, image-stricken medium that television had become.

Nowadays he barely earned enough to eat. Affording a wife

was out of the question, so he lived alone. No one called him anything but Trakker, and then with derision. He was tolerated in newsrooms only because he covered tragedy in the dead hours of the night.

But he wanted more than toleration. He wanted his life back; he wanted to rejoin the daylight living.

Gossett came off the phone abruptly, pointed his sharp nose at the Plexiglas assignment board behind his desk, and said, "I've got just about all the film I need for today."

Trakker saw only half a dozen stories grease-penciled on the glass. He knew it took at least twice that many to fill an hour of news. But all he said was, "You'll want what I've got this time."

"All stringers say that. What is it—another fender-bender?"

Trakker shook his head, grinning.

"Not another fire, I hope."

"No—a murder," said Trakker.

Gossett's eyes narrowed but that didn't hide their glint of expectation.

"Throat slashed from ear to ear, among other things," the stringer added.

Gossett jerked open a desk drawer and rummaged for a film purchase form. After filling in Trakker's name the assignment editor asked, "What else have you got?"

"Victim was male, late sixties. Found in an alley behind an all-night café on Main Street. He—"

"Main Street!" Gossett interrupted. "What the hell was he, a bum?"

"Wino."

The assignment editor swore profusely. "Nobody's going to miss one drunk more or less. Where's the human interest?"

"I'm the only one who got film of the body."

Pretending to be disinterested, Gossett shook his head. But Trakker knew better. All assignment editors lived for exclusive film.

"You sure?" Gossett asked finally.

"I was the only cameraman there and they were loading the

body when I left. The coroner's probably working on him right now, so that lets out any more film."

"Okay. We'll process your stuff and take a look-see."

Trakker nodded. That was half of the battle. Once a TV station agreed to process a stringer's film, they were committed to replace it free with a fresh roll of 16mm, sale or no sale.

"How much?" Trakker asked.

"If we use it—the usual, seventy-five."

"It's exclusive. It ought to be worth a bonus."

"Seventy-five is pretty damn good for one night's work. It's more than I make."

"I'm lucky if I sell one film a week," Trakker answered.

Gossett shrugged. "A slashed throat means a lot of blood. We got to be careful what we put on the air during the dinner hour. We don't want our viewers losing their appetite."

"I was careful," Trakker said. "I shot around most of it."

"We'll see. I'll check with the fuzz right now." With a dramatic gesture Gossett punched on his desk speaker so that Trakker could listen in. It was another of his techniques designed to squelch stringers, since cops made just about any story sound dull and boring.

But for once a detective was unusually talkative. "That Trakker's a bloodsucker. He beat us to the body. A regular ghoul." The policeman paused. "This sounds hollow. Are we on a speaker?"

"Yeah," Gossett admitted.

"Trakker's probably standing right there, huh?"

The assignment editor grunted.

"Tell him to watch it with his film. Our killer's a weirdo. Did some fancy carving on the body and we don't want the details getting out. Otherwise, the next thing you know we'll be up to our butts in copycat killers."

"We'll play it cool," Gossett promised. "Anything official you can tell me about the killing?"

"It's too early. No positive ID yet. We think the murder

weapon was a straight razor, but you'll have to wait for the coroner's report before you can run anything on that."

Gossett hung up and turned to Trakker. "Since we can't use the fancy stuff, it's not worth more than seventy-five. No way."

"An exclusive should be worth something," the stringer complained. "It's not like the old days around here. Remember—remember the Kennedy story in Malibu?"

"Not that again!"

Trakker's eyes glazed over. "It was 1960, I think. Maybe '61. JFK was driving along the beach and suddenly decided to go wading in the surf. Only cameraman around was a stringer. He got a thousand bucks for that film."

"An accident," Gossett said. "A fluke. That will never happen again. The stations are bigger now, with a lot more film crews."

"No," Trakker protested, "a big story can still make a stringer." Gossett laughed at him.

A week later a second derelict was found with his throat slashed. And again Trakker was the first on the scene. Channel 3 paid him $100 for the film.

The *Times*, which had run the first killing on the back page of the second section, moved the new murder to the first section with a headline that read THE SLASHER STRIKES AGAIN. That made it official as far as TV was concerned. The Slasher was now big news.

Trakker·had to share the third body with another stringer. "You can't win 'em all," he told Gossett. But even though the film wasn't exclusive, the assignment editor kicked in for $150. Of course, the other channels were bidding, too.

Trakker was now riding high. Competition didn't bother him. He'd been in the business too long. He began to haunt skid row, living out of his pickup truck. He felt certain the next killing would be the magic number, the one to bring him a really big

221

bonus, maybe even rivaling the JFK scoop. He felt it in his bones.

But then things started to go sour. The TV stations made a deal with the police—favorable coverage in return for calls to standby crews whenever the next murder occurred.

"After all," Gossett told Trakker, "it isn't every day a maniac killer comes along. And you stringers aren't equipped to get us sound. We need sirens and interviews from bystanders to make these murders live."

"It's not fair."

Gossett laughed. "News is just like show business. You gotta keep coming up with better acts all the time or people will switch channels. You'd better go back to fender-benders, Trakker. You've lost your bargaining power."

You're no bargain yourself, Trakker thought, scowling at the assignment editor. But the unspoken back talk did nothing for the stringer's peace of mind. Here he was, a fifty-five-year-old free-lance-playing reporter. A man his age ought to be planning retirement, not chasing after a paranoid killer.

"How about putting me on as backup?" Trakker asked deferentially. "You never know when you might have an equipment failure."

Wide-eyed, Gossett stared at the stringer. "You? Hell, Trakker, I can pull another crew in as backup if I want. But you? You aren't even in the union."

That's not the half of it, Trakker said to himself as he left the newsroom. He wasn't even covered by Social Security. Some old age he'd have. He'd be filming fender-benders until they carried him away.

Feeling exhausted, the stringer climbed into his pickup, his face drawn at the thought of the long daylight hours until it was time to patrol the night in search of tragedy once again. What was the use of going home? No one was buying free-lance film. Something inside Trakker crumbled.

"I'm as much a bum as those winos," he muttered to himself. "Only I'm going to hell with a little more style." He viciously gunned the motor of the battered old pickup and headed for the skid row district.

At 4:30 the next morning he called Gossett at home.

"How'd you get my number?" the assignment editor grumbled.

"Never mind that," Trakker said. "I need a decision—now."

"Has there been another one?"

"What would you pay for a double murder—two throats cut?"

"I have a crew on standby, you know that."

"A double murder, plus an exclusive interview with the killer?"

"I—an exclusive? You sure?"

"I want two thousand dollars," Trakker said. "Double the JFK money."

Gossett made a strangling noise.

"I can always try another channel."

"I can't make that kind of decision," Gossett mumbled. "I'll have to call management."

"You got five minutes, that's as long as I can wait."

"What's your number there?"

Trakker read off the numbers of the pay phone.

Four minutes later Gossett called back. "A thousand's as high as we can go."

"It's got to be more than that."

They argued until the assignment editor said finally, "Twelve hundred. And that's the absolute limit."

Trakker smiled. Twelve hundred would make him the highest-paid stringer ever. He gave Gossett an address and then asked, "How soon can you get your crew there?"

"Fifteen minutes—no more."

"Done," Trakker said and hung up. He stepped out of the telephone booth, hurried back to the pickup, and opened the door so that he could read his watch by the overhead light while he smoked a cigarette.

His head throbbed from lack of sleep and the aftereffects of cheap wine. He locked the truck and trotted toward the Fifth

Street Bridge. The two winos still lay in the shelter beneath the arch, right where he'd left them when they had passed out.

Trakker's heart pounded and he had trouble focusing on the two unconscious figures. "Just like me," he muttered. "Only I'm going to be remembered."

Already he felt the hot strobe lights of fame on his face. He wiped the sweat from his eyes so he'd look better for the battery of cameras that would be aimed at him. Only then did he realize that the Channel 3 newswagon was in sight.

Not much time left, he thought. But enough. His laughter echoed under the bridge. What did it matter that he wasn't the original slasher? It would take the cops days, maybe weeks, to figure that one out. He knew all the tricks; he could really make it look good. Who would ever be able to say for sure that he was a copycat?

He stood poised for a moment as if searching for the best camera angle and then, straight razor in hand, he lunged forward. The two winos died quietly enough for the approaching newsmen to hear a single crisp command, "Roll it!"

William F. Nolan

....

William F. Nolan had an interesting variety of jobs between his birth in Kansas City in 1928 and his decision to write full-time in 1956: greeting card designer, cartoonist, mural painter, aircraft inspector, credit assistant, and California State Department of Employment interviewer. As a writer, his accomplishments have been equally diverse: biographer (of Barney Oldfield, Steve McQueen, and John Huston, among others), science fiction writer (most notably of the novel *Logan's Run* with George Clayton Johnson), film and television writer, book reviewer, and anthology editor. In the mystery field, he is best known as one of the leading authorities on the life and work of Dashiell Hammett, his study culminating in the biography *Hammett: A Life at the Edge* (1983). He has also created private eyes of his own: Bart Challis, who debuted in *Death is for Losers* (1968), and Sam Space, hero of the s.f./hard-boiled parodies *Space for Hire* (1971) and *Look Out for Space* (1984).

Of his many crime short stories, Bill Nolan believes "A Real Nice Guy," which first appeared in *Mike Shayne Mystery Magazine,* is among the very best.

William F. Nolan

·······················

a real nice guy

They called him "Deathmaster"—an accurate title. He never missed a target, never wasted a shot. Every city street was his personal shooting gallery.

Warm sun.

A summer afternoon.

The sniper emerged from the roof door, walking easily, carrying a custom-leather gun case.

Opened the case.

Assembled the weapon.

Loaded it.

Sighted the street below.

Adjusted the focus.

Waited.

There was no hurry.

No hurry at all.

He was famous, yet no one knew his name. There were portraits of him printed in dozens of newspapers and magazines; he'd even made the cover of *Time*. But no one had really seen his face. The portraits were composites, drawn by frustrated police artists, based on the few misleading descriptions given by witnesses who claimed to have seen him leaving a building, or jumping from a roof, or driving from the target area in a stolen automobile. But no two descriptions matched.

One witness described a chunky man of average height with a dark beard and cap. Another described a thin, extremely tall man with a bushy head of hair and a thick moustache. A third description pegged him as balding, paunchy, and wearing heavy horn-rims. On *Time*'s cover, a large blood-soaked question mark replaced his features—above the words WHO IS HE?

Reporters had given him many names: "The Phantom Sniper" . . . "The Deadly Ghost" . . . "The Silent Slayer" . . . and his personal favorite, "The Master of Whispering Death." This was often shortened to "Deathmaster," but he liked the full title; it was fresh and poetic—and *accurate*.

He *was* a master. He never missed a target, never wasted a shot. He was cool and nerveless and smooth, and totally without conscience. And death indeed whispered from his silenced weapon: a dry snap of the trigger, a muffled pop, and the target dropped as though struck down by the fist of God.

They were *always* targets, never people. Men, women, children. Young, middle-aged, old. Strong ones. Weak ones. Healthy or crippled. Black or white. Rich or poor. Targets—all of them.

He considered himself a successful sharpshooter, demonstrating his unique skill in a world teeming with three billion moving targets placed there for his amusement. Day and night, city by city, state by state, they were always there, ready for his gun, for the sudden whispering death from its barrel. An endless supply just for him.

Each city street was his personal shooting gallery.

But he was careful. Very, very careful. He never killed twice in the same city. He switched weapons. He never used a car more than once. He never wore the same clothes twice on a shoot. Even the shoes would be discarded; he wore a fresh pair for each target run. And, usually, he was never seen at all.

He thought of it as a sport.

A game.

A run.

A vocation.

A skill.

But never murder.

His name was Jimmie Prescott and he was thirty-one years of age. Five foot ten. Slight build. Platform shoes could add three inches and body-pillows up to fifty pounds. He had thinning brown hair framing a bland, unmemorable face. He shaved twice daily—but the case of wigs, beards, and moustaches he always carried easily disguised the shape of his mouth, chin, and skull. Sometimes he would wear a skin-colored flesh cap for baldness, or use heavy glasses—though his sight was perfect. Once, for a lark, he had worn a black eye patch. He would walk in a crouch, or stride with a sailor's swagger, or assume a limp. Each disguise amused him, helped make life more challenging. Each was a small work of art, flawlessly executed.

Jimmie was a perfectionist.

And he was clean: no police record. Never arrested. No set of his prints on file, no dossier.

He had a great deal of money (inherited) with no need or inclination to earn more. He had spent his lifetime honing his considerable skills: he was an expert on weaponry, car theft, body-combat, police procedures; he made it a strict rule to memorize the street system of each city he entered before embarking on a shoot. And once his target was down he knew exactly how to leave the area. The proper escape route was essential.

Jimmie was a knowledgeable historian in his field; he had made a thorough study of snipers, and held them all in cold contempt. Not a worthwhile one in the lot. They *deserved* to be caught; they were fools and idiots and blunderers, often acting out of neurotic impulse or psychotic emotion. Even the hired professionals drew Jimmie's ire—since these were men who espoused political causes or who worked for government money. Jimmie had no cause, nor would he ever allow himself to be bought like a pig on the market.

He considered himself quite sane. Lacking moral conscience, he did not suffer from a guilt complex. Nor did he operate from a basic hatred of humankind, as did so many of the warped criminals he had studied.

Basically, Jimmie liked people, got alone fine with them on a casual basis. He hated no one. (Except his parents, but they were long dead and something he did not think about anymore.) He was incapable of love or friendship, but felt no need for either. Jimmie depended only on himself; he had learned to do that from childhood. He was, therefore, a loner by choice, and made it a rule (Jimmie had many rules) never to date the same female twice, no matter how sexually appealing she might be. Man-woman relationships were a weakness, a form of dangerous self-indulgence he carefully avoided.

In sum, Jimmie Prescott didn't need anyone. He had himself, his skills, his weapons, and his targets. More than enough for a full, rich life. He did not drink or smoke. (Oh, a bit of vintage wine in a good restaurant was always welcome, but he had never been drunk in his life.) He jogged each day, morning and evening, and worked out twice a week in the local gym in whatever city he was visiting. A trim, healthy body was an absolute necessity in his specialized career. Jimmie left nothing to chance. He was not a gambler and took no joy in risk.

A few times things had been close: a roof door that had jammed shut in Detroit after a kill, forcing him to make a perilous between-buildings leap . . . an engine that died during a police chase in Portland, causing him to abandon his car . . . an intense struggle with an off-duty patrolman in Kansas City who'd witnessed a shoot. The fellow had been tough and dispatching him was physically difficult; Jimmie finally snapped his neck—but it had been close.

William F. Nolan

He kept a neat, handwritten record of each shoot in his tooled-leather notebook: state, city, name of street, weather, time of day, sex, age, and skin color of target. Under "Comments," he would add pertinent facts, including the make and year of the stolen car he had driven and the type of disguise he had utilized. Each item of clothing worn was listed. And if he experienced any problem in exiting the target area this would also be noted. Thus each shoot was critically analyzed upon completion—as a football coach might dissect a game after it had been played.

The only random factor was the target. Preselection spoiled the freshness, the *purity* of the act. Jimmie liked to surprise himself. Which shall it be: that young girl in red, laughing up at her boyfriend? The old newsman on the corner? The school kid skipping homeward with books under his arm? Or, perhaps, the beefy, bored truck driver, sitting idly in his cab, waiting for the light to change?

Selection was always a big part of the challenge.

And *this* time . . .

A male. Strong-looking. Well-dressed. Businessman with a briefcase, in his late forties. Hair beginning to silver at the temples. He'd just left the drugstore; probably stopped there to pick up something for his wife. Maybe she'd called to remind him at lunch.

Moving toward the corner. Walking briskly.

Yes, *this* one. By all means, this one.

Range: three hundred yards.

Adjust sight focus.

Rifle stock tight against right shoulder.

Finger inside guard, poised at trigger.

Cheek firm against wooden gun stock; eye to rubber scope piece.

Line crosshairs on target.

Steady breathing.

Tighten trigger finger slowly.

Fire!

The man dropped forward to the walk like a clubbed animal, dead before he struck the pavement. Someone screamed. A child began to cry. A man shouted.

Pleasant, familiar sounds to Jimmie Prescott.

Calmly, he took apart his weapon, cased it, then carefully dusted his trousers. (Rooftops were often grimy, and although he would soon discard the trousers he liked to present a neat, well-tailored appearance—but only when the disguise called for it. What a marvelous, ill-smelling bum he had become in New Orleans; he smiled thinly, thinking about how truly offensive he was on that occasion.)

He walked through the roof exit to the elevator.

Within ten minutes he had cleared central Baltimore—and booked the next flight to the West Coast.

Aboard the jet, he relaxed. In the soft, warm, humming interior of the airliner, he grew drowsy . . . closed his eyes.

And had The Dream again.

The Dream was the only disturbing element in Jimmie Prescott's life. He invariably thought of it that way: The Dream. Never as *a* dream. Always about a large metropolitan city where chaos reigned—with buses running over babies in the street, and people falling down sewer holes and through plate-glass store windows. Violent and disturbing. He was never threatened in The Dream, never personally involved in the chaos around him. Merely a mute witness to it.

He would tell himself, This is only *fantasy*, a thing deep inside his sleeping mind; it would go away once he awakened and then he could ignore it, put it out of his thoughts, bury it as he had buried the hatred for his father and mother.

Perhaps he had *other* dreams. Surely he did. But The Dream was the one he woke to, again and again, emerging from the chaos of the city with sweat on his cheeks and forehead, his breath tight and shallow in his chest, his heart thudding wildly.

"Are you all right?" a passenger across the aisle was asking him. "Shall I call somebody?"

"I'm fine," said Jimmie, sitting up straight. "No problem."

"You look kinda shaky."

"No, I'm fine. But thank you for your concern."

And he put The Dream away once again, as a gun is put away in its case.

In Los Angeles, having studied the city quite thoroughly, Jimmie took a cab directly into Hollywood. The fare was steep, but money was never an issue in Jimmie's life; he paid well for services rendered, with no regrets.

He got off at Highland, on Hollywood Boulevard, and walked toward the Chinese Theater.

He wanted two things: food and sexual satisfaction.

First, he would select an attractive female, take her to dinner and then to his motel room (He'd booked one from the airport.), where he would have sex. Jimmie never called it lovemaking, a *silly* word. It was always just sex, plain and simple and quickly over. He was capable of arousing a woman if he chose to do so, of bringing her to full passion and release, but he seldom bothered. His performance was always an act; the ritual bored him. Only the result counted.

He disliked prostitutes and seldom selected one. Too jaded. Too worldly. And never to be trusted. Given time, and his natural charm, he was usually able to pick up an out-of-town girl, impress her with an excellent and very expensive meal at a posh restaurant, and guide her firmly into bed.

This night, in Hollywood, the seduction was easily accomplished.

Jimmie spotted a supple, soft-faced girl in the forecourt of the Chinese. She was wandering from one celebrity footprint to another, leaning to examine a particular signature in the cement.

As she bent forward, her breasts flowed full, pressing against the soft linen dress she wore—and Jimmie told himself, she's the one for tonight. A young, awestruck out-of-towner. Perfect. He moved toward her.

"I just *love* European food," said Janet.

"That's good," said Jimmie Prescott. "I rather fancy it myself."

She smiled at him across the table, a glowing all-American girl from Ohio named Janet Louise Lakeley. They were sitting in a small, very chic French restaurant off La Cienega, with soft lighting and open-country decor.

"I can't read a word of this," Janet said when the menu was handed to her. "I thought they always had the food listed in English, too, like movie subtitles."

"Some places don't," said Jimmie quietly. "I'll order for us both. You'll be pleased. The sole is excellent here."

"Oh, I love fish," she said. "I could eat a ton of fish."

He pressed her hand. "That's nice."

"My head is swimming. I shouldn't have had that Scotch on an empty stomach," she said. "Are we having wine with dinner?"

"Of course," said Jimmie.

"I don't know anything about wine," she told him, "but I love champagne. That's wine, isn't it?"

He smiled with a faint upcurve of his thin lips.

"Trust me," he said. "You'll enjoy what I select."

"I'm sure I will."

The food was ordered and served—and Jimmie was pleased to see that his tastes had, once again, proven sound. The meal was superb, the wine was bracing, and the girl was sexually stimulating. Essentially brainless, but that really didn't matter to Jimmie. She was what he wanted.

Then she began to talk about the sniper killings.

"Forty people in just a year and two months," she said. "And all gunned down by the same madman. Aren't they *ever* going to catch him?"

"The actual target figure is forty-one," he corrected her. "And what makes you so sure the sniper is a male? Could be a woman."

She shook her head. "Whoever heard of a woman sniper?"

"There have been many," said Jimmie. "In Russia today there are several hundred trained female snipers. Some European governments have traditionally utilized females in this capacity."

"I don't mean women *soldiers*," she said. "I mean your nutso shoot-'em-in-the-street sniper. Always guys. Every time. Like that kid in Texas that shot all the people from the tower."

"Apparently you've never heard of Francine Stearn."

"Nope. Who was she?"

"Probably the most famous female sniper. Killed a dozen schoolchildren in Pittsburgh one weekend in late July 1970. One shot each. To the head. She was a very accurate shootist."

"Never heard of her."

"After she was captured, *Esquire* did a rather probing psychological profile on her."

"Well, I really don't read a lot," she admitted. "Except Gothic romances. I just can't get *enough* of those." She giggled. "Guess you could say I'm addicted."

"I'm not familiar with the genre."

"Anyway," she continued, "I know this sniper is a guy."

"*How* do you know?"

"Female intuition. I trust it. It never fails me. And it tells me that the Phantom Sniper is a man."

He was amused. "What else does it tell you?"

"That he's probably messed up in the head. Maybe beaten as a kid. Something like that. He's *got* to be a nut case."

"You could be wrong there, too." Jimmie told her. "Not all lawbreakers are mentally unbalanced."

"This 'Deathmaster' guy is, and I'm convinced of it."

"You're a strongly opinionated young woman."

"Mom always said that." She sipped her wine, nodded. "Yeah, I guess I am." She frowned, turning the glass slowly in her long-fingered hand. "Do you think they'll ever catch him?"

"I somehow doubt it," Jimmie declared. "No one seems to have a clear description of him. And he always seems to elude the police. Leaves no clues. Apparently selects his subjects at random. No motive to tie him to. No consistent M.O."

"What's that?"

"Method of operation. Most criminals tend to repeat the same basic pattern in their crimes. But not this fellow. He keeps surprising people. Never know where he'll pop up next, or who his target will be. Tough to catch a man like that."

"You call them 'subjects' and 'targets'—but they're *people*! Innocent men and women and children. You make them sound like . . . like cutouts in a shooting gallery!"

"Perhaps I do," he admitted, smiling. "It's simply that we have different modes of expression."

"I say they'll get him eventually. He can't go on just butchering innocent people forever."

"No one goes on forever," said Jimmie Prescott.

She put down her wineglass, leaned toward him. "Know what bothers me most about the sniper?"

"What."

"The fact that his kind of act attracts copycats. Other sickos with a screw loose who read about him and want to imitate him. Arson is like that. One big fire in the papers and suddenly all the other wacko firebugs start their *own* fires. It gets 'em going. The sniper is like that."

"If some mentally disturbed individual is motivated to kill stupidly and without thought or preparation by something he or she reads in a newspaper, then the sniper himself cannot be blamed for such abnormal behavior."

"You call what *he* does normal?"

"I . . . uh . . . didn't say that. I was simply refuting your theory."

She frowned. "Then who *is* to blame? I think that guy should be caught and—"

"And what?" Jimmie fixed his cool gray eyes on her. "What

would you do if you suddenly discovered who he was . . . where
to find him?"

"Call the police, naturally. Like anybody."

"Wouldn't you be curious about him, about the kind of person
he is? Wouldn't you *question* him first, try to understand him?"

"You don't question an animal who kills! Which is what he
is. I'd like to see him gassed or hanged . . . You don't *talk* to a
twisted creep like that!"

She had made him angry. His lips tightened. He was no
longer amused with this conversation; the word game had turned
sour. This girl was gross and stupid and insensitive. Take her to
bed and be done with it. Use her body—but no words. No more
words. He'd had quite enough of those from her.

"Check, please," he said to the waiter.

It was at his motel, after sex, that Jimmie decided to kill her.
Her insulting tirade echoed and reechoed in his mind. She must
be punished for it.

In this special case he felt justified in breaking one of his
rules: never preselect a target. She told him that she had a job
in Hollywood, that she worked the afternoon shift at a clothing
store on Vine. And he knew where she lived, a few blocks from
work. She walked to the store each afternoon.

He would take her home and return the next day. When she
left her apartment building he would dispatch her from a roof
across the street. Once this plan had settled into place in the
mind of Jimmie Prescott he relaxed, allowing the tension of the
evening to drain away.

By tomorrow night he'd be in Tucson, and Janet Lakeley
would be dead.

Warm sun.

A summer afternoon.

The sniper emerged from the roof door, walking easily, carrying a custom-leather gun case.

Opened the case.

Assembled the weapon.
Loaded it.
Sighted the street below.
Adjusted the focus.
Waited.

Target now exiting.
Walking along street toward corner.
Adjust sight focus.
Finger on trigger.
Cheek against stock.
Eye to scope.
Crosshairs direct on target.
Fire!

Jimmie felt something like a fist strike his stomach. A sudden, shocking blow. Winded, he looked down in amazement at the blood pulsing steadily from his shirtfront.

I'm hit! Someone has actually—

Another blow—but this one stopped all thought, taking his head apart. No more shock. No more amazement.

No more Jimmie.

She put away the weapon, annoyed at herself. *Two* shots! "The Phantom Sniper," whoever he was, never fired more than once. But *he* was exceptional. She got goose bumps, just thinking about him.

Well, maybe next time she could drop her target in one. Anybody can miscalculate a shot. Nobody's perfect.

She left the roof area, walking calmly, took the elevator down to the garage, stowed her gun case in the trunk of the stolen Mustang, and drove away from the motel.

Poor Jimmie, she thought. It was just his bad luck to meet *me*. But that's the way it goes.

Janet Lakeley had a rule, and she never broke it: when you

237

bed down a guy in a new town you always target him the next day. She sighed. Usually it didn't bother her. Most of them were bastards. But not Jimmie. She'd enjoyed talking to him, playing her word games with him . . . bedding him. Too bad he had to die.

He seemed like a real nice guy.

William Campbell Gault

Apart from stints as a shoemaker and hotel manager in his native Milwaukee in the 1930s and as an infantryman during World War II, William Campbell Gault has spent his whole adult life as a self-employed writer. After several years as a prolific contributor to the pulps, he won an Edgar award for his first mystery novel, *Don't Cry for Me* (1952). Through the 1950s, Gault's reputation grew as one of the best of the hard-boiled school. Following the publication of *Dead Hero* (1963), Gault left the mystery field for nearly twenty years, concentrating on more lucrative juvenile sports novels. He and his best-known private eye, ex–Los Angeles Ram Brock (the Rock) Callahan, returned to the mystery scene in the 1980s, most recently in *The Chicano War* (1986).

Gault's other series private eye, Joe Puma, appeared in several paperback originals and one hardcover novel between 1953 and 1961. "—And Murder Makes Four!" probably Puma's first recorded case, has not been reprinted since its original appearance in *Detective Tales* in 1951.

William Campbell Gault

....

—and murder
makes four!

$\mathbf{A}$t ten o'clock, Dick phoned the room. "I think I've got something hot, Joe," he said. "Stay there until I get there, right?"

"Check," Joe said, not quite as interested as he should have been, perhaps. Dick was new to Globe and fairly young, with just a touch of the amateur's optimism.

So Joe said, "Check," and went back to the report he'd been working on for two hours. The Old Man wanted a resumé of the case activity so far, and there'd been a long trail. Hackensack to Miami and then to the West Coast.

It had been a month and a half ago that the Old Man had called him into his office. He'd been really hot. "Nobody," he'd said, "nobody in this bleeding world is going to take Globe for half a million. This is your baby, Joe. I'm giving you Dick Verch."

Somebody *had* taken Globe for half a million, so the Old Man's words were only partially true. Four smooth, capable, and well-prepared characters had done that in the Currency Transfer Company office in Detroit.

"Dick Verch is kind of young, Chief," Joe said. "I—"

"Dick Verch is kind of smart, too," the Old Man interrupted, "and he doesn't load the swindle sheet. I guess you'll be eating the same food and sleeping in the same kind of room. That way I'll *know* what's what."

That was the Old Man for you. Out to get a half million back, but worrying about the expense account.

Joe said, "So he'll save you a hundred and lose us a half million. The kid isn't ready." Then he said something that had seemed, later, like a premonition. "These boys have killed two men already."

"Joe, it's a bad morning to argue with me. I'm giving you Dick Verch. I'll want a report every day. Good luck." That had been Joe's dismissal.

Hackensack had followed, on a pigeon's tip, a tip that had extended to Miami and fizzled out. The Calumet Beach tip had come from the local sheriff. The Old Man must have screamed at the reports coming in from Calumet Beach.

Because all the hotels were resort hotels, and resort hotels have their own quaint conception of rates. They were terrific. If the four were still together, they were living very high in Calumet Beach.

Dick Verch was beginning to learn about expense accounts, despite his youth. Joe liked the kid more every day; they got along.

And the kid was a worker, out early and late, the way Joe had been before the depressing weight of his thirty-eight years and the corrosive action of rye and cynicism had dulled his fire.

Now, at ten o'clock on a Saturday morning, the lad had something "hot." In Hackensack and Miami, too, he'd seen smoke but found no fire.

So Joe said, "Check," and hung up. For which he was to feel guilty later. He'd been an operative too long for work that sloppy. He should have asked for more information than that.

He went back to the reports, finished them, signed them, took them down to the lobby, and mailed them. Then he went into the coffee shop to await the return of eager Richard Verch, the working operative.

He had a small but succulent sirloin steak on toast and a really inspired tossed salad. He was on his second cup of coffee when he was paged for a lobby phone call.

The voice was soft and masculine. "Puma? This is Sheriff Quintito. We've got a body here at the morgue requires some identification. Your boy, I guess."

"I'll be right down," Joe said.

Calumet was a county seat, and the morgue was in the basement of the courthouse. Quintito was waiting in his office, the door open, and he came along down to the basement with Joe.

"Two soft-nosed .38 slugs," Quintito said. "More than half of his face is gone. He'd better be fixed before his wife sees him."

Joe thought of Dick's wife, and a coldness moved through him. She had an idea Dick was a combination of Dick Tracy and Lord Peter Wimsey. Joe thought of Dick's four-year-old daughter. She thought Papa was Superman.

"He's a long way from his wife," Joe said. "There'll be time."

They went down a flight of worn terazzo steps. Joe kept his hand on the railing for support. This wasn't something a man could build up a tolerance for, not this kind of dying.

The sheriff hadn't been wrong. One blue eye stared up at Joe impersonally; there was no other. The white bone of his skull and jaw showed through in ragged splinters. Most of the mouth was gone, along with the right side of his face.

But it was Dick Verch, and Joe nodded.

"There'll be some papers upstairs," the sheriff said. His voice was soft and respectful.

"Whoever it was wasn't taking any chances, was he?" Joe said quietly. "Two soft-nosed .38's in the face. Where was Dick found?"

"In the men's washroom of the Spanish House. That's—"

"I know where it is," Joe said. "And what it is." His eyes moved to the sheriff's dark, broad face. "Who found him?"

"The porter. Went in there to clean up, around noon, and—"

"Went in there to clean up?" Joe said. "You mean nobody heard any shots? Two .38 slugs and nobody heard any shots? What the hell kind of story—"

"Easy, Mr. Puma. The man was your friend and you're excited. He was found there; it does not necessarily mean he was killed there."

"Why would he be moved to a place like that?"

The sheriff shrugged. "Who can read the mind of a man who uses soft-nosed bullets?"

Joe said quietly, "And if he wasn't killed there, how do you know what kind of slugs were used? Don't tell me they were still in his skull."

The sheriff shook his head. "I'll tell you nothing but the truth. I'm glad you're angry. It's about time."

Joe said patiently, "About the slugs. . . ?"

"They were on the floor beside the body. The killer is not only depraved, evidently—he is also contemptuous." He put his hand on Joe's shoulder. "Let's go upstairs." With his free hand he pulled the sheet back over the mutilated face of Dick Verch.

The sheriff's office seemed warm after the coolness of the basement.

"No reporters?" Joe said.

"Not yet. The proprietor of the Spanish House called me directly, and I thought it best to notify you before I called in the newspapers."

Joe looked at the phone and the sheriff nodded. Joe put through a wire to the Old Man and hoped the hopeless hope that the Old Man would be tactful in notifying Dick's wife.

Then he sat next to the sheriff's desk and managed to light a cigarette. His stomach was queasy; his heart was pounding. He said, "This Spanish House . . ."

The sheriff was grave, his eyes distant. "The proprietor is one of the—the older residents. Before the artists came, even, and the tourists, he was here. These older residents have some privilege beyond the law. There's gambling, for one thing. The pro-

William Campbell Gault

prietor's name is Dommaz. I don't think he'd have anything to do with murder. He doesn't go for violence."

"Gambling is one thing, you said. What are some of the others?"

Quintito studied Joe a few seconds. "I can only guess. He has boats. Perhaps dope, or duty-free gems, which is just my romantic mind. The boats, though, are seaworthy. He doesn't haul waste or garbage in them."

"Or use them for fishing?"

"Some, but only for his own guests and the patrons of his restaurant." Quintito's voice maintained its geniality as he said, "He's a friend of mine. In any interrogation, you'll be on your own."

"Without interference?"

Quintito nodded. "Unless, of course, he's molested."

Joe looked at the bland dark face and wondered what went on behind it. "And the city police?"

"We're all older residents. We all hate murder, and that includes Mr. Dommaz." A pause. "I'm glad, as I said before, you are finally angry, Mr. Puma. But take your time. Be very careful."

It wouldn't do any good to ask him what he meant, Joe knew. This was going to be one of Quintito's cryptic days. It was his message that had brought Joe to Calumet Beach. A partially burned leather bag had been found. It had been checked against the bags used by the Currency Transfer Company. It was identical.

But it hadn't been traced to anyone in Calumet Beach.

Joe said, "I'll be careful," and stood up. He put his cigarette out in the big glass ashtray on Quintito's desk. His hand had stopped trembling. "If you want me, you can leave a message at the hotel."

He went out, a big man and an angry one and a sick one, and stood for a moment on the curb, in the bright sunlight. A half block to his right was the water; the town spread east, north, and south from that.

It contained from twenty thousand to fifty thousand residents, depending on the season and the day of the week. It had started

244

its growth as an artists' colony and been vulgarized by tourists, real estate dealers, and dilettantes. But its basic beauty remained, behind the neon and the pseudo-Spanish and the sterile *moderne*.

The crackpots were here in great numbers, and four of them were killers. Dick's death had almost established that as fact now.

He went down to the stucco, flat-roofed building that housed the services of Boone and Diegel, Morticians. Dick's wife would need some kind of a face to look at before they buried him. Women were like that.

Then he went over to the Spanish House. It was set into the curve of the cliff next to the yacht basin, its wide veranda over the beach, supported by immense wooden piles black with age and water.

It was dim, coming in from the street side, cool and high ceilinged and peaceful, the hum of traffic outside distant and meaningless.

Peter Dommaz sat a table in one corner of the immense room. He was reading a book and drinking a cup of coffee. There was a silver pot of it on the small table in front of him.

He looked up as Joe came over, and he put his book down. He rose. "I am sorry about your friend." He indicated the chair across from him.

Joe sat down and Dommaz asked, "Some coffee?"

Joe nodded. "Thanks, I will."

A waiter was already bringing another cup and another silver pot.

Joe's eyes were on the waiter's hands, pouring the coffee, as he said, "I wonder why my friend should have been brought here. I understand he wasn't killed here."

"There was only a smear of blood on the floor," Dommaz said matter-of-factly. He was a thin man, tall, and with a strong face. His lips were thin, his teeth very white. He seemed very composed.

Annoyance stirred in Joe. He sipped his coffee.

Dommaz's eyes lifted to the doors facing on the balcony on

the east side of the room. "There are some big games, as you probably know, which go on in those rooms up there every night. All types of men come here. Occasionally they make me a proposition of one kind or another, something they know I might handle and involving a worthwhile profit." He paused.

Joe lighted a cigarette and said nothing.

The other man's gray eyes were humorously alight. "There is very little that goes on in Calumet Beach of which Peter Dommaz is not aware. There is nothing exceptionally profitable that goes on without my permission. It has been that way for twenty-five years. I had an offer the other night involving the transportation of four men by water to Mexico. I turned it down."

Joe was suddenly tense. He didn't stare at Dommaz or show any undue interest. "Four men—fleeing the country?"

"I suppose. It's an easy country to leave for anyone who isn't *seriously* wanted by the law. The kind of money this man offered, I realized his crime, or theirs, must have been stupendous. It must have included murder." Dommaz's smile was cool. "Any gentleman's code has rigid limits. Mine is considerably this side of murder."

"And Dick Verch's death?" Joe's eyes met the gray ones.

"Was a warning to me. I don't doubt I'll be approached again. They probably assume they've frightened me."

"And if they approach you?"

"I will point the man out to you, or see that you are informed."

"How about Sheriff Quintito, or the city police?"

"We have an agreement. They don't bother me, and I don't bother them." The strong, thin face stiffened. "I hate a killer, a pointless killer. I have watched you, Mr. Puma, and I think you could handle them very well. You have undoubtedly had experience with the type."

"Some. What'd this man look like? Do you know his name?"

"Not his name. He was very discreet. He had a rotten, coarse face but a very quick mind behind it. He wasn't anything I could describe. He looked like a composite photograph of a dozen rogue's gallery portraits. He'll be back."

"I wish you had told me this before Dick Verch had to die."

"There were two reasons why I didn't. I didn't consider it your business before that. You were a different man before that."

"Different?"

"Soft. But not now, are you?"

"No." Joe saw a door open on the balcony and a very shapely leg start to come through. Then the leg went back and the door closed.

Dommaz followed his gaze to the balcony, saw only the closed door, and returned to Joe. "Young Mr. Verch was married?"

Joe nodded. "Why?"

"I was thinking of his wife. It will be a terrible blow."

"There's a four-year-old daughter," Joe added. "The state police never bother you, Mr. Dommaz?"

"Only my conscience ever bothers me, Mr. Puma, and that very rarely."

A hard-shelled cutie, Joe thought. He wondered how much moxie Dommaz really had under the surface.

Again the door on the balcony opened and the leg came through, but this time the rest of the woman followed. A dark and definitely Spanish beauty with an arrogant tilt to her head and a firmly modeled body.

Her hair was pulled straight back, without ornament, her dress was black lace over some shimmering white fabric. She stood there, one hand on the balcony, surveying the room below.

Again Dommaz's gaze followed Joe's frankly appraising stare, and this time Dommaz said, "My wife. Isn't she beautiful?"

"She certainly is," Joe said, and there was no apology in the smile he gave Dommaz. "You're very lucky." He stood up. "Thanks for the help. I'm going back to the hotel for a bath and some work that has to be done. I'll come back here tonight."

Dommaz nodded and extended his hand. It was dry and thin,

247

an old man's hand. Joe took another glance at the balcony and wondered just how lucky Dommaz was.

If the old pirate was running dope, Joe ruminated, he'd be having trouble with the Feds. They don't play politics, not *that* branch of the federal government. And there didn't seem to be any secret about Dommaz being on the outer fringes of the law.

He walked back to the hotel slowly, thinking of Dick. By the time he turned into the lobby, he was thinking of the lady on the balcony. That first appearance by her could almost have been an invitation. But she was Dommaz's wife.

The clerk said, "Sheriff Quintito left a message for you to phone him when you returned, Mr. Puma."

Joe phoned from the lobby booth.

Quintito said, "We found a witness to two shots, about eleven o'clock, in the Custer Cove area. Just the sound of them, you understand, coming from north of his house."

"Thanks," Joe said. "Anyone new in that area, recently moved in?"

"We're checking that now. I'll keep you informed."

Joe thanked him again and hung up.

In his room, he stretched on the bed for twenty minutes, rubbing the back of his neck and staring at the ceiling. Then he sat at the small desk and wrote a long letter to the Old Man.

He emphasized the fact that he didn't want another partner, that he felt he'd do better on his own. That should please the old miser: He wrote:

> . . . a strange setup; a gent named Dommaz seems to
> have the crime rights in the town and he doesn't like
> murderers, he tells me. Think he's given me a lead. At
> any rate he's given me a cup of coffee and a handshake
> and we're on the same side of the fence at the moment.

After that he soaked in the tub for a half an hour. The sense of guilt for Dick's death stayed with him; he was the senior of the team—and he'd been careless.

He ate dinner at the hotel and went over to the Spanish House.

Most of the tables were occupied, and he went out onto the veranda. It would be cold here later; now the day's warmth still lingered.

From the dining room he could hear the music of a gypsy trio and below him he could hear the sound of the water slapping the piers. The highway in front was a major state artery, but the incessant clamor of its traffic was effectively muffled by the solid construction of the building.

Peace and profits and protection—a sweet setup. With scenery and good food, with a lovely wife. Joe's rye and water was halfway to his lips when he saw the lady in lace coming through the glass sliding doors leading from the restaurant proper.

She headed directly for him, and he rose.

"Mr. Puma?" Her voice was soft and pleasant.

He nodded. "And you're Mrs. Dommaz? I saw you this afternoon."

She nodded absently and took the chair across from him. Joe went over to help, but he was too late. A waiter came, bringing her some green fluid in a liqueur glass. He went away.

"I'm worried about my husband," she said. "He—he's not equipped to deal with killers."

"I think you underestimate him."

She shook her head stubbornly. "Everyone else overestimates him. He has the reputation from his younger days. He has the loyalty of influential men and undiminished courage but it is not enough, not for the kind of men who would—" Her voice broke.

"Who would do what was done to Dick Verch?"

She nodded without speaking. Her dark eyes searched Joe's face. She was sitting stiffly in her chair.

Joe said quietly, "Your husband has a good right arm now. Or maybe I should say right hand. A hand holding a gun. Me. I'm equipped to deal with killers, Mrs. Dommaz."

William Campbell Gault

"Is one man enough, and one gun, against four men and four guns?"

"We can't be sure of that. Your husband confides in you, doesn't he?"

"Always."

Joe said, "I think you can be sure that nothing will happen to your husband, not in this town."

She smiled wearily. "Those are his words." A pause. "He wants to know if the name Meredith Bentley means anything to you."

Joe nodded quickly. Meredith Bentley had been a long-time employee of the Currency Transfer Company who'd disappeared a year before the robbery. In a routine check of all former employees, the total disappearance of Meredith Bentley had seemed strange.

"That is the man who approached him regarding transportation."

"He lives here in town?" Joe asked.

"North of town, in the Custer Cove region. He came in right after you left this afternoon. My husband does not, of course, want his name mentioned if you interview this man."

"Of course. I'll need a car. Custer Cove is quite a distance from here, isn't it?"

She nodded. "I have my car, and I know the house. I'll be glad to drive you over."

"I wouldn't think of—"

She raised a hand. "It's my husband's wish."

She might as well have said "command"; it was in her tone. She went to get a cape while Joe paid for his drink.

The sun was going down now, a red ball reflected in the quiet water. The little coupé cut off the ocean road into a canyon road that climbed east toward the Custer hills. There was a sharp S turn just before they came to the summit, and she handled it very well, Joe thought.

The water was way below them now, and here was a house, its back to the road, its front facing the sea.

Joe's .38 was in the pocket of his jacket and his hand was firmly on it as he went up the path to the house. If Bentley should prove to be one of the four, it was clear he had separated from the others. This house wouldn't hold four people.

There was a small concrete stoop, and glass in the upper half of the front door. A face appeared in the glass before Joe rang the bell.

It was, as Dommaz had said, a coarse face. It was, at the moment, a scowling face, about on a level with Joe's.

The door opened, and the man said, "What the hell you selling?"

"Your name Bentley, Meredith Bentley?"

The eyes looked over Joe, and there was fear in them. His voice was ragged. "What gave you that idea? My name's Porterfield."

"Sorry," Joe said. "I made a—"

"Come in," the man said, and held the door wide.

Joe kept his hand in his pocket as he came in, and his eyes made a sweeping survey of the entire room. There were no other rooms.

The door closed and now Bentley stood with his back to it. There was a gun in his hand. A .45 automatic.

Joe's eyes lifted from the gun to meet Bentley's glare. Joe said quietly, "You didn't think I'd come unarmed, did you?"

Bentley's hand was shaking. "You're a cop. Just like that other."

"Don't make a mistake of tightening your finger," Joe said. "I'd like an excuse to kill you."

"Cop!" the man almost shouted, and Joe saw the finger tighten. Joe heard the roar of the .45 before he started to pour some lead himself.

Joe's third shot must have hit bone, for Bentley slammed back into the door as though he'd been hit by a truck. Then he crashed.

Joe saw the bloody face of Dick Verch in his memory. He looked down and saw the blood coming out of Bentley's stom-

251

ach. Just before he got sick he saw the wad of cardboard on the floor.

Three minutes later he was phoning the sheriff at his home. Mrs. Dommaz stood in the doorway, her face white, her eyes shocked.

"You'd better go," Joe said. "You'd best not get involved."

The sheriff's soft voice said, "Hello."

Joe said, "Puma, Sheriff. I came up here to 1342 Canyon Road to investigate a lead, and the character pulled a gun on me. He's dead, Sheriff."

"I see. I'll bring Chief Fuller along." A pause. "Wait for us."

Chief Fuller was head of the city force. Joe went out onto the concrete stoop in time to see Mrs. Dommaz's coupé make a U turn and head down toward the sea.

Joe fingered the wad of cardboard and watched the coupé disappear around a turn. It wouldn't be wise, he decided, to tell Sheriff Quintito about the cardboard.

The men who came with Fuller and Quintito were county men, deputies. They'd come quietly without a siren and they were all there, going over the house, when the ambulance came, just as quietly.

Only it wasn't an ambulance—it was a hearse from Boone and Diegel, Morticians.

Joe stayed out on the stoop until the body was carried to the hearse. Then he went in.

Quintito said, "We've found a little under a thousand dollars, Mr. Puma. Mostly in twenties. That money, though, wasn't identifiable, was it?"

Joe shook his head. "No wrappers?"

"None. We've found a driver's license issued to Meredith Bentley and another, from this state, issued to Harry Porterfield."

"Meredith Bentley, a man by that name, was a former employee of Currency Transfer," Joe said. "They'll have his prints on file there."

Quintito said, "You look sick, my friend. Why don't you go out and sit in my car? We'll be through here in a few minutes."

Joe smiled his thanks and went out. He wasn't used to this kind of cooperation from either city or county officers, and there wasn't any reason why he should expect it. It made him a little uncomfortable.

In a few minutes the sheriff came along the path with Chief Fuller. The sheriff got behind the wheel; the chief sat in back.

"You'll want a statement now, I suppose," Joe said.

"Tomorrow will be all right. It seems pretty clear that this Bentley or Porterfield must have been one of the gang."

"I'd give odds on it," Joe said. "But how much closer am I? This will just scare off the others."

"Maybe," Quintito said easily. "But Bentley's been living here for a year, in that house, alone."

"A year?" Joe said. "That would mean before the robbery."

Quintito nodded. "We'll check with the stores and the utility companies to see if he was gone for a time, the time when that company was robbed. I'll phone you in the morning. Take it easy. You be careful."

Joe looked over at the sheriff, but it was too dark in the car to see his face clearly. This was the damnedest case.

"Nobody's going to leave town," the sheriff said, "except the tourists, and we're always happy to see that."

Chief Fuller said nothing at all.

They dropped him at his hotel, and he went into the bar. He had two double shots of rye before he went upstairs. He should write to the Old Man, but he'd written to him twice today and telegraphed him once. Tomorrow morning would serve as well.

He fell asleep around midnight.

He was awakened by his phone. It was Mr. Boone, of Boone and Diegel. Dick Verch was ready to ship. Did Mr. Puma care to see him? There was some pride of accomplishment in the voice.

Joe said, "No," and hung up.

* * *

It was a bright, clean morning and the air coming in from the ocean side was warm. It was a Sunday morning, and the beach would probably be jammed. Though it was still early.

He put on his swim trunks and robe and went down the steps to the hotel's beach entrance. The beach was deserted.

The water was chilly at first, but he moved through it in a steady eight-beat crawl and he could feel the warmth of improved circulation moving through his body. He could feel the loosening of his big shoulder muscles and then the lassitude came.

He floated for a while, way out, riding the gentle swells, seeing nothing but the bright blueness of the sky overhead and closing his mind to the day before.

He was alive. He lived and was strong. The sun was bright and the water pleasant. He stayed out there for half an hour and then swam back leisurely.

A girl was standing at the water's edge, adjusting her bathing cap.

Her body was slim and firm, beautifully proportioned. Her face wasn't quite as young as her body, but it would do in any league. He couldn't see her hair but the coloring and the light blue eyes would indicate it was blond.

She smiled and said, "You're not a professional, by chance? You looked good out there."

"Professional?"

"Swimmer. Where did you learn to swim like that?"

"At Coney Island."

She made a face.

He smiled. "I could have thought of a lie, I suppose. About being a former intercollegiate champion. Or Olympic. I hope I didn't spoil your day."

Her laugh was as cheerful as the morning. "Honesty is always refreshing." She appraised him openly. "You're a guest at the hotel, aren't you? I've seen you in the dining room."

"I spend a lot of time there," Joe admitted, "but how could you see me without my seeing you?"

Again she laughed. "Before this gets out of hand, I'm married." She stretched her shoulders and took a tentative step toward the water. "Happily." A frown now, and some doubt. "Happily—I think."

Then she was running into the water.

Joe was grinning as he turned to watch her. She hit the water flat, in a shallow, racing dive, and went churning toward the open sea. She'd evidently done a lot of swimming herself.

He enjoyed his breakfast. He had a table on the patio overlooking the beach and he read the morning papers with his coffee.

After that he wrote to the Old Man about Meredith Bentley and then phoned the sheriff. He said, "I didn't know if you realized last night that today would be Sunday, Sheriff. Be at your office a while yet?"

"Until noon, at least."

Joe was over there in twenty minutes and he made out his own report on the machine in the sheriff's office.

The sheriff said, "Bentley was gone from Calumet Beach for about two weeks in January. That checks, doesn't it?"

Joe nodded. "There's no doubt in my mind about him. It would need to be one hell of a coincidence if he was innocent. But who else? And the money?"

Quintito shrugged. His broad face was weary and his brown eyes heavy with fatigue. "I'm not thinking so well this morning. It will be their move next. Yesterday should smoke something out."

"I wish Meredith had lived long enough to talk," Joe said.

Quintito smiled. "That's a change from your state of mind last night. Last night you probably wished only that he had lived. This is more professional."

"Yesterday was a bad day," Joe told him.

He went down the bright street toward the sea. The ocean road was dotted with morning traffic now, and the beach was being populated.

Again there was that sense of seclusion as he left the bright street for the dimness of the Spanish House.

Peter Dommaz was out on the veranda. The silver coffeepot and the book were with him. There were only a few diners on the porch, and they were at the other end.

Dommaz smiled and gestured toward the coffeepot.

Joe sat down and shook his head. "Thanks, no. I've had four cups already this morning. Don't you think that was dangerous, sending your wife along last night?"

Dommaz said, "There is a line I read somewhere—'Look not too long from the bright face of danger.' Do you recognize it?"

Annoyance stirred in Joe. "No, but I'm practically illiterate. It probably wasn't meant for women."

"You're old-fashioned, Mr. Puma." The gray eyes were amused. "They fly, they engage in all athletics, they even wrestle in the mud."

Joe lighted a cigarette. "I wonder if this business will scare off the others."

"We'll have to wait and see."

"If the house was watched, they might have recognized the car. That would involve you."

"No more than I already am. Killers don't frighten me."

"They frighten me," Joe said. "They scare the hell out of me. Sane people are bad enough, but you can't figure a killer. I like to know what to expect."

"No, you don't, or you wouldn't be in this business." Then Dommaz was looking past Joe and frowning faintly.

Joe looked up to see Mrs. Dommaz standing there. "I wanted to say hello to Mr. Puma. And tell him how—how I admire him."

Joe was standing now. "Admire me?"

"The way you went up to that house, not knowing if there was one man waiting there, or if there were four. You looked so . . . heroic."

Joe smiled. "Sit down and have some coffee and tell me more, Mrs. Dommaz." He pulled out a chair and held it.

Dommaz seemed faintly displeased. Mrs. Dommaz had left her señorita role behind; she was in white linen today and looking scrumptious.

Dommaz said, "Mr. Puma is waiting for you to be seated, dear."

Her face showed no annoyance. She sat down, and Dommaz gestured to a waiter.

When the man came, Dommaz said, "Some more coffee, Alan."

But Mrs. Dommaz said, "Not for me. Rye and water, Alan."

Dommaz said quietly, "It's not yet noon. It's still morning, Eve."

The waiter paused, looking from one to the other. Mrs. Dommaz said, "Rye and water, Alan. And you, Mr. Puma?"

"The same," Joe said.

The waiter went away. Dommaz said, "Mr. Puma was just telling me how much killers frighten him."

She looked at Joe.

He said, "Every time, I get the heebie-jeebies. I must have met a million of them."

"If you do, you conceal it very well. You didn't look frightened last night, Mr. Puma. You looked very sure of yourself."

"I had a staunch ally," he said.

Dommaz said, "I don't like to be rude, but I must leave you. I've an appointment for eleven."

He rose with dignity and left.

Eve shook her head. "You wouldn't know that he started out as a fisherman, would you? Half Swede and half Portuguese and now he's got most of the town thinking he's a Spanish gentleman."

"And you're his señora."

"From Park Falls, Minnesota. Got stranded in this salt-water tank town, Mr. Puma, and he was the biggest frog in the puddle. I've had almost enough."

"What book is that he's reading?" Joe said. "It looks like the same one, in limp leather."

"It is the same one, a book of poems. Browning, I think, though I've forgotten. He's been carrying it for years. He must be a slow reader."

Joe finished his drink and said, "I wonder if all marriages are as happy as yours?" He grinned at her. "It's a cold, cruel world beyond these walls, Eve."

"Let's have another rye," she said. She beckoned to a waiter.

The drinks came, and she lifted hers high, in salute. Joe answered it and said, "I wouldn't treat Peter Dommaz with any scorn. You know better than that."

She looked at him steadily. "You *are* frightened. Peter was right about that."

"And you were, too, last night. That was no act. You were about two breaths away from passing out."

She looked at her glass.

"And now you're restless," Joe went on, "and still frightened. What cooks, Park Falls?"

She looked up to meet his gaze. "Nothing cooks. I'm fed up. I've been trying to remember what *young* men are like."

"Don't look at me," Joe said. "I'm thirty-eight." Then: "Dick Verch was a young man. Did you meet him, Mrs. Dommaz?"

Her eyes were stones. "Never. What are you saying, Joe?"

"Just putting words together. He was a good-looking boy. You'd have enjoyed knowing him. Had a lot of sparkle."

She finished her drink and stood up. "I don't think I want to hear any more about him." She turned and went back into the dining room.

Joe ate a big dinner that noon, keeping an eye peeled for the blond. But she didn't appear. He was up in his room when Quintito phoned.

"Another corpse," Quintito said. "That motel about two blocks from where you are, the El Rancho. You know it?"

"I know it," Joe said. "Redwood fence along the front?"

"That's it."

"In five minutes," Joe told him.

It was a standard western motel, with brands on the room doors instead of numbers, and on the furniture. With imitation Navajo rugs and pseudo-Remington prints. With refrigerator and electric range and steel shower stall.

This one varied from the others only because of the man on the floor.

A big man, with red hair, with a surprised look in his bleak blue eyes. With his throat cut from ear to ear.

Quintito said, "Slugged first and then sliced. Like a steer in the slaughterhouse. His registry name is Paul Duncan."

Joe said, "I've met him before. His police blotter name is Red Hogan and he's known as a rough lad in Chicago and Detroit. Find anything?"

"Six hundred dollars. Some wrappers." Quintito held them up, two stiff paper bands used to wrap currency. They were stamped CURRENCY TRANSFER COMPANY, DETROIT.

"When'd it happen?"

"We don't know yet. After we learn when he ate, we'll know better."

"I wonder why he died," Joe said.

Quintito said, "There were four men to divide a half million, and now there are two."

"I can't believe that anyone as experienced as Red Hogan would leave the company wrappers on stolen currency," Joe said. "It doesn't make any kind of sense. That's amateur stuff, and Red wasn't an amateur."

The black wagon of Boone and Diegel was again pulling up to the front of the unit. A small man with a small bag was climbing into his coupé a few units up. The doctor.

The sheriff said, "Expected Fuller would be here, but he's

259

taken the family on a picnic. Some guys only work six days a week."

Joe turned to face him. "You know more about all this than I do, don't you, Sheriff?"

Quintito's voice was mild, his face impassive. "You *know* everything I do."

"But you suspect some things?"

The sheriff looked at Joe steadily. "Nothing I'd voice. My imagination is active. You've no complaints, have you, Joe?"

"I've been treated very well," Joe agreed. "Only—and this is a big only—Globe Protection and Currency Transfer are kind of cold-blooded about a deal of this kind. They'd rather have the money than the men, especially when the money comes to half a million. I've got the damnedest feeling that I'm never going to see that money."

"Two men to go," Quintito said easily. "When you get to the last man, you'll probably get to the money."

"Not if I get to the last man dead," Joe argued. "This is beginning to look like an epidemic."

"The death of Mr. Verch," Quintito told him, "was the first murder in this county in eight months. The three deaths in the last two days can all be tied to the robbery."

They had Red on the stretcher now, and they were covering him with a sheet.

Quintito's voice went on: "Something that happened yesterday, something, probably, that Mr. Verch discovered has set off a fuse. Four men with half a million between them have had a month and a half to speculate on how easy it would be to raise their proportionate share. Yesterday they started to put their thoughts into action."

Joe was looking out the window. "A theory."

"But logical. Are *you* telling *me* everything you know, Joe?"

Joe didn't answer for a moment. Finally he said, "A private operative has certain loyalties to his sources of information—"

Quintito raised a hand. "Save it. Both Fuller and I are working with you and you know it. You wouldn't get this kind of cooperation anywhere else in the country. Isn't that right?"

Joe smiled at him. "That's right. Well, drive me back to the hotel, nice and slow, and I'll unburden my heart."

Now Quintito smiled. "Good."

Joe took it from the moment he'd left the sheriff's office the day before and told him every incident and bit of dialogue up to the present.

When he'd finished, Quintito didn't look so weary. He said, "I'm glad you told me all this. And you probably will be, too. Be very careful, won't you, Joe?"

Joe nodded and climbed out of the car. He paused a moment. "When the last one is dead, you'll tell me your side, won't you, Sheriff?"

The sheriff put out both hands, palms upward. "What I know, you know. What I think is not evidence and possibly not even pertinent. Keep in touch."

The car made a U turn and headed back toward the courthouse. Joe went into the hotel, up to his room, and picked up the phone. He put through a person-to-person call to the Old Man at his home—collect.

The old boy started to splutter as soon as he was on, but Joe interrupted. "I'm getting writer's cramp," he said. "You'll read, tomorrow or Tuesday, that I shot and killed a man named Bentley, Meredith Bentley, last night and another man was killed, but not by me, today. This man's name is Red Hogan, and there was some CTC money in his room. I want all the dope you can get on both of them. I'd like it in a night letter, tonight, if that's possible. Or a straight wire tomorrow. Got that?"

The Old Man's voice was exceptionally meek. "Got it."

"If I remember the dope on Bentley right," Joe continued, "he had a brother who'd taken off about the same time he did, or a little later. Will you check that?"

"Of course. Do you have to take long-distance time to tell me my business? How much money have you recovered?"

"A little under sixteen hundred, and we're not sure all of it is CTC money."

"Fine," the Old Man said. "Dandy. That should pay for your lunches. Sixteen hundred dollars! Goodbye."

Joe stretched out on the bed and rubbed the back of his neck, staring at the ceiling. He fumbled in his pocket for a cigarette and brought out the wad of cardboard instead. He looked at it for a moment and then flung it savagely at the opposite wall.

He was the guy in the middle and he had a million theories, but they weren't any more than that. Any operative above the hotel dick level would know just about what was going on, but nothing short of a Fed would be able to do anything about it.

He sat up on the edge of the bed, found a cigarette, lighted it, and stared moodily at the phone. A little later, he shaved and got dressed.

In deference to local mores, he wore no tie with his sport shirt. He slipped into a baggy and fuzzy tweed sport jacket and went down to the bar.

The blond was there. Only she wasn't a blond, she was a redhead and she looked as nice in white silk as she had in the bathing suit. She was at a table, all alone, and she waved.

Joe went over. "Waiting for someone?"

"My husband, but sit down anyway. I've come away without my purse. And I'm thirsty."

"Is your husband big?" Joe sat down and beckoned to a waiter.

"About fifty pounds lighter than you, I'd say. Very modern, too. He won't mind at all. Sometimes I wish he'd be a little more unreasonable."

The waiter was there now, and she ordered Scotch, Joe rye. Then she said, "What do you do?"

"I'm a lifeguard, up at Redondo. What do you do, besides wait for your husband?"

"Pick up lifeguards. Where's Redondo?"

"Up north a ways."

"Is it nice?"

"It's horrible. They're all horrible—Redondo, Manhattan Beach, Hermosa. Beach towns."

"This is a beach town."

"It isn't quite as bad. The girls are prettier."

She picked at the edge of the blotting-paper coaster with one scarlet nail. "I wonder what's keeping Don."

"Some blond. Married long?"

"Two years." She took a swallow of her drink and went back to picking at the coaster. "All men are wolves, more or less, aren't they? I knew that before I was married. But it doesn't mean anything, does it?"

"I refuse to answer on the grounds that I might incriminate myself. Look, I'm not Dorothy Dix. Don't say anything that you'll be embarrassed about later."

"I don't embarrass," she said, and looked at him. "I wasn't speaking personally, just making conversation. I'm from Ohio. Where are you from?"

"Brooklyn."

"Everybody out here's *from* someplace, aren't they? Aren't there any natives?"

"Some. That man who runs the Spanish House for instance."

She looked up quickly. "Are you speaking of Peter Dommaz?" Her eyes were wide.

Joe nodded, watching her face. "Know him?"

"Of course. You know about . . . You're teasing me."

"Believe me, Red, I'm not teasing you. What is it?"

"Eve Dommaz, that old man's wife. She's the one Don—" She broke off, shaking her head.

"Oh," Joe said.

"The señorita," Red said bitterly. "The gracious, ladylike, mysterious, beautiful—"

"She's from some place, too," Joe said. "She's from Park Falls, Minnesota."

"You're joking! Are you serious?"

Joe raised his right hand aloft. "Gospel truth. She told me

263

that this afternoon. She told me also she was getting fed up with the old goat and this salt-water tank town."

"Fed up with the town, with her husband? That might mean—"

"It might mean nothing. Her husband is very well fixed, and this town might not be perfect, but it's probably better than Park Falls. With girls like Eve, it's mostly talk."

"You don't know Don," Red said. "He's—he's irresistible."

"To you. Have another drink."

"I haven't hardly started this."

"Bottoms up," Joe said.

She downed her drink, closed her eyes, opened them, and smiled. The waiter brought over another pair and set them on the table.

She said, "What's your name?"

"Joe Puma. And yours?"

"Mary Delahunt. Mrs. Donald Delahunt. Don't forget that *Mrs.* if I get drunk."

"I'll try. What does Don do to keep the wolf from the door?" Joe asked.

"Investments. He sells investments. Stocks and bonds and like that. He does very well, too."

"And now you're on your vacation?"

She shook her head. "Don makes a living wherever we go. He's clever. He says the nice thing about his job, we can live anywhere, just anywhere."

Joe fiddled with his glass. She was young, but not that young. He asked, "How old are you, Mary?"

"Twenty-six, though *gentlemen* don't ask questions like that. What are you thinking about?"

"About Donald Delahunt. That's a nice job he's got. Maybe that's why he spends some time with Eve Dommaz. Maybe he's trying to sell her husband some bonds or something."

"You've seen her," she said. "If you knew Don, you wouldn't say that. He's susceptible to women like that, is all. But he'll come out of it. He's got to come out of it." Her voice was strained.

"If I had a wife like you—" Joe began.

But she interrupted with a whispered, "Here he comes now. Isn't he handsome?" Joe turned to look, rising from his seat.

The gent approaching the table had a crew haircut and a face that could have been twenty or forty. The hair was blond, sun-bleached, the smile engaging, the sport coat nothing you could pick up under a hundred dollars.

"He certainly is," Joe said.

There seemed to be, for only a fraction of a second, a hint of bleakness in the smile of Donald Delahunt. Then the charm came back into that boyish face and he smiled at Joe.

Mary said, "Don, this is Joe Puma. He's been trying to get me to run away with him."

"Without success," Joe said.

Don's handshake had the firm, friendly strength of all confidence men. He sat down, and Joe did, too.

Mary said, "Joe's a lifeguard, up at Redondo Beach."

"Is he?" Don's smile showed what he thought of *that*. "Are you drunk, baby?"

"Not yet. Where have you been?"

He was still smiling. "Later. We don't want to fight in front of the other man."

"Don't we?" She looked up at her husband, and she was no lightweight for the moment.

Joe said, "I'll be running along. I really shouldn't . . ."

Mary waved him to silence, watching her husband.

"Don't go," Don said. "I've been working on a pretty big deal, and I've got to go back. I just dropped in to tell you that."

"How big, Don? About a hundred and ten pounds?"

"You're sounding like a wife," Don said. "That's enough, kid." He wasn't smiling now.

She looked at him, started to say something, and was silent.

Joe wanted to reach over and get a good grip on the crew haircut. He wondered what a good right hand would do to that boyish face. He reached for a cigarette and lighted it like the heavy in a B picture.

Mary said, "Don, I thought we'd planned on driving up the coast. I thought . . ."

Don turned to Joe. "Tell her about the Sunday traffic. Maybe she'll listen to you."

Their drinks came.

Don lifted his and said, "Success." He sipped it and put it down. "Baby, if I close this deal today, you'll see so much of me you'll get sick. This one's the biggest yet, believe me."

She looked at him steadily. "I want to believe you, Don. But I've believed you before." She lifted her glass. "Success."

Don said to Joe, "She's a reasonable woman, most of the time. She wouldn't be human if she didn't get these little spells."

"I'll remember that in case she leaves you for me," Joe said. "Wives don't always understand about . . . business."

Don was smiling again.

Joe wondered if Don knew what kind of league he was playing in. Messing with Peter Dommaz's wife could be rockier than three-card monte.

Don finished his drink and stood up. "You be a good girl. I might not be back for a couple hours, or even longer." He turned to Joe. "Glad to have met you, Mr. Puma. Proceed with caution."

Joe nodded. "Luck, Mr. Delahunt."

Delahunt was almost at the door when Mary said, "Damn him! I've got all kinds of rotten words I'm thinking, Joe. But maybe he's telling the truth."

"Maybe."

"We've been here almost a year," she said. "A month and a half ago he went back east on some big deal. That was going to be the biggest one, too. After he came back from that, we were going to Rio. I'd love South America, he told me. Don was going to retire, at *his* age, and it was going to be such fun, in Rio."

And Donald made three, Joe thought. He said, "Did you ever meet a gent named Dick Verch, Mary?"

She shook her head. "Verch? No . . ." Then she was staring. "That's the name of the man who was killed in the Spanish House. That's the name that was in the paper this morning."

Joe nodded. "I knew him. I just wondered."

"Joe, the *Spanish House*. What's—"

"Nothing. Just coincidence. I was thinking of Dick because we were thinking of Eve Dommaz. There's no connection." He shook his head impatiently. "I'm hungry, aren't you?"

She nodded. "I suppose I shouldn't be, with all the unrequited love burning in me. But I am."

"Stay right here," he said, "and discourage all advances. I'll be back."

He went into the lobby and up to the desk. He asked the clerk, "Is it possible to rent a car on Sundays in this town?"

"Certainly, sir. I'll have one brought around. A convertible?"

"A nice, big flashy convertible," Joe said, and pictured the Old Man's wrath. "Will it take long?"

"About three minutes."

Joe went back to the bar. Mary had finished her drink. He asked, "Have you ever had shish kebab, or pilaf?"

"What's that?"

"Shish kebab is lamb, roasted on a spit. With roasted tomatoes and peppers. Pilaf is rice cooked in chicken broth."

She made a face. "I don't like rice."

"You've never had rice, not in Ohio. I personally guarantee you'll love every grain. It's a little Armenian place, up in the mountains."

"You're being kind," she said. "Why should I spoil your day?"

"How do you know you will? If you don't go, I'll go up there alone."

"Oh, Joe," she said and rose.

The convertible was a Buick, black as sin and big as a house. Joe cut it into the six-lane flow of Sunday traffic feeling like a king.

Mary said, "You're not really a lifeguard at Redondo are you, Joe?"

He kept his eyes on the road. "What makes you think I'm not?"

"They're big and dumb and they don't drive cars like this."

"I'm big and dumb, and I rented this car. Mary, try to have a good time. Try to grow up a little. You're going to have to, one of these days."

"You mean try to stop loving Don?"

"I mean try to stop thinking he's the sun and the moon. Try to think of him as another guy with a crew haircut in a world full of his kind. Stop thinking of him as special as much as you can."

"Is this a pitch?"

"No. He could disappoint you, is what I'm trying to say. And why not be a little ready for it?"

"I know," she said. "I'm twenty-six and I know what you mean. We left Cleveland in an awful hurry, and I wouldn't let myself think about the why of it. I've been afraid to ask myself any questions. I wanted it to be the way it seemed. I suppose that's infantile."

"A little of it's all right; we need it to live. You're wiser than I realized. Let's think about the pilaf."

At Gulliver's Gorge they left the pounding traffic of the highway and cut between the rolling hills in a steady climb.

"Park Falls," Mary said and started to chuckle.

Andrikian's was in the valley beyond Moravo, and Papa Andrikian was at the cash register near the door, a smile on his face.

"Welcome again," he said. "I told you you'd be back." He smiled at Mary. "And this is Mrs. Puma?"

"For the afternoon," Joe said. "How's the kebab?"

"Never better."

Andrikian hadn't lied. The outside crisp, the inside juicy. Mary ate more pilaf than any lady should.

"It's wonderful," she said. "I'm not even thinking about Don, much. It's delicious."

They had a few drinks after that and then took the Buick up into the Valos Migra hills, winding and climbing to the cliff that overhung the sea. He stopped in front of the stone bumper-barricade.

The moon was full and there was a radio in the Buick. Joe lighted a pair of cigarettes and handed one to Mary.

"It is beautiful, isn't it?" she said. "When all the people are around, you forget how beautiful this country can be. What it must have been before the people came."

He nodded, saying nothing.

"Do you want to kiss me, Joe?" she asked. "I wouldn't mind."

"I don't want to kiss anybody who wouldn't mind," he told her. "Mary, why don't you go back to Ohio?"

"Are you serious?"

"I've never been more serious. Your boy's no good, Mary."

"Joe! That's rotten."

"Mary, I'm not a lifeguard. I'm a detective, and a damned fool, to boot. Don knows I'm a detective. Your Don is a confidence man who's in love with his own superintelligence. Right now he's over his head and doesn't know it. He's smack in the middle of mass murder, and maybe he *does* know it, but I can't be sure."

"Joe, you're not . . . Why should I . . . How can I believe you?" Her hand was gripping his arm like a vise.

"You've got to believe me. And I think you do."

"You followed Don here?"

"I followed the gang. A gang who held up the Currency Transfer Company in Detroit in January, killed two guards, and took off with half a million dollars. Two of the men have been killed here in the last two days, a man named Meredith Bentley and another named Red Hogan."

"In Detroit—in January? Don sent me presents from Detroit in January. That was where the big deal was, at the time."

"Believe me now?"

She didn't answer. She was crying. She was crying quietly, and then she began to sob and Joe could feel the tremor of her body transmitted through the springs of the seat.

I am probably, Joe thought, the lousiest operative currently west of the Rockies. Spilling my guts to the gang through the wife of one of them.

She said shakily, "I—I can't go back there now. Knowing what I've suspected right along, Joe, I can't—"

"You can get another room."

"At another hotel. Joe, I can't face him. I'm frightened."

"You get another room for tonight," he said. "I'll see you tomorrow, and we'll figure something out. I'll want to have a talk with the sheriff, first."

"The sheriff?"

"And the chief of police. They're working along with me; they've been unusually cooperative. I don't hide anything from them."

He started the motor and backed around to take the road down. He said, "Some other time I'll kiss you, Mary, and you'll enjoy it. And if not me, some guy. This world is full of guys."

"Let's not talk," she said. "Let's not say anything."

They didn't. He drove back to Calumet Beach through the now thinning traffic, planning his moves ahead. What she was thinking of, he couldn't know, but she'd been all right.

He checked her in at another hotel and told her, "You can get by for tonight. Tomorrow you can have your stuff sent over."

"Okay. Be careful, Joe," she said softly.

"You too."

She stood on tiptoe to kiss him on the cheek.

He drove back to his hotel, thinking of everything and nothing. He left the Buick at the curb and asked the clerk, "Any calls?"

"A man to see you, sir. You're through with the car?"

Joe nodded. "The keys are in it. Where's this man?"

"In the corner of the lobby, over there, sir. He's been waiting two hours."

Joe saw the high chair in the shadows near the deserted cigar stand and the head protruding above the high back. He walked over. He had his key in his left hand; his right was inside his jacket.

The man sitting there was tall and his face was in partial shadow. "Detective Puma?" he asked.

Joe nodded.

"I've some information for you."

"Who are you? What's your name?"

"I'm a guy who's been on a long trail. My name is Fred Englestadt. That name mean anything to you?"

One of the guards who'd been killed in Detroit had been named Englestadt. Joe said, "A brother?"

"That's right. I've got a house I want you to look at."

"I'm not in the market for a house, Fred. If it's something to do with the robbery, Sheriff Quintito or Chief Fuller will help you."

"My brother's dead," the man went on. "I'm not looking for a cop. I've seen too many scared juries and crooked judges in my time."

"Your brother may be dead," Joe said easily, "but his name wasn't Englestadt. Because that gent didn't have a brother, just two sisters, both married. And if your brother's name is Bentley, he was framed; there was a blank cartridge in the firing chamber and the mechanism didn't work after the first wad of cardboard came singing out. I didn't know his gun was a lemon or I wouldn't have killed him."

"This thing I've got in my hand isn't a lemon," the man said.

271

Joe looked closer and saw it wasn't. It looked like a .38 from where he stood.

The man said, "I don't know if you've got a bellyache or if your hand's on your gun. But I could put five shots into you before you'd pull it, and then you would have a bellyache. Five soft-nosed slugs."

"What difference does it make if I die here or at the house," Joe said. He could feel the sweat running down under his arms and along his back.

"Maybe you've got a story," the man said, "and maybe it even makes sense. But I don't figure to hear it here. It's too close to the courthouse."

"You're always going to be too close to the courthouse," Joe told him. "You'll never get smart enough to get out of its shadow."

The man said, "You want to die here and now? Or see a house?"

The sweat was soaking Joe's collar now. He said, "I'll take a look at it."

"Put your hands down then at your sides and head for the door. I'll be behind you."

Joe stole a glance at the clerk, but he was busy at a writing desk, his view screened by the service desk all around him. Joe put his hands at his sides and headed for the door.

"Turn right," the man said, and Joe turned right.

There was a Plymouth coupé there, and the gun prodded Joe's spine. "Get in. Slide in behind the wheel."

Joe slid in. The keys were in the ignition.

Bentley said, "Turn the key all the way; that starts it. You know the way to the house."

Joe started the motor and headed for Custer Cove. He said, "You killed Dick Verch?"

"That's right. He was just another dick, but he had his uses."

"As a warning to Dommaz?"

"Dommaz had the idea he could cut down the split by cutting down the jerks. That would mean Red and my brother and me.

He put Verch on my trail. I gave him back to him. I left the slugs behind, so there'd be no doubt in his mind."

"Dommaz must have been the cutie who fixed your brother's gun," Joe said. "Why don't you go for him, instead of me?"

"I've got time for both of you."

"He fixed your brother's gun and sent me up there, loaded. You've got the wrong pigeon, Bentley."

"Maybe. I'm not bright. Dommaz is; he planned the deal. Meredith and I were here for a vacation, and we planned it all right there at the Spanish House. Dommaz did the thinking, him and Delahunt. They're still doing the thinking, and maybe you're in on it, huh?"

"You said it all when you said you're not bright, Bentley." Joe was moving along about forty now. "You're trigger-happy. You're going to shoot yourself out of half a million dollars. How long do you think Delahunt and Dommaz will be buddies? With Delahunt making time with Dommaz's wife?"

"A lot of guys have made time with Eve," Bentley said. "If Delahunt is, with that doll he's got, he's dumber than I figured."

"He won't be so dumb when he takes off for Rio with half a million coconuts."

"He won't be taking off for Rio, not unless he does it in the next twenty minutes. He's not going anyplace."

Forty-five now, and here was the road leading up. Here was the bluff, and Bentley said, "Cut it down, monkey."

Joe swung, as though cutting into the side road. But partway through the turn he straightened the wheels again. The nose of the Plymouth was headed right for the bluff.

Joe was braced. Bentley tried to brace himself too late. The Plymouth smashed into the bluff, and Bentley went up, crashing into the windshield.

For a split second, Joe was motionless, his wind gone from hitting the steering wheel. Then his hand was reaching for his gun.

He caught Bentley across the temple, just as his head turned. Bentley slumped forward, and Joe thought of Dick Verch. Joe slammed him twice more with the barrel of his .38, right at the base of the skull . . .

Beyond the sheriff's office, there was another, larger room and Joe went in there. A deputy lounged at the desk behind the railing, reading a colored comic section.

Joe said, "I've got a killer out in the luggage deck of his car outside. Man who killed Dick Verch."

The deputy got to his feet, frowning. "Oh, yeah. You're Puma. I'll be right with you."

Joe handed him the keys. "You might call the sheriff and tell him I'm going to the Spanish House. He'll probably be glad to hear it. He's probably been waiting to hear it."

The deputy grinned. "We couldn't be sure, and Dommaz is a big man around here. You want a couple of the boys to go along with you?"

Joe shook his head. "This is getting personal. That guy in the deck could be dead or alive. I didn't check."

"Fearless Fosdick," the deputy said and grinned again.

"And if you're not too busy," Joe said, "you could send a man or two over to the Hacienda to pick up Donald Delahunt. He was one of the four." He reached over and put Bentley's gun on the desk.

"Delahunt. That makes four, Puma."

"Yeah. Dommaz was a kind of fifth wheel, the brain. I'll walk over." He turned and went out.

It wasn't quite midnight, and the Spanish House was still doing business. About half the tables were occupied. So was the one in the corner, though there was no book there, or even the usual pot of coffee, tonight.

Dommaz looked tired and he didn't smile as Joe slid into the chair across from him.

"Waiting for Eve?" Joe asked.

Dommaz's chin lifted.

"She's out with Delahunt," Joe went on, "figuring what they're going to do with the half million."

Dommaz's eyes flashed and then dulled. "I've . . . It's apparent I've made some mistakes."

"Your first mistake," Joe told him, "was when you stopped selling haddock and started reading Browning. That put you in another league. You're just a busher, Peter. Your second mistake was marrying that señorita from Park Falls. But I think your biggest one was trying to play me for a fish. I've met too many really skilled operators. It wasn't enough to be the big man in this town—you had to send a raiding party to Detroit. That's a major-league town. And now you're nothing, you're a laughingstock. Even your wife is laughing at you—right now— in another man's arms. Browning isn't going to do you any good at all."

Dommaz opened his mouth and closed it. His hand went below the table, and when it came out there was a small pearl-handled revolver in it.

Joe ducked, but there was no need to.

Dommaz put the barrel of the gun into his mouth before he pulled the trigger . . .

The clerk said, "Seven o'clock, Mr. Puma."

"Thanks," Joe said. He got up and shaved and put on his bathing trunks. He inspected his hair and studied his profile and went lithely through the hotel lobby and down the steps to the beach.

The beach was deserted.

The water was chilly at first, but he moved through it in a steady eight-beat crawl and he could feel the warmth of improved circulation moving through his body. He could feel the loosening of his big shoulder muscles, but the lassitude wouldn't come.

He floated for a while, way out, riding the gentle swells, seeing nothing but the bright blueness of the sky overhead, thinking of Mary, but not looking toward the shore.

He was alive. He lived and was strong. The sun was bright and the water refreshing. He swam back leisurely, his head par-

275

tially submerged most of the time, careful not to look at the beach.

Everything must be the same as yesterday.

But when he finally came to the shallow water, when he finally stood up, the beach was still deserted.

Jerk, he thought. What a ham I am. She didn't even stay here last night. I took her to a different hotel and forgot all about it.

Quinito was smiling when Joe walked in. He held out a hand. "Congratulations."

Joe took it without smiling. "Who's talked, and what have they said?"

"Bentley talks and talks, saying enough. He's delirious."

"He didn't die?"

"No, though he was slugged hard enough. Did you want him to die, Joe?"

"Wouldn't it be best? As you said last night, where will you find twelve heroes? Where will you find twelve men without families, who will sit in judgment on a killer with friends? Justice can be a little twisted in a case like that. We're professionals, but those people in the jury box aren't. They've no desire to look at the bright face of danger."

Quintito smiled. "You're all wound up."

"Maybe. And now we get to you, which is along the same line. Your job, or one of them, is to apprehend criminals. You suspected Dommaz, didn't you? But he was a big man in this town. Too big for you to haul in on a murder rap."

"That's right. And if I was wrong, I would no longer be sheriff. And how many criminals would I apprehend without the job? We do the best we can, Puma, but we're servants of the people—and you know what the people are."

"All right. It's too early to argue. What about the money? What about Delahunt?"

"The money is in a safe-deposit box at the local Security National branch. Dommaz had a key and so did Delahunt."

"And Delahunt?"

"Made the mistake of resisting arrest." Quintito's voice was soft, his face bland. "He was killed, resisting arrest."

"That makes five dead here and two in Detroit. The only one that really mattered here was Dick Verch." Joe expeled his breath. "I'll be over at the hotel, if you want me. Mrs. Delahunt's in the clear?"

"If you want her in the clear," Quintito said.

"I do. She may go back to Ohio or she may even wind up in Brooklyn. But first we want to see if it's true what they say about Yosemite. I'm getting to like this country of yours."

Gary Brandner

Michigan-born Gary Brandner graduated from the University of Washington and worked as an advertising copywriter and an aircraft industry technical writer before becoming a full-time freelancer in 1969. He has written several novels, the best known of which, *The Howling* (1977), was made into a successful film. Brandner has contributed over fifty short stories to *Ellery Queen's Mystery Magazine*, and other periodicals, and has created two series private eyes, Adam Dukane and Stonebreaker.

"The Pigeon Hunters," which first appeared in *Alfred Hitchcock's Mystery Magazine*, is the only one of the Stonebreaker tales that has not been previously anthologized.

Gary Brandner

the pigeon hunters

I was too late. The black and white L.A.P.D. cars in front of the house told me that. As I parked my heap another police car, this one unmarked, pulled up and Dave Pike stepped out. Dave was a sergeant in Homicide. A few years back he and I worked together. That was before the Department and I disagreed about

278

how to conduct an investigation. Now I was part of Private Enterprise.

Dave saw me as I got out of my car. He told his new partner to wait while he walked over to talk to me. "Hello, Stonebreaker. Don't tell me you were just passing by."

"No, I'm here on business. A client of mine is worried about the man living in that house you're heading for."

"Reuben Vasquez?"

"That's the name."

"Your client can quit worrying. Vasquez is dead." Dave started up the walk to the neat stucco house.

"Mind if I come along?" I asked.

"Can you do us any good?"

"You never know."

I followed Dave to the front door. Like the other houses on Malabar Street in the El Sereno district it was small and clean. The people who lived here were Mexicans. Not Chicanos; Mexicans. Chicano is a slang word that used to be a put-down like pachuco. Most of the people who live in El Sereno and Boyle Heights and East Los Angeles would rather be called Mexicans. It's their heritage and they're proud of it.

Inside the house were the uniformed officers who had answered the call, photographers and print men, and a young man from the coroner's office.

There was also a corpse.

In the center of the living room a man sagged in a chrome and plastic chair. His face, where the flesh showed through the crusted blood, was oyster-gray. The chair stood in the center of a crimson pool that had soaked into the beige carpet. The coroner's man had laid a path of newspapers across the carpet so he could get close to the body. In spots blood was seeping through the paper.

Dave Pike read from a notebook handed to him by one of the patrolmen. "The victim is Reuben Vasquez, age thirty-seven, residence right here, currently unemployed. Body discovered by victim's wife, Linda Vasquez, and neighbor, Mrs. Nona Herrera. Cause of death . . ." He looked at the coroner's man, who was backing gingerly off the damp newspaper.

"Primary hemorrhage," the young man said, "resulting from multiple stab wounds. Most of the cuts on the face and torso are superficial, but here on the upper arm you can see where the knife blade sliced through the basilic vein and into the brachial artery."

"He bled to death," Dave translated.

"That's the way it looks. His heart went on pumping until the blood vessels emptied and collapsed."

"How long would that take?"

"An hour. Maybe two. It wouldn't be as fast as severing the carotid or femoral artery."

I didn't want to look at the dead man anymore, so I walked across the room, keeping away from the red pool, and peered through an open doorway into a bedroom. A dark-eyed woman sat on the bed staring at nothing while a policewoman fed her coffee. The widow, I guessed. She was a couple of years past being pretty, but her face had the strong Indian bones and the fine Spanish features that would always give her a kind of voluptuous beauty.

Dave Pike moved over to stand beside me. "Want to tell me what you know about this?"

I stalled for a minute while I sorted out the information I wanted to give him. I owed Dave something, but I stayed in business only as long as people trusted me not to blab everything I know; people like the old man who was my client.

A couple of hours earlier the old man had come to my office in low-rent downtown Los Angeles. He seated himself across from me with a fragile dignity while we got the business of my fee out of the way. My rates are cheap, but I don't work free.

The old man's name was Antonio Vasquez, and when he was ready he told me why he had come. "It is my son, Reuben," he said. "He is in trouble with the Mexican Mafia."

The Mexican Mafia is a deadly organization of Latin thugs out to build a reputation by putting fear into people. It started in the prisons and was now beginning to reach outside.

"What sort of trouble is your son in?" I asked.

The old man straightened his thin shoulders and stared past me through the sooty window. The words did not come easily. "My son is an informer. At Soledad he gave them names. They gave him a parole. Now he is free, but those *cabrones* know what he has done. The order has been given that my son is to be punished."

I had heard how the Mexican Mafia dealt out punishment. They called it pigeon hunting. The victims who died were the lucky ones.

For the record I asked, "Do you want to tell this to the police?"

His eyes snapped with contempt. *"Por qué?* To the police it would be just one less bad Mexican to worry about. Reuben is not a son to make me proud, but he is the only son I have."

"What do you want to do?" I asked.

"Make him know the danger he is in. I am old and weak, and Reuben laughs at my fears. But he knows the name Stonebreaker and he will listen to you."

I wasn't so sure, but I didn't argue.

The old man stood up, brushed down the suit coat that didn't match his pants, and walked out of the office.

When I drove up to Reuben Vasquez's house I had only a vague plan about getting him out of town for a while. When I saw the police cars I knew it didn't matter anymore. I was a little too late.

Now, standing next to Dave Pike with Reuben's gray-faced body sitting there, I thought I might still earn my fee by helping to catch his killers.

"How about it, Stonebreaker?" Dave prodded. "What do you know?"

I filled him in on the Mexican Mafia story, leaving out only the identity of my client. The police would be in touch with the

Gary Brandner

old man soon enough anyway. Dave listened and made some notes.

"What do you know about Reuben's record?" I asked.

"He was a scumbag. Assault, dope, child-beating, you name it. Some people would say the Mexican Mafia did the city a favor."

The words of Antonio Vasquez echoed in my head. "How hard are you going to work on this?" I asked.

The cords in his neck went taut for a moment. In an icy voice he said, "We'll work just as hard as we do on any killing."

Dave Pike was a good cop, and he meant what he said. It was not his fault that there were more man-hours allotted to some investigations than to others.

"Are you going to talk to the widow now?" I asked.

"Yeah. Don't let me hold you up if you have someplace to go."

"Don't get all huffy," I told him. "A little help from me couldn't hurt, and you won't have to bill the city for it."

"Okay," he growled. "Stick around, but try to stay in the background. With your size and that face you have a way of scaring witnesses."

He had a point there, so I walked over and leaned against the wall while Dave asked Linda Vasquez to tell him what happened.

"They came between five and six o'clock, while I was making dinner," she said. "Two of them. One had a knife, the other a gun. Reuben tried to talk to them, but the one with the gun hit him, and he didn't say any more. The men tied Reuben in a chair, and they tied my hands and feet and put tape over my mouth. Then they locked me in the bathroom."

The woman's eyes were dry and her voice was without emotion as she went on with her story. "I could hear Reuben cry out, but very softly, like they put tape on his mouth, too. In a while the front door opened and closed and I heard nothing more. I got up on my knees and I could move around a little that way. I looked all over the bathroom for something sharp. Finally

282

I found a little pair of scissors and used them to cut the ropes. I pulled the tape away from my mouth and called to Reuben. He didn't answer. The bathroom door was locked from outside so I climbed through the window. My neighbor, Mrs. Herrera, was out in back and saw me. She came with me to the front door, and we came in and found . . . what you see there now. I ran to Reuben to see if I could help him. He looked very bad, but I still ran into the bathroom for bandages. It was too late."

Dave asked her to describe the two men. She began the way civilians always do in giving descriptions. The assailants were Mexicans, average height, average build, no distinguishing marks or unusual clothing. While Dave tried to improve on this, I strolled out of the bedroom. A path of smeared rusty footprints led from Reuben Vasquez in his lake of blood to the bathroom where Linda had run for the useless bandages. I walked out the front door and around to the neat little backyard. In the short grass under the bathroom window were two red-smudged impressions of Linda's tiny feet.

Across the lawn Dave's partner was questioning a ponderous woman with heavy black eyebrows. I wandered close enough to learn that this was Mrs. Herrera, the neighbor. Her description of how they found the body tallied with Linda Vasquez's. When Mrs. Herrera saw me listening she scowled. I answered with my friendly smile that frightens dogs and small children. Her scowl deepened, and I went away so the cop could go on with his questions.

I mooched around while Dave Pike finished talking to the widow, then walked out to the street with him as the body was trucked away.

"Anything?" I asked.

"Sure. I've got a description that fits half the adult male population. An arrest is imminent."

"Well, good luck," I said.

"What are you going to do?"

"Maybe I'll hang around and talk to the lady a little more."

"Stonebreaker, you're not holding anything back?"

"Take my word for it, you know as much as I do."

Dave's eyes held mine for a moment, then he nodded, got into his car, and drove away.

As soon as the law had cleared out, Mrs. Herrera lumbered over from next door and stood protectively just inside the living room. I had to talk over her shoulder to the widow.

"Mrs. Vasquez, did anyone else get a look at those two men?"

"No, just me. There is no one else here since I had to send my little boy to live with my sister. Maybe now he can come home."

"How about anybody else in the neighborhood?"

"The police asked all up and down the street. Nobody saw anything."

Mrs. Herrera spoke up then. She was liking me a little better now that she knew I was not with the police. "Maybe those kids saw something."

"What kids?"

"Some of those gang kids that hang around. They were across the street by that garage with spray-paint cans. Maybe they saw something."

I said good night to the women and walked across the street. The sun had disappeared and the light was failing fast. Spray-painted on the garage wall was the intricate style of graffiti peculiar to the Latin street gangs. An older message, beautifully lettered in white paint, read *VNE 13*. In the coded shorthand used by the gangs this translated as *Barrio* (or *Varrio*) *Nueva Estrada*, a gang whose territory bordered El Sereno. The number *13* stood for the thirteenth letter of the alphabet, *M*, and bragged that the VNE members smoked marijuana. Next to this was printed *El Caballo*, which would be the moniker of one of the gang members. This name had been X'd out in fresh red paint, and the comment *Puto* added, this being a heavy insult. The latter work was signed *V San B*, the San Benito Barrio.

I drove over to San Benito Street and found most of the gang at a *Taco Pronto* stand. A couple of tall, skinny adolescents looked me over with hostile black eyes.

"You want something, man?" one of them asked.

"I want to talk to Rojo."

"You a cop?"

"No. The name is Stonebreaker."

While the juveniles were thinking that over, a freckle-faced, red-haired kid came out of the taco shop and saw me.

"Stonebreaker," he said with a grin. *"Qué pasa, amigo?"* In spite of the fact that he looked like a slim, teenage Arthur Godfrey, Roberto "Rojo" Chacon was Mexican all the way, from around Guadalajara.

When the two skinny lieutenants saw that the big ugly stranger was no threat they got interested in something else.

"How can I help you, my friend?" Rojo asked. A few months back I was able to get his sister out of a nasty situation, and in the barrios they remember a favor.

I said, "Were some of your boys painting up a wall on Malabar Street earlier? Five or six o'clock?"

"Maybe. Why?"

"Relax, Red, I'm not on a cleanup drive. Somebody in your bunch put the "X" to El Caballo on a garage wall today. They may have seen a couple of hoods go into a house across the street. If they did, I'd like to know about it."

"I'll find out."

He walked a few yards away and went into a huddle with some of his buddies. They talked briefly in staccato street-Spanish, then Rojo came back.

"Yeah, we saw the two guys," he said. "What you want them for, Stonebreaker?"

"They tied somebody in a chair tonight and cut him to pieces."

"Friend of yours?"

"No. Business."

"Then you better forget it. Those two are very bad people."

"Bad people are my business. Who are they, Rojo?"

"Okay, but it's on your head. They're the Garza brothers—

Gary Brandner

Joe and Ignacio. Mexican Mafia. They won't be glad to see
you."

"Where do they hang out?"

"The Ruidoso. You know it?"

"I know it. See you, Rojo."

"Adios." He looked worried.

Here is where a good citizen would have turned the information over to the police and stepped out of the way, but I knew
what would happen then: the police would question Rojo, he'd
deny everything, the Garza brothers would not be touched, and I
would lose a friend. Which is why I did not call Dave Pike.

The Ruidoso was a beer joint and pool hall on Marengo near
Soto Street. I parked out front in a loading zone and walked in.
The place smelled like a latrine.

"I'm looking for the Garza brothers," I told the bartender.

"I ain't seen 'em," the man answered quickly, but his eyes
flickered back toward a pool table in the rear where a game had
halted when I came in. I started back and the two men immediately began playing again. One was thin as a blade, wearing
an electric-blue jacket and aviator shades. The other was short
and solid like an oil drum.

I reached down and picked up the cue ball as Blue Jacket
was lining up a shot.

"Hey, what's the idea, man?" he said in a whiny voice.

"I'm looking for the Garza brothers. You wouldn't be them,
would you?"

Usually I am not slow. In the kind of work I do, a little bit of
slow can make you a lot of dead. But this time I was a fraction
of a second behind the action when the thin one snapped, "Hit
him, Joe!"

I had barely started to turn when the weighted end of a cue
stick slammed the side of my head and the lights went out.

There was a foot in my face when the world came back. A ham-
mering pain in my temple kept time with my heartbeat. When I
could focus my attention away from the pain I saw I had been

crammed onto the floor in the rear of a car. My own car, I realized, on hearing the familiar grind of the transmission.

By peering upward through a slitted eye I saw that the foot in my face grew on the stocky leg of Joe Garza. That meant Ignacio must be driving. An emptiness under my arm meant they had lifted my gun. No doubt it was now pointed at one of my vital areas.

The car jounced as Ignacio drove up over a curb, and the mushy feel under the wheels told me we had left the pavement.

We jolted to a stop. Joe Garza's size twelve bore down on my sick head, and I clamped my jaws together to keep from yelling.

"This is good enough," said Ignacio's whining voice from the front seat.

That was the end of the conversation as the brothers both got out and started tugging at my feet to drag me from the car. Evidently the Garzas were scared and panicky, and now they were going to kill me. They must have wanted to use my car to get away, or they would have blasted me where I lay.

Without showing visible signs of life, I made myself as awkward as possible for them to pull out. When they had my lower half draped over the doorsill I managed to hook my jacket sleeve over the seat adjustment lever. Joe Garza gave a couple of futile tugs, then swore in Spanish. He leaned into the car to free whatever was hanging me up. When he took hold of my sleeve I reached across and grabbed his wrist with my free hand. I levered his arm down over my shoulder and grinned to myself when his elbow cracked and bent the wrong way.

Joe Garza bellowed in pain, and something heavy dropped out of his other hand and bounced off the back of my leg. I thrust myself out of the car and scrabbled around in the dark until I came up with my .38 Detective Special. I rolled onto my back in time to see Joe Garza, one arm dangling, his good hand gripping a knife. He lunged at me. Behind him I could hear Ignacio yelling at him to get out of the way.

There was no time to pick a spot, so I aimed at the broadest part of the onrushing Garza and fired. Joe grunted as the bullet punched him in the chest. He lumbered several steps past me before crashing to the turf.

Something popped away angrily behind me, and I turned to find Ignacio Garza shooting at me. It was a little toy of a .22 pistol, but they can make a hole big enough to kill a man. That was my last conscious thought before Ignacio shot me and I went down and out tasting blood.

There has been a rumor that my head is made of granite. Not true. In one evening it had been bashed with a pool cue and creased by a .22 bullet. The damage to the outside was obvious. Inside, my brain was as active as a lump of mashed potatoes.

After a while I decided I wasn't dead. Dead men don't feel pain. In easy stages I raised my head from the cool grass and looked around. Nobody in sight. My car was there. Faithful old car, one door open, reaching out to comfort the wounded master.

Moving one section of my body at a time I stood up. The dark landscape tilted left, tilted right, finally leveled off. Some part of the mashed-potato brain recognized where I was: Hazard Park just off Soto Street. Awkwardly, like a windup man, I walked to my car and climbed in. I was not alone.

Slumped far down in the passenger seat was Joe Garza. He had a hole in his chest and a faraway look in his eyes. I opened the door on his side and pushed him out.

When I twisted the key in the ignition nothing happened. This occurred about 75 percent of the time. I reached under the dash and jiggled the wires to make the connection. Ignacio wouldn't have known about that. When he couldn't get the heap started after gunning me down he must have panicked and beat it, leaving brother Joe behind. Joe wouldn't care.

I drove out of the park and headed south on Soto. A message tried to get through telling me there were urgent things to do, but my head wasn't taking any calls. Street lamps and headlights kept fading and coming back, fading and coming back. Before they blacked out completely I turned up a familiar street, drove a couple of blocks, and parked.

Somehow I must have staggered up to the house, but I don't

remember it. My next memory was of looking at the ceiling in the Vasquez bedroom. Linda Vasquez's face, looking frightened, floated above me while something cool and wet swabbed my battered face.

"Can you hear me, Stonebreaker?" she said. "Are you awake?"

"Yeah," I groaned. "Call the cops."

"Yes. Right away. Are you going to be all right?"

"Who knows? Call the cops."

She went away and left the damp washcloth over my eyes and forehead. Her heels clacked on the bare living room floor. Somebody must have removed the blood-soaked carpet. I heard her pick up the telephone and start to dial. As I began to drift back to slumberland there was a commotion at the front door, and another pair of feet rapped across the floor.

The whiny voice was higher and more excited than when I last heard it in the park.

"I told you what would happen to you if you talked to the police. Now I'm gonna make you real sorry before I kill you."

"No, don't," Linda Vasquez pleaded. "I didn't tell them anything. I said I couldn't remember what either of you looked like."

"Shut up! You told Stonebreaker, and now my brother is dead. I should have let Joe kill you too when we took care of your husband, but I was too soft. I said, 'Just tie her up and put her in the bathroom. She won't talk.'"

The woman was making little whimpering sounds.

When I pulled the cloth away from my face the light stabbed my eyeballs. I swung my legs off the bed and sat there for a slow count of five, gathering the strength to stand up.

From out in the living room came the solid smack of a fist on flesh and bone. A body thumped to the floor and Linda Vasquez began keening in a terrified voice.

"Oh, no, please don't do it. Please don't. I didn't tell anybody. Honest!"

I fitted the .38 into my hand and stood up. The bedroom door was open about six inches. I stumbled over and punched it open the rest of the way. Ignacio Garza was aiming his little pistol at the woman, who cowered on the bare floor.

When Ignacio saw the broken-faced apparition in the doorway his jaw dropped open. Then surprise gave way to hate and he swiveled the gun in my direction. Before he could pull the trigger I shot him directly in the mouth.

I finished the call to the police that Linda had started, and we waited in the kitchen for them to arrive.

I said, "Before the cops get here I want to ask you something."

"What is it?" She was fairly calm now, with a big red splotch on the side of her face where Ignacio had hit her.

"Was your husband dead when you came in and looked at him the first time?"

"You heard what I told the police. And what Mrs. Herrera told them."

"I mean when you came in alone, Linda."

Her mouth opened to form a denial, then she gave it up and slumped a little in her chair. "I don't know. He was still bleeding a little. Maybe he was alive. Maybe I could have saved him."

"But you didn't try."

"No, I didn't try."

"Why not?"

"You see that picture on top of the TV, Stonebreaker?"

I looked through the square arch into the living room at a framed photo of a somber-eyed boy of about four.

"That's my son, Manny," she said. "A month after that picture was taken Manny's father died. A year later I married Reuben Vasquez. In that picture Manny has all his fingers. Now his right hand has only three because Reuben got mad when he cried and he held Manny's hand over the gas flame. I hoped that when Reuben came out of prison this time he would be a better man. I asked him if I could bring my boy back to live with us. Reuben said if I did he would cook Manny's other hand."

"So what happened tonight?" I asked.

"It was as I said. I cut the ropes and crawled out the bathroom window, only I did it sooner than I said, and nobody saw me. I came in the front and found Reuben sitting in all that blood. If he wasn't dead he was soon going to be. I went back into the bathroom and watched through the window until Mrs. Herrera came out. Then I called to her and climbed out as I did the first time. We went to the front door together. This time there was no doubt. Reuben was dead. I ran to the bathroom and pretended to unlock the door to get bandages."

She sat staring at the tablecloth for a minute, then looked up at me. "How did you know, Stonebreaker? How did you know that when I came in with Mrs. Herrera it was not the first time?"

"You keep a neat house, Linda," I said. "You would have found those scissors a lot faster than you told the police. Then there were your footprints under the bathroom window."

"But I was very careful to put my feet in the same place both times."

"You forgot to clean your shoes. The grass had a smear of blood where you stepped. To pick that up you had to walk through the living room."

"What will you tell the police?"

"The truth. That Joe and Ignacio Garza killed your husband. What are you going to tell them?"

She looked at me for a long time out of those black unreadable eyes. Then the police knocked at the front door and she went to answer it.